D1808009

Speak To Me!

Shane Beaver

Published in 2014 by FeedARead.com Publishing

Copyright © The author as named on the book cover.

First Edition

The author has asserted their moral right under the
Copyright, Designs and Patents Act, 1988, to be identified
as the author of this work.

All Rights reserved. No part of this publication may be reproduced,
copied, stored in a retrieval system, or transmitted, in any form or by
any means, without the prior written consent of the copyright holder,
nor be otherwise circulated in any form of binding or cover other than
that in which it is published and without a similar condition being
imposed on the subsequent purchaser.

A CIP catalogue record for this title is available from the British
Library.

PROLOGUE

Friday, 9 January, 1987

Another cold and frosty January morning lay ahead for the residents of the village of Brockley, including those living on Gold Crescent and its adjoining side streets. Wrapped up against the elements, one or two had set off with their dogs for their customary jaunt along the nearby footpaths and fields, whilst others could be seen and heard scraping away at their car windscreens. Children were being prepared for junior school, whilst others were still struggling out of bed.

As the bells of St. Matthew's church struck 8.00 a.m. a procession of vehicles made its way slowly along Gold Crescent before pulling up outside number thirty-three. For the most part they had aroused no suspicion; nor did they wish to. Three men alighted from the first of these vehicles, their breath mixing with the cold air as they made their way down the path towards the front door in silence.

The curtains were drawn in the window on one side of the door and the blinds were down in the other, but a light could be seen coming from behind the latter to indicate that someone was up and about. One of the men knocked on the door and it was opened within seconds by a rather sad-looking woman in her mid-fifties, with short, dark grey hair and equally grey eyes.

'Yes?' she murmured, with a look of puzzlement on her face.

'Mrs. Fordham – Mrs. Joan Fordham?'

'Yes, that's right.'

'We're from Derbyshire CID,' said the first man with some authority as he proffered his identity card. 'I'm Detective Chief Inspector Thornley. This is Detective Constable Richardson and Police Constable Graydon,' he said nodding to the others.

The woman seemed somewhat flustered as she continued to dry her hands on the tea towel. 'What is it?' she asked, with a sense of nervous anxiety in her voice.

'We'd like to speak to your son, if we may?' replied the Inspector, as he and the other two policemen brushed past her and stood brooding in the hallway.

'But…but…well he's still in bed and…'

'Would you wake him then, please?' interrupted the Inspector rather brusquely.

With that the woman led the policemen down the hallway. The first door on the right was slightly ajar and evidently led to the living room, as the TV could be heard in the background. The second door on the right was closed, but she knocked lightly and entering gingerly she whispered 'Peter? It's mum.'

The policemen followed her into the room and stared with mouths agape at the sight that confronted them. The walls were covered with drawings, paintings and other graphic representations of what appeared to be humans with wings, some of which were clearly flying around the sun.

'Have you got that drawing, Richardson?' muttered the Inspector to his colleague, who immediately withdrew an A4-sized sheet of paper from the inside pocket of his coat and handed it over to his superior. 'It's just as I thought – Daedalus and Icarus!'

Meanwhile the woman had approached the bed, which was facing the door, and gently shaking the sleeping figure that lay beneath the sheets she again whispered his name. 'Peter? There are some policemen here to see you.'

The figure came to life and it was that of a young male in his late teens. His thick, dark brown hair lay strewn across his forehead, but his face lit up as he rolled over onto his side to be greeted by his mother's smile – albeit a weak one. However, this charming scene was suddenly broken by the voice of the Inspector.

'Peter Fordham? I'm here to arrest you on suspicion of murder.'

As the young man turned to face the figures standing in the doorway, a look of panic and terror spread across his face, and as if to emulate his hero, Icarus, he literally flew out of his bed in t-shirt and boxer shorts in an effort to flee from the scene.

'Grab him!' barked the Inspector.

'You can't do this!' screamed the young man's mother in protest.

As the two policemen grappled with the terrified youngster and sought to restrain his distraught mother, a man's voice came booming down the hallway.

'What the bloody 'ell's goin' on 'ere!'

An angry-looking man with greasy grey hair, several days of stubble and traces of egg yolk at the corners of his mouth suddenly burst into the room. There was a time when Trevor Fordham was not to be messed with, but the Inspector had no trouble grabbing him by the arm and throwing him up against the bedroom wall.

'We believe your son has committed a serious crime,' snarled the Inspector. 'And to that end we're going to take him in for questioning.'

'But you can't!' screamed Joan Fordham, barely able to control her emotions. 'He won't be able to say anything – not now! Not after this! He's...'

The Inspector cut her off once more. 'After what he's done, he'll speak to me whether he likes it or not!'

'But 'e 'asn't done anything', said Trevor Fordham, struggling to free himself from the vice-like grip.

'That'll be for a court to decide,' replied the Inspector. Without taking his eyes from the anguished father, he ordered the two other policemen to put a blanket around the young man and take him to one of the waiting cars. 'You and your wife can accompany me in one of the other cars.'

And that was it. It hadn't taken long. Indeed, it had all gone relatively smoothly – for the most part. So like some funereal funeral procession the vehicles thus left Gold Crescent almost as quickly as they had arrived – only now they contained three very unwilling and equally unhappy passengers.

Vera Hartley could barely contain herself. The events of the last few days had caused quite a stir among the people of Brockley and tongues had been wagging from the very beginning, but the curtains of number 26, Gold Crescent, had been twitching from the moment that the three vehicles pulled up across the road that morning.

The elder of two sisters, Vera had something of a reputation within the community. She had always taken a keen interest in the affairs of others and it was no secret that she was regarded as the village gossip. Indeed, it was almost as if she wore that appellation as a badge of honour! The village store and its attached post office was like a second home to her, and from there she directed her daily diet of what can only be described as "shit stirring"!

But it was from behind the curtains of the modest bungalow that she shared with her husband, Dennis, that she had witnessed the comings and goings from number 33, and provided him with what can only be described as a running commentary – not that he was actually listening.

'There you go!' she said triumphantly. 'What did I tell you? They've got him!' The excitement in her voice was palpable.

'That right?' muttered her husband, his face hidden behind the Daily Mail.

'I always said there was something wrong with him.'

'S'ppose you'll be 'appy now then?' he replied, with a hint of sarcasm.

'Well I did tell them that when they came to the door a day or so ago.'

He was aware of that, of course. He had been there when the police were conducting their door-to-door enquiries. But she had to take over the conversation, didn't she? *She* had to let them know what *she* thought. And *she* had seen the lad follow the girl down the footpath. Oh yes, *she* made much of that! And now there would be no stopping her.

'Wait till I tell our Val,' she chirruped, as she made her way excitedly into the hallway and to the telephone.

'What do you want to go and tell her for?' he shouted forlornly.

But she wasn't listening. She had already picked up the receiver to call her sister and tell her the good news!

'That you Val? Guess what?' he heard her say. But before continuing she closed the living room door behind her, preventing him from hearing another word. No doubt she'll be on that bloody phone for hours now – and barely pausing for breath! So it was with some surprise when she re-entered the living room less than five minutes later with a look of shock and puzzlement on her face.

'Well I never!' she exclaimed.

'Now what have you gone and done?' he asked with some irritation.

'She put the phone down on me!'

'Can't say I blame her!' he said, rising from the easy chair and throwing down his paper before heading to the kitchen.

'All I did was tell her that they'd taken the Fordham's lad away and she hung up on me!'

The reaction of her sister would be a source of some bewilderment to Vera Hartley thereafter. Indeed, it would be some considerable time before the subject came up in conversation between the pair again.

It was 8.45 a.m. when the procession of vehicles carrying Peter Fordham and his parents arrived at Leverton police station. Normally around this time of the day the station was a hive of activity, but apart

6

from the desk sergeant everyone had gathered in the main office – and one could cut the air with a knife.

Needless to say, there was some commotion as the vehicles emptied and everyone entered the building. At this point Detective Constable Richardson broke off from the group, and poking his head around the door of the main office he clenched his teeth, punched the air and shouted 'We've got the bastard!'

The reaction inside the office was like that when England have won a penalty shoot-out against the opposition – the place erupted! Backs were slapped, hands were shaken and out of nowhere someone produced a bottle of whisky. The old man wouldn't begrudge them that surely? It was a team effort and they had all worked so very hard to bring this about.

And yet not everyone was celebrating. A young police constable rose unsmiling from a desk in the corner of the room, donned his cap and was about to leave the office when a colleague shouted to him above the cacophony.

'Hey, Sniffer! Where are you off to?'

'Work to do,' replied the young policeman.

'What? Aren't you gonna join in the celebrations?' asked his colleague.

'What is there to celebrate?'

This was enough to wipe the smile from his colleague's face, and he made to move over to the young policeman. 'Here, are you trying to tell me something?'

'Such as?'

'Are you trying to tell me that we've got the wrong man?'

'I just don't believe that we've mounted a thorough investigation, that's all.'

The look of exasperation on his colleague's face was tangible. 'Oh, for crying out loud. It was you who found the body! You saw what that bastard did to her?'

The young policeman looked long and hard into his colleague's eyes, but then made to move out of the room once more. 'If you'll excuse me,' was all he could muster.

But the celebrations went on without him. Little did anyone know at the time that this case would figure again in the coming years and not only for the young policeman who was affectionately known to his colleagues as "Sniffer"!

PART 1

SPEAK TO ME

Chapter 1

Sunday, 2 July, 2017 (p.m.)

Keith Jackson was hardly likely to forget the combination in a hurry, was he? The day he joined the Army was a day that he would remember for the rest of his life! It was a Monday morning on September 6, 1982, when he enlisted in the Worcestershire and Sherwood Foresters, and it was a decision that he never regretted. Great times, but above all a great bunch of guys!

He'd always found it difficult to make friends at school – he wasn't one of the gang. But from the moment he joined up he knew that he was part of a team – part of a family. Yes, there was the order and the discipline, but it was the comradeship – the camaraderie – that he loved most of all. He and the lads did everything together and went everywhere together – Warminster, Cambridge, Omagh, Cyprus, Tidworth and of course the tours to Bosnia and Afghanistan. Okay, so he got demoted to Corporal for slapping that recruit, but in spite of it all his mates were always there for him – and he for them.

And what of him now? Reduced to mowing the lawns of the local toffs and looking after that bloody cricket pitch! Still, at least there was always the guarantee of a good piss-up at the pub after the match – home or away! And that's where he'd been for the last couple of hours or so, although there hadn't been a match earlier as the team had being playing away the day before. He really ought to show his face at the care home though; he hadn't seen his mother for a couple of weeks.

And so it was that slightly the worse for drink and dressed in Army field jacket, camouflage t-shirt, combat trousers and Army surplus boots, he tapped in the numbers 6982 and opened the outside door of the care home to gain access. Noting the time (8.05 p.m.), he duly filled in the visitor's book and entered the foyer.

Oh my God, it was like walking into a sauna! The heat was overpowering and for the umpteenth time he wondered why the central heating system had to be on full blast during the summer months. Shaking his head, he stopped briefly to look at the large aquarium in the corner to his left and smiled to himself as a Red Eye Swordtail darted away to hide behind one of the fixtures. Beyond this was a corridor to the left leading to the office of the manageress, but she had gone home at 5.00 p.m. and now there was only a skeleton staff to look after the residents. However, they seemed to be conspicuous by their absence at this particular moment in time.

In front of him was the lounge, in which two female residents had apparently fallen asleep whilst watching an episode of *Dad's Army* – although that was probably not the fault of one of Britain's classic comedies!

There was yet another corridor to his right and he made his way along this until he came to his mother's room, which was the third on the right-hand side. Just as he was about to enter he suddenly stopped and noticed that the door to the room immediately opposite had been left open for some reason. The name on the door meant nothing to him, but ever the opportunist he glanced furtively around and with not a soul in sight he instinctively decided to take a peek inside.

The room was evidently empty and although the curtains to the window in front of him were drawn, the bedside lamp had been left on, allowing him to discern that someone had recently been sleeping in the bed immediately to his left. The covers had been casually cast aside and the occupant had probably been taken for a bath or shower, he surmised. Not every room had a toilet, but this one did. As with his mother's room it was situated beyond the bed on the far left, and its door was closed. Wardrobe, dressing table and chair were to his right, and on this chair was a handbag. Residents weren't supposed to leave money or valuables lying around in their rooms, but you never know, do you? And Jackson was no kleptomaniac!

Quietly easing the door shut behind him, he made for the handbag. Aware of the fact that he had to act quickly, he rifled through the handbag with a dexterity one might associate with an eminent surgeon, but he was somewhat peeved to discover that this particular resident seemed to have adhered to the Home's monetary rules and regulations.

Turning his attention to the drawers of the dressing table, he found it equally frustrating that the top and middle drawers contained only underwear. However, on opening the bottom drawer he came upon a few towels, beside which was a carrier bag bearing the unmistakeable logo of the Tesco supermarket. Could there be something of value inside this perhaps? He took the bag out of the drawer and peering inside he was able to make out that it contained what appeared to be a small, brown exercise book. What's more, he could feel that there was something inside of the book that was making it bulge. At that precise moment he heard voices approaching down the corridor outside.

'Shit! That's all I bloody need,' he grunted to himself.

Keeping hold of the carrier bag and the contents therein, he quickly closed the drawer and made for the toilet. It was like the covert operations he had undertaken with the Army, and he silently prayed that the "enemy" would not enter the room and discover him. To his immense relief, however, the voices carried on past and along the corridor. And yet the return of the occupant had to be imminent, so it was time to get out of there before he really was discovered. Leaving the toilet clutching the bag to his chest, he tiptoed towards the door and gently easing it open he made sure that the coast was clear before darting across the corridor to his mother's room opposite. Phew! That was a close run thing!

Safely ensconced within, he looked down to his left to find his mother fast asleep with mouth agape and making the most hideous guttural sounds. Clearly oblivious to his presence, he wondered if there was any point in him staying as she appeared to be out for the count, so to speak. But he decided to give her twenty minutes or so, and if she was still in the land of Nod by the end of that time then he would leave and make his way home. Now was the time to discover what was making that bloody book bulge!

Opening the bag once more, he removed the book and as he did so something dropped out and disappeared underneath his mother's bed. At the same time three crumpled ten pound notes also fluttered to the floor. His mission to the room opposite had obviously paid off! Thirty pounds wasn't much, but it was better than nothing. Bending down to retrieve the notes, he then crouched down on his hands and knees to search for the other item that had dropped to the floor beneath the bed. Fortunately it lay within reach and stretching his arm out he discovered that it was a small circular clip-on badge, the size of a fifty pence piece, upon which were the faded images of the cartoon cháracters *Tom and Jerry*.

As much as he enjoyed watching the cat and mouse antics of these two well-loved rascals in his younger days, the money was of far more importance, and so he pocketed the notes and placed the badge back into the carrier bag. He was about to do the same with the exercise book, but curiosity got the better of him and he decided to flick through the pages to see if there was any more money.

As it turned out there was one "note", but this was merely a written one to the occupant of the room just down the corridor, thanking her for 'knitting the two Aran sweaters for my Jim.' And as a token of her thanks the author of this particular note (who apparently went by the name of Beryl) had attached thirty pounds. Oh well, beggars can't be choosers. At which point this note also slipped from the book and fell to the floor. He picked it up, but as he was carefully placing it back inside the book he suddenly froze.

'What's this all about?' he heard himself say.

A name leaped from the page before him and it was the name of someone he knew well. His eyes moved down the page and the name came up again and again. More importantly, the individual concerned was being accused by the author of having committed the most heinous of crimes, *namely that of murder*!

He looked up from the book and whistled softly to himself. This was some revelation! Could there be more? And what had prompted the author to make such an accusation? There was only one way to find out, so he opened the book at the beginning and began to read.

It was almost an hour later before he finally put the "book" down, for it was more like a diary or an autobiography of the woman in the room opposite really – and the name *still* meant nothing to him! It was a tale of sadness, tragedy, frustration and anguish, and those of a more sensitive and sympathetic disposition would have seen it that way. But Keith Jackson did not see it that way, for he had begun to devise a plan and one which would solve most – if not all – of his problems; or so he believed.

Several times he had looked up and glanced at his mother whilst reading the book, but she was still fast asleep. It was now time for him to go. Before leaving the room he took the badge from the carrier bag and put it into the left-hand pocket of his jacket. Placing the book inside the bag, he then put this package into the middle drawer of his mother's dressing table, underneath her underwear. He would come and see her again in a couple of days.

Closing the door quietly behind him, he made his way down the corridor, and at that moment one of the two female residents emerged from the lounge. She had evidently woken from her slumber somewhat miffed at having missed the episode of Dad's Army, and was now attempting to make her way back to her room with the help of a Zimmer frame.

She greeted Jackson with a smile and an 'Evening luv,' but he did not return the compliment. 'Uh, talk to your bloody self then,' she snarled as Jackson signed out and left the building. He had more important things to consider, didn't he?

As he climbed into his white Citroen Berlingo van and drove off, a self-satisfied smirk appeared on his face, for tomorrow he would put his plan into action, and he was confident of success. Too confident, as it would transpire; for Keith Jackson couldn't have known then that he had less than twenty-four hours to live!

Chapter 2

Monday, 3 July, 2017 (p.m.)

Every Monday to Friday just after 4.00 p.m., Ken Watson made a point of setting off for a stroll around the village of Brockley with his beloved eight-year-old West Highland White Terrier, "Wilf". Leaving his bungalow on Gold Crescent, their route would invariably include Blackthorn Lane and the surrounding fields, but it would always culminate with a visit to *The Wheatsheaf Inn* along the way and a pint (perhaps a pint and a half) of one of their cask ales ('and a bowl of water for "Wilf", please') before returning home. Such was the case on this late Monday afternoon in July.

Ken surprisingly possessed boundless energy for his age (he was born on September 1st 1939, the day that the Second World War broke out). It would have certainly surprised his late father, who always sarcastically referred to his only son as a 'pen-pushing little jobsworth!' He had expected Ken to follow him down the pit, and so it came as a huge disappointment when the lad announced to his parents that he'd got a job at the regional offices of the National Coal Board! The fact that Ken became an able administrator, with a talent for responsibility and leadership, did nothing to assuage the disdain that Watson senior felt for his offspring.

There was a slight cessation of hostilities between the years of 1957 and 1959, when Ken was obliged to do his National Service. He was always proud of this episode of his life, when he served as a dog handler with the Royal Air Force Police. To this day he seldom went anywhere without a tie bearing the RAF Police logo and *Fiat Justicia* (Let Justice Be Done) emblazoned upon it. Oh, how he would boast of his time at RAF Scampton to anyone who cared to listen. During the war Scampton had been home to the famous 617 or "Dam Busters" Squadron and in May 1958 the Squadron did indeed reform and return to Scampton. However, it was only when a former RAF colleague placed a letter in the local rag years later – asking if anyone knew of Ken's whereabouts – that it was established that he had never been at Scampton at all. He had spent the entire two years of his National Service at RAF Strubby, near Alford, in Lincolnshire. That caused some embarrassment to our Ken and he had his work cut out trying to cover it up!

And yet those two years were to provide him with a sense of discipline that he maintained throughout the rest of his life. Furthermore, his time in the RAF helped him to adopt strong personal values, which proved invaluable in the face of his father's renewed hostility when he returned to his job with the Coal Board. In fact he went from strength to strength and subsequently rose to the lofty heights of head of Area No.5 (Leverton) in the East Midlands Division.

Marriage to Margaret Trueman came in 1966, followed by the birth of a son, Michael, three years later, and his ambition to create a prosperous family seemed to be well within his grasp. The family moved from the town of Grimley to the rural tranquillity of Armisfield and everything in the garden was rosy for a while, but dark clouds eventually loomed on the horizon. The National Coal Board was dissolved in 1987 and Ken was out of work for the first time in his life. For someone who was used to being in control of others and of his own destiny, this was a massive blow to his ego and it was several months before he found alternative employment as a gatekeeper at a local storage depot. He was no longer in control of others, but at least he had the power to determine who came in and out of the depot; or so he told himself.

And then within a couple of year's Michael dropped the bombshell that he was moving to Australia. Father and son had never really seen eye to eye and the boy had always been closer to his mother, but it was some years later when he arrived on his parents doorstep unannounced (together with wife and three children) that Michael deemed that now was the time to inform his mother that it was his father's overbearing, pretentious attitude and attempts to control every aspect of his life that had caused him to emigrate. Margaret was naturally upset, but she remained typically stoical to the end and never revealed the details of her conversation with Michael to her husband.

Ken finally retired in 1999 and a few years later he and Margaret moved into the bungalow on Gold Crescent. Her death in 2013 hit him hard and he let it be known that he felt 'completely flat' without her. Nevertheless, he immersed himself into the gardening and swiftly became head of the local Allotment Association; although it irked him somewhat that he was continuously overlooked as head of the Parish Council. His real passion, however, was Brockley Cricket Club and on match days he was a regular fixture, complete with navy-blue blazer (RAF badge of course), tie (RAF Police logo of course), cream Panama hat and cream slacks!

As a matter of fact it was the forthcoming match with Coote's Abbey that occupied his thoughts as he and "Wilf" made their way down to the main road that led from Grimley to Derby. No blazer or Panama hat today, just a buff-coloured short fleece jacket, grey slacks, brown shoes and a checked flannel shirt complete with tie (RAF logo of course).

There had been light rain earlier in the day, but it had brightened up considerably and he deemed it unnecessary to wear anything to cover the bald patch on his crown or what was left of his wispy grey hair that he had attempted to style into a combover à la Bobby Charlton! Bespectacled as always, the sad grey eyes were a testament to the major disappointments in his life.

After a few polite words of acknowledgement to fellow villagers, he and "Wilf" crossed the main road and then headed down Blackthorn Lane. This was once an old turnpike road, whereby travellers had to pay a toll many moons ago. Indeed, the only building along the lane was called The Old Turnpike House, but Ken would be cutting off and heading across the fields before he reached there.

There weren't many blackthorn bushes in evidence nowadays either, but nevertheless it was still a pleasant route for walkers or ramblers as well as cyclists. Here and there the hedgerows were interspersed with the odd oak tree or horse chestnut, and red campions flourished along either side of the lane. It was a narrow lane though, with barely enough room for two vehicles to pass by each other.

Ken was mulling over the probable line-up for the match at the weekend as he and "Wilf" approached a sharp left-hand bend in the lane. The height of the hedgerow rendered him blind to what lay beyond, but at that precise moment a black Range Rover came tearing around the bend towards him and almost forced him into the nearby ditch. He wasn't tone deaf – yet; but he *still* hadn't heard it coming.

'Bloody idiot! What do you think this is – a bloody racetrack?' he bawled as the vehicle disappeared up the lane.

Not one for making expletives at the best of times, he blushed slightly as he sought to regain his composure – and control of "Wilf". He was still chuntering to himself as he came to the stile on the left-hand side of the lane that would take him across the fields to the pub.

However, had he continued further along the lane, he would have been passed by another vehicle a couple of minutes later; a silver Renault Twingo, bearing the registration number HK15 TDG. But the pub beckoned for Ken Watson and he had put Blackthorn Lane behind him.

Chapter 3

Monday, 3 July, 2017 (p.m.)

It had been another busy day at *The Wheatsheaf Inn*. A modest little hostelry, it had a reputation for fine ales and quality food, with the *Moules Marinière* a speciality and highly popular with the customers. Standing alone on the main road from Grimley to Derby, it was now the only pub in the village. *The Fox and Hounds* had suffered the fate of many pubs in recent years and was demolished four years previously to be replaced by what was loosely termed 'luxury flats'.

Mine hosts at *The Wheatsheaf* for the last three years were Tony and Sally Dawkins. They had previously run several successful pubs throughout the Nottinghamshire and Derbyshire areas, although it must be said that Sally insisted with some conviction that this success was due entirely to *her* brains and brawn!

Indeed, although her husband had only left the pub forty-five minutes previously, it was his absence that was causing her to become anxious. He wouldn't be gone long (he said); pick the car up from the garage (he said); ten minutes or so at the cash and carry (he said). Knowing him as she did it would be a damn sight longer than that (she'd said). And with only two other staff to help her she already felt run off her feet!

'Thank you. I hope you both enjoyed the food?' she beamed as another satisfied couple returned the compliment and made their way out through the front door to the car park.

A natural performer, she had always thrived on entertaining and taking centre stage; which is why she had wanted to follow her father into the licensing trade for as long as she could remember. But at fifty-six she would be the first to acknowledge that she was showing signs of her age.

The long, flowing locks had long gone and her blonde hair was now cut very short. And with every passing year there seemed to be more and more wrinkles upon her face and forehead. She would have liked to have put that down to the stresses of being married to a dimwit, but she grudgingly accepted that it was more likely due to her smoking habit. The figure-hugging skirts and dresses were a thing of the past too, for she had convinced herself that her backside was getting bigger and bigger. For crying out loud, she was getting enough exercise, what with looking after the pub and keeping an eye on her other half, but none of the diets had worked either and she was now reduced to wearing trousers or shorts. She had never been blessed with a large bust, so what was the point in wearing a revealing outfit if there was bugger all to reveal?

But what she lacked in curves and contours she more than made up for with leadership, exuberance and charm. She was the boss and everyone knew it! That included Ken Watson, who entered the pub with his dog shortly before 5.00 p.m.

'The usual, Ken?' shouted Sally from behind the bar.

'And a bowl of water for "Wilf", please.' he replied curtly before taking his seat at the table nearest the door.

She pulled him a pint of John Smith's and gazed across at him with a puzzled look on her face. Ken wasn't one to say a great deal at the best of times – unless it involved cricket of course – but she had to admit that he did look somewhat flustered. He had obviously taken the death of his wife very hard, but he could be a right bloody show off when the occasion arose. She would take his pint and bowl of water over to him and try to make the conversation as brief as possible.

'There you go, Ken.' she said cheerfully as she placed his pint on the table and the bowl of water on the floor for "Wilf". 'That'll be three pounds and ten pence, please.'

He looked up and seemed to grimace all the more at her last words, but saying nothing he duly proffered the three pound coins and ten pence piece.

Smiling again, she deemed it wise not to say anything more, so she turned away and muttered 'miserable bugger' as she made her way back to the bar!

If there was one customer that Sally Dawkins disliked above all others then it was most definitely John Sheldon. Although he had yet to cause an affray in the pub, it was common knowledge that he had been in trouble with the law. There were rumours of unprovoked attacks elsewhere and it had been suggested that he had been a bully at school. Not to put too fine a point on it, the guy had trouble written all over him; and he thought a lot of himself too. For one thing his voice had to be heard above everyone else's, but he always wore those bloody tight-fitting t-shirts to show off his physique and his tattoos. Horrible man, thought Sally, as she contemplated going outside for a cigarette. He wasn't even from Brockley. He lived at nearby Thraplow with that slut he called his partner. No doubt she would be showing her ugly mug later – and no doubt *her* husband would be all over her!

Sally was just about to reach for her packet of Mayfair when at just before 5.15 p.m. Sheldon walked through the door. He was a relatively tall man at just under six feet, complete with shaven head and yes, a tight-fitting white t-shirt that emphasised his bulging biceps. The fact that he also wore a pair of khaki-coloured shorts failed to impress Sally. There was clearly no love lost between the two of them, but he made his way to the bar with a smirk on his face and ordered a pint of Stella Artois. As Sally poured his drink, he turned and noticed Ken Watson sitting brooding at the table near the door as "Wilf" lapped at his bowl of water.

'You gonna be at the game on Saturday, Ken?' Sheldon bellowed from the bar in a voice that was almost ear-splitting, causing everyone to jump and all the glasses on the nearby tables to shake as if the pub had been hit by a slight earth tremor.

'What?' replied Ken, as if he had been in a trance. 'Oh yes – yes I'll be there. Hope you take a few wickets and...'

But Sheldon ignored him and turned to face the bar once more. Smirking again at Sally, he threw a five pound note across to her and then taking his change and his pint of lager he made for a side room and the pool table, where some equally unpleasant individuals awaited him. Sally shuddered before grabbing her packet of Mayfair and as she sat at the table just outside the front door of the pub, she inhaled deeply on her first cigarette for several hours.

Sally was back behind the bar several minutes later when in walked Christopher Ibbotson. Tall, slim and wiry (he was six feet and two inches in height), with wispy, collar-length grey hair (parted down the right-hand side), she had taken to calling him a 'la-di-dah stick insect.' And he seldom went anywhere without a tweed jacket and a bow tie. Originally from Sidcup in Kent, he came to Brockley in 2011 and around the same time he opened an antiques shop in Derby. With access to things of great value, he liked to pass himself off as someone of supreme importance, and all the more so within a couple of years when he became head of the parish council *and* captain of the village cricket team. Clearly well-educated, he seemed to dazzle and seduce everyone around him, but to Sally Dawkins he came across as an arrogant, superior know-all, with a sense of entitlement.

Ibbotson had hardly set foot in the pub when he was waylaid by a clearly agitated Ken Watson.

'Mr. Ibbotson?' pleaded Watson as he half rose from his chair. 'I'd like a word with you if I may?'

Somewhat irritated, Ibbotson tried to brush off this attempt to grab his attention. 'If you don't mind, Ken, I need to speak to Mr. and Mrs. Dawkins about an urgent matter. Council business, you know.'

Leaving Watson open-mouthed and frustrated, he made his way to the bar, parked his backside on an empty stool and ordered a large glass of Panataia Pinot Noir!

Ibbotson was still seated at the bar at 5.45 p.m. when Ken Watson abruptly rose from his chair and with a 'Come on, "Wilf",' he made for the door. At that moment the burly figure of Simon Collins entered the pub, but Watson brushed past him without saying a word and headed home to Gold Crescent.

'Watcha Ken!' shouted Collins in his inimitable East London brogue, as Watson crossed the main road and disappeared out of sight.

Oh my God, thought Sally Dawkins, here comes the original Cockney wide boy in the traditional West Ham United kit of claret and blue (complete with crossed hammers and castle logo), white shorts and sandals! She would have put him down as being more overweight than burly, but he wasn't a bad looking guy for his age.

Plaistow's finest was now fifty-four, with dark, close-cropped hair and blue eyes. There were faint traces of a scar just above his right eye. He claimed to have fallen off a ladder, but Sally had got it into her mind that he had probably upset one of the local villains or successors to the Kray Twins. He wasn't all that tall (he was five feet and nine inches in height), but she could see why women might fall for him. And he had the gift of the gab too. More importantly, he was a self-made millionaire was our Mr. Collins!

Whilst slaving away at the docks one day, he decided to bring the future into the present by turning his interest into a prosperous, successful enterprise. And the only thing that Simon Collins was ever interested in was betting and gambling. The guy was prepared to bet on anything – and not just horses and greyhounds. Whilst on holiday in Australia some years ago he ate a plateful of live, raw Witchetty grubs for a bet – and he won!

But from the moment he opened his first betting shop he believed in his vision and brought it to fruition. By his mid-forties he was responsible for an empire of over thirty betting shops, with the result that he came to dwell in a realm that few others have access to. And then in 2009 he suddenly left London altogether, claiming with some authority that 'the East End ain't the East End no more,' and settled in South East Derbyshire with his wife. Having bought what can only be described as a "hacienda" at the nearby village of Armisfield (complete with outdoor swimming pool), he opened two more betting shops in the area. An astute businessman, he has undoubtedly earned both the power and the prestige that his business has brought, but he does enjoy exuding this over others.

Preferring a drink with the lads at *The Wheatsheaf* to throwing parties and entertaining, Collins spotted Ibbotson at the bar and swaggered over before tossing a twenty pound note onto the bar. 'Pint o' Guinness for me, darlin', get Chris another and 'ave one for yourself.'

'I'll have a dry white wine if I may?' replied Sally trying to look grateful.

Collins had been roped into playing for the Brockley cricket club as a number three batsman and a slip fielder by none other than Ibbotson, but he would be the first to admit that he 'couldn't catch a bleedin' cold!' Not that cricket was on his mind at that particular moment.

'Everything okay, Simon?' asked Ibbotson

'Yeah, you know. Bleedin' wife – nag, nag, nag all the time. Told myself it was time I 'eaded to the pub!'

That was hardly likely, thought Ibbotson as he sipped at his wine. He'd probably been screwing one of the girls from the betting shop at Grimley or Leverton, and the wife was probably stretched out by the pool on her second bottle of gin by now!

At that moment the tall figure of Tony Dawkins entered the bar from the rear, looking slightly dishevelled in spite of the fact that he wore a shirt and tie. His receding, collar-length grey hair didn't appear to have been combed, but as always he tried to look cheerful for all and sundry. The smile was soon wiped from his face.

'Where the bloody hell have you been?' snarled wife Sally

'I told you.' he protested. 'Drop his nibs off and then go to the garage to see if the car was ready, but…'

'And call at the *Miners Arms* judging by your bloody breath!' she hissed with some venom.

'I only had a swift half!' he replied unconvincingly before looking around to see if anyone was watching their confrontation (they were).

'Swift half my arse!' she snapped. 'Bet you've spent the last couple of hours ogling at that barmaid's tits if I know you!'

Collins and Ibbotson tried to hide their amusement at the poor man's obvious discomfort, but he only made matters worse.

'The car wasn't ready when I got there, so…'

'I'm not interested in any of your pathetic excuses!' She cut him short again before turning to smile at someone standing at the bar and then glared at her husband once more. 'Well, don't just stand there looking gormless – there are customers waiting to be served!'

For someone who was an eternal optimist and lived for the moment, it had been a very uncomfortable few minutes for Tony Dawkins. The former lorry driver was wishing that he had never pulled into that motorway service station all those years ago, but he had become so dependent upon his bloody wife. He desperately tried to avoid conflict with her, so he either kept out of her way or attempted to please her and cater for her every whim, but in doing so he risked losing his own identity and losing sight of his ultimate goal. And she was due any moment.

Originally from the Derbyshire town of Scatwell, Angela Radford had always loved the sun, the sea and the sand. So much so that she had worked in the travel industry since she left school, and now at the age of forty she managed the Co-op travel agency in Grimley. The archetypal team builder, it is widely acknowledged that she provides leadership to those around her, commanding loyalty from them at all times.

Passionate and flashy, she has always been determined to experience life to the fullest, using charm, intrigue and seduction to achieve her goals, which are to build relationships and connect with others. Indeed, her charm lies in an almost theatrical and sensually pleasing visual experience. Petite in stature, her long blonde hair and blue eyes enable her to stand out in a crowd, but she is quite busty too and frequently takes to showing off her cleavage outside of working hours. Her long nails are painted in a turquoise colour, but she has also taken to following the latest trend by having intricate tattoos on her shoulders and thighs. In short, she has an instant effect on the opposite sex due to *her* sex appeal.

Sally Dawkins, on the other hand, has always regarded her as a slut – and a dangerous one at that. If anyone can make a man pursue her then it was Angela Radford! To make matters worse, husband Tony fancied his chances. But Angela was drawn to dangerous men herself, and according to Sally there were none more dangerous than Angela's partner, John Sheldon. But Angela was the kind of woman who always felt incomplete without a partner. She had never liked being alone or single, so she had a tendency to want to control every aspect of *her* partners life. That was never going to be easy with a man like Sheldon, which would go a long way to explaining why their relationship was somewhat rocky at the best of times.

There was another thing that Sally Dawkins disliked about Angela Radford too, and that was the fact that she was infuriatingly loquacious. And just after 6.00 p.m. as Sally was returning from a visit to the loo she heard that familiar ghastly high-pitched voice enter the bar.

'Hiya.' screeched Angela as she went over to chat to one or two female friends before heading to the bar to order a glass of Sangria.

Unaware that his wife was watching, Tony Dawkins had been waiting for this moment and as he poured her drink he greeted Angela with one of his lewd comments.

'Judging by your tan you've been stripping off in the back garden again, haven't you, my little kitten?' he grinned lasciviously. 'You must let me know next time you go out and I'll come around and help you with the suntan oil!'

'Oooh Tony.' she giggled. 'You are a cheeky monkey.'

Tony Dawkins was unaware that John Sheldon had re-entered the bar too, and as he nodded in the direction of Ibbotson and Collins he took Angela by the arm and literally ordered her to keep away from the landlord.

'For God's sake, he's harmless.' scowled Angela, before releasing his grip and joining her girlfriends to talk about holidays.

Both Ibbotson and Collins witnessed the incident and shook their heads. As Dawkins moved over to join them briefly, Ibbotson pointed through the window to a vehicle in the car park.

'That's Jackson's van out there, isn't it?' he said with a puzzled look on his face.

'Oh yes,' replied Dawkins. 'He was in earlier having a skinful and throwing money about like confetti. Must have won on the horses or something.'

'Someone take him 'ome?' asked Collins inquisitively.

'Yes,' confessed Dawkins, 'I did!'

Chapter 4

Tuesday, 4 July, 2017 (a.m.)

Brockley is a rural community that lies on the main road from Grimley to Derby. It takes its name from 'Broca's woodland clearing,' or a wood where badgers are seen (and still can be seen in the vicinity). Its population as of the 2011 census was 2,784. It had once been part of the South East Derbyshire coalfield, but the local colliery was closed in the 1960's and there is now a set of allotments on and around the site.

Indeed, this and most of the collieries in the area were once owned by the Frankland-Moore family, who still reside at Brockley Hall. Surrounded by woods, the Hall is a late 18th century Georgian mansion set back from the main road and is approached along an avenue bedecked with magnificent lime trees. There is a large lawn at the front of the building and it boasts a fine garden at the rear, complete with a grass tennis court.

On one side of the Hall is the picturesque setting of St. Matthew's Church and vicarage (also surrounded by woods); the present incumbent, the Rev. Peter Cox, being installed less than a year beforehand. The church still holds records for births, deaths and marriages going back to the seventeenth century. Memorials to the Frankland-Moore family are located to the rear of the cemetery, but what makes it so attractive is the presence of numerous trees of the *Taxus baccata* variety, or the yew tree. Although the leaves and seeds are poisonous the aril – or fleshy seed covering – isn't, and Bullfinches flock to the trees to feed on the berries.

It was the Frankland-Moore's who endowed the village school, which lies between the Hall and Gold Crescent. Indeed, the endowment still continues to this day, despite the fact that the school is now administered by the local authority. Although the school capacity is 175, it is perhaps a reflection of our times that the actual number of pupils at the school is 209, all overseen by headmistress, Mrs. Louise Smedley. The Chair of Governor's, Mrs. Rachel Garvey, is one year into her term of office, which ends in 2020.

A public bridleway (little more than a dirt track) leading from Gold Crescent to Delves Lane separates the Hall from Steadman's Woods on the other side. The woods themselves form part of a nature reserve that surrounds a large pond or lake. There are several bird hides located throughout the woods and fishing in the pond is granted to those with a licence. At the top of the dirt track to the rear of Gold Crescent lies the Brockley village cricket club, complete with a splendid-looking pavilion. Every other Saturday (mostly) the sound of leather against willow (together with a few expletives) can be heard throughout the community. Gold Crescent itself lies off the main road and along with its two side roads – Sword Close and Juno Close – is occupied almost entirely by bungalows.

On the same side of the road and heading towards Grimley, the village of Thraplow can be reached via a small side road or country lane. Just past this junction are the 'luxury flats' which were built to replace the *Fox and Hounds Inn*, followed by a few small terraced houses that were formerly miner's dwellings. Just beyond these are the allotments and what used to be the colliery. Further back from there is the old disused railway line that was used to transport the coal until Dr. Beeching's axe fell so ingloriously. There is then a sharp right-hand bend before one comes to Moor Farm, which has been in the same family for three or four generations at least. From there until one reaches the outskirts of Grimley there are nothing but fields of rape.

Across the road from Moor Farm and almost directly opposite is the Little Orchard Nursing Home, which is now in its twenty-sixth year of existence. Coming back towards the village there are a number of semi-detached buildings, including those which form a small cul-de-sac on the sharp bend. There then used to be a newsagent's, a hairdresser's shop and an off-licence at one time, but these have been converted into reasonably-priced homes. The only shop that remains is the post office, which also acts as the village stores and is moderately successful in these very trying times.

We then come to *The Wheatsheaf*, which is open seven days a week, noon till eleven on weekdays and Sundays, but closes midnight on Saturdays. There is a small car park at the front of the building and a larger one to the rear. Running alongside this car park is a footpath (one of several this side of the main road), which leads to the fields beyond and to Blackthorn Lane. The houses thereafter are largely detached and the abode of the wealthier inhabitants of the village.

Shortly before another sharp right-hand bend and opposite the village school there is a narrow lane which leads to the community hall. There are a couple more detached houses on the bend, and then there is a large field beyond which is a dirt track leading to Dawson's Farm. This lies opposite St. Matthew's Church and vicarage. More fields lie on the other side of the track until one comes to Blackthorn Lane, which comes to an abrupt end with a metal bar field gate at The Old Turnpike House. Beyond this the lane is for pedestrians and cyclists only, and during the summer months it can get very busy.

The trouble with Brockley was that there were too many outlying farms and isolated buildings, thought Postwoman Shaminder Kaur Johal as she began her delivery that morning, and this was one of them. The long drive down Blackthorn Lane to The Old Turnpike House was never one of the most popular drops on her delivery and she was always glad to get it out of the way, but this morning she had a large parcel for the occupant and as it was a Recorded Delivery it would require a signature.

Shaminder was a member of the Sikh community from Derby. The eldest of three sisters, she was now forty-three and married with two children, but she and her sisters were still very close. Cheerful and exuberant for the most part, she was also very vocal, especially when she and her sisters were together, and to some extent this belied her given name of Shaminder, which means 'quiet and gentle!'

Although she resided in Derby, she had been based at the Leverton Delivery Office since 2002 and was the only Asian member of the workforce. Having settled into her job and her environment very quickly, she soon gained a reputation among her colleagues for gossip and spreading rumours. They would be the first to say that she had a tendency for allowing drama to veer into melodrama, whereas others would acknowledge that she was terrified of falling out of favour. There was, however, one incident that brought her back down to earth and one which she never liked being reminded of, and that came about when she was first required to use a Royal Mail vehicle. No one had told her that all company vehicles were diesel-powered, so when it was discovered that she had pulled into the petrol station one morning and filled up with unleaded her colleagues had a good laugh at her expense. For someone who does not like being ridiculed or upstaged, that did not go down well at all!

Nevertheless, that was now all behind her as she drove the diesel-operated Royal Mail van down Blackthorn Lane that morning. At five foot three she was barely able to see above the steering wheel and it didn't help that the road to The Old Turnpike House was bumpy and full of potholes. Pulling up outside the building in a swirl of dust, there appeared to be no sign of the white Citroën Berlingo van that often stood outside the house or any other vehicle; nor were there any walkers, ramblers or cyclists. With her long hair tied in a bun and attired in the Royal Mail uniform of red t-shirt and blue trousers, she climbed out of the van and went to the rear. The nearby hedgerows and trees teemed with birdsong, whilst up above vapour trails criss-crossed the morning sky. It was a pleasant day and she was going to make the best of it.

As she retrieved the parcel addressed to Mr. Keith Jackson, curiosity got the better of her and she attempted to hazard a guess as to what the contents might be. It was quite light and easy to handle. He was a gardener; she was aware of that. So it had to be something like garden shears or even pruning scissors. She would make a polite and discreet enquiry to that end if he came to the door; just to stimulate the conversation.

She opened the small wrought iron gate and went up the path to the door. There was no bell so she gave the door a good solid rap. At that moment a cyclist manoeuvred his way through the field gate and then made his way up the lane to the main road without saying a word. Receiving no reply, she knocked on the door for a second time and then a third, but there was nothing. Thankfully the letterbox was halfway up the door and level with her navel, so growing impatient she decided to open it and call his name – he was sometimes still in bed when she called at the house. If that failed then she would fill out one of the red Royal Mail 'something for you' cards, explaining why she couldn't deliver the item and showing how it could be collected or a re-delivery arranged.

Lifting the outside flap of the letterbox she crouched and made to peer through, but as she was about to call his name she suddenly squealed and reeled back in horror on seeing what appeared to be the legs of a man dangling from the lintel above the inside door of the house. Cupping hand to mouth, she stood frozen to the spot for several seconds and literally fought back the urge to be sick. After several seconds she re-gathered her composure and went back to look through the letterbox one more time, if only to verify that what she had seen was for real. It was.

Leaving the parcel by the door, she staggered back down the path to the gate and then took out her mobile phone. Dialling 999, she gave her story and was told to remain where she was until emergency services arrived. She climbed back into the van, oblivious to the cyclists and those who now passed by the house walking their dogs. It was like a bad dream, only she had actually seen it with her own eyes. It suddenly dawned on her that she had to call the office and tell them what had happened. They'd never believe it.

'He was dangling there before my very eyes!' she screeched excitedly down the phone.

'What have you been on, Shaminder?' replied the office manager with a chuckle.

'It's true I tell you!'

And by the time she had got around to calling one of her sisters she was in full flow; only now she was making it known that a man had actually 'hung himself' on her delivery, as if she had carried out the post mortem *and* the investigation herself in five minutes flat!

One thing was for sure. Shaminder Kaur Johal would be the talk of the town when she got back home, and she was going to make the most of it.

Chapter 5

Tuesday, 4 July, 2017 (a.m.)

It is often said amongst locals that the town of Leverton has very little going for it nowadays, and it would be difficult to argue with them. Situated in the southeast corner of Derbyshire and roughly equidistant from Derby and Nottingham, Leverton was at one time a thriving, bustling community that owed its prosperity largely to the advent of the Industrial Revolution. Coal, steel and hosiery were the major industries and all were aided and abetted by the canals and then the railways.

There had been a history of coal mining in the area for centuries, but this was only on a small scale. Beginning in the last quarter of the eighteenth century, its extraction became a major occupation. The next stage of development began in 1828, and this was followed by further expansion in 1872 and then again in 1898, culminating in the General Strike of 1926. The coal industry – as with others – was nationalised after the Second World War, but it was downhill all the way thereafter, and the last pit in the area ceased operations in 1966.

One of the biggest and most important local employers was the Welham Ironworks, which was a continuation of a long-standing tradition of iron working in the area. As with coal mining, the iron and steel industry took off on a huge scale in the 1780's and by the mid-nineteenth century there were several blast furnaces. However, its heyday came after 1945, with the British Steel Corporation, but here too work gradually declined. It was taken over by a Belgian company in 1985, but the last casting came in 2007 and it is now a large industrial estate and business park.

Up until the 1880's the hosiery industry had been dominated by men, but then a growing number of women were admitted to the industry. All that changed with the First World War, and thereafter women formed the basis of the workforce at the numerous large factories that sprung up in and around Leverton. These too suffered a decline after the 1970's, but there are still one or two hosiery businesses in the area, but only on a small scale.

The Edgeley Canal was opened in 1779 and runs alongside the river of the same name. It was initially built to carry coal to the Welham

Ironworks, but was later used to transport coal to the Trent and Mersey Canal and thence to markets in Loughborough and Leicester. It is now used for recreational purposes only.

By 1832 colliery owners (including the Frankland-Moore's) grew concerned at the charges levied by the canals and decided to build their own railway. After much debate and some minor disagreements, work began on the East Midlands Railway in 1837. Taken over by the Midland Railway in 1847, the line (running from what became known as Leverton South station) soon made a profit with the transportation of the valuable coal traffic. In 1923 the Midland Railway merged with others to become the London, Midland and Scottish Railway (LMS). The line was closed in 1967, but there are plans to re-open it in 2018.

Work began on another line in 1867, from what became known as the Leverton North station. Initially run by the Great Northern Railway (GNR), it became a constituent of the London and North Eastern Railway (LNER) following the Railways Act of 1921, but it too closed in 1964. The site lay derelict up until the 1990's.

So the core industries have changed, the railway system has been much reduced and the canal system altered almost beyond recognition. But there is still a police presence in Leverton.

For as long as anyone could remember, the police station at Leverton was always located close to the town centre, just off the market square and opposite the council buildings. A Victorian structure of Derbyshire gritstone, it loomed over the nearby buildings and residential housing until the Co-operative Store was erected alongside it in the 1950's. Indeed, such was its imposing character pedestrians would occasionally be seen to cross the road to avoid having to pass the building, even though nothing more sinister occurred there than the locking up of the town's drunken, brawling revellers on a Friday and Saturday night.

And then in 1997 it was decided that the town needed a more modern building for its police force, so they turned their attention to the derelict site where the Leverton North railway station once stood. The new building was erected amid much pomp and ceremony the following year, and the old police station was transformed into a number of small offices and business units.

Following yet another major restructuring of the police forces of the United Kingdom in 2011, extensions were added to the new building and Leverton henceforth became part of the East Midlands Regional

Police (EMRP), which were now to comprise three divisions, namely North (Derbyshire), South (Leicestershire, Rutland and Northamptonshire) and East (Nottinghamshire and Lincolnshire). The Chief Constable of the East Midlands Regional Police is based in Nottingham. He has three Assistant Chief Constables; one based in Derby, one based in Leicester and the other in Lincoln. The North Division has four area CID units, namely Derby (representing the city), Ashbourne (representing the Peak District), Chesterfield (representing the north and northeast of the county) and Leverton (representing the south and southeast of the county). Since 2015 the head of Leverton CID has been Detective Chief Superintendent Roger Annable – and he now faced a dilemma.

'Bugger!' muttered Annable to himself as he put the phone down. There was nobody available to take charge of the case and now the bloody Deputy Senior Investigating Officer has gone and had a stroke! For an experienced, organised and methodical officer like Annable, this was not the way to start to the day!

A born leader, Annable was driven by the need to wield power, so that he was always anxious for everyone to know that he was in charge and control; even to the point where he deemed it necessary and expedient to alter his appearance. At just over six feet in height, he cut an imposing figure and with hands like shovels he also maintained a commanding presence throughout the station, especially when those hands were placed on hips and legs were spread wide apart. This image is given further credence by the almost permanent frown that seems to bring his glaring brown eyes closer together all the more. Formidable as all of this may seem, the Superintendent has taken to touching up the roots of his short but thick dark brown hair (parted down the left-hand side) to hide the grey hairs; or so his secretary is willing to testify after catching him unawares one morning when taking him a cuppa.

It has to be said that there was little sign of a weight problem either, but he would put that down to enjoying a regular round of golf and drinking very little; unlike some other officers under his command. However, if there was one thing that enabled Annable to make his presence felt then it was his voice. Loud and penetrating (booming even some would say), he had the capacity to make actor Brian Blessed seem soft-spoken and reserved at the best of times. Indeed, such was his determination to exercise control and prevent chaos that he had a tendency to shout and lose his temper quite a lot, especially with the male officers. For this reason they referred to him as "Annable the Cannibal", although he was much milder and conciliatory-sounding with the female members of the force. His secretary insisted that he was a 'pussycat really,' but perhaps she wouldn't have said as much had she known that he had actually shot and killed a machete-wielding rioter when serving with the Metropolitan Police some years previously. Fortunately for Annable, the subsequent inquest found that he had acted in self-defence and he was allowed to resume his career.

But as the son of a Chesterfield steelworker he had worked hard to get where he was, but he had a bad habit of letting everyone know it; everyone except the Assistant Chief Constable that is. And Mrs. Annable it would seem. He may have liked to portray himself as the authoritarian, does-everything-by-the-book control freak, but maybe his secretary had a point to some extent, because there were times when he could be nauseatingly subservient to his superiors – and to his wife.

Annable was very much a family man and as if to prove it he had placed two photographs on either side of his desk; one of his wife, Julie, and the other of the two of them with their three children. A creature of habit, he had taken to polishing them without failure every day; and always first thing in the morning before seating himself at his desk. Happily domiciled at their detached house close to the golf course at Armisfield, there were actually very few bones of contention between pair, although Mrs. Annable's insistence that they always spend their summer holidays in the Caribbean did rankle him somewhat, especially as his desire was to travel the length and breadth of Italy. However, they did share a passion for the theatre and a love of Shakespeare, and to the annoyance of others he would frequently quote from one of the bard's illustrious works. Nevertheless, his secretary always knew when Mrs. Annable rang her husband's office, for a smile would come to her face as she heard the familiar 'Yes dear, no dear, three bags full dear!'

But today his secretary was on leave. Indeed, everyone was on bloody leave, or so it seemed to Superintendent Annable. So he picked up the phone and asked to be put through to the Assistant Chief Constable in Derby. He didn't have to wait long before she came on the line and his demeanour changed immediately.

'Yes, Ma'am,' he said with an air of despondence. 'We seem to be short of sta…'

But the Assistant Chief Constable interrupted him.

'Oh, so you've heard about Detective Sergeant C…?'

She cut him short again.

'Yes, yes, so it would app…'

If only he could get a word in. But then he suddenly sat up straight.

'From Nottingham you say? And we can expect their arrival tomorrow? Well that's splendid,' he shouted triumphantly.

But as the Assistant Chief Constable continued, the ingratiating side of Annable's character came to the fore. 'Yes, Ma'am, but of course, Ma'am, I understand perfectly, Ma'am. I'll look forward to introdu...'

The Assistant Chief Constable had made her point.

'Thank you, and…'

The line was dead, but rubbing his hands together he rose from his desk as though he had just been selected to play for the European team in the Ryder Cup. Opening the door to his office he marched swiftly down the corridor until he came upon the Desk Sergeant.

'Scattergood!' he barked

The Desk Sergeant had heard the footsteps coming down the corridor and recognised them instantly. Moving quickly, he hid his copy of *The Sun* and his morning cuppa under the desk, and was ready and waiting for whatever the Superintendent was going to throw at him with a half-hearted smile.

'Yes, Sir?'he said slightly nervously.

'We shall be having a new officer on our team tomorrow,' shouted Annable, 'albeit temporarily. A Detective Sergeant Fletcher, as I understand. Let me know the moment they arrive.'

'Would that be Detective Sergeant Fletcher from Nottingham, Sir?' queried the Desk Sergeant with a note of anxiety in his voice.

'Yes, that's right. Do you have a problem with that, Scattergood?'

'Erm, no. Not at all, Sir.' replied the Desk Sergeant truthfully. However, he knew a man who would, but he wasn't going to be the one to tell him!

'And I do wish that you would cut out the smoking and the takeaway's, Scattergood!' snorted Annable as he pointed to the tell-tale signs of cigarette ash and food stains on the Desk Sergeants uniform. 'What kind of message do you think that sends to the public?' he continued. 'At the end of the day it reflects badly on this station, of which I am the Chief Superintendent, in case you haven't noticed. And I won't have it! Do I make myself understood?'

'Yes, Sir!' replied the Desk Sergeant sheepishly and with head slightly bowed.

'And get hold of Inspector Clarke.' bellowed Annable, as he turned and marched back to his office. 'I want him in charge of the case!'

'But he's on leave, Sir,' pleaded the Desk Sergeant. 'Doing a spot of decorating, so he said.'

'Not now he isn't!' retorted Annable as he continued along the corridor without looking back over his shoulder. 'Get him up to Brockley – now!'

The Desk Sergeant slumped back onto his swivel chair, shook his head and muttered to himself 'At the end of the day he's not going to like this. He's just not going to like this!'

Chapter 6

Tuesday, 4 July, 2017 (a.m.)

Bob Scattergood was well liked and respected, not only by his colleagues at the Leverton police station, but by the community as a whole. Open and honest, he possessed the ability to understand how to get along with a wide variety of people; the post of Desk Sergeant could have been tailor-made for him. However, although he came across as being quite a jovial and friendly sort of chap, he was a man of deep feelings and it would not be too unkind to say that he had been experiencing great personal pain for some time.

Leverton born and bred, he was from a coal mining family, but then so were most of the kids he went to school with. So when the sandy-haired, blue-eyed lad from Ashover Street was asked what he wanted to be when he left school and excitedly announced to the class and the teacher that he wanted to be a policeman, it came as no surprise that he received a lot of stick from his mates. But Bob Scattergood could look after himself; it was a case of having to in those days. And true to his word, he joined the police immediately after leaving school and never looked back.

There was one girl in the class who would never give Bob any stick. On the contrary, Maureen Lister swelled with pride the day Bob put his hand up and said that he wanted to join the police, for the simple reason that they were childhood sweethearts. To be happy and unconditionally loved were goals that he had set himself from an early age, and the day he married Maureen (both were eighteen) he felt that he had fulfilled his desire and found paradise.

Four children followed (three girls and one boy), and it would be true to say that he was the quintessential family man, grateful for what he had and committed to each and every one of them. When his son joined the Army he was the last of the children to leave home, but Bob had prepared himself for that eventuality. What he dreaded most of all – what absolutely terrified him – was losing the love of his life, Maureen, and he just hadn't prepared himself for that.

So when Maureen lost her battle with cancer at the age of fifty in 2012, Bob's whole world fell apart. He had lost the love of his life and that life was never going to be the same again. The prospect of coming home to an empty house was more than he could bear and he even considered quitting his job and moving elsewhere. Thankfully everyone rallied round and persuaded him to carry on. So that's what he did – to the best of his ability.

His daughters were all married and had families of their own, but they didn't live too far away and so they were regular visitors. One of them still comes around once a week to clean, hoover and tidy – and cook him a decent meal now and again. Otherwise he relies almost entirely on takeaways; as the stains on his uniform will testify. He was never very good around the house anyway, so these visits are a godsend. Needless to say, he dotes upon his grandchildren, and they take up much of his spare time. He is immensely proud of his son and his service with the Army, so he always looks forward to seeing him when he's on leave. At just over six feet in height, he's a couple of inches taller than his father, as he is always fond of reminding him.

His only other means of escape from what he considers to be the banality of his existence is fishing, so it has come as a welcome surprise to find that one of his grandchildren appears to have become addicted to the sport. Indeed, the lad is only too happy and willing to get up during the early hours to accompany him down to the canal, but especially so during the summer break. What's more, Bob turns a blind eye to the fact that the lad takes a swig from his can of Abbot's ale when he thinks granddad isn't looking!

However, the lad's mum certainly doesn't approve of Bob's drinking; she even called him 'portly' a few weeks ago. Okay, so he's put on a bit of weight over the last five years, but there's nothing wrong with propping the bar up down at the local once or twice a week, is there? And maybe he does smoke too much, but so what? That doesn't make him a bad person or a bad copper, does it? And he's always been a bloody good copper – contrary to what Superintendent Annable may think!

He had tampered with the idea of becoming a detective at one time, but he gave up on this when his wife was diagnosed with cancer. If his kids helped him get over her death, then his colleagues were just as supportive and he has never regretted taking their advice and carrying on as Desk Sergeant at Leverton. There was one member of the force in particular who stood by him and persuaded him to soldier on, and now he had the unpleasant task of informing the man that he was no longer on leave.

The Edgeley Canal is not renowned for its bustling activity these days. Starting from the River Trent at Dernley, it runs roughly parallel to the River Edgeley for twelve miles or so to the Braidley Junction basin (also known as the *Bridge Inn* basin), near Grimley. Halfway between Grimley and Leverton is the Croxley Wharf, which at the turn of the 20th century was busy with the transhipment of coal from the nearby collieries to narrow boats on the canal. This lasted until 1952 and the top section of the canal was closed ten years later. In 1968 the Edgeley Canal Preservation and Development Trust (ECPDT) was formed with the purpose of restoring the canal to its full navigation, and their goal was duly achieved and celebrated at the *Bridge Inn* in 1973. Reclassified as 'Cruising Waterway Standard' by the British Waterways Act of 1983, the canal is actively used by pleasure cruisers of all shapes and sizes.

Just below the Wharf is Croxley Lock, which is one of fourteen locks along the canal. There is also a bridge over the canal at this point, besides which stands the old lock keeper's cottage (still occupied). Both bridge and cottage are connected to the main Grimley to Leverton road by a narrow lane, known locally as Long Lane. About a hundred yards or so below the lock, the narrow boat *Emily* is moored on the port side of the canal and facing the direction of Grimley. The occupant of the *Emily* has secured planning permission for long-term mooring, as the boat is his sole place of residence (for the occupant is most definitely a male), and has been for three years. A silver Ford Focus is parked a dozen or so yards away from the *Emily*, which can be accessed from Long Lane by a dirt track.

The *Emily* is a forty-five feet long, two-berth narrow boat in need of a lick of paint here and there. Fed up with living in rented accommodation, the occupant splashed out on a run-down narrow-boat in 2014, renovated it to the best of his ability and renamed it *Emily*. Actually the occupant didn't do a bad job the first time around, choosing to paint the vessel navy blue with a white roof and trimmings. However, not to put too fine a point on it, the occupant has been guilty of some neglect over the last three years, as those walking along the towpath have been quick to observe.

The steering area of the *Emily* is referred to as 'Cruiser Stern,' whereby the hatch and rear doors are further forward than on a traditional boat, creating a large open deck protected by railing. Either side of the rear doors the built-in seating has been removed and replaced by plant pots containing herbs, such as mint, parsley, thyme and coriander, amongst others. Other features include a 200-gallon water tank which supplies hot and cold running water, and full radiator diesel control central heating.

Entering the cabin by the rear doors, it becomes immediately apparent that oak flooring has been laid throughout the boat. Two steps lead down to the galley or kitchen area, which is equipped with a four-burner gas cooker (complete with grill and oven) and refrigerator on one side (complete with fridge magnets), and a sink unit and washing machine on the other. Indeed, the kitchen area appears to be clean and clear of crockery and cutlery, but there is a microwave oven on one worktop and a kettle and much-used slow-cooker on another. There is plenty of storage space too and a shelf containing several cook books has been affixed to the wall beside the sink unit. There is a large rectangular window above the latter and another above the gas cooker on the other side, but in each case the curtains are drawn. A clock hangs above the steps and a large litter bin stands aloof beside the washing machine.

The galley leads into the saloon, which acts as a living room and dining room area. It is carpeted for the most part, but there are one or two signs of wear and tear visible to the naked eye. It is also furnished with two comfortable armchairs and a pull-out table upon which is a laptop, printer and lamp. Facing these on the starboard side of the vessel is a large screen TV, mounted on a cabinet containing DVD's/DVD player and CD's/CD player. On the wall between the sink unit and the TV screen is a framed picture of Pink Floyd's *Wish You Were Here* album cover, depicting two men shaking hands, one of whom is on fire. Directly opposite are two paintings, one of which is a woodland scene with fallow deer and the other a rustic scene from the Derbyshire Peak District. As with the galley, there are two more large rectangular windows in the saloon and here too the curtains are drawn. At the top end of the saloon is a stove and on same side as the TV is a slide door which leads to the bathroom area.

Spacious and light, this part of the cabin is dominated by the shower suite, which is immediately to the right of the door. The occupant has always preferred a shower at the end of each working day to a long soak in a bath, for the simple reason that 'it's a quick in-and-out job.' Up against the wall opposite the shower is an electrically-operated flush toilet and a wash basin, above which is a mirror. There is a shaver socket too, but the occupant has no need for this, as will become apparent. Unlike the galley and the saloon, the bathroom area has two portholes on either side of the vessel (curtains drawn), but another slide door on the starboard side leads to the bedroom.

Much of the space here is taken by a large double bed (facing the fore deck), beside which is a small table complete with bedside lamp, alarm clock and small black and white photograph of a young couple on their wedding day. Furthermore, there is also a half empty bottle of Laphroaig (pronounced La-froyg) single malt whisky and a small glass still containing a good measure of the distinctive, richly-flavoured liquid. At the foot of the bed is a wardrobe with a set of drawers and another mirror. The wardrobe contains very few clothes, but there is an acoustic guitar propped up inside (left-handed of course). Again, there are two portholes either side of the boat and these too are drawn.

However, lying face down and asleep upon the bed in a black t-shirt and dark grey shorts is a middle-aged man about five feet and ten inches tall, with brown eyes and short but thick, greying hair that was once dark. Needless to say, the hair is unkempt and one night be mistaken for thinking that he hasn't shaved for a number of days, but the fact of the matter is that he has always had a close-cropped beard since his mid-twenties, and yet it does occasionally give the appearance of being stubble. The beard has now turned grey too and is trimmed on a weekly basis (that's if he remembers). Furthermore, he prefers to turn to a pack of Gillette Blue II *Plus Slalom* disposable razors rather than use an electric variant for the removal of unwanted facial hair (that's when he bothers).

There is a case for arguing that he is slightly overweight too, but this is not due to lack of exercise or the consumption of fatty foods; rather a predilection to beer and spirits over the years, but especially the latter. And he sure as hell hit the bottle the night before judging by what remained in the bottle on the bedside table!

This *Felix caeli dormitabis* was suddenly interrupted by the chiming of clocks and the ringing of alarms that marked the introduction to the track *Time* from Pink Floyd's *Dark Side of the Moon* album, and which acted as the ringtone on the man's mobile phone. It had the desired effect of waking the man with a start, but to all intents and purposes he was still practically comatose as he reached out here and there with his hand for his mobile. After what seemed to be an eternity he found the offending piece of apparatus on the pillow just above his head and he answered it with a barely audible grunt.

'Clarke?'

The Desk Sergeant had second guessed that the Inspector would probably still be asleep and suffering from a hangover, so with some trepidation and yet with a cheerful disposition he announced himself as quietly as possible.

'Scattergood here, Sir. Hope I haven't disturbed you?'

'Of course you bloody well disturbed me, Scattergood.' mumbled Clarke. 'And there's no need to whisper. I'm not bloody deaf!'

The Desk Sergeant also surmised that the Inspector had not kept to his word and set about decorating his boat whilst on leave, but he still pressed ahead.

'Hope the decorating is going as planned, Sir?'

'Just get to the bloody point will you man!' grumbled Clarke with some irritation.

'Well, it's just that there's been a suspicious death out at Brockley, Sir.' continued the Desk Sergeant somewhat gingerly.

'What's that got to do with me?' protested Clarke. 'I'm on leave, as you well know.'

'Yes, Sir, but Superintendent Annable has asked me to tell you that he wants you to attend, Sir.' The Desk Sergeant felt somewhat relieved that he'd made it clear that this was the Superintendent's decision and not his.

By now Clarke had stirred sufficiently to manoeuvre himself to the edge of the bed, where he now sat with head throbbing and realising that any further resistance was futile.

'Oh well, if the Superintendent wants me to attend then I don't suppose I've got a bloody option, have I?' retorted Clarke a trifle sarcastically.

'No, Sir.'

'Has Sergeant Coates been notified?'

Scattergood paused slightly before replying. 'Erm, I'm afraid that Sergeant Coates had a stroke at the weekend, Sir.'

'What?' shouted Clarke with some disbelief. 'Well who the bloody hell...?'

But Scattergood was expecting just such a response and politely interrupted the Inspector. 'It's all in hand, Sir. We're to expect a temporary replacement in the morning.'

'Do we know who this replacement is?' queried Clarke

Scattergood paused again. 'Erm, not as yet, Sir,' he lied, 'but Constable Webster has gone to Brockley to co-ordinate the initial response, Sir.'

'That's a start, I suppose.' said Clarke, more to himself than to the Desk Sergeant. 'Okay, tell Webster I'll be there within the hour,' he continued. 'And let's just hope that the new Sergeant is up to the task!'

The phone went dead and Scattergood slumped back onto his swivel chair once more before muttering to himself 'He's not going to like it. He's just not going to like it!'

Chapter 7

Tuesday, 4 July, 2017 (a.m.)

Within one hour of the body being discovered, the scene at the Old Turnpike House had been transformed. The Royal Mail delivery van was still there, as was the postwoman, but now numerous other vehicles had arrived, including an ambulance and those belonging to the police, the police surgeon and Scenes of Crime Officer's or SOCO's. The house itself had been sealed off and all passers-by were being told to turn around and go back from whence they came, including ramblers and cyclists.

Clarke had taken a quick shower following the call from Scattergood, and he was in the silver Ford Focus and on his way to Brockley within twenty minutes. In many respects this was just the excuse he needed to get out of having to paint the narrow boat. His head still throbbed and he'd taken a couple of paracetamol caplets since rising, but he'd also drank plenty of water, and there was a small bottle of Buxton sparkling water beside him on the passenger seat as he turned right at the top of Long Lane and onto the main road that ran from Leverton to Grimley. He surmised that it wouldn't take him long to drive through Grimley and on into Brockley before arriving at the scene, and having navigated the various bumps and potholes of Blackthorn Lane he pulled up outside the Old Turnpike House fifteen minutes later.

He had donned a pair of grey slacks, white long-sleeved shirt (sleeves rolled up and top button undone) and navy blue tie (loosely knotted) prior to leaving the *Emily*. The familiar dark grey bomber jacket had been deemed unnecessary due to the heat – it was a very warm and sunny morning. Climbing out of the car, he took in the pleasant surroundings and smiled to himself briefly as he heard the unmistakeable sound of a Chaffinch, but just as he was putting on the requisite personal protective clothing he spotted the familiar ever-jovial figure of Detective Constable Matthew Webster coming towards him.

'Morning Sir.' began Webster with a smile stretching from one side of his face to the other. 'Bad news about Sergeant Coates, isn't it?'

Clarke said nothing at first, but as he bent down to pull on the protective footwear he merely answered Webster's question with one of his own.

'What have we got?'

'Well, it looks like he was very highly strung, Sir!' replied Webster flippantly as he was barely able to suppress yet another huge grin.

Clarke straightened up and shook his head. 'Not now, Webster. Not now.'

Difficult as it undoubtedly was to carry on an important conversation with one who frequently makes quips to lighten a sombre atmosphere, Clarke was accustomed to Webster's facetiousness and sense of frivolity. Ever the jester and practical joker, it was common knowledge that at secondary school he was the one who supplied the girl's hockey team with laxatives prior to an important game, and needless to say they lost! But then he always had been blessed with charisma and magnetism, all of which made him a man of mischief. It's just that he dreads becoming bored and with a lack of stimulation.

He's certainly not unattractive either, although he has made it clear that he has no desire to commit himself to any relationship as yet. As with many young men of today he is elegantly coiffured. His thick, dark hair is cut short, parted to one side and brushed over to the other. He has long sideburns too, but no facial hair to speak of. At five feet and nine inches he is not a tall man, but what he lacks in height he more than makes up for in his appearance. He has brown eyes and olive skin, leading others to believe that he is of a Latino extract. His response is to suggest that he may be a 'quarter Italian on his mother's second cousin's grandmother's side!' When not biting his thick lips, he will almost always provide a broad grin or smile, revealing a set of perfectly aligned white teeth.

Strangely enough, he always wanted to be a comedian or comic actor from an early age, much to his father's exasperation. This led to arguments, because his father wanted 'the lazy bugger to do something with his life' and become a fireman like him! Young Matthew ("Matt") did just enough to get his GCSE's, so it was with some surprise to everyone (father included) when he went to Leicester De Montfort University after leaving school, to undertake a BA with Honours in Criminal Investigation with Policing Studies. Again, doing just enough to get his degree, it was with even greater surprise to all that he joined the police immediately after leaving university. It was a proud Webster senior who saw his son become a Detective Constable at the age of twenty-five in 2014, because he had 'done very little to achieve the bugger!' Assigned to his home town of Leverton, this 'lazy bugger' still has difficulty staying on task, but in spite of this he is loyal to his boss and he now provided him with a brief account of what was known so far.

'Single white male in his mid-fifties, Sir.' said Webster a trifle more tactfully. 'Postwoman came upon him as she was delivering a parcel.'

Clarke briefly transferred his gaze towards the red van before heading for the house with Webster alongside. 'What time was this?' he asked.

'About a quarter past nine, Sir.'

'Do we know the man's name?'

'Jackson, Sir – a Mr. Keith Jackson.'

'There doesn't appear to be a vehicle?'

'No, Sir. There's no CCTV camera's either and we've been unable to find the victim's mobile phone.'

'Terrific!' was Clarke's rather sardonic reply.

As they passed through the gate and headed up the path, Clarke recognised the familiar face of the police surgeon in the hallway, squatting over the body which, as Webster pointed out, had been hanging from the lintel and had since been taken down for a preliminary examination. As he continued to administer to the body, the surgeon seemed to be in a world of his own and was happily singing away to himself with an unmistakeable lilting Borders accent.

'Oh, better for to live and die…'

'Morning, Alex.' interrupted Clarke. '*Pirates of Penzance* if I'm not mistaken?'

The surgeon looked up somewhat startled. 'I thought you were on leave?' he said with some surprise.

'So did I!' replied Clarke with an element of exasperation in his voice.

As the surgeon struggled to his feet he winced and grasped his knee. 'Bloody thing!' he said with a grimace.

'The old war wound taking its toll I see.' said Clarke sympathetically.

It wasn't that Dr. Alexander Fraser FRCPath had ever served in Her Majesty's armed forces, but Clarke was conscious of the fact that there was a time when he could have had the distinction of playing international Rugby Union as a second-row forward for Scotland whilst at University. Unfortunately a knee injury put paid to that and at fifty-six he was still suffering the consequences.

Although born in Edinburgh in 1961, Dr. Fraser spent most of his childhood years in the Scottish border town of Selkirk. The son of a pathologist of the same name, there was never really any doubt that he was going to follow in his father's footsteps, so after leaving school in 1977 he spent five years undergraduate training at the University of Edinburgh Medical School before registering with the General Medical Council. Having developed a love of rugby at school, he was first choice for the number five shirt with the university rugby first fifteen until his injury. He remained at the university for a further two years to complete the UK Foundation Training Programme, and afterwards attended the Royal Infirmary of Edinburgh to undertake five years of basic histopathology training. He then joined the Royal College of Pathologists and remained at the Infirmary as a forensic pathologist.

During his first years at the Infirmary he met Jean MacLeod whilst on holiday on the Isle of Skye and they married in 1989. They have three daughters, namely Fiona, Isobel and Catriona. In 2003 the whole family left Scotland and moved to Derbyshire, where he took up his present job at what was then the new, state of the art Queen Elizabeth II Hospital on the outskirts Leverton. The fact that this gave him quick and easy access to the Peak District undoubtedly played a part in his decision to accept the post. It also enabled him to join the Derby Gilbert and Sullivan Company, membership of which has brought him unparalleled joy.

The archetypal pathologist, he and Clarke have developed a mutual understanding and not merely because of their shared love of rugby. Reflective at the best of times, Clarke sees him as a sort of "spiritual mediator", in that he has the ability to explain complicated ideas and theories in ways others can grasp. Having said that, he can be easily-ruffled and irritable when others fail to catch on to his "vision", so to speak, or fail to harness their excitement. Constable Webster would almost certainly fall into that category. This would probably explain why Webster hid behind the Inspector as Dr. Fraser straightened up and tried to shake off his (hopefully) temporary affliction.

At just over six feet he didn't so much as tower over the two detectives – and certainly not Clarke anyway; but like the great Sandy Carmichael he could make his presence felt, with or without the ball. Bill McLaren would have probably described him as a 'raging bull with a bad head' during his playing days, so maybe Webster was probably fortunate not to have come face to face with him in a ruck! Somewhat overweight now, the mousy-coloured wavy hair was rapidly fading to grey like his eyes, but his mind was as razor sharp as ever. Rubbing his bearded chin between the forefinger and thumb of his right hand, he suddenly turned to face Clarke once more and prepared to deliver his preliminary findings.

'Well it isnae suicide, that's fer sure!' he said confidently in his Border brogue.

'I might have bloody known it,' replied a somewhat disappointed Clarke. 'What makes you say that then, Alex?'

'Okay, he was found suspended from a hook in the masonry lintel above the inside door by what appears to be the washing line cable, which has a steel core protected by PVC. At first glance it looks like suicide, I'll grant you, but take a closer look here.' Warming to his theme, he crouched down once more and beckoned the two detectives over to the body. 'There are two abrasions, not parallel with each other, on the front of the neck – see?' Clarke and Webster peered over his shoulder and duly nodded in agreement as the doctor continued. 'The upper abrasion is that made by the ligature, whilst the one beneath is accompanied by bruising. The upper mark has no bruising and was produced *after* death, whilst the lower abrasion is a ligature mark from strangulation. This would suggest that he was suspended for simulation of suicide after being strangled.'

As always Dr. Fraser had carried out his task assiduously and made his point clearly and succinctly, but Clarke still pressed him further.

'And you're certain about this?' he asked politely. 'He was definitely strangled?'

'Och aye.' replied Fraser. 'In my view it was a poor attempt to disguise murder, but that's for you to establish.'

'And do we know when the crime was committed?'

'I'd say about eighteen or nineteen hours ago – or thereabouts.'

'So, that's between 4.00 p.m. and 5.00 p.m. yesterday afternoon?'

'Aye, but I'll be able to be more exact after the post mortem.'

'Thanks, Alex. Much appreciated as always.'

With that the detectives and the police surgeon bade their farewells and the body was taken away to the mortuary. People were still coming in and out of the house at this time and the SOCO's were continuing to carry out their forensic examinations, but at least now the detectives had a victim and it was time to find out more about him.

Clarke and Webster duly began their search of the downstairs rooms, beginning with the kitchen and dining room. Hygiene was clearly not one of the victim's strong points, as the sink was still full of unwashed pots and pans, and there was a half-eaten plate of fish and chips sitting on the draining board. The gas cooker didn't appear to have been cleaned for ages and the litter bin alongside clearly hadn't been emptied for some time either. The cushion flooring in the kitchen was filthy and there was a large damp patch in front of the sink unit, which was traced to a leak in one of the pipes behind the cooker. The windows were closed, but they must have been open at some time in the previous twenty-four hours or so as there were flies everywhere. The table in the dining room area provided evidence of the victim's habits and lifestyle, as there were several betting slips and two empty bottles of vodka. Most interesting of all were a series of letters, all signifying that the victim had money problems. Most were from the victim's bank, but there were a couple of letters with the National Debtline logo at the top left-hand side of each page, and these showed that he was at least receiving some help and advice.

The living room was untidy too, and it appeared that the victim had been sleeping on the sofa. There was just one easy chair in the room, but like the sofa the covers were full of holes. Beside the chair was a small table, upon which lay a number of DVD's. Some were classic wartime favourites such as *The Longest Day* and *The Great Escape*, but others were clearly of a pornographic nature. There were stains all over the carpet and the curtains clearly needed to be replaced. Over in the far corner there was a TV set and a DVD player nearby, but it was the photographs that caught Clarke's eye. There were three on the mantelpiece above the gas fire, all of which showed the victim in his younger days and in Army uniform. One was a photograph presumably showing the victim with his parents, whilst the other two showed him with a group of comrades and obviously in far happier times. To the left of the door was a cabinet, upon which were two more photographs. One of these was a black and white snap that showed a couple on their wedding day, but again this had to be the victim's parents. The other was a colour photograph of two children (a boy and a girl), smiling happily for the camera. Curiously there was no photograph of their mother. Whilst Webster went upstairs, Clarke searched through the drawers of the cabinet, but although he found nothing of importance he couldn't help feeling that someone else had been there looking for something.

Whilst Webster continued his search upstairs, Clarke went through the back door and out into the garden, most of which was overgrown. There was a path either side of the door and posts at each end, suggesting that this was where Jackson hung is washing. But there was no washing line now of course; that had been used on the victim!

In the far left corner of the garden was a rowan tree and a buddleia to the right, but everything else was just bracken, nettles and what Clarke correctly assumed to be cow parsley. There was no lawn, but Clarke surmised that Jackson or the previous occupant had attempted to grow vegetables of some kind. There were three or four outbuildings full of garden equipment and machinery, most of which was in need of repair. The path to the right led to a dilapidated gate which was closed. Clarke went through this and discovered a lean-to garage in which two SOCO's were hard at work.

Clarke returned to the house and was heading for the front door just as Webster was coming down the stairs.

'Anything?' inquired Clarke

'Nothing really, Sir.' replied Webster. 'There's a bathroom and toilet – both of which are filthy. And three bedrooms – one of which is crammed with all sorts of paraphernalia. Everywhere could do with a good dusting, Sir.'

There was barely a cloud in the sky outside the Old Turnpike House and little in the way of breeze. The midday sun therefore beat down almost without mercy and the heat increased in intensity. The small wall surrounding the house was covered in moss and dandelions interspersed with sedum protruded from the base.

Looking down at these, Clarke seemed to be in deep contemplation for several minutes, gathering his thoughts and taking stock of the situation. If it had been a suicide then surely the victim would have left a note explaining why he had taken this course of action? But they had been unable to find such a note, giving further credence to Dr. Fraser's insistence that it was murder. The drawers and cupboards didn't appear to have been ransacked, but then the killer wouldn't do that if he or she was trying to make it look like a suicide? Nevertheless, they may *still* have been searching for something. Therefore, had they found what they were looking for, or were they disturbed? And surely the victim had a vehicle of some sort? That had to be found and bloody quick! It might give them some idea as to who was the last person to see him alive. Of course it would have made the whole job a damn sight easier if there had been CCTV cameras, but hey ho! That was a stroke of luck for the killer. Was he or she aware of this? Webster's voice suddenly brought him out of his reverie.

'Is it okay for the postwoman to return to her duties, Sir?' he asked

'Has she revealed anything of any importance?'

'She says that she rarely saw the guy and knows nothing of any family.'

'Okay, take her statement and then she can go.'

Webster nodded to the uniformed officer standing alongside the Royal Mail van, and after two or three minutes postwoman Shaminder Kaur Johal sped off into the distance and back up Blackthorn Lane to reveal to her colleagues, family and friends how *she* had found the body.

In the meantime Clarke informed Webster of the immediate action to be taken. He was aware of a community hall in the village just off the main road; that was to be the Main Incident Room (MIR).

'And if anyone complains, tell them to get in touch with me,' he barked through gritted teeth.

He then gave Webster the onerous task of putting a team together (minus a Deputy Senior Investigating Officer for the time being), but he trusted the lad enough to get the right people for the right job. He was also to issue a preliminary press release, including a request for possible witnesses, especially ramblers, dog walkers and cyclists who were in the vicinity of The Old Turnpike House between the hours of 3.00 p.m. and 5.00 p.m. on the previous day. Door-to-door enquiries were to be initiated, but only throughout the community of Brockley for the time being. It wouldn't need an army of recruits, so to speak, but if there were any problems he was to be notified immediately. The public were to be asked primarily for details of the victim – his possible movements, his family, his work, his car and any information on his military service – but also for witnesses and suspects too. Someone was to visit the local betting shops to find out more about his lifestyle and whether or not he had won any substantial amounts of money recently. Furthermore, they were to visit the victim's bank *and* contact the National Debtline to find out more about his debt problem.

'I want a report of everything on my desk at the Incident Room first thing in the morning,' he demanded, 'including post-mortem results if ready, forensic results where possible, results of door-to-door enquiries *and* feedback from the banks and National Debtline. Think you can manage that, Webster?'

'Yes, Sir.' replied the Detective Constable with a befuddled look on his face.

'And there will be a team briefing at the Incident Room at 10.00 a.m. sharp!'

Clarke had made it back to his car and was removing the protective clothing when Webster came running after him.

'Sir, I almost forgot this.' Webster produced an evidence bag containing what appeared to be a circular badge, the size of a fifty pence piece and complete with clip or pin at the back. 'I don't know if it's relevant to the case, but SOCO's found it under the cabinet near the inside door and at the foot of the stairs.'

Clarke took the bag from Webster and a look of puzzlement appeared on his face. The image on the badge was somewhat faded (probably as a result of the elements), but Clarke was able to make out that it depicted the cartoon characters *Tom and Jerry*. Webster was about to make one of his humorous quips, but Clarke stopped him in his tracks.

'Don't even go there, Webster. Don't even go there!'

Chapter 8

Tuesday, 4 July, 2017 (p.m.)

When is a cob not a cob? When it's a bread roll, according to the menu at the *Railway Tavern* in the village of Clavermill, which lies about six or seven miles north of Brockley. Clarke still had a thick head, but he was feeling a little peckish now and thirsty too, so after leaving the murder scene he headed out to a little watering hole he hadn't been to for some years. Yes, he remembered now. He and his then wife, Lesley, had popped in one Saturday evening on their way back from Dovedale during the summer of 1999. They had sat outside beside the river, mesmerised by the movements of the brown trout – well he was anyway. It was a picturesque setting and little had changed, but the heat was now so intense that he decided to sit inside where hopefully it was cooler.

He had opted for a pint of refreshing Thatcher's cider, but couldn't decide on what to eat. A ham and tomato cob would have sufficed, but as he gazed at the menu all he could see were baguettes and bread rolls with fancy names. He remembered the time when he had got off the plane at Luton Airport many years previously, and having made his way to the railway station he called in at the restaurant for a bite to eat before catching the train back home. Stomach rumbling, he pointed to what he thought was a salad cob, only to be told in no uncertain terms that it was a bap!

At that moment, as he stood there ruminating on what to eat, the barmaid came over with his pint.

'Decided what to eat yet, luv?' she asked rather seductively. She had noticed that he had undone his tie and the top button of his shirt, but there were the tell-tale signs of sweat underneath his armpits too.

'Think I'll go for the Cajun Chicken with chips and side salad, please.' replied Clarke somewhat hurriedly.

'I'll bring it over to your table when it's ready.'

'Much appreciated, thanks.'

'That'll be twelve pounds and forty-five pence altogether please, luv,' she said with a smile that would have normally melted Clarke's heart.

However, he looked up sharply and with a stone face he reluctantly handed over a ten pound note, two pound coins and a fifty pence piece.

'Thanks,' he replied rather brusquely, 'put the change in the charity box.'

And with that he headed for a table in one corner of the bar with his pint, mumbling to himself and making a mental note that he wouldn't be coming here again for a bite to eat – not at those prices!

Sitting down at the table, he wasted no time in gulping back the first few draughts of his cider. It was bliss! Indeed, all his aches and pains seemed to disappear in a matter of seconds – including the throbbing head. It would have been nice to have shared these moments with someone else, he thought for a second or two, but then he had always preferred his own company and did not mind being alone. He was used to it.

Whilst waiting for his meal he turned his thoughts and attention back to the crime that had been committed at The Old Turnpike House, and proceeded to contemplate the *Who*, the *What*, the *When*, the *Where*, the *Why* and the *How*!

He had given Webster the task of finding out *who* the victim was, so *who* was the offender – the person or persons who killed Keith Jackson? Indeed, did the offender act alone or was there more than one person involved? If acting alone then the offender had to be strong, well-built and physically fit to have committed this particular crime. That ruled out the person who found the body, namely the postwoman.

And then there was the old chestnut about the last person to see the victim alive, so the sooner they found that out the better.

Jackson lived alone, but there were photographs of children, so he must have been married or had a partner at one time? Surely his ex couldn't have done this? But she might now have a boyfriend or partner who did…? Check this out Clarke!

Could it have been a former Army comrade? Doubtful, he thought to himself, but it had to be followed up.

Was it a contract killing perhaps? And if so, who might be behind it?

One thing was for sure in Clarke's mind; and that was the likelihood that the victim knew the killer and vice-versa! If only they had his mobile phone – that might give a clue as to who committed the crime. Again, Clarke was certain that they were looking for just one person and very probably a male of the species.

Clarke was making a few notes when the barmaid came over with his meal. It looked very appealing – but then so did her cleavage as she leaned across and laid the plate on the table before him!

'Any sauces to go with your meal, luv?' she asked politely but seductively once more.

Clarke tried to make out that he was completely unruffled by her deliberate attempt to encourage his advances and simply spluttered 'Erm, no. No thanks. This will be fine.'

As she turned and made her way back to the bar, Clarke had a quick glance around the room to see if anyone had witnessed the incident. There were at least half a dozen or so other people in the bar at the time, but they all seemed to be engrossed in their food and drink or in each other, so he began to consume his meal whilst continuing to make notes from time to time.

Where were we? Oh yes, *what* were the sequence of events and actions of those involved?

It was originally thought (by whom?) that the victim had committed suicide, but there was nothing to suggest as much, not even a note? But then the preliminary examination by the police surgeon had confirmed that the victim was initially strangled with washing line cable, and then subsequently suspended from the lintel using the same to simulate suicide – and poorly according to the police surgeon! So the victim would have been unconscious within fifteen seconds at least and death would have occurred minutes later. All this would confirm his suspicions that the offender was a male and that he was strong, well-built and physically fit. And there was one more thing, thought Clarke. Had the offender done this before?

Taking a bite of his Cajun chicken, he then turned his attention to *when* the crime was committed. The police surgeon had estimated that Jackson was murdered in the late afternoon, between 4.00 p.m. and 5.00 p.m.. Therefore, was the offender absent from work for some reason (a day off maybe)? There is the possibility that they had finished work early of course? Or perhaps their job afforded them the opportunity to be in the area at that particular time. For all Clarke knew the offender could have been unemployed! This was going to be a tricky area, make no mistake!

Clarke had almost completed his meal when he moved on to the location of the crime; *where* Jackson was killed.

The Old Turnpike House was a remote and isolated building, and if the offender was using a vehicle then there was only one point of access and exit – down Blackthorn Lane from the main road. And if the offender was lying in wait, then where did he (again, Clarke was sure it was a he) park his car – if he was using one? There was the lean-to at the side of the building and the dirt track alongside – unless they parked directly in front the building? Nah, surely not?

There were other escape routes of course, but only if one was on foot, and Clarke had his doubts about that. One thing was for sure; whoever killed Jackson was taking a huge gamble, because the lane and surrounding countryside was popular with ramblers and cyclists no matter what the time of day!

There was one other thing to consider. Had the offender been to the house before? If only there had been bloody CCTV cameras!

Wiping his mouth with the napkin (bugger the etiquette!), he took a swig of the cider and moved on to the *why*. Why had Keith Jackson been murdered?

The man was clearly in debt – the letters on the table to the National Debtline were proof of that. But there were also betting slips lying around, so he had sufficient funds to have a flutter now and again. How was he able to manage that if in debt? Had he been lucky on the horses recently? Webster and the team would be making enquiries at the local betting shops, so hopefully they might be able to come up with something. They might get lucky with the banks too and there was also the National Debtline.

Jackson had been in the Army at one time, so he must have signed up to the Armed Forces Pension Scheme? Had he blown it all? Did he have a job? The sheds outside were full of lawnmowers, hedge trimmers, spades and the like, which would indicate gardening of some kind, but was that a seasonal occupation and how much did he earn?

It would appear that he was a heavy drinker (the empty vodka bottles). Again, if so, how was he able to afford it? They were clearly going to have to find out who he was in debt to. So, had he borrowed money from someone and not paid it back, or was he blackmailing someone? Or was there something more sinister? There was definitely a rational motive for the murder, of that Clarke was certain.

He had almost finished his drink and would have loved to have ordered another pint of Thatcher's, but he decided that he wasn't going to succumb to the temptation. He had almost completed his notes too, but there was still a matter of *how* the crime was committed.

The offender clearly wasn't armed when he (it was now definitely a he in Clarke's mind) arrived at the scene, for he obviously used what was at hand and in this instance it was the washing line cable. That would suggest that he had been at the rear of the house, and coming upon the washing line cable decided that this would suffice as the weapon of murder. Again, that begged the question, had he done this sort of thing before? Worth thinking about, thought Clarke.

And there was another question that suddenly came to mind. Had he been to the house before? Almost certainly! Having armed himself with the washing line cable, the offender must have waited somewhere outside before striking. Did he wear gloves at the time of the murder? Must have done, surely? See what forensics come up with.

He looked through his notes one more time, drained the last dregs of his pint and was about to leave when he suddenly remembered the *Tom and Jerry* badge that Webster had shown him. The question was, did it have any significance to the case? Sometimes cases *do* hinge on seemingly insignificant things like this and the more he thought about it, the more he became convinced that the two cartoon characters were indeed going to play some part in solving this particular case. The team were going to have to take this into account when making enquiries.

He placed the plate and empty glass on the bar and was glad that the barmaid was nowhere to be seen at that moment in time, so he turned and made his way to the door.

As he did so he noticed a man and a woman almost hidden away in the far corner of the bar near the door. They were clearly engrossed with each other, so to speak. The woman had her back to him, so he couldn't see her face, but she had mousy-coloured hair and it was in a ponytail. Furthermore, she was wearing a red t-shirt, jeans and riding boots.

The man on the other hand was a burly figure with dark, close-cropped hair and what appeared to be a scar just above his right eye. Clarke guessed that he was about the same height as himself – maybe slightly smaller. But what stood out for Clarke was the fact that the man's eyes seemed to be the same colour as his t-shirt, which was light blue. The sleeves were claret, as was the badge on the left breast; a badge with two crossed hammers over a castle. It was the away kit of West Ham United Football Club!

Clarke had almost reached his car when his mobile suddenly erupted into life. He was feeling so much better after his meal and a drink, so he hoped that the call would be important and relevant to the case. It was.

'Clarke?' he answered officiously.

An excited Constable Webster was on the other end with the news that door-to-door enquiries had already revealed more about the victim, beginning with the whereabouts of his car.

'It's a white Citroën Berlingo van, Sir. And it's here – at *The Wheatsheaf*!'

'Well done, Webster.' replied Clarke, clearly impressed by the swiftness of the young officer's part in the investigations. He was about to issue further orders when Webster interrupted him.

'And that's not all, Sir. The landlord says that he drove the victim home from the pub yesterday afternoon about 4.00 p.m.!'

Webster sounded smug, almost like a little boy boasting that his idea is better than all the others put together!

'Alright, alright!' protested Clarke, who was trying to bring an element of calmness and normality to the conversation. 'No need to burst a blood vessel, Webster! Is the landlord there?'

'Yes, Sir. But he's got an appointment at the dentist at 4.30 p.m. and...'

'Well he hasn't now! I want him down at the Incident Room immediately and I want a statement from him. Is that clear?'

'Yes, Sir. But...'

'Then I want Jackson's van taken away for examination. And then do the same with the landlord's car!'

'Yes, Sir. But...'

'What?' Clarke was clearly getting annoyed at Webster's constant interruptions.

'That's what I'm trying to tell you, Sir. The landlord was driving a courtesy car at the time.'

'Oh, for God's sake! Well find out what garage he went to and get that bugger examined as well! Do you think you can manage that?'

'Yes, Sir!' replied a not-so-smug Detective Constable Webster.

With that, Clarke rang off, climbed into his Ford Focus and headed back to Leverton to inform Superintendent Annable of the situation. It was a good start to the investigation, he thought. They now knew the identity of the man who was almost certainly the last person to have seen Jackson alive – apart from the killer of course; unless that person *was* the killer?

And they also had a pretty damn good idea when he *was* killed; the results of the post mortem the following day should confirm it. Hopefully Annable would be pleased.

Clarke left Annable's office shortly before 5.00 p.m. that day, slightly more irritated and despondent than when he went in. At the end of the day it was all about results – and the quicker the better; and all so that he (Annable) could take the glory and look good in the eyes of his superiors. At the end of one of these days Superintendent Annable was going to get a smack in the mouth, thought Clarke as he headed for home and a glass or two of Laphroaig!

Chapter 9

Tuesday, 4 July, 2017 (p.m.)

Around the same time that Clarke was leaving Superintendent Annable's office, the regulars started to arrive at *The Wheatsheaf*. Most of them were completely unaware of the day's events, but were now obviously keen to find out why there seemed to be a large police presence in the village, why Jackson's van was being taken away from the pub car park and what had become of the landlord, Tony Dawkins. His wife was able to put them *all* in the picture.

It had all happened so suddenly. Just after 3.00 p.m. two policemen – one a plain-clothed detective and the other one in uniform – had entered the pub wanting to speak to the landlord and/or the landlady. There had been an incident down Blackthorn Lane at The Old Turnpike House, and the policemen were gathering information on the occupant, a certain Mr. Keith Jackson.

'What kind of incident?' asked a very severe-looking Sally Dawkins.

'A suspicious death, ma'am.' replied the detective. 'Is there somewhere we can talk privately?'

Tony Dawkins then seemed to appear from nowhere. 'What's going on here?' he asked somewhat nervously.

Ignoring her husband's remarks, Sally Dawkins then ushered them all into a side room and left the bar in the capable hands of one of the barmaids.

A number of questions were asked and it was clear that Sally was going to do the talking. Furthermore, she was able to provide them with just about all the answers – and more.

Yes, she knew the deceased and where he lived. 'That's his van in the car park – the white one.' At this the uniformed policeman was told to go outside and have a look at the vehicle, whilst Sally continued. 'He was in the pub yesterday afternoon and he had a right skinful. In fact I asked my husband to take him home.'

Told him more like, thought the detective as he turned to Tony, who seemed to be in a world of his own. 'Is that right Sir?'

'What? Oh yes, that's right. He was very drunk, so I took him home.'

'Presumably that would be in your car then, Sir?'

'No, no, no.' protested Tony. 'My car was in for service, so I used the courtesy car. I dropped him off and then went to see if my car was ready.'

The detective was busy scribbling notes when his uniformed colleague returned to the room. They conversed with each other briefly and then the questioning continued. Was Jackson a regular? Again it was Sally who answered and this time there was no stopping her.

'I wouldn't call him a regular; more of a loner really.' She lit a cigarette and continued. 'He didn't seem to have any friends – not that you could speak of. But he liked a drink, that's for sure. Vodka was his tipple. And he was always running up a bloody tab. Then he'd have a win on the horses – he liked a flutter on the gee-gees – and then he paid it off.'

The detective nodded his head whilst continuing to add to his notes, and then he fired the next question at her. Did she know if the victim owed anyone a large sum of money?

There was a pause as she inhaled deeply on her cigarette. 'Not that I know of, but I wouldn't be at all surprised.'

The detective then moved on to the subject of employment. What kind of work did the victim do?

'As far as I know he just did gardening work in and around the area, as well as for some of the pub regulars.'

'Don't forget the cricket club.' interjected Tony, to the annoyance and irritation of his wife. 'He was the groundsman.'

'Really?' replied the detective. 'How interesting.' Sally had the impression that the detective wasn't in the least bit interested and just shook her head in disbelief as he then turned to the subject of family. 'Was Mr. Jackson married?' he asked, looking straight at Sally once more.

Again, Sally was only too happy to oblige. 'He was at one time, but they went their separate ways – no doubt it was down to his drinking and gambling.' She stubbed out her cigarette and continued. 'Patricia – that's her name – she's got a riding school over at Sapworth, across the way there.' she nodded over to her left. 'She's doing very well apparently.' she added. 'The kids never come to see their dad though. The lad's in the Army, isn't he?' she turned to Tony for confirmation, but he was clearly miles away and so she returned to the conversation. 'The girl's a student in Derby – she's close to her mum.' She gave the detective time to finish his notes before she suddenly remembered something else that might be of interest. 'Oh, and his mum's in the care home at the other end of the village.'

'His mum?' queried the detective.

'Yes, old Mrs. Jackson – lovely lady. His dad died some years ago, so I'm told.'

Both Sally and Tony were unable to shed any light on the victim's Army career, so that was it basically, but for a few minor details. The detective thanked the couple before adding that they may need to speak to them again. Not that the useless lump that passed for her husband had contributed much, thought Sally.

And then within a matter of minutes they were back, taking Tony off down to the community hall where he was to make a statement about having taken the victim home from the pub the previous afternoon.

'He's still there as far as I know,' Sally told an attentive-looking Christopher Ibbotson. Indeed, clearly in her element, she readily imparted all of the afternoon's events to him and anyone who cared to listen. Simon Collins was there too, but he was busy sending text messages on his mobile, much to her irritation.

'Well, fancy that?' sighed Ibbotson, as Sally went off to serve another customer. 'I've been at an auction in Leicester and it looks like I've missed all the action.' Collins was still tapping away on his mobile as Ibbotson looked down into his glass of wine. 'I wonder who will take over as groundsman now?' he said quizzically.

Other than that, there seemed to be very little empathy for the unfortunate Keith Jackson or the manner of his demise. Not even the fact that Tony had very probably been the last person to have seen him alive.

Collins was *still* tapping away, but then he suddenly seemed to spring to life. 'Yeah, me too. I've been at my shops in Derby and Grimley.' And then he jumped from his stool, threw a twenty-pound note on the bar and ordered another round of drinks. 'Look, I've got a call to make. Shan't be long. Another Guinness for me, glass o' wine for Chris and 'ave one for yourself, darlin'.' And with that he made a dash for the front door of the pub.

'Business I expect,' said Ibbotson.

'Mmmm,' replied Sally with a shrewd look on her face. 'I wonder!'

Collins was back a couple of minutes later. Knocking his pint of Guinness back in one go, he threw yet another twenty-pound note on the bar before ordering yet another round of drinks.

It was Ibbotson who spoke next. 'I wonder who could have done the dirty deed?'

'What's that?' replied Collins, almost as if the entire conversation had passed him by.

Sally returned with the drinks. 'Shall I tell you who I think did it? she whispered to the two men. 'Him over there,' she nodded in the direction of John Sheldon, who was enjoying a game of pool with his mates.

'What makes you say that?' asked Ibbotson.

'I just don't like him!' replied Sally sharply as she handed Collins his change.

The latter then broke into the conversation once more. 'Where's old Ken tonight? Thought 'e would 'ave been 'ere by now?'

'Funny you should say that,' said Sally. 'He was in earlier. Moaning about how the police had stopped him going down Blackthorn Lane.' She leaned further across the bar and as all the heads drew closer she continued almost in a whisper again. 'I asked him if the police had been to his place and he said that he'd been out all day. When I told him what had happened and that they were looking for witnesses, he just turned around and shot off without touching his drink!'

At that precise moment Tony Dawkins returned from the community hall having made his statement to the police. Naturally, he made light of his trip, much to the annoyance of his wife once more. She had been run off her feet – so she claimed. Now she was going to take time out and put her feet up.

Ibbotson leaned across to Collins and whispered 'While the cats away...!'

Needless to say, several minutes later in walked Angela Radford, full of the joys of spring and oblivious to the day's events. 'Hiya!' she shrieked to everyone, before making her way to the bar, where Tony Dawkins greeted her with the usual lascivious comments accompanied by the equally lascivious grin.

'You're looking particularly hot today, kitten,' he leered.

'Now, now, Tony!' she replied somewhat coyly.

The pugnacious John Sheldon had been chalking his pool cue when Angela walked in, but it hadn't escaped his notice that Tony Dawkins was all over her as usual. How he wanted to deck that bastard, but Angela always managed to assuage his anger. He suddenly put down his cue and made his way menacingly towards the two of them. At the last minute Dawkins saw him coming over out of the corner of his eye, and swiftly handing Angela her change he abruptly ended their conversation before joining Ibbotson and Collins.

But Dawkins needn't have worried, because Sheldon wasn't coming for him. It was Angela who was the object of his attention. Grabbing her forcefully by the arm he literally tried to drag to one side, but as always she threw him off.

Over Dawkins shoulder, Ibbotson could see the pair arguing, but he couldn't hear what was being said. Had he been a gentleman he would have come to her rescue, but he remained glued to his seat. Suddenly Angela put her hand up to her mouth, as if she had been shocked by what her partner had just said. What were they talking about, wondered Ibbotson? And then it dawned on him that Sheldon was probably telling her about what had happened to Jackson. Or was he? He just couldn't be sure. Infuriatingly Dawkins then moved slightly to one side and Ibbotson was no longer able to see what was going on. Damn and blast, thought Ibbotson. Damn and blast!

Sally Dawkins had been right. Ken Watson was really put out at having been turned away from Blackthorn Lane by the police. He'd spent most of the day watching Derbyshire struggle against Somerset at the County Ground in Derby, and having returned home about 4.00 p.m. he was looking forward to taking his beloved "Wilf" for a stroll across the fields to the pub. So when the policeman at the top of Blackthorn Lane told him in no uncertain terms that nobody was allowed to go down the lane he was understandably miffed!

All the policeman would say was that there had been an incident and that he would have to turn back. Consequently he had no alternative but to walk to the pub along the main road, which is what he did.

He was still muttering to himself and to "Wilf" as he entered the pub to order his pint. Yes, Sally Dawkins had asked him if the police had called at his place – they were conducting door-to-door enquiries apparently.

'No, I've been out all day, watching the cricket in Derby. Has something happened?' he asked inquisitively.

'I'll say,' replied Sally. 'They've been here, asking questions.'

'Questions about what?' Ken was beginning to sound frustrated.

'About Jackson. Summat's happened to him and they're looking for witnesses.'

'Witnesses? Witnesses to what?'

'Jackson's dead and they want to know if anyone saw anything suspicious yesterday afternoon about 4.00 p.m., down Blackthorn Lane!'

My God, thought Ken. The bugger that nearly ran me over! Ken suddenly turned on his heels and made his way out of the pub as if he had seen a ghost, leaving a stunned and speechless Sally holding his pint of John Smith's!

Unbeknown to Sally, Ken had gone straight out of the pub and into the village store next door, where he bought a copy of the Derby Evening Telegraph. As he stepped out of the store he began flicking through the pages until he found what he was looking for. There it was, in black and white:

'Police are looking for possible witnesses to an incident that took place around 4.00 p.m. yesterday afternoon (the third) at The Old Turnpike House on Blackthorn Lane, Brockley. We would like to hear from anyone who may have seen anything suspicious (ramblers, cyclists, dog walkers). Anyone who can help with our enquiries could they please get in touch with Leverton CID on either 01773-565444 or 01159-323833.'

Ken made his way home in an excited state, with poor "Wilf" struggling to keep up with him. Almost as soon as he closed the door behind him he picked up the phone and dialled the second of the two numbers on the newspaper before him. After what seemed like an eternity someone eventually picked up the phone at the other end, and Ken barely gave them the chance to introduce themselves.

'I understand that you're looking for witnesses to a crime that took place yesterday on Blackthorn Lane here in Brockley?'

It was Sergeant Scattergood at the other end and he corrected him. 'Ye-es, that's right. There was a suspicious *incident*, Sir.'

'Well, I've got something that may be of interest to you,' said Ken somewhat haughtily and in that pretentious manner of his. And so he proceeded to tell the Sergeant all about *his* incident with the 'maniac' on Blackthorn Lane the previous day.

Scattergood took down all the details (including Ken's address and phone number), before ending the conversation by saying that someone would come out to see him first thing in the morning.

Ken had expected someone to come out immediately, but he wasn't too put out. He could wait until the morning. For the time being he could gloat on the fact that *he* was probably going to play a vital part in the solving of a major crime. 'Wait until they hear about this in the pub and at the cricket club!' he chortled to an equally excited "Wilf"!

Later that evening a middle-aged woman was pacing up and down her kitchen in an agitated state. Biting her nails, she suddenly darted for the mobile phone on the table and dialled a number. A man answered.

'I told you never to call me on this number!' he snapped angrily.

'I know, but the police are going to want to speak to me. What do I tell them?' she replied tearfully.

'Well you don't tell them about us!'

'When can I see you again?'

'I told you. We need to keep a low profile for a while.'

'But...'

'Look, I've got to go. I'll call you in a few days.'

With that the man rang off and the woman made her way into her living room, where she collapsed onto the sofa weeping uncontrollably.

Around the same time a man poured himself a brandy, made his way into his conservatory and then dialled a number on his mobile phone. It was answered by another man almost immediately.

'Yeah, what is it?' The voice was composed but curt; he clearly recognised the voice at the other end.

The man who had made the call could hear a TV in the background, but he spoke softly and yet with a slightly threatening tone. 'I hope you haven't been opening your mouth?'

'What do you take me for?'

'If I found out that you've said anything...'

'Well I 'aven't!'

'The last thing we need is someone else in on this. We've got to keep our nerve and let things blow over for a while.'

'If you say so.'

'I do say so!' And with that he ended the call before knocking back the glass of brandy.

Chapter 10

Wednesday, 5 July, 2017 (a.m.)

Clarke had slept reasonably well during the night; he had risen only once to use the lavatory and was sound asleep again within a couple of minutes. He woke just after seven in the morning and lay there on his back in the double bed trying to recollect what he'd been dreaming about.

That was it! He'd been playing a guitar solo live on stage at the Leverton Recreation Ground; left-handed just like Jimi Hendrix. The whole town was there and familiar faces were in the crowd – some he liked, but some he didn't. Only he wasn't playing Hendrix, he was playing the blues à la Eric Clapton – another hero. If only he could remember the song. And then it came to him. Of course, it was *Before You Accuse Me*! And now as he rose he couldn't get the bloody tune out of his head!

A bowl of cereal and a glass of fresh orange juice straight from the refrigerator were just the ticket before he took a shower and brushed his teeth. There was no point in having a shave; bugger what Annable said!

He opened the doors to the narrow boat and looked outside – it was another fine, dry day, although he could detect the pungent smell of elderflower in the air. He went back inside and donned a white shirt, dark grey slacks and black slip-on shoes. And of course there was the bloody tie! How he hated wearing them – ever since Grammar School. Nevertheless, he picked out a dark green one and leaving the top button of his shirt undone he made a half-hearted attempt to put it on. Better take the bomber jacket just in case, he thought. Satisfied that he looked okay, he locked up the narrow boat, climbed into the silver Ford Focus and set off for the Incident Room at Brockley.

The Community Hall at Brockley was built in 2003, on the fiftieth anniversary of the Queen's coronation. It was located down a slip road leading off the main road and was roughly opposite the village school. There was a car park to the side and rear, with room for up to thirty vehicles, but it was chiefly surrounded by fields, with panoramic views across the surrounding countryside and Leverton in the distance.

The main door was at the front of the building and slightly to the right. Access was via a ramp that had been installed for the disabled and for wheelchair users. On entering the building one first stepped into the foyer, immediately in front of which was a cupboard. To the right lay a store room, besides which were the toilets. To the left one passed along a corridor that led to the main hall. On one side of this corridor was a kitchen, complete with a modern gas cooker and oven, refrigerator, sink unit and several cupboards. The requisite microwave oven and electric kettle were also at the disposal of whoever was allowed access to the hall. On the other side of the corridor was a small office, ostensibly for the head of the parish council, but this too was used by others, such as the head of the pre-school and the leader of a weekly dog training programme. Waist-high indoor windows had been installed from one end of the office to the other, including the door. Thankfully there was also one outdoor window. The hall itself was very light and spacious, with modern insulated vinyl flooring, central heating and air conditioning. All in all, he couldn't have chosen a better location.

When Clarke arrived at the Incident Room that morning just after 8.30 a.m. the place was already a hive of activity, although a couple of uniformed members of the team were taking a break to have a fag outside. As he passed by he acknowledged them, but the smell of nicotine almost made him retch, and yet he couldn't bring himself to complain. Why would he? He would have joined them at one time.

An avid smoker from his teenage years, he used to go through more than forty a day until he packed in fifteen years ago. His then wife, Lesley, was forever going on about how she hated the 'filthy habit'. And then he suddenly stopped. It was March 22, 2002 – the day after he was promoted to Detective Sergeant. He'd celebrated the event by having a drink or two (make that six or seven, if not more), but he also smoked a number of cigars too, and after he'd gone to bed that night he was violently sick. That was it as far as he was concerned – no more fags or cigars. And he stuck to it, much to the surprise of his colleagues. At least Lesley was pleased – for the time being.

Leaving the smokers to finish their fags, he entered the building and made his way to the kitchen, acknowledging other members of the team in the process. He couldn't see Webster, but when he gave instructions for the latter to set up the Incident Room he told him to make sure that the refrigerator was stocked with small bottles of Buxton spring water (sparkling of course), and he was pleased to see that Webster had performed that particular task. There was a light smile on his face as he removed one of the bottles and headed for his office.

Very nice, he thought to himself as he opened the door, but the outside window was still shut and he made it his first priority to open it – wide. That was much better, and he stood there for several seconds taking in the fresh air before turning his attention to his desk. As requested, all the up-to-date reports had been placed upon the desk for his perusal, so having put down his shoulder bag and bottle he sat in the swivel chair and began to read through them.

Door-to-door enquiries had proved to be very fruitful from the outset, and they had revealed much about the victim. In addition to his name, they had established that he lived alone and was separated from his wife, who now ran a nearby riding school. There were children, but they had left home and he had little to do with them. His father had passed away, but his mother lived in a nearby care home. He had few – if any – friends and seemed to prefer his own company; although he did frequent the local pub and more often than not built up a hefty tab. He was a heavy drinker and a gambler, but he apparently earned some sort of living as a gardener and groundsman at the village cricket club. What's more, he had been in the Army at one time. Yes, not a bad start at all.

'Now then, what have we got here?' said Clarke to himself. Ah yes, bank enquiries had revealed that the victim had little in his account, but he owed over ten thousand pounds on one credit card and over five thousand pounds on another. 'Phew,' Clarke whistled softly to himself before picking up the next report. This revealed that National Debtline had confirmed that the victim was heavily in debt and that he had a gambling habit combined with alcohol abuse. However, there was no suggestion of drug addiction or substance abuse. Relevant local groups had been suggested to the victim, but he appeared not to have taken any interest whatsoever. Pride or pig-headedness, Clarke wondered? The next report revealed that the victim was a regular customer at the Simon Collins betting shop in Grimley, but staff there confirmed that although the victim was fortunate enough to have had two or three big wins in the past, he rarely won and certainly hadn't done so on the day of the murder or in the previous week.

Clarke then turned his attention to the statement made by Tony Dawkins, and it didn't take him long to read through it. Everything seemed to be above board and there was little to suggest that he was the killer, but stranger things have happened, thought Clarke, and it was clear that he would have to go through the statement with the landlord of *The Wheatsheaf* in the next day or two. Besides, it was a good excuse for a swift half or even a wee dram!

That left forensics – including the results of the search of the victim's van and that of the courtesy car used by Tony Dawkins – and the results of the post mortem. Clarke sat back in the swivel chair, placed his hands behind his head and looked up at the ceiling. There was a lot to think about, but there was one thing that kept nagging away at him; what was the significance of the badge? Because he was sure that it held the key to solving this particular crime.

He was still reflecting on this and other aspects of the reports when there was a knock on the office door, and in stepped Webster.

'Hope everything's to your satisfaction, Sir?' he asked with a hint of trepidation.

'You should know by now that I'm never satisfied until justice has been done, Webster!'

Webster should have known that his question would meet with just such a response, but he simply replied meekly 'Yes, Sir.'

'Was there something else, Webster?'

'Well, thought you might like to know that we've got a potential witness, Sir.'

'Have we now!' said Clarke as he rose swiftly from his chair. 'Who might that be?'

'A guy from just up the road, on Gold Crescent, Sir. Reckons he saw a getaway car.'

The address didn't immediately register with Clarke. 'Getaway car?'

'That's what he says, Sir. I've sent someone up there to get a statement.'

Clarke was just about to issue a response when there a commotion along the corridor and voices were raised. 'What the hell's going on out there?' he asked.

'Erm, it's Superintendent Annable, Sir,' replied Webster somewhat nervously. 'And it looks like he's got the new Deputy Senior Investigating Officer with him.'

'About time!' shouted Clarke, as he stood up, attempted to straighten his tie and don his bomber jacket.

And then the door swung open and in strode Annable, looking like he meant business. 'Ah, there you are Clarke. Let me introduce your new Deputy Senior Investigating Officer – Detective Sergeant Fletcher, this is Detective Chief Inspector Clarke.'

As he looked up, Clarke's legs visibly buckled and there was a look of sheer horror on his face as Detective Sergeant Jacqui Fletcher smiled and held out her hand. Oh my God, he thought! The new Deputy Senior Investigating Officer is a woman!

Strangely enough, Eric Clapton was still strumming away in his mind as she stood before him, but it was no longer *Before You Accuse Me*. No, the tune now was *I Shot the Sheriff*!

Chapter 11

Wednesday, 5 July, 2017 (a.m.)

Still reeling from the shock of meeting his new Deputy Senior Investigating Officer, Clarke was almost in a trance-like state as he joined the other members of the team in the hall, where Superintendent Annable was now about to introduce them to Detective Sergeant Fletcher.

He had been completely in the dark as to who was going to replace Sergeant Coates, but from the moment that Sergeant Scattergood was informed of the fact that it was to be Sergeant Fletcher from Nottingham, he had been unable to keep the news from everyone else on the team.

'Guess what?' he confided to Constable Webster. 'Sniffer's got a new sidekick – and it's a woman!'

'He's not gonna like that,' replied Webster.

'That's what I said!'

So as Clarke joined the others for Annable's hopefully brief little homily, everyone turned their heads in his direction in an effort to gauge his reaction to the fact that Sergeant Fletcher had been added to the team. Naturally Webster made one or two amusing little quips out of earshot of his boss, with the result that some of the other females on the team were barely able to suppress their giggles.

However, this was Superintendent Annable's moment and he quickly brought those assembled before him to order. This was yet another example of the fact that the man was determined to show everyone present that he was in total control. Conscious of his appearance as always, he looked resplendent in his uniform and with hands on hips and legs apart he stood before his audience as if he were addressing the troops before the Battle of Agincourt. Thus he made his formal introduction of Sergeant Fletcher to the team.

'Saddened as I was to hear that Detective Sergeant Coates had suffered a stroke at the weekend,' he began, 'at the end of the day (there were audible groans) we are here to provide a service, and in order to do so we require men and women of the highest integrity, diligence and character.'

'Get on with it!' muttered one of the uniformed officers.

'What a load of bollocks!' another was heard to say.

Oblivious to the frustrations of those present, Annable waffled on for another five minutes or so before finally introducing Sergeant Fletcher. There was generous if half-hearted applause, but he clearly hadn't finished, because he couldn't resist ending by quoting from William Shakespeare, much to the chagrin of Clarke, who considered the works of the bard to be unintelligible tripe and therefore to be consigned to the dustbin of history.

'And finally, just before leaving I would like to quote from *A Midsummer Night's Dream*,' he shouted above everyone (there were more audible groans). 'And though she be but little, she be fierce.' A clever touch, he thought. Not so, Inspector Clarke!

As Annable left the building and made his way to his car, Clarke came after him with a face like thunder.

'And whose bloody idea is this then?' he bawled.

'For your information it was the Assistant Chief Constable,' replied Annable as he reached his car.

He was about to add that it was on the recommendation of the Chief Constable in Nottingham, who just happened to be on friendly terms with Sergeant Fletcher's parents, but Clarke cut him short.

'I might have bloody known – that incompetent dimwit!'

'Your recalcitrance is a long-standing issue in this force, so I would be very careful what you say, Inspector!'

'Well, everyone knows that she only got where she is because she's a woman – it certainly wasn't through intellect or hard graft! And besides, I've got no time for her bloody politically correct, box-ticking claptrap!'

'You've got no time for women period!'

Clarke was visibly taken aback by Annable's comment. 'And what's that supposed to mean?'

'It's no secret that you have a long-standing bitterness towards women. Look at you – you're a bloody misogynist man!'

'I am not bloody bitter! I…I… just…don't...' Clarke was clearly losing the battle of words and Annable sensed it.

'I'm not interested in your personal feelings, Inspector. This has come from the top!' And then almost as an aside. 'And I sanctioned it.'

'You did what?' bellowed Clarke. 'Has the name Maxine Greenhough suddenly escaped you?'

Annable seemed to show signs of embarrassment as he was about to climb into his car.

'Look, I am perfectly aware of the events of eight years ago,' he replied, 'but at the end of the day you are going to have to learn to work with Detective Sergeant Fletcher whether you like it or not! Do I make myself clear?'

Suddenly a morbid fear came over Clarke and he began to sense that there was more to Sergeant Fletcher's appointment than met the eye. They've never liked him at Division – he doesn't do things by the book for starters. So are they pushing for his early retirement and is she being lined up as his replacement? Is this why he was kept in the dark?

No, it's worse than he thought. She's a bloody plant! In spite of the fact that he was cleared of any wrongdoings or involvement in the Maxine Greenhough case, the buggers *still* don't trust him! The Chief Constable, the Assistant Chief Constable and bloody Annable have given Fletcher the task of keeping her eye on him so that she can report back to them with her findings. That's it! That's what this is all about!

'Well I'll bloody well show them!' he muttered under his breath.

At that moment Annable popped his head back out of the car to give Clarke one final reprimand.

'And smarten yourself up, Inspector!'

Clarke turned on his heels and headed back to the Incident Room full of rage, but as he did so he couldn't resist one final parting shot. 'And it's *Detective Chief Inspector*!' he shouted defiantly over his shoulder.

Chapter 12

Wednesday, 5 July, 2017 (a.m.)

The altercation between Clarke and Annable had not gone unnoticed by those in the Incident Room, including the new Deputy Senior Investigating Officer, Detective Sergeant Jacqui Fletcher. One or two of the female members of the team had come over to make themselves known to her, but every now and again she was able to peer through one of the windows and witness the scenes outside. Of course she couldn't hear what they were saying, but judging by the flailing of arms and the pointing of fingers it was pretty damn heated.

Constable Webster wasn't slow at coming forward either. At twenty-eight he was eight years her junior, but he'd never let a thing like age difference stop him before and he certainly wasn't going to now. Slim, slender and slightly smaller than him, her medium-length dark brown hair had been pulled back in a ponytail, leaving a fringe above her thick, brown eyebrows and big brown eyes. Her skin was quite pale, but she had a long, arched nose and thick lips, which seemed to spread right across her face when she smiled. Upon opening her mouth she revealed a set of perfectly aligned teeth. There was some make-up around her eyes, but that was all. What's more, she hadn't taken to painting her nails either. However, it has to be said that she looked highly fashionable in her contemporary dark blue, single-breasted, two-button jacket with matching trousers and white blouse. She wore a couple of small earrings, but there were no rings on her fingers. Yes, thought Webster – play your cards right son and you might just be in with a chance. And with that he made his way over to her.

'They love each other really,' he quipped, nodding to the two detectives outside in the car park.

'I hardly think so,' she replied somewhat haughtily. Well-spoken, there was little sign of an accent. There seemed to be little interest on her part either, but Webster persevered.

'They'll kiss and make up later, you'll see. By the way, I'm Matt,' he added holding out his hand.

Unfortunately for Webster she didn't return the compliment. Instead she turned to look him straight in the eyes. 'No,' she said with both authority and assuredness. 'You're Detective Constable Webster and your reputation precedes you.' Oh dear, one of the girls must have forewarned her. 'What's more,' she continued, 'from now on you address me as Sergeant or Detective Sergeant. Do we understand each other?'

Suitably chastened, Webster could only reply 'Yes, Sergeant.'

As she watched him walk away with tail between his legs, a slight smile appeared on her face. It was undoubtedly a smile of satisfaction, but then she had always sought to prove her worth by overcoming adversities and rising to every occasion in what she saw as a man's world.

She had been born in Kensington, London, in 1981, the daughter of a middle-class civil servant and a qualified neurologist. However, at the age of five her parents divorced and she moved with her mother and elder brother to Nottingham. She was immediately enrolled at the Nottingham High School, whilst her mother remarried and became a Consultant Neurologist at the Queen's Medical Centre in 1988.

She enjoyed her time at school and established a lifelong friendship with at least one of the other girls. However, she also learned to appreciate her own character strengths, among other things, and in doing so developed a keen sense of self-reliance. Indeed, this aspect of her character became predominant at an early age, so that her primary concerns were her independence (of which she is fiercely proud) and the fulfilment of personal goals.

After leaving school, she attended the Liverpool John Moore's University and obtained a BSc with Honours in Forensic Psychology and Criminal Justice. On her return to Nottingham she immediately joined the police and quickly rose to the rank of Detective Sergeant.

Competent, focused and determined to succeed in spite of the odds, the posting to Leverton had come as little surprise to her, and she resented the suggestion that it was all down to her parents 'friendship' with the Chief Constable. No, it was all down to her accomplishments in Nottingham – that's the way she saw it.

There was no disputing the fact that she had achieved much in such a short space of time, but in the eyes of her former colleagues this had led to her becoming a trifle arrogant and haughty. It was as if she was always striving to prove herself – they said. She was over-ambitious – they said. To hell with what they thought! The post of Deputy Senior Investigating Officer was hers – and she was going to rise to the occasion!

Clarke entered the foyer of the Community Hall after his clash with Superintendent Annable and attempted to slam the door behind him, but the felt pads along the edge of the door frame provided just enough soft cushioning to slow down the door as it closed. This only seemed to add to his anger and he stormed off into the kitchen. Opening the door of the refrigerator, there was only one bottle of Buxton water left, so he grabbed this and was about to slam the door when he stopped in his tracks. No, there was no point in getting worked up about this, so he closed the refrigerator door calmly and sat down at the table to contemplate what Annable had said.

He recalled Annable describing him as a misogynist. Him a misogynist? What a load of b..! He stopped short of actually swearing to himself and took a large swig of water. Shaking his head, his mind went back to the day he got married in 1995.

A year earlier he'd been posted to the Drugs Squad in Derby as a Detective Constable and shortly afterwards he met Lesley in the beer tent at a village fete – and she was slightly tipsy at the time. The daughter of prominent local barrister and later District Judge, Lionel Deering and his wife, Miriam, Lesley was undoubtedly a very attractive woman. A friend likened her to actress Kim Basinger and he had to admit that there was indeed a strong resemblance. The pair seemed to hit it off and their relationship progressed accordingly. After some time Lesley kept dropping hints that they should settle down and get married, but he was keen to further his career and seemed happy for things to stay as they were for the time being. However, peer pressure from friends eventually prompted him to take the plunge, and the pair were duly wed at the parish church of St. Michael's at Lindley, to the north of Derby.

From the very beginning Lesley had made it clear that she didn't want children, and he seemed happy to go along with this at first. However, he later confided to a colleague that this was undoubtedly one of the major regrets of his life.

Then there was Lesley's father. The man had never taken to his son-in-law from the outset, making it abundantly clear that Clarke wasn't good enough for *his* daughter. What an inveterate snob!

Promoted to Detective Sergeant in 2002, Clarke remained in Derby with the CID, but his dedication to the job and his 'obsession' (her words) with seeing justice done forced Lesley into an affair, and one day in 2005 he came home from work early and caught the couple together. He made the on-the-spot decision to leave, and taking only the clothes he stood up in and his Pink Floyd collection with him he found temporary accommodation with one of his colleagues (which he hated).

It was a year later that he discovered that the woman who didn't want children had become pregnant and they divorced in 2007. What's more, Lesley went on to marry the father of her child (a consultant paediatrician), and they later moved to New York. He never saw or heard from her again. The break up of his marriage certainly affected him deeply and the knowledge that she later had a child by her lover didn't help matters. But him, a misogynist?

Nevertheless, he entered into a relationship with a married woman by the name of Carol Vaughan in 2009. She subsequently declared her undying love for him and that she wanted to spend the rest of her life with him. However, within days of her making this confession she apparently had a change of mind (he never did find out why, but put it down to his occupation). Several few weeks later she was seen with a builder from Nottingham and before long they were living together! But him a misogynist?

And then to cap it all there was Detective Chief Inspector Maxine Greenhough – his boss at the time. They had never really seen eye to eye, but then that was probably not his fault. However, what really stuck in his throat was the day back in 2009 when she suspended him from duty for allegedly stealing confiscated drugs and then supplying them back to criminal gangs. All along he had protested his innocence, claiming that he had been deliberately set up and accused of doing something he hadn't done. This terrible part in his career came to an end when it was discovered – during a sting operation – that it was actually Greenhough who had committed the crime as part of her involvement in a major drug supply conspiracy. Although he was exonerated of any wrongdoing and allowed to return to his duties, he always suspected that his superiors never really believed him. But him, a misogynist? More like a bloody misanthrope if truth be told!

He had tried to put all of these things behind him; of course he had. Work was the key. And his music too; music from the golden era – Floyd, The Stones, Cream, The Who, Zep, The Eagles, Santana and many, many more. All washed down with a bottle of Laphroaig now and again! That helped him forget. Or did it? Maybe it was the whisky that kept those bad memories very much alive? And now this!

Convinced that the new Deputy Senior Investigating Officer was a plant for one reason or another, he now faced a dilemma: how to keep her out of his hair whilst conducting a murder enquiry. His thoughts were suddenly interrupted by a knock on the kitchen door. It was Webster.

'Erm, everyone's waiting, Sir.'

'Sorry?' replied Clarke looking up.

'The briefing, Sir. 10.00 a.m. you said.'

'So I did. I'll be with you in a minute or two.'

He *had* almost forgotten. Taking a last swig of the sparkling water, he felt slightly refreshed as he rose from the table, although uncharacteristically nervous too. Get a grip man, he said to himself as he made his way to his office.

Picking up his notebook he then headed down the corridor and into the main hall, where everyone suddenly stopped talking and turned their heads in his direction. Christ! It was as if he was going to deliver a speech to the bloody nation! Or tender his resignation! Oh, for God's sake, pull yourself together man! Reaching the top of the room, he looked around at everyone present and then began the briefing.

It was clear from his voice that the appointment of Sergeant Fletcher and the subsequent 'disagreement' with Superintendent Annable had left him rather shaken, but he covered each and every detail in his usual eloquent manner.

There had been a suspicious death at The Old Turnpike House on Blackthorn Lane. They had the name of the victim at last and that the cause of death was very probably strangulation by washing line cable; the subsequent post mortem report should confirm this. The offence occurred between the hours of 4.00 p.m. and 5.00 p.m. on Monday the third at the victim's home address. This was somewhat isolated from the rest of the community and access was via a country lane. The victim had been married at one time and had two children, but at the time of his death he was living alone. His estranged wife lives in a neighbouring community and his mother lives in a care home at the other end of the village. The victim had also been in the Army at one time. He was a gambler and an alcoholic, but he was also heavily in debt. He was also something of a loner. He made a living chiefly from gardening, but he was also the groundsman at the cricket club. Forensic searches have been carried out at the scene, but they have revealed very little so far. They are still awaiting the results of further searches of the victim's vehicle and that of the last person known to have seen him alive. The latter has provided a statement confirming that he took the victim home and that the victim was still alive when he dropped him off. This was around 4.00 p.m. A potential witness has apparently come forward and is currently being interviewed prior to making a statement.

Having outlined the details of the victim and the crime, Clarke then began to issue orders. Door-to-door enquiries were to continue throughout the village, looking for the victim's movements on the day of the crime, any possible friends and associates, and any likely suspects. The enquiries may be expanded to include nearby communities (there were groans from some of those present), but not yet. The press will need to be updated on the case too. Webster was given the task of informing the victim's estranged wife of his death and asking her to identify the body. Clarke had decided that he would first visit the care home in the company of Detective Constable Laura Preston, who would act as Family Liaison Officer, before heading to *The Wheatsheaf* to interview the landlord about his statement. There was one final point that he wished to make before sending everyone on their way.

'There is one piece of evidence that was found at the scene and it's just possible that it may have some bearing on the case.' He then held up an artist's impression of the *Tom and Jerry* badge. 'We need to find out what – if any – significance this has. So bear that in mind when making your enquiries. Any questions?' he asked tentatively. 'Good! Let's get cracking then.'

Satisfied that he had covered everything, he was just about to depart when a voice over his shoulder stopped him dead in his tracks.

'I'd like to get involved if I may, Sir?' It was Sergeant Fletcher. 'Perhaps I could interview Mrs. Jackson or…'

Clarke cut her short. 'No!' he said firmly. 'I want you to co-ordinate everything from here.'

'But, Sir…'

Clarke said nothing. He didn't have to. The look he gave Fletcher was enough. She had been put in her place. He then made his way out of the room, and as he did so a wry grin appeared on his face as he muttered under his breath 'Me, a misogynist? Uh!'

Chapter 13

Wednesday, 5 July, 2017 (a.m.)

Lying at the far end of Brockley and the last building on the right hand side of the road before entering Grimley, the Little Orchard Nursing Home was one of the more recent additions to the community. Opened in 1991, the home is set in peaceful, tranquil grounds, surrounded by fields for the most part and giving those same panoramic views as the Community Hall down the road. There are those in the twenty-six years of its existence who have complained about the smells from the farm across the road, but they are few and far between!

Providing residential care in a 'warm and friendly atmosphere,' the residents are encouraged to personalise their rooms as they wish. There are sixty rooms in total, each with en-suite WC, TV points and a call system. There is also a good mobile network and Wifi available. The home has various communal areas, including a light airy conservatory, main lounge, piano room and coffee lounge, where residents can relax with family and friends. Overseeing all of this since 2014 is the tall, slim, bespectacled figure of Audrey Bostock, originally from Hitchin, in Hertfordshire.

With her brown hair in a bob, brown-eyed Audrey was always attired in a jacket, blouse and trousers, but never high heels – God forbid! In essence she was the model professional – and she looked it! She was in fact a qualified nurse before going into the care industry, but she and her family (she has two boys) came to Derbyshire when her husband became a lecturer at Nottingham University. Everyone seemed to have settled well in the area, eventually moving into a large detached house in the more affluent area of Grimley (if there was such a thing!). However, Audrey has never quite got used to the local dialect and the propensity for local people to drop their aitches!

Motivated by the desire to care and protect others (she always opens every interview with 'We provide the highest quality of residential and dementia care'), her thirst for knowledge does leave her open to new ideas. Compassionate to a fault, she is therefore willing to take risks in pursuit of helping those in her care. However, this can lead her to worry about the possibility of burn-out. Her attachment and dedication to her job has undoubtedly put pressure on her marriage, but thankfully her husband has been sympathetic for the most part. Some of the staff think she is a bit of a know-all, with a tendency to consider herself five steps ahead of everyone else! It must be said, however, that although she is terrified that one day she may be proved wrong, her education and training has taught her to listen to her gut.

On this particular morning as it approached noon she sat in her office ruminating about her forthcoming holiday to Italy; the family never went anywhere else! Audrey simply loved everything Italian – food, wine, language and of course holidays. In August the family would be going to the upmarket fishing village of Portofino, with its picturesque harbour and historical association with celebrity and artistic visitors.

The very thought of mixing with the crème de la crème of society enthralled her; which is why they also took time out to visit the skiing resorts during the winter months. Indeed, unbeknown to the staff at the home, Audrey once got very drunk whilst on holiday in Cortina d'Ampezzo, where she had the good fortune to find herself in conversation with Italian skier and local hero, Kristian Ghedina. She has always kept *that* particular incident very close to her chest!

Just before 11.30 a.m. her blissful reverie was interrupted by a knock on the door and she was politely informed that there were two police officers wishing to see one of the residents.

Having arrived at the care home, Clarke and Constable Preston had been asked to sign in and then wait in the foyer for the manageress. It didn't take long for her to appear and introduce herself.

'Good morning,' she said with kindly smile. 'My name is Audrey Bostock and I'm the manageress. How may I help you?'

Clarke was a pretty good judge of character at the best of times and he correctly surmised that the woman before him was a thorough professional. He also correctly guessed from her accent that she probably hailed from the London area or thereabouts.

'Good morning.' he replied softly and with an equally engaging smile. 'This is Detective Constable Preston and I'm Detective Chief Inspector Clarke of Leverton CID. I understand that a Mrs. Jackson is one of the residents here?'

He didn't look like a policeman in his bomber jacket, but Audrey was impressed by his manner. 'Yes, that would be a Mrs. Valerie Jackson. Is anything wrong?' she asked.

'I'm afraid we have some rather bad news regarding her son.'

'Oh no. Is it very serious?'

'I'm afraid so. Would it possible to see her?'

Clearly shaken, she seemed confused at first, but soon recovered herself. 'Erm…yes, but of course. Let me take you to her room, Inspector.'

As she led them down the corridor, Clarke was pleased and relieved that she didn't appear to be one of life's more officious bureaucrats. He had a profound dislike of bureaucracy and red tape, but an even greater antipathy towards those who actually enforced it!

When they reached the room Audrey knocked on the door and entered, followed by Clarke and Constable Preston. Mrs. Jackson was sitting up in bed and watching her TV as Audrey made the introductions.

'Mrs. Jackson? There are two police officers here to see you.'

As she turned to face them, Mrs. Valerie Jackson gave a smile that would have normally melted Clarke's heart. It was the smile of a woman who had overcome many hardships in her life, but remained stoical and resilient in the face of all of her adversities.

'I hope you haven't come to arrest me?' she joked.

Audrey explained that Mrs. Jackson still maintained most of her faculties and was not suffering from dementia or other associated ailments. 'Nevertheless,' she whispered to Clarke, 'I'd ask that you be sensitive at a time like this.'

'Of course,' replied Clarke as he sat beside the bed.

And so he broke the news to Mrs. Jackson that there had been an incident at The Old Turnpike House and that her son had been the victim of a terrible crime. That was enough for her to break down uncontrollably and it was clear to everyone in the room that she was too upset to answer any questions for the time being.

'I think it would be better if you came back some other time, Inspector,' hinted Audrey as she leaned over Clarke's shoulder.

'Yes, I think you're right,' he replied. Rising from his chair he turned to Audrey and said in a firm but soft voice 'I'd like to leave Constable Preston here if I may, as Family Liaison Officer?'

Audrey nodded in agreement. 'Yes, that will be fine.'

'Is there anyone else you can think of who can be with her?' he asked politely.

'She has a sister who lives quite close and comes fairly regularly,' pondered Audrey. 'I'll see if I can contact her.'

And so leaving Constable Preston with the distraught Mrs. Jackson, both Clarke and Audrey stepped out of the room and into the corridor, where he explained that he would have to call back again and at a more appropriate time. They parted company amicably and he made his way to the door. It had been a trifle disappointing, but only to be expected under the circumstances. As he was passing the main lounge the door opened and a female member of staff emerged carrying a tray full of crockery, and he almost bumped into her.

'Ooops, I'm very sorry,' he said apologetically.

'Allan?' she replied with a frown on her face. 'Allan Clarke?'

'That's right. Who wants to know?'

'It's Maria. We were at school together. Remember?'

He stared at her for a moment and then it all came back to him. Of course, it was Maria Bukowski. It must have been forty years since they had last seen each other, when they went their separate ways after leaving junior school. And even after all those years she had recognised him.

She was a frail eleven-year-old at the time, with long dark hair in a ponytail and big brown eyes. Oh and not forgetting the flared trousers! The woman standing before him now was about five feet and five inches tall, with a slim figure and a small bust. What's more, she now had mousy-coloured hair in a sleek bob (parted down the left-hand side) and a feathery fringe. Well, women were always colouring their hair, weren't they? Her eyebrows had been plucked, but there was very little evidence of make-up, other than that around her eyes. The flares had long gone, but she wore a blue smock and trousers – presumably the regulatory uniform for care home staff, he thought. She also wore a gold necklace with what appeared to be a heart; a locket perhaps? Her earrings were small, but he was able to discern that she wasn't wearing any ringers on her fingers. She must have been married at one time though? Indeed, although she was by no means a glamorous-looking woman, she could have easily passed for someone younger.

Well, well, well. Who would have thought it? Little Maria Bukowski. She was the youngest child of Polish Army veteran, Wladyslaw Bukowski, who had fled his homeland following the German invasion of Poland in September 1939. He had married Joyce Redfern in 1949 and they had six children together – two boys and four girls, all of whom were raised as Roman Catholics. She was already a pupil at the Pawley Junior School when he came to the village following his parent's untimely death in a car accident towards the end of 1974. That was right, he lived with his grandparents on the small council estate and she lived at the other end of the village, in a row of terraced cottages just off the Derby Road. In fact she was one of the very first pupils (if not *the* first) at the school to actually speak to him. Yes, of course. She had offered him one of her liquorice allsorts!

'Yes, of course I remember,' ventured Clarke. 'But I can't believe its….is it really you?' For once he was lost for words.

'Yes, it's me,' she replied a trifle coyly.

'I'm surprised that you can remember me though after all these years?'

'How could I forget you?'

The reply took him by surprise and he almost blushed, but it had been made in all sincerity. She had never forgotten the shy boy who had sat at the desk beside her on his first day and captured her heart almost immediately Thereafter they were practically inseparable, to the extent that some of the other boys thought he was a tad queer; until he turned on one of them and felled him with one punch. Needless to say the young boy went running home to his mum, and thereafter neither she nor Clarke's grandmother ever spoke to each other again!

It was around this time that the other lads started calling him "Sniffer", and Maria never did understand why. As long as they were together, that was all that mattered to her. And of course the six weeks school holidays in July and August were a magical time that seemed to go on forever. They would go for walks together around the village and through the fields, where they could both be at one with nature. Then they would help out at the farm when it was baling time, and there was the day when they had their *Cider With Rosie* moment during a break in the work. Except that it wasn't cider; it was orange squash! She remembered all of these things because they weren't just best of friends in her eyes; they were like childhood sweethearts.

And then it all came to an end when he passed his eleven-plus and went to Leverton Grammar School and she went to the Roman Catholic school in Derby. It was 'all part of growing up', or so she was told, but to her mind it was as if someone had just switched the lights out on a beautiful friendship and a beautiful time, and she missed him terribly. They still lived in the same community, but their paths never crossed and so it just wasn't the same any more. They never saw each other again – until now.

Her last remark had caught him off guard, so to speak, and recovering his composure slightly he sought to turn the conversation in a different direction.

'So, how long have you been working here then?' he asked.

'For the last two years. Before that I was at a care home on the outskirts of Nottingham.'

'You like the job then?'

'Yes, I've always liked the job.'

Was she being a little economical with the truth, thought Clarke before continuing? 'Do you live locally?'

'I've been at Grimley for five or six years.'

'Well I never.' He paused for a few seconds and then looking down at the floor he put another question to her. 'Have you ever married?'

'Yes, but I'm divorced.'

'Me too,' he said without looking up. 'Any kids?'

'Two boys. And you?'

'No, she....we...' Clearly finding it difficult to explain himself, he went back to his original response. 'No, there are no kids.'

She sensed that he was holding something back. 'Do you regret that?'

'Sometimes. Yes, sometimes I regret that.' Looking up once more he noticed that the clock had struck noon. 'Look, I really must dash. It's been lovely to see you again after all these years.'

'And you too. Will we be seeing you again?'

'It's possible. Yes, it's very possible.' And with that he turned to go.

'In what capacity I wonder?' she shouted after him.

'Oh, didn't I tell you?' he said as he opened the outer door. 'I'm a police officer and I'm in the process of investigating a suspicious death.'

Chapter 14

Wednesday, 5 July, 2017 (p.m.)

Well that was a turn-up for the books, thought Clarke as he made his way back to his car. Ostensibly he had gone to the care home to inform a frail old lady that her son had met a suspicious and untimely death, but he spent the greater part of his time there in conversation with a friend from junior school – a very special friend. He was still thinking of that special friend when he received a call on his mobile phone. It was Dr. Fraser with the results of the post mortem.

'Hello Alex. What have you got for me?' asked Clarke anxiously.

'It's as I said, Allan. He was strangled first and then suspended from the hook to make it look like suicide.'

'And the time?'

'Around 4.00 p.m. – give or take fifteen minutes.'

'Brilliant, Alex. Is there anything else?'

'Well, he doesn't appear to have had much to eat within the previous twenty-four hours, but examination of his liver would suggest that he was suffering from acute cirrhosis.' He paused briefly, but then couldn't resist a little dig. 'By the way, do you still have shares in the Laphroaig Distillery?'

'Very droll, Alex,' replied Clarke. 'Very droll.'

'I'll get my report typed up and you can have a copy.'

'Okay, thanks Alex.'

Again, Clarke had a lot of time and respect for Fraser, but it was mutual. Admittedly his sense of humour occasionally bordered on the deadpan, but he would never hold that against him. And now he had given the green light for the case to become an official murder enquiry. With that in mind he climbed into his car and was just about to turn the ignition on when the phone went again. This time it was Webster.

'What is it, Webster?' said Clarke somewhat irritably.

'I've been to see the victim's ex…I mean estranged wife…like you said.'

'I trust that you were the soul of discretion, Webster?'

'What? Oh, yes Sir. Although…'

'Just get on with it for God's sake!'

'Well, just to say that she's consented to identify the body, Sir.'

'Thank you,' said Clarke somewhat relieved. 'Go with her to the mortuary and I'll join you there about two o'clock. Do you think you can manage that?'

'Yes, Sir.'

Clarke shook his head as he ended the conversation, turned the ignition on and set off down the road to *The Wheatsheaf*.

Wednesday was "Pie Day" at *The Wheatsheaf* and by the time that Clarke pulled up in the pub car park just after 12.30 p.m. several customers had already arrived to select from a wide choice of pies, including Chicken & Mushroom Pie, Steak & Ale Pie, Steak & Kidney Pudding, Lamb Shank Pie, Game Pie, Fish Pie and Three Cheese & Potato Pie.

It had been many a year since Clarke had last called at *The Wheatsheaf*, but he couldn't recall the cuisine being anywhere near as tempting as that on offer today. Admittedly he was feeling rather peckish, but he was there to interview the landlord with regard to the statement he'd made, and he settled for a pint of Theakston's Old Peculiar before asking Tony Dawkins to join him at a table well away from the bar.

As they took their seats Sally Dawkins pretended to look busy behind the bar, but every now and again she couldn't resist looking over in the direction of her husband and Clarke, as if she were frightened to death of missing something. In reality of course she was frightened to death that her stupid husband might say something incriminating!

Clarke savoured the first few swigs of his ale before pressing ahead with the interview.

'You probably know why I'm here today, Mr. Dawkins?'

'I clean my pipes every week – honest gov!' was Dawkins considerably irreverent reply and one that left Clarke stupefied.

'Pardon?'

'Just trying to lighten the atmosphere, that's all.'

Clarke just wasn't impressed. 'Well, if we could just stick to the narrative, if you don't mind, Mr. Dawkins.'

Duly chastened, the stupid grin disappeared from Dawkins face, as Clarke put it to him that he may have been the last person to have seen the victim alive.

'Well he was very much alive when I dropped him off!' protested Dawkins.

Clarke looked him in the eyes briefly and then continued. 'Perhaps if we started at the beginning. When did Mr. Jackson enter the pub and how long was he there for?'

'It's all there in my statement!'

'Well I want to hear it from you. Now if you don't mind, please?'

'I can't remember exactly what time Jackson came in the pub, but he was in there for a couple of hours or so. That I do know.'

'And you say he was drunk?'

'Too bloody right he was. Absolutely plastered. Knocking back the vodka's like there was no tomorrow!'

Clarke remembered the empty vodka bottles on Jackson's dining room table. 'Was there a reason for this? For example, was he celebrating something, like a win on the horses maybe?'

'I couldn't tell you, but he was throwing money around like confetti.' Dawkins paused briefly before continuing. 'Oh, and he paid off a large bar tab.'

'And what time did he eventually leave?'

'Well, my missus, she suggested that it was time he left. This was coming up to four o'clock.'

Clarke quickly glanced at the bar and noticed that Mrs. Dawkins was pretending to clean some glasses. But he was conscious of the fact that she was watching the pair of them. He then continued.

'Did he protest or cause any trouble at this?'

'No, he came quietly, shall we say,' sniggered Dawkins at what he thought was an amusing quip.

'It says here that you drove him home. Did you use your car?'

'No, like I said in my statement, *my* car was in for a service. I took it in earlier that morning. They gave me a courtesy car and since I'd still not heard from the garage I decided to use that to take Jackson home.'

'Did you go into the house with Mr. Jackson?'

'No bloody chance! I stayed in the car. I thought he was going to be sick, so I pushed him out smartish and drove off.'

'Did you wear gloves at any time?'

The question puzzled Dawkins. 'No, I never do when I'm driving.'

'Was there anyone else about – ramblers, cyclists?'

'Not that I can recall.'

'What did you do next?'

'I drove straight to the garage, but the bloody car still wasn't ready, so I went to the cash and carry.'

'How long were you there for?'

'About an hour I suppose.'

'Do you still have the invoice?'

He nodded over to the bar. 'My missus will have put it somewhere safe.'

'And then?'

Dawkins looked over to where his wife was standing, as if to make sure that she wasn't listening in to the conversation. 'Then I called at the *Miners Arms*. I was only in there for ten minutes when the garage rang at last.'

'Can anyone verify this?'

Dawkins looked sheepish before answering. 'Yeah, there were one or two folk in there at same time as me.'

'So you went to pick the car up? What time was this?'

'Be about a quarter-to-six.'

'And then you went home?'

'Yeah, got back just after six.'

'Is there anything else that you can add?'

'Not that I can think of.'

'And you're certain that you saw nothing suspicious or out of the ordinary?'

Dawkins had clearly had enough. 'Like I said in my statement, I wasn't there long enough!'

Then Clarke seemed to remember something and pulled out the artist's impression of the *Tom and Jerry* badge to show Dawkins. 'Does this mean anything to you by any chance?'

'Nope,' he replied almost indifferently. 'Looks like some sort of kiddies badge to me.'

Clarke rose from his seat. 'Okay, Mr. Dawkins. That's all for the time being, thank you.'

Dawkins sighed. 'You mean I can go?'

'Yes, but we will need to corroborate your story and very probably speak to you again.'

Dawkins looked up to the ceiling before turning and heading back to what he deemed to be the safety of the bar.

Never one to waste his drink, Clarke savoured the last few dregs of his pint before leaving. Climbing into his car, he looked into the rear mirror and noticed Mrs. Dawkins having a cigarette at the back of the pub. He turned the ignition on, fastened his safety belt and wound the window down. And then he heard it. Indeed, the whole village probably heard it too. He looked in the mirror again and Mrs. Dawkins had evidently been joined by her husband. What's more, she was giving him one almighty bollocking! Poor chap, thought Clarke. And then a wry smile came to his face as he drove off.

Chapter 15

Wednesday, 5 July, 2017 (p.m.)

Patricia Jackson was feeling very nervous. She had consented to formally identifying the body of her estranged husband, but she wasn't looking forward to it. Why, oh why did she say yes? She sat fidgeting beside Detective Constable Webster in the waiting room outside the mortuary at the hospital at Leverton, as they both awaited the arrival of Detective Chief Inspector Clarke.

It had started clouding over outside and so she had donned her khaki-coloured anorak before departing the riding school at Sapworth. Nevertheless, she was still concerned about her appearance on an occasion such as this. Underneath the anorak she wore a light blue vest-like top and jeans. She was worried that her riding boots would be inappropriate, so she had changed into a pair of beige-coloured casual shoes before leaving.

As was almost always the case, her mousy-coloured hair had been taken back into a ponytail and her sad, blue eyes seemed to mirror the occasion perfectly. She wore no make-up, but her face and features looked weather-beaten, as if she had spent a lifetime working outdoors – which was true to some extent. And she was only fifty!

Born in the Hampshire town of Andover in 1967, she grew up in the nearby village of Grateley, the younger of two daughters of the local butcher, George Rickman. Hers was a happy childhood, in and around the local farmland with its ancient footpaths and droveways. After leaving school in 1983, she studied gardening at was then Cricklade College (now Andover College). Upon receiving the relevant qualifications she began working for the local council at Andover, tending to the town's parks and gardens. There were numerous boyfriends at the time, but her job always came first. Working outdoors in all weathers never bothered her and she wasn't afraid of getting her hands dirty. That would explain why she felt so at home at the riding school – literally! And it was clear that she wanted to return there as soon as possible.

'What time is the Inspector due?' she asked Constable Webster.

'He should be here any minute now, Mrs. Jackson.'

'Patricia, please.'

Her voice was soft, gentle and with barely a trace of an accent, but Webster could sense that she was both anxious and nervous.

At that moment the outside door opened and in walked Clarke. She had expected him to be wearing a suit and tie, so she was moderately surprised to see him wearing a bomber jacket. He also had what appeared to be a week's growth of stubble on his face, but other than that he wasn't a bad looking guy, she thought.

'Mrs. Jackson? I'm Detective Chief Inspector Clarke and I'm the Senior Investigating Officer looking into the death of your former husband.' There was a vague semblance of a smile on his face as he stretched out his hand.

As she stood up to shake hands with Clarke, she guessed that he was only a few inches taller than she was, but she answered him as she had answered Webster earlier.

'Patricia, please.'

'If you wish,' he replied. And then looking into her sad, blue eyes he suddenly began to frown. 'Haven't we met somewhere before?' he asked politely.

'I doubt that very much, Inspector,' she replied before turning away from him abruptly.

He was just about to press the issue when the doors to the mortuary opened and Dr. Fraser popped his head out.

'Will ye no come in?' he said, beckoning them to join him.

The two policemen and Patricia Jackson thus entered the mortuary and as Dr. Fraser pulled back the sheets to reveal her former husband's face, she was asked to identify him.

'Yes,' she said quietly and without emotion. 'That's my...' She was about to confirm that it was her estranged husband, but then she seemed to correct herself. 'That's Keith Jackson.' She then turned away.

As Clarke thanked him, Dr. Fraser replaced the sheets and the two policemen and Patricia Jackson went out into the waiting room once more. Webster was told to return to the incident room and departed forthwith. However, Clarke asked Patricia Jackson to remain as he needed to ask her some questions.

'If I must,' she shrugged.

'I'm afraid so.' And with that curt reply he escorted her to the hospital restaurant.

When they arrived at the hospital restaurant on Level 3 there was very little activity, other than two young couples heavily engaged in conversation. Clarke ordered a coffee for Patricia and a glass of fresh orange juice for himself. She had chosen to sit at a table near one of the windows, and when he joined her she was staring blankly at the sky outside. It had started to spit with rain and the weather seemed to mirror her melancholy demeanour.

'I can't imagine you being married somehow,' she said as he sat down opposite her and passed her the coffee.

'What makes you say that?' he asked.

'Something about you – I can't quite put my finger on it.'

He looked down at the table. 'Well I was married once.'

She continued to press him. 'What happened?'

'It just didn't work out.' He continued to stare at the table.

'You drink a lot, don't you?' she said abruptly. 'Is that why the marriage ended?'

Clarke was taken aback. 'No, it was nothing like that…'

'But you do drink a lot?'

She was persistent; he had to give her that. 'I don't…' He was getting quite flustered now. 'Look, can we…'

'Keith drank a lot. You know that, don't you?'

Thank goodness the inquisition appeared to be over. 'It has been suggested, yes.'

'He gambled a lot too. Loved a flutter, did Keith.'

Clarke grabbed this opportunity to take control of the conversation. 'So, how did you meet?'

She sighed. 'We met at *The Angel*, a pub in Andover. He was with some of his mates from the barracks at Tidworth. You could tell them a mile off – the Army guys. But he was good fun. He made me laugh.'

'Do you know what unit he was with?'

'Yes, it was the Worcestershire and Sherwood Foresters. They'd not been long at Tidworth. Think they were in Cyprus before being transferred.'

'So you started seeing each other?'

She smiled weakly. 'We had what you might call an *on-off* affair.'

'How do you mean?'

'I finally decided that it was time that I settled down and had kids, but he preferred to be with his mates.' She paused briefly. 'Yes, he was *always* with his bloody mates.'

'And yet you ended up getting married?'

There was another sigh. 'I fell pregnant, didn't I? Like I said, we'd been seeing each other for three bloody years – on and off…'

'And he did the decent thing?'

'Oh, can't fault him there – ever the gentleman. He proposed immediately, and we were married six weeks later.'

'When was this?'

'1996 it was. And I had Matthew – our son – later that year. A week or so after the birth of his son he was off with his regiment to Bosnia.'

She went on to describe how she missed her job, but being a full time mother somehow made up for that. After all, marriage and motherhood were her ultimate goals, except that her husband was away for long periods. He was sent to Bosnia again in 1998, shortly after being promoted to Sergeant.

'I think that was the happiest day of his life – the promotion. It was certainly the proudest.' She seemed to be lost in thought for a while.

Clarke pressed her further. 'You had a daughter, or so I'm told?'

'Yes, Adele. She was born a few months later, in 1999.' Again, her mind seemed elsewhere, but Clarke continued.

'It must have been difficult for you, bringing up two kids like that – practically on your own?'

'I was a soldier's wife – you just had to get on with it.'

Clarke thought carefully before putting the next question to her. 'And in your husband's absence – were there any temptations?'

'What are you suggesting?' she snapped.

This time it was his turn to sigh. 'Was there anyone else in your life during this time, Mrs. Jackson?'

'It's Patricia! My name is Patricia – I told you!' She was beginning to lose her composure – and her temper.

'So you did – Patricia.' Clarke squirmed before continuing. 'Well, was there anyone?'

There was a long pause before she replied, almost in a whisper. 'It was nothing.'

'So, there was someone else? Was he a married man by any chance?'

At this point she began to fiddle with her fingers, and then without looking up she nodded her head.

'Did your husband ever find out?' Clarke had regained the initiative.

'No,' she replied adamantly. 'Not that I know of. Anyway, I put an end to it after only a few weeks.'

'A few weeks?' replied Clarke unbelieving.

'Yes, a few weeks,' she hissed. 'I felt ashamed – and guilty. And I thought of my kids.' Then her voice rose again. 'Look, I thought you wanted to know about my husband?'

'Indeed I do. Please feel free to continue.'

So she went on to tell him how Jackson was demoted to Corporal in 2002, for slapping a young recruit who *he* thought wasn't coming up to standard. That hurt, that did! Two years later and the regiment was sent to Afghanistan, and he took part in *Operation "Herrick"*. It was 2005 when he finally quit the Army, but she readily admitted that his departure left a huge void in his life. And what with his experiences in Bosnia and Afghanistan, his character changed completely. That was when he began drinking *and* gambling heavily.

A year after leaving the Army the couple took over the first of several pubs in the Andover area, but unfortunately the rows over his drinking and gambling intensified. He was even thrown out of the regimental veteran's group because of his drinking. She had to think of the children; and she considered herself a good mother – responsible, nurturing and protective. Unfortunately for her this led to a period of self-neglect. And then in 2012 Jackson's father died and to her dismay he wanted to return to Derbyshire, to be near his mother.

'I'd never really left that part of Hampshire, so it was a big wrench for me – and the kids,' she explained earnestly.

'So what persuaded you to come in the end?'

'He promised to give up the drinking and gambling.'

'And you believed him?'

Again she nodded her head. 'I thought that we could start all over again when we got the pub at Armisfield.'

'Would that be *The Royal Standard*?'

'Yes, do you know it?'

'My boss is known to show his face in there from time to time, so I am led to believe.'

There was a hint of sarcasm in his voice, but she didn't seem to notice and just continued with her story.

'Everything went well at first, but then our son joined the Army a year after we moved here, and a year after that our daughter became a student in Derby.' She started fiddling with her fingers again. 'That was difficult for me.'

'In what respect?'

'I found it difficult to let go.' She then looked up once more. 'You don't have kids, do you?'

Well, she was straight and to the point, thought Clarke. And it was the second time today. 'No, I don't have any kids.' He shuffled uncomfortably and then tried to change the subject. 'So, what went wrong?'

There was a long pause before she replied. 'Like I said, it all went well to begin with. I tried to create a good impression – in order to please him and keep him from going off the rails.'

'But he turned to the bottle again?'

She nodded. 'Big time – and the gambling too.'

Clarke leaned forward. 'Was there a reason for this – for going back on his word and returning to type?'

'It's called a *relapse*.' she said with some authority.

'Okay, so why the relapse?'

She shrugged her shoulders. 'Who knows?' was all she would say.

'And how did this affect you?'

'You don't let up, do you?' She looked up at him again.

'It's my job, Patricia.'

'Naturally I became depressed, with periods of low self-esteem and loss of confidence. It didn't help that the kids had left home, as I've said already.'

'You lost your identity?'

'That's about it.'

'And how did you get things back together again? Did you receive help?'

'Sort of.' She didn't seem to be very forthcoming.

'Would you care to expand on this?'

'I was encouraged to go after my dreams. I'd always had a creative and imaginative streak, and I loved the outdoors. So I hit on the idea of a riding school.'

'Who encouraged you?'

'A friend.' She would say no more.

'And was this when the marriage came to an end?'

'Keith's drinking and gambling got worse, so towards the end of 2015 I just couldn't take any more and so I left him.'

'And where did you go?'

'I went back to my parents to begin with – they were very helpful. I told them that I wanted to set up a riding school here in Derbyshire, so they gave me the money to buy the run-down farm buildings at Sapworth. The farmer rented out the small cottage alongside and I moved there.' And almost as an aside she added. 'I wanted to be near my daughter. She lives in Derby.'

Clarke wasn't sure whether to believe her or not, but he continued nevertheless. 'I understand that the stables are doing well?'

'Moderately so,' she replied.

'And what became of your husband?'

'Well he couldn't stay at the pub, could he? Not the way he was carrying on. I heard he'd moved into the house down on Blackthorn Lane.'

'Did you see much of him after you parted company?'

'Once or twice maybe.'

'You were no doubt aware that he was in debt?'

'For crying out loud, he was always in bloody debt to someone or something.' She was clearly getting tired of the questioning.

'Just a few more questions, Patricia, and then we're done.' If he was honest with himself then he too would be glad when the questioning was over. 'What was your relationship with your mother-in-law?'

She put her hand on his arm. 'Does she know what's happened?' It was almost as if she were pleading with him.

'I broke the news to her earlier. As you can imagine she's very upset.'

'To be honest I rarely saw anything of her – but then neither did Keith until she moved into the home last year.' She could see that Clarke was looking at her quizzically. 'It's alright, Inspector. A friend of mine works there – she keeps me informed, so to speak'. She paused briefly. 'But the old girl doted on Keith; that I do know.'

Clarke wasn't looking forward to the next question, but it had to be asked. 'And has there been anyone else in your life since…'

She cut him short. 'Too busy, Inspector. I have a riding school to run.'

Well, she didn't waste time in answering that particular question! But that's nothing to go by. He smiled briefly and then asked her the penultimate question.

'Who do you think could have killed him?'

Again her response was swift. 'Where do you want me to start?' She cocked her head to one side as she looked at him. 'It could have been any one of a dozen or so people, Inspector, but it wasn't me! Oh, there were many times that I wanted to…' Her speech tailed off. 'But I loved him too much – once.'

Clarke rose from his chair. 'Well, thank you Mrs…' He swiftly corrected himself. 'Thank you, Patricia. Thank you for being so patient.'

'You mean I can go now?' she asked with a sense of relief.

'Erm, just one more thing. Does this mean anything to you?' He pulled out the artist's impression of the *Tom and Jerry* badge. 'We found the original near the scene.'

She blew and shook her head. 'No, it means nothing to me.'

'Any significance to Keith? Something to do with his Army days?'

'If it was then he never said anything about it to me.'

And with that they parted company.

He took his time in returning to his car, mulling over several aspects of the interview. He was fairly certain that she was being economical with the truth at times; particularly with regard to the financial aid she said she had received from her parents. And then there was this so-called "friend" who had allegedly encouraged her to pursue her dreams. She was definitely holding something back there, he thought. And he was pretty certain that there *was* or had been someone else in her life too. It was then that he saw her, at the far end of the car park and standing beside an olive green Y-reg Land Rover Defender with white roof. She was talking to someone on her mobile and the conversation looked quite heated. Funny how everything about this case so far seemed heated – including the weather. And just at that moment he felt a drop or two of rain on his head. By the time he reached his car the heavens had opened. What was all that about heat?

Chapter 16

Wednesday, 5 July, 2017 (p.m.)

Not accustomed to being rebuffed in any way, Detective Sergeant Jacqui Fletcher was clearly not a happy bunny. The goal-oriented, independent-minded and suitably-qualified lass from Nottingham was determined to succeed at her new post, but she had now come up against a stumbling block in the shape of Detective Chief Inspector Allan Clarke.

He had to be a traditionalist with his head stuck in the past, she thought. Worse still, a bloody bigoted misogynist to boot, I'll bet! And to an ardent feminist like her that was bound to present a challenge – and probably a clash too. But if it was a fight he wanted then she was more than up for it! Times have changed and she saw herself as an agent for *positive* change (albeit with a propensity to embrace political correctness), and nobody was going to derail her plans. So, who was this man who dared to oppose *Unternehmen "Jacqui"*!

Shortly before 3.00 p.m. Fletcher was reading one of the case reports when she heard the outside door of the Community Hall open. Within a minute or two there was laughter coming from the kitchen; Webster must have returned from the mortuary, she thought.

Sure enough, the ever-cheerful and cringingly-cocksure (in her opinion) Detective Constable appeared in the main hall with a cup of steaming hot tea in his right hand. As he was passing a couple of uniformed colleagues he couldn't resist cracking a joke or two, and needless to say they all fell about laughing. Out of the corner of his eye he noticed the attractive figure of Sergeant Fletcher sitting alone at her desk, but he deliberately chose to ignore her. It made no difference.

'Webster,' she called to him, perhaps a trifle seductively.

'Oh, it's you Sergeant,' he replied coyly. 'I didn't see you sitting there.'

She ignored the blatant lie. 'Could I have a minute or two of your time, please?'

Shit, thought Webster! What does *she* want with me? 'Yes, Sergeant. Of course.'

'Pull up a chair. I'd like to have a chat with you if I may?'

'What about, Sergeant?' he replied warily.

'How long have you been at Leverton, Webster?'

He puffed out his cheeks and blew. 'About three years now.'

'Have you known Inspector Clarke all of that time?'

'He was here before me and he's always been my boss – if that's what you mean?'

She ignored *his* question. 'What's he like to work with?'

'He's okay, I suppose.'

'Would you care to expand?'

Clearly unaware of Fletcher's intent, Webster certainly wasn't going to be backwards at coming forwards.

'Well he seems to prefer his own company and comes across as a bit of a loner. This gives some of my colleagues the impression that he's unapproachable, but I've always found him to be open. You know, keep the right side of him and he's fine, but touch a nerve and it's a different matter altogether.'

'How do you mean?'

'Well, he can get a bit touchy if you question is judgement or intellect – I've seen him blow a fuse on more than one occasion. In spite of that he is highly respected by everyone in the force – even Superintendent Annable.'

'Really, how interesting?' She sounded surprised, but then she continued. 'Does he have any friends?'

'Not that I know of and certainly not in the force; although he and Detective Sergeant Coates seemed to get on well, but only on a professional basis. Like I said, he tends to keeps his private life to himself'

Fletcher seemed to sense that Webster was holding something back. 'Go on,' she said leaning forward.

'I shouldn't really say this, but there's his drinking – he does like a drink every now and again.'

'Takes to the bottle, does he?'

'Oh yeah! He's been known to go on a right bender every so often, has Sniffer!'

'Sniffer?' she said with a puzzled look on her face.

'Yeah, he's always been called that for as long as I can remember.'

Still significantly puzzled, Fletcher pressed Webster for an answer. 'Why Sniffer?'

'Buggered if I know.'

Fletcher let the matter drop before returning to the previous issue. 'And do we know why he – Sniffer – drinks?'

'I don't believe he's had much success with women – he seems to lack confidence with them.' Unlike you, thought Fletcher, as Webster continued. 'It's not that he doesn't like women, but ever since his marriage broke up they reckon he's become embittered, if you know what I mean.'

Oh, she knew exactly what he meant and she immediately saw a way of exploiting this apparent chink in Clarke's armour, but she wasn't going to say as much.

'Embittered – why is that do you think?'

'Well, apparently Sniffer's wife was knocking somebody else off and he caught them at it – *in flagrante delicto*, so to speak!'

Webster was about to go into greater detail and say something lewd about Mrs. Clarke's infidelity, but Fletcher put her hand up – she got the gist of what he was saying. If only he would be a little less frivolous and stick to the point. Nevertheless, she paused and reflected on what he had just said for a moment, but her thoughts were interrupted as Webster clearly had the bit between his teeth.

'Then there are the events of eight years ago.'

'I'm all ears,' she replied excitedly.

'A bit before my time, but the word is that Sniffer was alleged to have stolen confiscated drugs and sold them back to some of the local villains.'

Fletcher feigned astonishment. 'Wow! What happened?' she cried.

'Well, he claimed to have been set up, but he was still suspended from duty. And then it was discovered that he was telling the truth after all. It wasn't him that had been stealing the drugs – it was his boss!'

'His boss!' repeated Fletcher incredulously.

'Yeah, they mounted a sting operation and they found out that she'd been involved in a major drug supply conspiracy.'

'She?' replied Fletcher, barely able to conceal her surprise and disappointment. 'So it was a female officer?'

'That's right.'

'And do we know who this was?'

'Greenhough – Detective Chief Inspector Maxine Greenhough!'

It was at this point that Webster excused himself and made for the kitchen. Whilst making himself another cuppa he happened to look up and through the window he watched as Sergeant Fletcher drove off in her car. He was already beginning to wonder if he'd said more than he should have.

An hour or so later Clarke returned to the Incident Room still preoccupied with his conversation earlier, with Patricia Jackson. As he entered the hall he looked around and spotted Webster with his feet on his desk, using rubber bands to fire paper clips at a female colleague. He quietly came up behind the unsuspecting Webster and gave vent to his observations.

'Is that what they pay you for, Webster?' he bellowed.

Webster's reactions would have probably won him the Olympic Gold Medal for the high jump such was his surprise at Clarke's presence.

'Yes, Sir...I mean no, Sir,' he spluttered.

'Can't leave you alone for five bloody minutes, can I?' Clarke continued. 'Where's Sergeant Fletcher?'

'Erm, she's gone home, Sir.'

The relief on Clarke's face was palpable. 'Has anything come in during my absence?'

'There's a statement from a probable witness, Sir.'

'Oh yes. And who might that be?'

'A Mr. Watson, Sir – a Mr. Ken Watson. Lives on Gold Crescent here in Brockley. Says he was taking his dog for a walk along Blackthorn Lane around the time that the victim was murdered.'

'And...?'

'Oh yes. Says he was almost run off the road by a car, Sir.'

'What sort of car?'

'Dunno, Sir. All he could say was that it was a "big black bugger".'

'And that's it, is it?' Clarke wasn't at all impressed. 'Looks like we'll be paying him another bloody visit!'

Clarke went into his office and shut the door behind him. He stayed there for another thirty minutes or so – ruminating. Webster remained at his desk, but refrained from firing paper clips at colleagues.

Shortly before 5.00 p.m. Clarke decided to call it a day. Webster indicated that he was going to stay on a while longer, so truce having been unofficially declared Clarke bade him farewell and headed for the car park. Having decided on making his way home through Grimley, he was just passing *The Wheatsheaf* when he spotted two large black Range Rovers parked at the front of the pub. He continued along until he was able to do a u-turn, and then made his way back in the direction of the pub. Interesting, he thought to himself. One of them had what appeared to be hedgehog stickers on the bumper. Making a mental note of the licence plate number (SC13 TTT), he did the same with the other (MA55 TMR), and then pulling out his mobile phone he hoped that Webster hadn't left the incident room. He was in luck.

'Ah, Webster. Glad I've caught you,' he said in a kindly manner. 'I'd like you to run a vehicle check on the following number plates for me.' He read the numbers out and waited.

It wasn't long before Webster came back on the phone. 'Sir, the first one belongs to a Simon Collins of *Hacienda Jalisco*, Church Lane, Armisfield.'

'And the other?' interjected Clarke.

'The other belongs to a Christopher Brian Ibbotson, of Thraplow Lane, Brockley.'

Clarke thanked Webster and then turned the car around in the pub car park before heading home. It *had* been an interesting day, he thought. Very interesting indeed.

Chapter 17

Thursday, 6 July, 2017 (a.m.)

After Wednesday's intermittent showers, Thursday morning dawned bright and sunny in the village of Brockley, with the prospect of some glorious weather for the days ahead. There were still a few puddles here and there in the Community Hall car park, but at least nobody was going to get wet today.

Clarke had arrived at the Hall attired in khaki bomber jacket and dishevelled tie shortly after 8.30 a.m. He had a clear head (for once) and as such he began the day in a positive frame of mind, letting it be known that there would be a team briefing at 9.30 a.m. He entered his office and went through some of the reports once more, before turning his mind to the events of the previous day.

Satisfied that all was in order, he duly called everybody together at the specified time and began by confirming that they were now involved in a murder enquiry. Naturally this caused heads to turn and tongues to wag, but he managed to regain control within a matter of seconds.

They now know more about the victim, he said, but more needed to be known of his movements before he entered *The Wheatsheaf*. Scenes of Crime had produced very little so far, other than the fact that the only fingerprints on the washing line belonged to those of the victim. So it would appear that the landlord of *The Wheatsheaf* was telling the truth. A potential witness has come forward, however, but he has given them very little to go on. Consequently Clarke now began to issue orders.

'We need to speak to the witness again. Surely to God he can come up with something better than a "big black bugger"!' He clearly had someone in mind for this task. 'Webster, get on up to Gold Crescent and see if you can prise some more information from the dog walker.'

'But of course, Sir,' said Webster with a touch of exasperation.

'In the meantime we continue with door-to-doors – and don't forget to ask everyone about the badge!' At that he sent everyone away, but he was aware of the presence of someone over his right shoulder, and he knew what was coming next.

'Sir, I'd like to interview the old man if I may.' began Sergeant Fletcher. I'm more than…'

But Clarke cut her short. 'No!' he snapped. 'I've told you once already that I want you *here* to co-ordinate the enquiry. Now, do I make myself clear?'

Fletcher said nothing at first, merely biting her lip to suppress her rising anger. Clarke turned to go, but Fletcher had one question that she put to him through gritted teeth.

'And where will you be going, Sir?'

Somewhat surprised at her intervention, Clarke replied. 'I hope to be interviewing the landlady of *The Wheatsheaf*.'

'Sure you won't need someone to come and hold your hand?' she muttered under her breath.

Clarke pretended not to hear; but he heard alright. And as the female members of the team sniggered at Fletcher's sarcastic comment, it dawned on him that someone had been tittle-tattling behind his back!

When Clarke pulled up outside *The Wheatsheaf* there was still an hour or so to go before opening time, and they were evidently in the process of receiving a delivery. The front door was shut, but he knocked nevertheless and before long the glamorous figure of Sally Dawkins stood before him in a low-cut blouse, shorts and slippers. He proffered his card and introduced himself. Sally's demeanour changed immediately.

'You'll be wanting to speak to my husband again?' she inferred, pointing towards the rear of the pub.

'Actually Mrs. Dawkins it's you I'd like to talk to if I may?' he replied forcefully.

Sally picked up on this immediately, and fluttering her eyelashes at him she gave a winsome smile as she pointed to one of the tables at the front of the pub.

'Why don't we sit here?' she said seductively. 'I'll just see that everything's okay behind the bar and join you shortly.' With that she disappeared inside for a few minutes and left him to admire the hanging baskets around the door.

He could hear voices raised inside at first, but then it went quiet and when Sally finally re-appeared he could have sworn that she had applied more of her red lipstick *and* undone one of the buttons on her blouse – not that there was much to see!

'Hear I am,' she giggled, thrusting her chest at him, 'all yours, Inspector.'

Ignoring her blatant attempt at flirtation, he began by confirming that she had been seen by the police during their door-to-door enquiries and that her husband had been interviewed about his statement. Sally nodded her head in agreement and then lit a cigarette, much to Clarke's distaste. He then went on to ask if the names Simon Collins and Christopher Ibbotson meant anything to her.

'Yeah, of course,' she said confidently. 'They're both regulars in here; they come in most days.'

'Were they both in here on Monday – that would be the third?'

'Yeah,' she replied blowing smoke out of the corner of her mouth.

'Can you remember what time they came in the pub?'

She looked up and paused briefly before replying. 'They both came in some time between half five and six o'clock, that I do know.'

Clarke made a few notes. 'What can you tell me about them? Let's start with Mr. Collins?'

'Cockney Harry, you mean?'

'Cockney Harry?' repeated Clarke with a puzzled look.

'Yeah, he's from the east end of London. Had a few betting shops down there. Now he's got a couple up here; one in Grimley and one in Derby, I think.' She paused again whilst Clarke scribbled on his notepad, and then continued. 'Oh, and he plays for the local cricket team, although I don't think his heart's really in it.'

'And what about Mr. Ibbotson?' said Clarke without looking up.

'Oh *he* plays cricket alright. He's the bloody club Captain, isn't he?'

'Is he?'

'Yeah, and he's head of the parish council. Thinks a lot of himself does Mr "lah-de-dah" Ibbotson.'

'You don't like him?'

'Bit of a snob – know what I mean?'

'And what does he do for a living?'

'He's an antiques dealer, isn't he? Got himself a shop in Derby.'

'Is that right?' said Clarke with a hint of sarcasm. 'Are both men married?'

'Collins is, but not Ibbotson. Never seen him with a woman.'

'Does Mrs. Collins come in the pub?'

'Nah,' she replied stubbing out her cigarette – to the relief of Clarke. 'She spends her time getting pissed... I mean drunk... by the swimming pool all day *and* every day.'

Clarke said nothing in response to her last comments, but put another question to her instead. 'Is there anything else that you can tell me about Mr. Collins or Mr. Ibbotson?'

She leaned forward and almost in a whisper said 'Well between you and me, word is that Mr. Collins has got a bit on the side.'

Clarke sighed inwardly. Women and gossip, he thought to himself. And yet he felt duty bound to pursue the matter. 'And do we know who the lady is?'

'Well, I'm not one to name names, Inspector, but rumour has it that Mr. Collins does like to spend a lot of time in the saddle – if you know what I mean!' said Sally with a wink and a rather smug expression on her face.

Clarke was about to shake his head, but he thought better of it. 'I see,' was his curt reply. He made a few more notes and then changed the tack of his questioning.

'Do you know if Mr. Jackson owed anyone any money?'

Sally blew out her cheeks. 'I wouldn't be surprised – he was always in debt.'

'And did he have any enemies?'

'None that I can think of – he kept himself to himself,' she replied almost disinterestedly. And then her eyes narrowed as a look of anger appeared on her face. 'Not unless he upset John Sheldon!'

'John Sheldon?' repeated Clarke. 'And who's he?'

'He's a CCTV and alarm installer – lives out at Thraplow. He's always in here – and he plays for the cricket team too.'

'I take it you don't like the man?'

'A nasty piece of work – I wouldn't put *anything* past him!'

'Pugnacious, is he?'

'Pug what...?' she replied with perplexed look on her face.

'Never mind, Mrs. Dawkins,'

Clarke finished making his notes and thanked Sally for being very co-operative. As the pair stood up, she leaned forward and sticking her chest out again she asked him if he would like to stay for lunch.

'That's very kind of you, Mrs. Dawkins, but I'm afraid that I have to return to the Incident Room.'

'Well you're more than welcome, Chief Inspector,' she purred seductively. 'Anytime.'

Clarke was about to make for his car when he remembered the badge. 'There is one more thing that I would like to ask, Mrs. Dawkins.'

'Oh please call me Sally,' she pleaded.

Dawkins just smiled. 'Do you know anything about a *Tom and Jerry* badge and its possible significance?'

'Sorry, I haven't got a clue.'

He thanked her again and then swiftly made for the car. He was somewhat relieved when he shut the door behind him and sat behind the wheel. Not his cup of tea, Mrs. Dawkins. She might be wearing shorts today, but he had a sneaking suspicion that the woman would much rather prefer to be seen wearing the trousers!

As he turned the ignition on and pulled out of the car park, he looked into his rear mirror and noticed Tony Dawkins laughing and joking with the driver of a delivery vehicle. 'Poor sod,' he muttered to himself.

Chapter 18

Thursday, 6 July, 2017 (p.m.)

It was that time of day and his stomach was rumbling again. He'd turned down the offer of a meal at *The Wheatsheaf* and he was buggered if he was going to have a bloody bap or baguette at the *Railway Tavern* at Clavermill! He wasn't one for takeaways, fast food or pizzas, but now and again he liked to call at the chippie. That was it! He fancied fish, chips and mushy peas, and he knew where there was a decent chippie nearby. Chips and peas was known locally as a 'mixed,' but had he gone to Derby or anywhere outside the Grimley and Leverton areas then they wouldn't have had a clue what he was on about. So when he called at the chippie on the Market Place at Grimley he confidently ordered a 'fish and mixed,' safe in the knowledge that the staff knew precisely what he wanted!

He would have preferred to have had his 'fish and mixed' in an old newspaper, just like when he was a nipper, but he had to accept that those days were long gone – more was the pity. He'd ask for them to be wrapped, as he intended to eat them elsewhere and *al fresco*, so leaving the chippie absolutely ravenous he headed back to his car and set off for Stubbs Pond, on the outskirts of Grimley.

Stubbs Pond was part of a small nature reserve. It was popular with local ramblers and birdwatchers, and also those who enjoyed a spot of fishing. There were quite a few vehicles in the car park when Clarke pulled up, but fortunately he spotted a vacant bench near to the waters edge that afforded him a view of most of the lake. As he unwrapped the meal before him, there was a rustle in the alder trees to his right and left, and a robin flew off into the bushes behind him. Smiling to himself, he began to tuck into the delicious contents within. Looking up, he watched as a coot chased off an intrusive moorhen. Several swans seemed to drift by gracefully in the distance, intermingled with the obligatory Canada geese. A common blue damselfly flitted by before settling briefly on the sausage-shaped seed head of a reedmace plant. Nearby and to his rear he could hear the distinctive sound of a song thrush, and at that moment he suddenly felt a pang of sadness. This is what he would undoubtedly miss most of all when it was his time to leave this world, he thought; the sights and sounds of nature.

He was so grateful to his grandfather for introducing him to the great outdoors and especially to the wildlife that abounded in the fields surrounding the village of Pawley. Had his parents not been killed in that car crash when he was seven, then he would have no doubt spent his entire childhood enclosed within the concrete of the grim streets of Leverton and the hustle and bustle of urban life; but fate had decreed that he should be relocated to the tranquil, more appealing environs of Pawley and the slower pace of rural life, and he took to it from the outset. He never forgot his working class roots or the down-to-earth character of the people of Leverton and nearby communities, but he always regarded himself as something of a 'country boy,' and for that he had to thank his grandfather, Harry Clarke.

Shaken out of his whimsical, melancholic state by an elderly man approaching with a border terrier, the two men nodded to each other as the dog casually cocked its leg up and urinated against the bin that stood beside the bench. As the old man and his dog moved on and out of view, he looked down at his meal once more and bit off a large portion of the battered fish. At that precise moment the ringtone of his mobile went off. Who the hell can that be now, he heard himself say? It was Webster.

'Trust you to call me when I've got my mouth full of fish and chips, Webster,' spluttered Clarke. 'It had better be good.'

'It's about that witness, Sir,' said Webster in an unusually excited state.

'What about him?'

'Well, I went to see him, Sir – like you said – and he now seems to recollect that the registration number of the vehicle that nearly knocked him down on the day of the murder might have begun with an "M",'

'Might have, Webster?' groaned Clarke (having finally managed to swallow the large piece of fish). 'Is that the best you can do?'

'I'm sorry, Sir.'

'It's something to go on though, I suppose,' said Clarke thoughtfully. 'Whereabouts are you at the moment?'

'I'm back at the incident room, Sir.'

'Good! Here's what I want you to do. Find out if this guy Ibbotson has been interviewed during the door-to-door enquiries. If not, then he has an antiques shop in Derby. Get hold of him there and find out where he was and what he was doing at the time of the murder. Got that?'

'Right you are, Sir. I'll get cracking on that now.'

But Clarke hadn't finished. 'Hang on, Webster, hang on. There's something else that I want you to do for me.'

'What's that, Sir?'

'I want you to run a PNC check for me.'

'What – now?' replied Webster sounding somewhat puzzled and perplexed.

'That's right.'

'What – on this guy Ibbotson?'

Clarke was clearly getting frustrated. 'No, no, no,' he snapped. 'On a guy by the name of John Sheldon.'

'John Sheldon?' repeated Webster.

'Yes, it's a name that's come onto our radar, shall we say.'

Webster immediately set about running the PNC check on John Sheldon, whilst Clarke attempted to finish his meal. Within a matter of minutes Webster was back on the line.

'Are you still there, Sir?'

'Yes, I'm still here,' replied Clarke with a wry grin upon his face. 'Have you found anything?'

A triumphant Webster duly read out to him the results of the PNC check. A John Sheldon was caught stealing electrical equipment as a teenager, for which he was fined and given a slap on the wrist. He was also caught stealing a microwave to the value of seventy-nine pounds at the age of nineteen, for which he received a court conviction; he was fined and jailed for six months.

At this point Clarke smiled as his mind flashed back to the sketch from the TV comedy series *Only Fools and Horses*, where Del Boy is held on suspicion of stealing a microwave by the hated Chief Inspector Roy Slater.

'Is that it?' enquired Clarke.

'There's more, Sir,' replied Webster.

The latter continued to read from the results of the PNC check, which showed that Sheldon also received a five-year sentence for actual bodily harm at the age of twenty-eight, when he hit someone with a pool cue and punched them, causing bruising and cuts; this was apparently for trying to chat up his then girlfriend. That was the end of the file on John Sheldon.

Quite a character, thought Clarke; and it would appear that Sally Dawkins was right – a nasty piece of work.

'Will we be speaking to this John Sheldon, Sir,' asked Webster, 'about the murder of Keith Jackson?'

'It's very possible, Webster,' replied Clarke. 'But not for the moment.'

'I'll see if I can find this guy Ibbotson then shall I, Sir?'

'You do that, Webster – and let me know how you get on. I'd better go see Annable and keep him up-to-date.'

But Webster couldn't resist a little quip before leaving. 'Come not between the dragon and his wrath,' he intoned.

'What *are* you on about, Webster?' queried a flummoxed Clarke.

'Not sure which act or scene, Sir, but it's from *King Lear*. And knowing how much you like Shakespeare…'

A veritable flood of expletives were directed at a smiling Webster from the other end of the line and brought the conversation to an end.

As Clarke switched off his mobile, he looked down at what was now a somewhat cold tray of mostly chips and peas. Besides, he was well and truly replete after such a large meal. Why do they always give you a vast amount of chips, he thought? Wrapping what was left of his meal in the paper it came in, he threw it all in the bin beside the bench. Making his way back to his car he noticed one or two other people around the lake feeding bread to the swans and other wildfowl – and very likely chips too. He would never consider doing such a thing, as he was a firm adherent of the argument that bread and chips were no substitute for the proper diet that the birds can seek out for themselves. He would have preferred to have stayed beside the lake for the rest of the afternoon, but a dragon in the shape of Superintendent Annable awaited his presence.

It had been six weeks since Annable had touched up the roots of his hair with the dark brown dye. Nobody was around, so now was as good a time as any, or so he thought. Of course he was unaware that his secretary knew of his little secret, but she was on an errand at this specific moment in time, so he opened the bottom drawer of his desk and was about to withdraw the bottle and brush when there was a knock on the door

'Erm, just a minute,' he shouted uneasily as he hurriedly replaced the bottle and brush. 'Come in.'

The door opened and in stepped Clarke. 'Hope I haven't disturbed you, Sir?'

'Erm, no. Not at all. Please take a seat.'

Clarke suspected that he had disturbed him and that it had something to do with hair dye, but he wasn't going to say anything. He merely muttered 'Thank you, Sir', and then sat down opposite his boss.

'Well, how is the case going? Do we have any idea who killed this fellow Jackson yet?'

Clarke knew that Annable expected results pretty damn quickly, so in order to keep the man satisfied he was always prepared to mix a few half-truths with the truth. They had already determined a couple of suspects and were confident of getting their man within a matter of days.

'Good!' boomed Annable with a satisfied look on his face. But Clarke suspected that something else was coming and he wasn't wrong. 'And how is Detective Sergeant Fletcher doing by the way?'

Convinced that there was a conspiracy of which Annable was part, Clarke now decided to forego the half-truths and elected for a whopper, 'She's settling in well, Sir, and playing a vital role in the case!'

'Splendid!' was Annable's almost ecstatic response, as he rose from his chair and donned his cap. 'At the end of the day (Clarke groaned inwardly), we must all get along with each other, mustn't we?'

'Indeed we must, Sir,' replied Clarke in a mildly compliant manner.

As the two men headed for the outside door side by side, Clarke was almost praying that Annable would leave without quoting from Shakespeare, but he was to be disappointed. Annable opened the door for Clarke and just as the latter was about to bid him farewell for the day, Annable quoted a line from *The Tempest*.

'We are such stuff as dreams are made on, and our little life is rounded with a sleep!'

What is the daft sod on about now, thought Clarke. 'So I've been told, Sir,' was his curt response!

The two men parted company and crossed the car park in different directions. Judging by the look on Clarke's face it was extremely likely that he could have shot Superintendent Annable there and then; he would almost certainly make it a capital offence to quote from the works of Shakespeare if it were left to him. 'Bloody rubbish,' he said out loud as he opened the door of his car. He was about to utter one or two other distasteful expletives aimed at the bard when the phone went. Webster was on the other end again.

'Ah, Webster, have you managed to find Ibbotson by any chance,' enquired Clarke.

'Yes, Sir,' replied a rather subdued Webster.

'Good man! And…?'

'Bad news I'm afraid, Sir. He's got an alibi.' Webster removed the phone from his ear in anticipation of the deafening reaction.

'What!' Clarke's reaction was ear splitting.

Glad to have got that over with, Webster proceeded to inform Clarke of Ibbotson's whereabouts on the day of the murder.

'I caught him at his shop in Derby, Sir. He told me that on the day Jackson was murdered he was at an auction in Leicester, leaving the shop in the care of his assistant – he could provide numerous witnesses, he said. Oh, he did return to the shop, but that was before 4.00 p.m. – his assistant would vouch for him. He locked up about five-ish and then went to *The Wheatsheaf.*'

'Damn!'

Webster waited a few seconds before giving his response. 'What do we do now, Sir?'

'Well, we'd better question the owner of the other "big black bugger", hadn't we?' Clearly frustrated, Clarke suddenly had an idea. 'Look, I want you to go to chez Collins first thing tomorrow. Find out what our friend from London was doing on the day of the murder.'

Clarke then rang off and Webster went home. Slumping into the seat of his car, Clarke cursed again – several times. Just when it looked like they were on to something at last…

But wait a minute, lad. What if the witness had got it wrong? What if the witness was mistaken as to the registration number? Indeed, what if the witness was in fact lying? Oh, go home and forget about it for now, he told himself. He was going to the care home in the morning. Perhaps Mrs. Jackson will spring one or two surprises?

Chapter 19

Friday, 7 July, 2017 (a.m.)

Well, it wasn't called *Hacienda Jalisco* for nothing, thought Detective Constable Webster as he pulled into the driveway of the home of Simon Collins. Named after a hacienda in the Sierra Madre Mountains above Puerto Vallarta, Mexico, Simon Collins took to it the moment that he saw it; especially as the building backed onto the Armisfield Golf Course. His wife did not share his enthusiasm. Largely hidden from view and set back off the road, Webster almost drove past the entrance as he was cruising down Church Lane, Armisfield, on that hot, sunny Friday morning shortly after nine o'clock. It was completely out of character with the surrounding area, or so he thought, but even he had to admit that it had its charms.

The main building was a cream colour with the versatile concrete roof tiling so typical of haciendas. There were four upstairs windows all of which led to a balcony. Below this was a porch fronted by five archways; there were two more at either side of the porch. Behind the central archway was the main door and either side of this were two windows. There was a small outbuilding to the left and a large garage to the right; the black Range Rover Autobiography was parked in front of the latter. Between the garage and the main building was a large wrought iron gate, and behind this Webster was able to discern a large swimming pool. There was a small wall in front of the archways; in front of this a path led around to the rear of the building and through the gate. The vast courtyard had been concreted over in a style that complimented the main building perfectly. As Webster pulled up, a stocky, well-built man appeared to be loading golf clubs into a brand new Katsura-Orange Nissan sports car. Webster climbed out of his blue Toyota Aygo and introduced himself.

'Mr. Collins? Mr. Simon Collins?'

'Yeah,' the man replied in what was clearly an East End accent and without looking up, 'who wants to know?'

'I'm Detective Constable Webster of Leverton CID.' He proffered his identity card. 'No doubt you've heard of…er...the suspicious death at Brockley last Monday?' said Webster hesitatingly.

'Yeah, what about it?'

'Well, we've been conducting…er…door-to-door enquiries in and around the Brockley area with a view to…er…finding out as much as we can about the victim – a Mr. Keith Jackson. Did you…er…know the victim by any chance?'

'Nah, not really. Only saw 'im at the cricket club from time to time – and even then we never spoke. Bit of a loner apparently.'

'Did you…er…know that Mr. Jackson was in debt?'

'Like I said, I didn't know 'im.'

Webster wasn't looking forward to the next question, but he had been told to ask it all the same. 'So you…er… never lent Mr. Jackson any…er…money?'

Collins slammed the boot of the car, straightened up and confronted the young detective. 'Look, what's this about? Am I a suspect or somefink?'

Clearly intimidated, Webster stepped back. 'No, no, no. Not at all. It's just that…er…well, on the day of the murder Mr. Jackson was apparently…er…throwing money about like it was…er…going out of fashion. He hadn't had a win on the…er…horses, so we were…er…wondering where he…er…got the money from?'

'Well 'e didn't get it from me!' snarled Collins, who promptly made to go back indoors.

'There was just…er…one more thing, Mr. Collins,' shouted Webster after him.

Collins stopped and turned to face Webster once more. 'What?'

'Where were you around four o'clock on the afternoon of Monday the third, Sir?' asked Webster without *any* hesitation.

'For your information I was at my shops in Grimley and Derby. Now, can I get on wiv my life?' And with that Collins turned and walked away once more.

Webster attempted to thank him for his co-operation, but Collins had already slammed the door behind him. With a sense of relief Webster climbed back into his car. Indeed, he was glad that it was all over and done with. As he sped off down the driveway he was tempted to look in the rear mirror and take one last glimpse of *Hacienda Jalisco*, but he thought better of it!

There was one thing that Webster did do before heading off back to the incident room, and that was make a call to Inspector Clarke and inform him of his meeting with Simon Collins.

'Looks like *he's* got a good alibi too, Sir.' announced a frustrated Webster.

'Mmmm,' pondered Clarke. 'There's something not quite right about all of this, Webster. You know what I think?'

'What's that, Sir?'

'I've got a feeling that they're all lying – including the bloody witness!'

As Webster carried out his questioning of her husband, Dawn Collins had made her way quietly and yet very unsteadily downstairs to the kitchen, where she poured herself a large gin and tonic – no doubt the first of many.

At five feet and four inches tall, with short blonde peroxide hair and blue eyes, she looked rather older than her fifty-three years, and especially so first thing in the morning – not that she was usually up before noon. No, more often than not she was still abed, sleeping off the previous day's hangover; but today was different. It hadn't always been like this of course.

The daughter of a market trader who had played cards with the Kray twins in the large antechamber of the men's toilets at Shoreditch Town Hall, she was a stripper at Raymond's Revuebar in Soho when she met Simon Collins in the 1980's. Although somewhat loud and brash, she was sensual, charismatic and exuberant, with an air of seduction about her. She had an instant effect on the opposite sex because of *her* sex appeal and that was undoubtedly what attracted Collins to her in the first place. It had always been her desire to enjoy life to its fullest, so when she married Collins in 1989 she not only became accustomed to being the wife of a self-made businessman, but she was able to fulfil that desire and live a life of luxury.

From the outset, however, she was aware that her husband was a bit of a 'Jack the Lad' and had something of a 'roving eye,' but she always tolerated his little indiscretions. Of course she was jealous, and it was that which led her to engage in a number of affairs herself, especially with younger men, but in the end she always remained loyal. That all changed when the couple left London and moved north to Derbyshire. She never liked it from the very beginning and she soon started taking to the bottle. This got worse when she began to suspect that her husband was having a full blown affair. Indeed, it became an obsession with her; it was as if she was being rejected and she got it into her head that she was falling out of favour. To counter this she decided to have cosmetic surgery, which she believed would make her more physically attractive. She started with liposuction, but then she had her boobs enlarged, and she took to showing them off when they had guests for dinner. She had always preferred entertaining rather than going to the pub, so she would flirt with the male guests in an effort to make Simon jealous, but it all came to nothing and her drinking then became much worse. She made it clear that she wanted to return to the London area, whilst maintaining the lifestyle to which she had become accustomed, but Simon would have none of it.

And now there was the possibility that her husband was involved in a murder – why else would the police question him? More importantly, the murdered man was the former husband of the woman who Dawn Collins suspected *her* husband of having an affair with! She had overheard the entire conversation between her husband and the policeman, and now it was her turn to ask him a few questions.

Collins was in a foul mood after his contretemps with Webster; hence the slamming of the door when he re-entered the house. He paused for a few seconds as if to control his emotions and then swore a couple of times before heading to the kitchen and the fridge; he had evidently forgotten to take a cold drink with him. Unaware that his wife was up and about, there was a genuine look of astonishment and surprise on his face when he saw her standing before him as he entered the kitchen.

'What you doin' up at this time?' he mumbled before making for the fridge.

'You always used to call me "babes",' she replied with a slight slur. 'Remember?'

'Did I?' There was a brief pause as he removed the bottle from the fridge 'Well, that was before you started drinkin', wasn't it? How many is that since you've been up?' The tone was harsher.

She ignored his question and asked one of her own. 'So, you were at the shops in Derby and Grimley on Monday, were you?'

'That's right.'

'Then you're a liar!' she screamed and spat at him. 'I rang both shops and they said you 'adn't even been in!'

He turned to face her and scoffed. 'What? You'd be too pissed to pick up the bleedin' phone, woman. So don't come that cobblers wiv me!'

The tears were coming now. 'You were wiv that slut, weren't you?'

Collins put a hand to his forehead. 'For God's sake, don't start all that crap again!'

'You fink I don't know?'

Collins was in no mood for another argument. 'I'm outta 'ere!' And with that he stormed off.

'That's right. Go back to your slut!' she screamed after him. Collins had just reached the door when she screamed again in that unmistakeable East End accent. 'You barstard!' And launching a full glass of gin at him it smashed into smithereens just above his head and to his right.

Collins was out of the door in a flash and for the second time that morning he slammed it behind him. As he jumped into his car and turned on the ignition, there was another smash of glass against the door. He could have been mistaken of course, but he was willing to swear that it was a bottle this time – and probably a full one!

Chapter 20

Friday, 7 July, 2017 (a.m.)

They were sisters, but other than their appearance there was little to suggest that Mrs. Valerie Jackson and Mrs. Vera Hartley were in any way related or connected. The old chestnut of 'chalk and cheese' was indeed a true reflection of the two elderly widows.

Separated by three years, Vera was the elder of the two Greatorex sisters. She found work in a hosiery factory after leaving school, and after a whirlwind courtship married bus driver, Dennis Hartley, in 1956. They had the one daughter, Paula, who was doted on by her mother until she too married and left the Grimley area. Eventually Vera and Dennis moved to nearby Brockley in the early nineteen eighties and settled in a bungalow on Gold Crescent. After Dennis died in 2008, Vera chose to remain in the bungalow and became an ardent member of the local Women's Institute. Other than that she spent much of her time in the post office, where she was renowned as the village gossip.

But that was Vera all over. Driven by the desire for attention, she just loved to be centre stage, where she obtained tremendous satisfaction from knowing that if there was a story or a rumour to be passed around, then she must be the one who started it! What's more, she had a tendency to exhibit extreme jealousy towards those who were already 'in the know,' so to speak; she was terrified of falling out of favour and being regarded as a has-been.

Born in 1938, Valerie Greatorex was a different kettle of fish altogether. In fact she had very little to do with her sister as she grew up, preferring the company of Maureen Chapman, whose family lived on the same street at Grimley. The two were inseparable and she spent much of her time at the Chapman's, where she got to know other members of Maureen's family. Unlike her sister, Vera found work as a domestic servant at Brockley Hall after leaving school, but she was forced to leave very abruptly under a dark cloud after only a few months.

She married Derek Jackson in 1959 and they made their home in a small terraced house at Grimley. She had undoubtedly found the love of her life – which had been her lifetime's ambition – and under his protection she felt so safe and free from harm. When son Keith came onto the scene in 1964 she was naturally driven by the maternal instincts of nurturing and compassion, so she also became motivated by the desire to protect and care for him. This she did until the time came when he chose to leave home and join the Army. She had to admit that she found it difficult to let go and she missed him terribly. In fact it was only when husband Derek died in 2012 that she got to see more of Keith and his family, when they decided to move to Derbyshire. However, crippled with arthritis, Vera moved to the Little Orchard Care Home in 2016. Having occupied herself with knitting for much of her life, she found solace in the television – especially the soaps!

Indeed, with her hair in a grey wavy perm and her blue-grey eyes hiding behind her spectacles, she had been sat up in bed in her dark grey dressing gown and nightie watching *This Morning* on the ITV channel when her sister had popped in to see her (the Family Liaison Officer accordingly departed for the lounge for the time being). She did this two or three times a week, but although Valerie was grateful for the company she could hardly ever get a word in edgeways. So she would turn the sound down and pretend that she was listening to Vera rabbiting on about the vicar's latest boyfriend, Mrs. Thornhill having run off with him at number twenty or Mrs. Jordan's varicose veins. Today, however, she had expected Vera to offer her condolences – which she did – and be a little more sympathetic considering her loss – which she was to some extent; but as she sat opposite Valerie with her grey collar-length hair in a fringe above her grey-blue eyes and dressed in a dark grey pant suit and white blouse (her spectacles were hanging from a chain), she just couldn't resist that one little piece of gossip that was bound to impress her sister.

Leaning forward she whispered 'Her at number fifty-two has been sunbathing topless in the garden again!'

'Who's that then?' replied Valerie with a heavy sigh.

'You know – her with the two miniature pinscher's.'

Valerie hadn't got a clue who Vera was on about, but she thought it would be better if she played along. 'Oh, her,' she said disinterestedly.

'And at her time of life too – disgusting if you ask me.'

Vera was just about to provide a detailed account of what she thought of 'her at number fifty-two' when there was a knock at the door and in stepped the manageress, Audrey Bostock; and standing behind her was a rather scruffy-looking man in a bomber jacket and tie.

'Ah, Mrs. Jackson, you have company,' said Audrey apologetically.

'That's okay, Audrey. My sister was just leaving,' replied Valerie. At which Vera's eyes narrowed in a look that could be best described as spiteful.

'It's just that there's a policeman here to talk to you, about…well, you know.'

Vera Hartley rose from her chair, leaned across to kiss her sister and bade her farewell for the time being, promising to return in a few days. She then brushed past Audrey Bostock and Inspector Clarke of Leverton CID without so much as a by your leave, but it was clearly a 'I know when I'm not wanted' moment! Unseen by the people left in the room, she then turned right and headed for the toilet along the corridor.

For the second time Audrey Bostock introduced Clarke to Valerie Jackson and having offered a few words of advice she promptly left the room and headed down the corridor to her office.

'Hello again, Mrs. Jackson,' began Clarke. 'Please accept my condolences on the loss of your son.'

'Thank you, Inspector,' she replied with a hint of a smile. 'You don't look like a policeman – oh and please call me Valerie by the way.'

It wasn't the first time that Clarke's appearance had led others to be deceived as to his profession, so he took her comment in his stride. And yet as he pulled up a chair he couldn't help thinking once more that her smile hid a lot of pain, both physical and emotional.

'I think you know why I'm here, don't you, Valerie?' he said compassionately.

'I take it you want to know more about my son?' she replied with head bowed.

'I'd be very grateful, please.'

'Where do you want me to start?'

He shrugged his shoulders. 'Childhood I suppose – what was he like as a child?'

Valerie was just about to respond to the question when Clarke put the forefinger of his right hand to his mouth, as if to call for silence and then rose from his chair. Reaching the door, he noticed that it had been opened slightly since Audrey Bostock left the room and so he pulled it open sharply to reveal a startled Vera Hartley, who was clearly trying to listen in to the conversation between her sister and the detective.

As she jumped back in surprise, Clarke smiled at her politely.

'Something we can do for you, Mrs. Hartley?' he said in a calm voice

Lost for words, she attempted to put together an excuse. 'I...I...thought that...I...I...might have left my...spectacles in the room.'

'No, Mrs. Hartley. They're on the chain around your neck!' And then pointing down the corridor in the direction of the outside door he continued. 'Now if you don't mind I'd like to speak to your sister in private if I may?'

Issuing a garbled apology, Vera Hartley scuttled off down the corridor with tail between legs, obviously miffed that the detective had frustrated her attempts to earwig the conversation that had been taking place in her sister's room.

Clarke closed the door behind him and returned to his chair, whilst a perplexed Valerie Jackson wondered what on earth had caused him to leave the room. He made some excuse about one of the residents having a spot of bother in the corridor, and then attempted to resume his conversation with her.

'You wanted to know about my son, Keith,' she said.

'That's right,' he replied somewhat apologetically. 'What was he like?'

So Valerie told him about Keith's childhood, and how he particularly enjoyed being 'one of the lads.' He never got into any serious trouble, but boys being boys there was the occasional fight; and yet Keith could always look after himself. Joining the Army seemed such a natural choice after he left school; he was going to be with another group of lads, wasn't he? And when he did come home on leave he never stayed long; he wanted to get back to his mates and Army life. She and Derek were pleased when he got married, but again she rarely saw him, his wife or the grandkids. When Derek died it was as if a light had gone out of her life, so it was a blessing of sorts when Keith and his family moved to Armisfield.

'Where you aware that he had a drinking and gambling problem?' asked Clarke purposefully.

'Yes,' she replied rather shamefacedly, 'and I blame myself entirely.'

'Why should you want to do that?'

'Because I had clearly done something wrong in the past, during his childhood. And now I was being punished for it.'

Clarke recalled Patricia Jackson saying that quitting the Army had left such a huge void in Keith's life, so he was unable to understand why his mother should take the blame for his later problems.

Valerie went on to stress that in spite of those problems she remained optimistic and willing to believe the best about her son; even when he came begging for money.

Clarke's face was a picture of astonishment. 'He actually came to you begging for money?'

Valerie nodded. 'Oh, I know that you will think me naïve and gullible, Inspector. I suppose that I was being exploited, but he was still my son.'

Clarke felt it best that he should leave the conversation there, so he duly thanked Valerie for her co-operation at such a difficult time and began to rise from his chair once more. It was then that he remembered the badge.

'There was one more thing, Mrs. J…' She looked at him over her spectacles in a slightly disapproving manner. 'I'm sorry…Valerie. We found a *Tom and Jerry* badge at the scene of the crime. Does it mean anything to you?'

She shook her head. 'I'm sorry, but I can't help you there, Inspector.'

Thanking her again, he then made to leave, but as he reached the door he suddenly stopped and stood for a while as if reminiscing about something. After a few seconds he spoke.

'I'll tell you something, Valerie. I was never fortunate enough to have children and I look upon that as one of the biggest regrets of my life.'

She paused for a few seconds before replying. 'Yes, it's one of mine too.'

For the second time Clarke looked at her in stunned amazement. 'I'm sorry, but did I just hear you right? Are you saying that you've never had any children of your own?'

She looked back at him in surprise. 'Oh, I thought you knew. Keith was my adopted son, Inspector!'

Chapter 21

Saturday, 8 July, 2017 (a.m.)

Saturday morning broke with barely a cloud in the sky and it was clearly going to be another glorious day for Southeast Derbyshire. For the most part the Edgeley Canal was calm and the peaceful backdrop was disturbed only by the sounds of waterfowl and a Jet2 Boeing 737 which had just taken off from the East Midlands Airport.

It was almost 8.30 a.m. when Clarke woke from his deep slumber aboard the *Emily*. More often than not he was able to recollect the content of his dreams without too much difficulty, even after a few glasses of whisky the night before, and this morning was no different. As he rolled onto his back he clearly remembered that in his dream he had been back to his teenage years, but as an adopted child and not one raised by his grandparents. As a young teenager he had been bullied at Leverton Grammar School for three years, but eventually he snapped and turned on one of his tormentors. In his dream he was being bullied again, only this time he was standing up to and taking on each and every one of them. If only he had done that forty years previously!

Enough was enough, he told himself. He hated every minute of his time at Grammar School and he was buggered if he was going to lie there ruminating over such a detested part of his life – dream or no dream!

Heading for the toilet, he decided that he would have a wash and a shave later. He then put on a pair of beige coloured big size three-quarter length shorts, a black t-shirt and navy blue slippers before making his way outside via the rear doors. He would never countenance leaving a sink full of pots and pans for the following morning, so they had been washed and dried the night before, leaving the kitchen area clean and clear. Climbing the steps and opening the doors he stepped outside and took in the air and the scenery for a few minutes. That was it, he decided; a bowl of cereal and a glass of fresh orange juice outside for a half hour or so, then get the washing machine on and do some cleaning before preparing the evening meal in the slow cooker. That would leave the afternoon free for a pint or two at *The Navigation*; a damn sight better idea than going to that bloody cricket match at Brockley, which was his original intention.

It took him nearly all morning to complete most of the afore-mentioned tasks (and others), but shortly before 11.00 a.m. he finally opted for a Chicken Jalfrezi for his evening meal. Just before he began to prepare the ingredients he selected a CD from his collection – a little music whilst cooking was just the ticket; and especially when the CD in question was Pink Floyd's *Wish You Were Here* – his favourite album.

As the CD opened with Part I of *Shine On You Crazy Diamond*, his mind went back to the first time that he had heard the track. It had been shortly after his parents were killed in the car accident in 1974, when the infant Clarke had been given his father's record collection, which included every album made by Pink Floyd up until then. Inquisitively he had placed the album on the record player – if it was anywhere near as good as *Dark Side of the Moon* then he was in for a treat! It was. But it was *Shine On You Crazy Diamond* that had simply blown his mind that day – and it still did!

As he finally placed all the ingredients for his evening meal into the slower cooker, the album came to an end and he felt exhilarated. He was still on a high as he finished washing the pots, but it was almost noon and he decided to have a couple of sandwiches outside before having a wash and shave (leaving the stubble). Thirty minutes later he was heading for the bridge over the canal at Croxley Lock and back along the towpath towards *The Navigation*.

It was a fifteen minute walk to the pub and he delighted in the sights and sounds of the wildlife and nature around him. On the opposite side of the canal a couple of mallards were making their way quietly along in the same direction. Here and there dragonflies and damselflies flitted around or settled on isolated lily pads. And in the hedgerow up ahead he could hear the unmistakeable song of the yellowhammer, calling for a 'little-bit-of-bread-and-no-cheese.'

There was of course one other perfectly logical reason for calling at *The Navigation*; and that was the outside chance of seeing the very amply-bosomed landlady, Diana Marshall. Strangely enough, when Diana and her partner first took over the pub a year or so before, Clarke had been their very first client. He was never likely to forget the occasion, was he?

When he walked through the door that day there was nobody about – or so he thought. But then he heard that earthy, seductive South Yorkshire accent for the first time. 'Be with you in a moment.' And then she suddenly popped up from behind the bar to reveal a truly massive 38GG cleavage! What's more, he was able to discern a partially hidden tattoo of Marilyn Monroe on her left breast, which was all made possible by her tight-fitting light blue vest-like top. Wow!

Taking one's eyes away from her cleavage was always going to be a difficult task, but one thing that could be said for Diana Marshall was that she was undoubtedly a woman of glamour. Then, as always, her wavy, shoulder length auburn hair was complimented by her dazzling blue-green eyes, which to Clarke suggested that she was a woman of passion. Her predilection of applying light blue eye-shadow to her eye-lids merely added to this concept, and it seemed only natural to him that there was seldom very little evidence of any eyebrows.

Her long, slender nose was thankfully free of rings or studs, but she almost always took to wearing a pair of very large circular earrings. However, if there was one aspect of her appearance that Clarke found nigh on impossible to resist it was her peach-coloured pouting lips, and he always found himself wanting to taste the delectable allure of her mouth.

Deeply tanned and bronzed, he guessed (correctly) that she was a sun-worshipper, but he also suspected (correctly) that she took to visiting the tanning salon or sunbed parlour from time to time. This not unnaturally caused her skin to age and yet she didn't appear to be frightened of showing her wrinkles. That might have made it difficult for others to estimate her age, but Clarke guessed (correctly) that she was at least four years older than him.

She was about two inches smaller than Clarke, but as she was standing behind the bar at the time it had the effect of making it look like she was actually taller.

'What can I get you, luv,' she had asked seductively as he stood before her literally mesmerised by her bust.

Temporarily incapacitated as it were, it was only the arrival on the scene of Diana's partner, Graham Chambers, that caused him to snap out of his trance-like state and order his drink.

'Pint of Abbot's, please,' he spluttered nervously.

As she provocatively pulled his very first pint, he was able to take his eyes away from her bust long enough to observe that she had painted her very long oval-shaped nails in a burgundy colour, and that she had rings on almost every finger. It was then that introductions were made and from that moment he was a fairly frequent visitor to the pub.

That was his first experience of the seductive allure of Diana Marshall and her massive cleavage, but looking back he was unable to recollect *any* occasion when she *wasn't* showing off her cleavage. And then there were the short skirts and high heels, especially on a Saturday night during the summer months. There were a couple of prominent varicose veins on the back of her legs, but they caused her no discomfort and so she saw no reason to consult her GP. But at the age of fifty-five she could get away with this, for the simple reason that she was able to boast a very fine figure. It was all genuine – boobs included; but then there was nothing fake about Diana Marshall.

Of course there was more to Diana than just her appearance and her voluptuous figure. A Sheffield lass through-and-through, she was born Diana Staniforth, the second daughter and third child of a steel worker. Leaving school at the age of sixteen in 1978, she initially found work at a local supermarket. Not content with this line of work, she got a job as a waitress at the Hallamshire Golf Club, near Sheffield, two years later. Here she met the man who was to become her husband, golf professional Wayne Marshall, who was four years her senior. Although she was looking for intimacy, here was a chance to live life to the fullest and she grabbed it.

Naturally seductive, she has always had an instant effect on the men in her life due to her sex appeal, and this is what undoubtedly attracted Wayne. They married when she was nineteen and they went on to have three children – a boy and two girls. They lived very well for a while, but from the outset Wayne couldn't keep his hands to himself, and when the youngest child left school in 2007 Diana decided it was a case of 'anything you can do!' Indeed, Wayne's infidelity caused her to engage in multiple sexual encounters herself, seeking a constant stream of conquests purely for her own pleasure. But then she was charming, charismatic and fun too, inciting arousal and passion in others. She undoubtedly loved the sex, but there were times when she was rejected and this damaged her self-esteem to some extent.

Eventually Diana and Wayne divorced after 29 years of marriage in 2010, when she was aged forty-eight. To celebrate the occasion she hit the champagne big time, which is when she caused something of a stir by climbing onto one of the tables and dancing topless at the Code nightclub in Sheffield!

With a very reasonable divorce settlement, she then decided to go into the hospitality trade and took over a pub on the outskirts of Sheffield. Two years later, in 2012, she met former coal miner,

Graham Chambers, who was a divorcee from Bolsover. She persuaded him to join her and they took over a pub just outside Chesterfield, but it was her name above the door.

It was as if she had gone full circle, back to those moments of intimacy that she had shared with her husband. She was initially willing to accept the fact that he too enjoyed a game of golf, but when it became apparent that he was also something of a Lothario she was subsequently heard to lament to one of the regulars that she was a 'bugger for punishment!' Perhaps it was her fear of being alone, but she put up with his little peccadillos and in April 2016 they took over *The Navigation* at Leverton. Again, the pub was in her name, but more importantly she liked the place and the people; they were down to earth, no nonsense folk and it would have to take a lot more than a promiscuous partner to get her to leave the area.

Dating back over 200 years, *The Navigation* stands beside the Edgeley Canal and it was at one time well placed to quench the thirsts of passing boatmen. As well as being popular with locals, it is now also ideally situated to serve the needs of leisure boaters, walkers and cyclists. Access for motorists is via Canal Street, which separates the largely working class Gartland area of Leverton from the relatively new Woodend estate. A narrow hump-backed bridge is used by pedestrians and cyclists to get from the pub to the towpath on the other side of the canal, and to a footpath that leads to a small wetland nature reserve. There is a large car park to one side of the pub that backs onto the canal, as does the beer garden at the rear. The pub itself has undergone substantial renovation in recent years, with a conservatory being added at the rear alongside the toilets, and a state-of-art kitchen installed beside the bar on the left. The bar is L-shaped, facing the front door as one enters the pub and then round and down towards the toilets on the right. The door leading to the upstairs quarters is located beside the toilets at the bottom right-hand side of the building. Deliveries to the pub are made every Thursday at the rear and beside the car park. At the front of the pub there is a porch decorated with hanging baskets during the summer months. The outside door remains open between midday and eleven in the evening most days, and then one enters the pub using the inside door. Either side of the porch and in front of the windows there is bench seating complete with tables and chairs.

As Clarke began to cross the hump-backed bridge that led to the pub he felt his heart pounding. What would the delectable Diana be wearing today, he wondered? As little as possible with any luck! Entering through the porch, he opened the inside door and to his utter dismay there was no sign whatsoever of the woman who had been occupying his thoughts for the last hour or so; come to that there was no sign of her partner either. Instead he was greeted from behind the bar by a young lass in her late teens, beaming from ear to ear and dressed in an all-black outfit with the pub logo on her left breast.

'Hi there,' she chirruped. 'What can I get you?'

Feeling somewhat deflated he replied 'I'll have a pint of Spitfire, please.'

As she poured the amber liquid he felt the urge to enquire as to the whereabouts of Diana, but then he thought the better of it. She'd probably get the wrong idea (or the right one, depending on how one looked at these things). Instead he looked around disconsolately and watched as two or three other customers ordered food from the mouth-watering menu. There was an old chap in a cloth cap seated beside the door behind him who he recognised, but he couldn't put a name to him, and yet the pair nodded in acknowledgement. The young lass then returned with his beer.

'Anything else I can get you?' she asked the rather sad-looking man.

'No thanks, luv,' he replied.

'That'll be three twenty, please.'

He handed her a five pound note. 'I can give you the twenty pence if that'll help?'

'I'd appreciate it,' she said with some relief.

Handing her the twenty pence, he received two pound coins in return – for which he thanked her. And then with a weak smile he took his beer and headed outside to the garden at the rear.

He preferred this time of day as there weren't usually too many people about, and so he was reasonably pleased to find that the only occupants of the beer garden were a young couple who sat at the top end, and were seemingly oblivious to everything that was going on around them. There was a table that was partially in the shade, but if he sat with his back to the pub he would be able to watch the comings and goings on the canal, and so he chose that one.

The peace and tranquillity was a blessing after the week he'd had, but try as he might he just couldn't get the case out of his mind. For crying out loud, he was supposed to be relaxing, but what with the alibis from Collins and Ibbotson, not to mention the witness statement, he gave up on any idea of relaxation!

He was almost certain that blackmail was at the heart of the case *and* that the badge was the key to solving it. But he was equally certain that Collins was lying and probably Ibbotson too, and that the witness was also being a tad economical with the truth. He'd said as much to Webster, hadn't he? And now it transpires that the bloody victim was adopted! To cap it all he'd been saddled with a bloody woman as his deputy!

Shaking his head, he had almost drained his pint when his deliberations were disturbed by that familiar earthy South Yorkshire accent coming from over his shoulder.

'Penny for them,' she said inquisitively.

Clearly caught off his guard, he turned around sharply and found himself confronted by the seductive smile and voluptuous cleavage of Diana Marshall, who was wearing a black low-cut blouse with denim shorts, and was smoking one of her More Red 120 long brown paper cigarettes.

'Erm…I…thought you might be…out for the day?' he enquired nervously.

'I've been to the cash and carry,' she replied. 'It looks like you could do with another drink.'

With his hand shaking he proffered the almost empty glass. 'Erm…I wouldn't say no to another pint of Spitfire.'

That seductive smile was still on her face as she took the glass from him, and with a calm, unhurried demeanour she disappeared inside. He turned to look in the direction of the young couple further up the garden to see if they had witnessed his brief conversation with Diana (and his nervousness), but they were thankfully still engrossed with each other. He kept telling himself to calm down, but he was still shaking when Diana reappeared with his drink; all the more so as he watched her boobs bouncing up and down as she made her way towards him. Then he recalled her telling him once that she rarely wore a bra!

'There you are, luv,' she said huskily. And as she bent down to place the brimming glass on the table, he could have sworn that he saw Marilyn Monroe winking at him from the tattoo on her breast! He attempted to produce some money for his drink, but placing her hand on his she brushed aside his offer. 'Don't be silly. This one's on the house.'

'Thank you,' he replied. 'That's very good of you.'

'I'm that kind of girl,' she said seductively once more; and then moving around to park her very delectable derrière on the other side of the table she lit another long brown paper cigarette, before leaning forward and blowing the smoke away to one side.

Although a smoker himself at one time, he had come to find the habit distasteful over the years, but with Diana it just seemed to add to her sex appeal. Barely able to take his eyes away from her very ample cleavage, he decided to enquire as to her partner's whereabouts.

'Oh, he's off on one of his golfing weekends with his mates. They've all gone to La Cala, near Malaga, and left me here all on my own,' she replied suggestively. And how Diana hated being alone.

God knows she had the capacity to make a man pursue her, thought Clarke, but whereas she had always seemed just out of reach beforehand, now it was as if she was there for the taking. And yet although he was clearly smitten with the woman, something made him pull back.

Diana was immediately able to sense a lack of confidence in the man and probably vulnerability too; and yet he had an innocent quality about him that made him irresistible. Aside from her seductive qualities, she was also motivated by the desire to get to the truth in all things, and she could see that all was not well with the man who sat opposite, so she suddenly changed tack and tried to get him to talk about what was troubling him.

'So, what's eating you then, sweetheart?' she asked earnestly.

'Is it that obvious?' he replied.

'I wasn't born yesterday, luv.'

'If you really want to know I fear for my job.'

Diana was aware that Clarke was a policeman of some sorts, but his reply still surprised her. 'What on earth makes you think that?'

He proceeded to tell her about the appointment of Detective Sergeant Fletcher, but she still failed to see how that could result in him losing his job.

'She's a lot younger than me for one thing,' he said purposefully. 'And they're probably lining her up as my replacement.' He then looked her straight in the eye and added with more seriousness. 'But there's also the possibility that she's a plant.'

'Don't talk daft,' she scoffed. 'Surely you're over-reacting?'

He then told her how he was suspended from duty earlier in his career and that in spite of the fact that he was exonerated he had always believed that his superiors never really believed him.

'Don't you see? Fletcher could have been given the job in order to look into my past and the possibility that I was always guilty after all!' he said with some alarm.

Diana began to appreciate his anxiety. 'Wow!' she exclaimed. 'I see where you're coming from.' She then placed her hand on his once more, and as he looked down at her long, beautifully-manicured burgundy-coloured fingernails she was about to say something more when her mobile suddenly went off and it was as if the spell had been broken. 'Damn!' she muttered. 'It's my partner, Graham.'

'I'd better go,' said Clarke regretfully.

'Why don't you come along tonight?' she pleaded. 'There's live music.'

And probably not the sort of music that he liked, so he declined and making an unconvincing excuse he bade her farewell. He walked away from the table despondently and Diana reluctantly answered her phone. As he crossed the car park he could hear her swearing and shouting down the phone at her partner. Some guys have all the luck, he thought to himself.

Chapter 22

Saturday, 8 July, 2017

For the cricket-loving Ken Watson, spring and summer were always his favourite times of the year. If he wasn't watching the test matches on Sky Sports or trotting off to watch Derbyshire at the County Ground, then you could guarantee that every other Saturday – weather permitting – he would be cheering on the first eleven at the Brockley Cricket Club; not that they really had a second eleven. And since there was barely a cloud in the sky on this particular Saturday, all boded well for a veritable feast of cricket against old rivals, Coote's Abbey.

At 10 a.m. precisely, he set off at a brisk pace along Gold Crescent with his beloved "Wilf". Resplendent in navy-blue blazer (RAF badge of course), tie (RAF Police logo of course) and cream Panama hat with slacks, there could be only one place where Ken was heading at that time of the day, and everyone knew it. With a smile on his face he issued a 'good morning' here and a 'lovely day' there to disinterested neighbours, before making his way down the dirt track that led to the ground. He took along with him an apple, a few sandwiches and a flask of tea, and of course his folding camping chair. Seated alongside the pavilion with Steadman's Woods as a backdrop as always, he was as happy as a pig in the proverbial!

Another of Brockley's residents also rejoiced on this fine Saturday morning in July, if not more so. Christopher Ibbotson was not only captain of the Brockley Cricket Club, he was the opening bat, and he was looking forward to giving Coote's Abbey a good hammering! What's more, they had found someone to replace the late Keith Jackson as groundsman. Another cricket-loving local had offered his services, and he had ensured that the pitch was in perfect condition.

Having won the toss, Ibbotson chose to bat first and just before 10.30 a.m. he came out of the pavilion and headed for the square with his colleague, swinging his arms and performing a number of other exercises before shouting to the umpire 'middle and leg, please.' Off the mark with a couple of runs first ball, he added another run before the end of the over. Feeling more and more at ease, he attempted to play a defensive shot with the first ball of the second over, but he missed the ball completely and it hit him on the pads. 'Please God no,' he said to himself as he looked up towards the umpire with dread, and as the latter raised the finger of his right hand he felt that familiar sickening feeling in the pit of his stomach as he realised that he had been given out leg before; and it was only the second over!

'Shit, shit, shit,' exclaimed Ibbotson as he made his way back to the pavilion, passing Simon Collins on the way. Chortling to himself, Ken Watson clearly took pleasure in Ibbotson's dismissal, even though he was without doubt Brockley's most ardent supporter.

Collins was not really up for this game. For starters he had not returned home after the row with his wife the day before. After his game of golf he had headed to *The Wheatsheaf* where – despite some initial reservations by Sally Dawkins – he managed to persuade the couple to put him up for a few nights; he would see them right – and he did! Tony even offered to lend him some of his old clobber, even though he was a size or two bigger than Collins. And then of course he had left his cricket gear at home too. Thankfully he was able to find a spare kit in the pavilion, but this was a size smaller and he felt a proper Charlie when he walked out to the crease in the tightest of trousers. He needn't have worried. He was only there for a few minutes when his stumps were sent flying by an unplayable yorker from the Coote's Abbey fast bowler. Two down and Brockley weren't even in double figures. Ken Watson wasn't chortling now!

Another two wickets went down within the half hour before up to the crease stepped the tall, slim and flame-haired figure of fifty-one-year-old Rupert Frankland-Moore of nearby Brockley Hall. Appearances were deceptive, however, because in spite of his somewhat lithe frame, Rupert was regarded as an indomitable foe on the cricket pitch, and so it proved on this occasion. Brimming with self-confidence, he put on a performance that mirrored Ian Botham's 149 not out in the second innings of the 3rd Test against Australia at Headingley in 1981, hammering the Coote's Abbey bowling to all corners of the ground – and beyond. Indeed, two balls were lost amid the flora and fauna of the surrounding woodland!

Ken Watson sat watching the performance with ever-increasing rapture. Even he was hard-pressed to recall a better innings during all the time that he had been coming to the ground, although he was forced to miss Rupert making his half-century as he had to go to the toilets to make a call of nature.

That was when he heard them – Ibbotson and Sheldon; embroiled in an angry confrontation at the rear of the pavilion. The window was open, but try as he might he just couldn't make out what they were arguing about. He returned to his chair just as Sheldon appeared from behind the pavilion with a face like thunder. Probably a good thing, thought Ken. Might be just the incentive he needs to demolish the opposition with his bowling.

Nevertheless, Ken was there to see Rupert make his century, and thirty minutes later the home side declared at 167 for 7, with Rupert finishing at 114 not out.

After a brief interval for lunch, the two sides returned to the pitch, but the Coote's Abbey performance was something of an anticlimax as they were all out for 79, thanks chiefly to the fast bowling of John Sheldon who, it has to be said, came in from the pavilion end like a demented demon! The wicket-keeping of Frankland-Moore was first rate too, but then it had to be since Christopher Ibbotson dropped two relatively easy catches whilst fielding at second slip; much to the chagrin of Ken Watson, who went home after the game in the firm belief that the latter should be replaced as team captain!

Anna Frankland-Moore hated Saturday's. Life at Brockley Hall wasn't exactly a bed of roses at the best of times, but Saturday's were especially irksome at this time of year, and for one reason – the bloody cricket!

It wasn't so much the game itself; she had seen England play at Trent Bridge and at Lords, and she enjoyed it. No, it was the manner in which her husband reacted to victory or defeat having played for the village cricket team on any given Saturday. If Brockley won, then the phone would ring and she would have to collect Rupert from *The Wheatsheaf*, and that would invariably mean that he was inebriate. If the team lost, however, then he would come home in a foul temper and *then* proceed to get drunk. And Rupert did *not* like losing – no matter what the circumstances.

It was like that when they first met at the Nottingham Theatre Royal in 1989, following a production of *Richard III*, starring Derek Jacobi. Anna was quite a catch back then – and Rupert was determined to pursue her. The daughter of a West Bridgford bank manager, she was then in her final year at the University of Nottingham, where she was studying for a BSc in Finance, Accounting and Management. With her long brown hair and dark piercing eyes, she was only a couple of inches smaller (and four years younger) than the handsome, ginger-haired young trainee lawyer and heir to both Brockley Hall and the

Frankland-Moore law firm, but she was undoubtedly flattered by his attentions.

Having gained a first-class degree later that year, she made it known that she valued her independence, but Rupert was persistent and it was only a week or so later that the couple announced their engagement. At a party at Brockley Hall to celebrate the event, there was an 'incident' and it took all the skill and dexterity of Anna's future mother-in-law, Monica Frankland-Moore, to pass it off as a 'misunderstanding.'

The couple married in 1993 and within a matter of weeks they were starting a new life together in Brussels, where they had both found employment with the European Union; he as a lawyer and she as an accountant. They made their home in the affluent area of Le Vivier d'Oie in Uccle, although Rupert was frequently called upon to travel the length and breadth of the continent as part of his job.

Three years later and Anna suffered a miscarriage. Needless to say, it was a traumatic time for her, but Rupert was in Rome on business and to her astonishment and dismay he refused to return and be by her side. She had suspected for some time that he might have been having an affair, but this only served to add to her fears. When he eventually did return she decided to confront him, but he simply brushed aside her concerns and accused her of being delusional or suffering from post traumatic stress disorder.

They spent a long weekend back in England shortly afterwards, and Monica made it abundantly clear that she took her son's side; but then he could never do wrong in her eyes. More to the point, Monica also wanted an heir for Brockley Hall, so it came as a huge shock to Anna when her mother-in-law blamed *her* for the miscarriage.

What was she to do? She felt alone and isolated for the first time in her life; as though everyone was against her. She had few friends – here in the UK or in Brussels; but she had always been committed to any undertaking and considered marriage to be sacrosanct. It was 'an act of union in the eyes of God, irreversible and permanent.' she was sometimes heard to say. It was for that reason that she decided to soldier on and work even harder at *her* marriage, come what may.

However, Rupert's infidelities continued and slowly but surely the couple grew apart. It was then that Anna made a momentous decision, but it was to be one that she kept from *everyone*.

And then in 2014 Rupert's father died. Anna and Rupert returned to England, but whilst he succeeded his late father as head of the family law firm, both he and Anna were forced to share Brockley Hall with his mother; a prospect that Anna was most definitely not looking forward to – and with good reason. Although Anna 'tolerated' Monica to some extent, there was clearly mutual dislike between the two of them. Mercifully for Anna, she found an outlet for her talents and ideas, and so she decided to write a book about the history of the European Union. To the outside world it may have seemed that she was socially lacking (even she had come to regard herself as something of a "Plain Jane"), but she had always preferred the company of books rather than people, and so she was able to spend hours in the library at the Hall, researching for her project.

And so it was that on this particular late Saturday afternoon Anna sat in the library immersed in her books, waiting for the phone to ring or for Rupert to return from the match in a foul mood. Neither was a particularly pleasant prospect, but she had become accustomed to one or the other. She looked up and out through the window as Monica removed the spent blooms of roses in the garden. But then Monica was always a stickler for tidiness – inside and outside the Hall. The library wasn't vast by any means, but the Frankland-Moore's were able to boast a fine collection of books, many of which were understandably a testament to the family's long-standing connection to the legal profession.

The old grandfather clock in the corner of the room to her right had struck six thirty a couple of minutes beforehand when she heard the phone ring in the hallway outside. It could only mean *one* thing; the team had won and Rupert was drunk. With a sigh she rose from her chair and made her way slowly out of the library and into the hallway. Sighing again, she calmly picked up the phone.

'Brockley Hall – may I help you?'

It was Tony Dawkins and he was in a bit of a flap. 'Mrs. Frankland-Moore?'

'Hello Tony,' she replied. 'What is it this time? Has he fallen off one of the tables?'

'You'd better get down here quick, ma'am. Things are getting out of hand!'

'I'll be down there in five minutes, Tony.'

She put down the phone and made her way out to the garden at the rear, where Monica was still happily snipping away at the dead roses.

'It looks like they've won again,' she shouted. She never even gave Monica a chance to reply. Returning inside, she picked up the car keys from the small table in the hallway and then went out through the front door where her white Ford Fiesta awaited. Monica would know what she meant anyway – and what lay in store for the rest of the evening.

Following their victory over Coote's Abbey, most of the Brockley cricket team had made straight for *The Wheatsheaf*, where Sally Dawkins had put on a spread in anticipation. However, both she and Tony – in fact the whole bloody team – knew what this meant; Rupert would be getting shit-faced again – and they weren't wrong!

The trouble with Rupert was that he just didn't know when to stop! Others tried to keep up with him, but they soon fell by the wayside, as they did on this occasion. Even Simon Collins seemed to have had one Guinness too many, whereas Christopher Ibbotson was suffering a bout of maudlin self-pity with a glass or two of wine following yet another poor innings. As expected, John Sheldon just stood brooding over the pool table with a pint of Stellar, but everything changed when his partner, Angela Radford, walked in.

'Hiya,' she screeched to everyone before making her way to the bar, but to her surprise Tony Dawkins uncharacteristically darted into the kitchen on her arrival.

However, that was not for fear of retribution from her partner. No, he had foreseen that Angela's arrival would be the signal for Rupert to force himself upon her, and in his inebriate state he wouldn't be taking no for an answer. Then of course all hell would break loose. As he peeked through the kitchen door, Tony watched as Rupert staggered over to the bar with a double Jack Daniels and began to try is luck with Angela. Time Mrs. Frankland-Moore was here, thought Tony, and so he took out his mobile and called the Hall.

Meanwhile Angela was clearly getting somewhat agitated with Rupert's dogged attempts to chat her up.

'That's enough now, Rupert,' she snapped. 'You've clearly had way too much to drink.'

But Rupert persisted. 'Aw, come on, just a little peck,' he slurred as he placed his hand around her waist.

How she wished that they would hurry up with her drink. 'Go away,' she shouted. And then she suddenly froze as she felt his hand slowly but surely moving down to her rear.

That was the moment that John Sheldon saw red. Sending tables, chairs and drinks flying in all directions, he surged towards the bar and grabbed Rupert from behind. As Rupert turned, Sheldon head-butted him full in the face and he fell back onto the floor in a heap. Sheldon was about to pounce, but Angela tried to pull him away.

'No, John, please don't,' she screamed.

Sally Dawkins appeared on the scene and called for her husband. 'Tony, get your arse here now!' But coward that he was, there was no way that he was going to get involved at this stage.

So it was left to Simon Collins and Christopher Ibbotson to restrain Sheldon. Just as they were pulling him off the helpless figure on the floor, Anna Frankland-Moore walked through the door to be confronted by the sight of her husband with blood streaming from his nose.

'I take it that you won today?' she said looking down at him and with just a hint of sarcasm.

Rupert looked up. 'Oh, hello darling,' he said with a stupid grin on his bloodied face. 'Just having a bit of fun, don't you know!'

At that Simon Collins stepped in and offered to help Anna get Rupert into the waiting car, but before he could do so Ibbotson turned to Angela and persuaded her to leave together with Sheldon. As they headed for the door Sheldon turned and jabbed his finger in the direction of Rupert.

'He so much as touches my woman again and I'll fuckin' kill him!' he bellowed.

Sally Dawkins watched the pair storm off. 'Just like you killed Keith Jackson,' she said to herself.

Chapter 23

Saturday, 8 July, 2017 (p.m.)

At 3.20 p.m. that Saturday afternoon, Fletcher arrived back at her apartment in the Basford area of Nottingham having completed her shopping. Not one of life's most enthusiastic shoppers, she was more of an outdoor girl and would have much rather preferred to have been hiking in the Peak District than fighting her way through the packed throngs in Nottingham city centre. These things had to be done, however, so it was something of a relief when she finally closed the door behind her and headed towards the kitchen to unpack.

She was extremely happy with her apartment, which was actually a former Victorian mill building. Combining most of the original features, including the traditional high ceiling and the original staircase, the building was blessed with a large, spacious lounge, bedecked for the most part with Art Deco furniture (which almost certainly would *not* have appealed to the Chief Inspector), ornaments and paintings. The kitchen area was equally expansive, although she would be the first to admit that she wasn't the world's greatest (or enthusiastic) cook. The two bedrooms were more than adequate, as was the bathroom and the walk-in shower, which for some reason she rarely used. And of course all of this came with central heating and double glazing. To cap it all there was allocated car parking and communal areas in the courtyard outside. Yes, everything was very much to her liking.

As she began to unpack her shopping, she was joined by her domestic shorthair tabby cat, "Benji", who immediately began to weave his way between her legs, purring rather loudly and demanding attention – and food. Unable to ignore the demands, she briefly broke off from unpacking to open a tin of cat food. Placing the bowl beside the refrigerator, she watched as her beloved "Benji" tucked into the meaty morsels.

Ten minutes later she poured herself a glass of Tesco's finest Argentinian Malbec red wine and then slumped onto the sofa feeling utterly shattered. She began to doze, but her all-too-brief reverie was brought to an end by "Benji" who – replete from his meal – had decided that now was the time to curl up on his owners lap.

What was she going to do with herself for the rest of the day? She thought about the murder of Keith Jackson and the events of the previous week, but then she decided that now was not the time to get wound up about that misogynistic bugger that made her hackles rise back at Leverton. No, don't even go there Jacqui, she told herself. She felt hungry, but she just couldn't be bothered to get up and fix herself even a light repast. She picked up the remote and turned on the TV, but after flicking through all of the channels she decided that there was nothing worth watching.

However, she'd begun to watch the Royal Shakespeare Company's 1978 production of *Macbeth* on DVD a few nights previously, and finally opted to continue watching that for the time being. Starring Ian McKellen and Judi Dench, the character of Lady Macbeth was arguably Shakespeare's strongest female lead, and a role many actresses aspired to play. Moreover, it was a character that Jacqui felt that she could identify with, and served as something of an inspiration for her. She had left the disk in the DVD player, so all she had to do was pick up the remote once more and press "resume". So with "Benji" snoozing contentedly on her lap, she sat absolutely enthralled by the performance of Dench in this marvellous production of the Scottish play.

She had only been watching for twenty minutes or so when she heard the doorbell ring. 'Damn,' she said to herself. 'Who the hell can that be?'

Pressing the pause button on her DVD, she shuffled off languidly towards the door expecting to be confronted by Jehovah's Witnesses or some irritating little man selling double-glazing when she opened it, so it came as something of a surprise when she looked through the peephole and saw the five feet six inch frame of her old friend, Isobel Jennings, standing outside. Swiftly removing the chain, she unlocked the door and flung it wide open.

'Izzy!' she exclaimed with unbridled delight. 'What are you doing here?'

'Lance is in Auckland for the Rugby,' replied her friend, 'and I was bored, so I thought a drive up the M1 to see my chum might help me out of my current malaise.'

'Who's Lance? Don't tell me you've got another boyfriend?'

'Oh he's just someone I picked up at the London Fashion Week back in February. Look, dahling, are you going to let me in or not?' pleaded Izzy in her highly fashionable and upmarket manner of speaking.

Stepping inside, the pair embraced; although Izzy was careful not to get *too* close to her friend in case her make-up was disturbed – especially her bright red lipstick! So with a 'mwah, mwah', she broke away and handed over her bags and accoutrements to Jacqui as if the latter was no more than a domestic servant girl, and then began to look around the apartment.

An inveterate snob, she was never slow to pass judgement on others and their tastes, and she looked down her long, thin nose as if to show her displeasure.

'Is this the best that Nottingham has to offer, dahling?' she said with a sneer.

Fletcher was used to comments like this from her friend. 'Well I like it and that's all that matters.'

Izzy tossed back her long, wavy, mousy-coloured hair. 'I don't suppose you've got any Chianti, dahling? I could kill for a glass of Chianti?'

Fletcher pointed to the bottle of Malbec on the kitchen worktop. 'Sorry to disappoint you. That's all I have I'm afraid.'

'I suppose it will have to do,' replied Izzy with a deep and disgruntled sigh.

Well, she certainly hadn't changed, thought Fletcher. 'Look, I'm famished. How about we go find ourselves a restaurant and you can bring me up to date on the London fashion scene?'

'What a *good* idea. They do have a decent Italian restaurant in Nottingham then?'

'*Piccolino's* over at Weekday Cross. I'll give them a call and see if they've got a table free.'

They were in luck. There was a table free at seven o'clock, so Fletcher suggested that Izzy should make herself at home whilst she had a shower and got herself ready. She would book a taxi later for six thirty.

Izzy waved off her friend with the back of her hand. 'Go, go, go – I'll be fine, dahling.'

With yet another deep sigh, she began to rifle through several magazines which lay strewn upon the small rectangular glass coffee table in front of the sofa. Every so often there was an audible "tut tut", as if she was disgusted by the contents of the magazines. But that was Izzy.

Born to a wealthy company director in the Wembley area of London in 1981, she was six years old when the family moved to Nottingham (she had an older brother). She attended Nottingham High School, where she met up with Jacqui Fletcher; although even then she had a tendency to look down on her great friend. Displaying a talent for creativity and imagination, she attended Cambridge University after leaving school, but here too she alienated her friends with what they perceived as her superficial high-mindedness.

After leaving Cambridge she moved to London, where she began working for a fashion designer. However, her desire to create things of enduring value led her to become something of a perfectionist, in the sense that her pursuit of the 'ideal' had a tendency to make her somewhat insatiable and inconsolable when the results of her work met with disapproval. This and her fear of failing to keep up with the latest trends and fashions induced her to become editor of her own fashion magazine, through which she has been able to demonstrate her other talents for influence and exuberance. Occasionally, however, she does display her love for the timeless and classic standards of fashion, and her friend has always insisted that had she lived through the sixties Carnaby Street would have been a virtual paradise for her.

As an individual she has always been self-reliant, and in many ways she has come to represent a woman's autonomy and ability to pursue a life of her choosing. In many respects her primary concern has always been for her independence, along with the fulfilment of personal goals, and these are the aspects of her character that predominate. For that reason she comes across as being aloof, emotionally unavailable and to some extent even cruel – as many of her boyfriends have discovered to their cost. Needless to say, they always play second fiddle, and she disposes of them readily and at will.

Driven by her desire to be comfortable in her own skin, she set her sights on cultivating her individuality and a stylistic point of view that reflects her whole being. She is innately stylish and always impeccably attired, because every aspect of presentation has to be carefully considered, not just visually but socially as well.

Indeed, she had arrived at Fletcher's in a blue, low-cut Talitha Robe by Misa of Los Angeles; *very* elegant and *very* expensive. And as Fletcher reappeared after her shower in a cream-coloured tailored short-sleeve utility pencil dress, she couldn't help thinking that Izzy had known all along that they would be going to an Italian restaurant that evening, and had prepared herself accordingly beforehand. So it was with some trepidation that she asked her friend what she thought of *her* appearance.

'How do I look?' she enquired with a modicum of apprehension.

'Well I certainly wouldn't have chosen to wear *that* dress, dahling,' was her friend's characteristic reply.

No, I dare say that you wouldn't, thought Fletcher, who then rang for a taxi to take them to the restaurant.

Located in the Lace Market area of Nottingham, Weekday Cross was at one time the main market area in the city, before the market moved on to the Old Market Square. Serving only the best and freshest seasonal produce, *Piccolino's* proudly boasts an open kitchen, cocktail bar and fair weather alfresco terrace. To Jacqui's surprise and relief (not to mention undisguised delight), Izzy appeared to be mightily impressed by the surroundings, and made for the cocktail bar as if she were queen of all she surveyed. Ordering a Mojito, Izzy grabbed at the wine list and her eyes lit up on seeing the Chianti Classico Riserva from Tuscany.

'How absolutely divine,' she shrilled. 'We've simply got to have a bottle of that, dahling.'

Fletcher had opted for a Piña Colada and was somewhat aghast at her friend's expensive tastes. 'Hang on a mo, Izzy,' she whispered. 'Let's not get carried away.'

'Nonsense!' replied her friend. 'Besides, I'm paying – the evening is on me!'

'I can't let you do that, Izzy.'

Her friend seemed taken aback. 'I've come all this way to see you and here you are rejecting my good intentions?'

Realising that there was little point in arguing the matter when Izzy was in this mood, Fletcher shrugged and the pair went on to peruse the menu.

Having placed their order, Fletcher couldn't help notice that there was a book sticking out of her friend's handbag.

'I see that you've brought Mary with you as always,' she inferred, nodding to the object in question.

'But of course,' replied Izzy. 'You should know by now that I never leave home without her.'

For her sixteenth birthday, Izzy had received a copy of Mary Quant's autobiography, *Quant by Quant* (first published in 1966), and she habitually takes it everywhere with her; even having the good fortune to get the lady in question to autograph *her* copy on one occasion.

Cocktails duly quaffed, the pair were then directed to their table outside; after all, it was a glorious summer's evening. Starting with a first course, Fletcher had settled on a salad, which contained gem lettuce, chicken, crispy pancetta and parmesan cheese. Izzy had plumped for a bruschetta, consisting of broad beans, goat's cheese and toasted ciabatta. In between bites they reminisced about their time together at Nottingham High School, and invariably they were reduced to fits of giggles as they recounted some of the antics that they got up to.

For the second course Fletcher had opted for baked sea bass with potatoes, black olives and capers, whereas Izzy had decided on marinated and char-grilled chicken escalope with peperonata. It was whilst they were awaiting delivery of their respective dishes that Izzy demanded to know about the progress of Jacqui's career.

'Don't ask!' snarled Fletcher.

'We seem to have touched a nerve,' replied Izzy as she poured herself and her friend another glass of Chianti. 'What *has* happened to bring about this current state of affairs?'

And so Fletcher proceeded to recount the events of the previous week; about how she had been assigned to Leverton CID and appointed to the post of Deputy Senior Investigating Officer on a case involving the murder of a former Army veteran fallen on hard times. All well and good so far, but she then revealed her frustrations with the man in charge of the case and how she believed that he had sidelined her, giving her mundane tasks which she saw as being obstacles to her achieving her goals.

'Sounds like a *ghastly* man, dahling,' snorted Izzy as she emphasised the adjective by inserting an "r" into the word when there wasn't one!

'Oh he is,' replied Fletcher, 'and he's a drinker!'

Izzy glanced guiltily at the almost empty bottle of Chianti, most of which she had imbibed, and refraining from ordering another bottle at that particular moment she decided to turn the conversation to the subject of the murder enquiry.

'A murder, don't you know;' she said excitedly. 'How positively super! Are you anywhere near getting your man – or woman?'

'There are a couple of suspects, but they both seem to have alibis. In fact there's very little to go on at the moment.' There was a long pause before she continued. 'Apart from this badge I suppose.'

'Badge?' repeated her friend. 'What sort of badge?'

'All I can say is that it's a badge depicting the cartoon characters *Tom and Jerry*,' said Fletcher forlornly before going on to describe the badge in more detail. 'And as yet nobody seems to know its significance.'

'Well I can give you the answer to that right now,' said Izzy somewhat smugly as the waiter arrived with the second courses.

Fletcher looked at Izzy in stunned amazement, but she waited until the waiter had disappeared before responding to her friend's outburst. 'What are you trying to tell me? Do you know something that I and the rest of Leverton CID don't?'

'Oh yes,' replied Izzy. "When I was at Cambridge there was a sort of boys club – if you could call it a club. Members of this club would regularly get drunk, take drugs and cause all sorts of mayhem and destruction wherever they went.'

'And the name of this club?' asked Fletcher with some frustration.

'Didn't I say?' replied Izzy. 'They called themselves the *Tom and Jerry Club* and members wore a badge like the one you described.'

Fletcher flopped back into her chair. 'Well bugger me!' she said to herself.

Izzy went on. 'Apparently the term *Tom and Jerry* became a euphemism for rakish or riotous behaviour in the early nineteenth century, and that's where they got their name from – or something like that.'

Sometimes one needs a bit of luck in my profession, thought Fletcher. Wait till they hear about this back at the Incident Room! She leaned forward and stared her friend in the face.

'Well, are you going to order another bottle of Chianti or not!'

Chapter 24

Saturday, 8 July, 2017 (p.m.)

Clarke's journey back from *The Navigation* was largely uneventful, but that was probably due to the fact that his mind was a complete whirl.

He looked back on his conversation with Diana with mixed emotions. Of course he was surprised and pleased (elated would probably be nearer to the truth) that she had taken the time to sit with him and engage in conversation with him in the first place, and yet he was so disappointed that it all came to an end so quickly and so abruptly. She had seemed so attainable, but she had a partner and that was the stumbling block. That's what caused him to hesitate and refrain from making any advances towards her; and then there was that bloody phone call!

Or was it his lack of confidence? Yes, that was it. 'Admit it man, you blew it,' he told himself. 'You always bloody do!' And he was convinced that she had picked up on that.

As he stepped onto the narrow boat and unlocked the door, he began to regret the fact that he had turned down her invitation to return to the pub later that evening. It was playing on his mind as he checked on the Jalfrezi in the slow cooker. Deciding that the meal was almost ready, he turned his attention to the rice and the naan bread.

Twenty minutes later he was sitting outside in the glorious sunshine enjoying his meal, together with a glass of Laphroaig. And yet he was *still* undecided as to what to do with the rest of his day. Oh, for crying out loud man, make your bloody mind up!

And with that he finally cracked. He would make his way to *The Navigation* about half past eight, but in the meantime he would wash the pots and then as a reminder of when he had actually seen Pink Floyd live at Earls Court in October 1994 (during their *Division Bell* Tour), he would watch his *Pulse* DVD of that actual concert.

And that's what he did. Only he dropped off halfway through *Us and Them*, and didn't wake up until twenty minutes to nine!

It wasn't like him to panic, but he was in and out of the shower faster than Usain Bolt at the 2016 Olympics! Donning a pair of jeans, a light blue open-necked shirt (sleeves rolled up) and a pair of navy blue canvas slip on shoes, he was ready to set off down the towpath once more by nine o'clock.

He could hear the noise coming from *The Navigation* as he approached the pub, and he correctly surmised that the place would be packed. A four-piece, all-male band calling themselves The Fourmidables (vocalist, guitarist, bass guitar and drums) were belting out *Meet Me on the Corner* by Lindisfarne as he fought his way to the bar, and needless to say many of those present were joining in with the sing-along. To his disappointment there was no sign of Diana as he reached the bar, but he soon caught the eye of one of the barmaids and managed to order yet another pint of Spitfire.

Generous applause greeted the band as they ended one song and immediately moved on to another, with their rendition of *Born on the Bayou* by sixties rock band, Creedence Clearwater Revival. His feet were beginning to tap and in spite of Diana's absence he started to feel so much better for coming along. There was a time when he had seen some of the great bands of the seventies – Led Zeppelin, The Who, Genesis, Yes and of course Pink Floyd – and although he hadn't been to a gig for some years, he had never lost his love of music. He had taught himself to play guitar (left-handed) and he still had his old faithful acoustic guitar back at the narrow boat. Indeed, he was just thinking how he would have liked to have joined the band on stage when there was a tap on his shoulder. He turned around and there was the smiling face – and mighty cleavage – of Diana. Dressed in a white, low-cut short-sleeved blouse, jeans and high heels, she was forced to shout above the music.

'You had a change of heart then?'

'Glad I did,' he shouted back.

The smile on her face suggested that she was glad too. She had been outside collecting glasses when he first arrived and she noticed that his glass was almost empty now.

'Care for another?' she shouted once more.

'Thought you'd never ask,' was his equally loud reply.

She brought his drink over and he didn't see her again until the band had finished just before eleven thirty. It had been en enjoyable evening, with music to his taste too. As the band members were loading their van, he ordered another pint (his fourth) and went to sit outside at the front of the pub. Diana had seen him go out and a couple of minutes later she stepped outside too and lit one of her long brown paper cigarettes.

'Mind if I join you?' she asked in that earthy, seductive voice.

'You shouldn't need to ask,' he replied, as if the beer had given him new found confidence.

'We never did get to finish our conversation earlier, did we?'

Clarke shrugged. 'I don't suppose that we did.'

'Tell me, why were you suspended from duty?'

And so he explained to her about being set up by his boss and that it was she who had in fact been the guilty party all along. Somewhat sheepishly he then admitted that he had become mistrustful of women ever since. There was a genuinely sad look on Diana's face at this, but as customers started to leave the pub she bade them farewell with a joke here and there, intermingled with a 'Night luv – safe journey home.' But she suspected that there was more to come from Clarke and she was determined to press him further.

'So there's nobody in your life then?' she asked.

Clarke looked down at his pint and tried to make light of his response. 'Only me and a bottle or two of whisky here and there.'

The sad look was still on Diana's face. 'You drink a lot, don't you?' It was more of a statement than a question; and Patricia Jackson had put exactly the same question to him earlier in the week.

'Are you always so matter-of-fact?'

'I like to get to the truth at all times,' she explained, 'and I expect the same from others.'

'Maybe I do drink more than I should, but I never let it interfere with my work.'

'Would a nightcap help now?'

A rather weak smile appeared on his face as Diana rose from her seat and suggested that they head back inside the pub. Choosing a stool at the corner of the bar, he watched as Diana poured herself a glass of Courvoisier and then a double Glenfiddich. God, what a woman, he thought to himself – and what a body! The drink was certainly beginning to take effect. As she rejoined him, her massive cleavage almost breached the front of her blouse as she mounted the stool, but she never batted as much as an eyelid; which was more than could be said for Marilyn Monroe!

At this point the bar staff were about to take their leave, so she reassured them that she would lock up before retiring. As they made their way outside, they could be heard giggling and sniggering – no doubt they were making the odd suggestive comment about the couple remaining in the bar. Diana took no notice as she was still intent on getting to the truth behind Clarke's drinking habit, but then her experiences in life had brought her wisdom and a worldly-wise approach to just about everything.

'So tell me, Allan, why *do* you drink?' she asked abruptly. 'I suspect you've not had much luck with women. Am I right?'

He nodded as he took a large swallow from his glass of whisky. 'One or *two* women actually.' He went on to tell her about his failed marriage to Lesley and the affair with Carol Vaughan. 'To tell the truth, Diana, both left me feeling a tad scarred and embittered.'

Her reply was simple and honest. 'I've been there myself, babe, so I do know what it's like.'

'It's as if I'm on a downer all the time – depressed, flat and impotent.'

'Hitting the bottle is only gonna make things worse, babe.' And then she placed her hand on his once more.

He liked that – and the fact that she kept calling him 'babe'. Looking into her eyes, they both leaned forward slightly and simultaneously as their mouths came together in one blissfully delicious moment of mutual passion.

'Stay here tonight,' she pleaded as they broke apart. 'I hate being alone.'

'But what if your partner finds out?' It was if he was looking for an excuse to leave there and then.

Diana gave full vent to her frustration. 'Oh, for God's sake!' she shouted. 'Do you want to go to bed with me or don't you?'

With his right hand he gently stroked her face. 'You know I do – you've always known.'

She took his hand and climbed down from her stool. 'Then let's bloody well go!'

As she was leading him out of the bar she stopped and kissed him once more. 'Besides,' she whispered, 'he's probably having it off with some Spanish tart!'

Still holding his hand as they made their way upstairs, she put her arms around him as they entered the bedroom and then they kissed again. Breaking apart once more, he watched as she sensuously removed her blouse to expose her breasts – and Marilyn Monroe in her entirety! As he hurriedly removed his clothes, she pulled the sheets back and climbed into bed naked.

'What's this about you being flat and impotent,' she purred.

'Well, you certainly weren't lacking in confidence tonight, were you?' said a satiated Diana to Clarke as he rolled onto his back.

Still breathless after making love, he openly confessed to her that it was undoubtedly the most fantastic sexual encounter he had ever experienced, but then he had expected it to be so. As she put her head on his shoulder, he responded by putting his arm around her and they lay there for several minutes before she spoke.

'Will you do something for me, babe' she implored.

At that particular moment in time it would be safe to say that he would have been prepared to move heaven and earth for the woman who lay beside him, but he merely made a curt response.

'What's that?' he said.

'Please don't be bitter or use the break-up of your marriage as an excuse for your present circumstances.'

It was a heartfelt plea and he knew it. 'You're right of course.'

'And don't let your personal feelings or opinions interfere with your work – just try and be more objective. That's all I ask.'

She had a way of putting things that made sense and again he couldn't argue with the woman. He kissed her gently on her forehead and felt happier than he had done for some considerable time. With that he fell into a deep sleep, and dreamt of Marilyn Monroe reassuringly telling him that all was going to be well from now on.

Chapter 25

Sunday, 9 July, 2017 (a.m.)

It was 8.20 a.m. on the morning after his night of passion with Diana Marshall that Clarke woke with a slightly thick head. Indeed, it took him a few seconds to realise that he wasn't even in his own bed. Turning over slowly, he was disappointed to discover that Diana was no longer lying beside him. He needn't have worried. A couple of minutes later she reappeared in her dressing gown and she was carrying a tray with two steaming hot mugs of tea. Oh dear!

'I hope you don't mind,' he said apologetically, 'but I don't drink tea.'

'That's no problem,' she replied with a winsome smile. 'I can get you a coffee if you like?'

To Clarke her voice was seemingly earthier first thing in the morning, and she looked just as glamorous as she had done when they had made love the night before. He guessed correctly that she'd already had one of her cigarettes, but he didn't mind in the slightest. However, he did have another apology to make.

'I don't drink coffee either, I'm afraid.'

She put the tray down on the bedside table. 'Well, what *do* you drink first thing in the bloody morning then?'

'I usually have a glass of fresh orange juice.'

Picking up her pillow, she playfully hit him over the head with it. 'You could have bloody well told me!'

Pulling her back into bed, there was still a sense of euphoria from the night before for the two of them, and seductively removing her dressing gown to expose her breasts once more, she readily thrust them towards his eager mouth as they made love yet again.

It was another exhilarating experience and he wondered where he'd got the energy from, but such was the effect that Diana had on him. They reluctantly broke apart once more and she placed her head on his shoulder again. Wrapping his arms around her, he pulled her closer.

'Where do we go from here?' he said after a few minutes.

'I don't know, babe,' she replied with some hesitancy.

One thing was for sure as far as Clarke was concerned; he didn't want this to be a one-off experience. Yes, the sex was absolutely fantastic, but he genuinely liked the woman and he felt that the feeling was mutual. However, there was of course the small problem of Diana's partner, who was due to return from Spain the following day. If they were going to get together at any time, would it always have to be in his absence?

For her part, Diana was undoubtedly attracted to the man who lay beside her; there was an innocence about him that appealed to her. But he was clearly troubled by the fact that she had a partner – and a partner who was partial to a bit on the side all too bloody frequently. She dreaded the thought of becoming a wallflower or being alone, and although she had made that clear to Clarke, was this going to be their only time together and would he be deterred from ever coming back to her? It was she who eventually broke the silence.

'Bar staff will be arriving soon,' she said as she almost absent-mindedly pulled at the hairs on his chest.

'And I've got to get some shopping done, amongst other things,' he replied with a heavy sigh.

He climbed out of bed and started to put on the clothes he had worn the night before, whilst she donned her dressing gown once more and lit one of her cigarettes. He followed her down the stairs to the outside door, which she opened before peering out to see if anyone was about. As she turned to face him, he ran his finger gently across her lips, and he could have sworn that a tear had started to well up in her eye as he bent down to kiss her.

'Go on,' she said persuasively. 'Get off now.' Then she watched as he made his way towards the hump backed bridge and the towpath. 'Remember what I said last night,' she shouted after him.

He then disappeared from sight, and as he did so the tears began to stream down Diana Marshall's face like a waterfall.

Back at the narrow boat, Clarke made a beeline for the shower. Whilst it was wonderful to feel the hot water pouring forth from the shower head and enveloping his whole body, he couldn't stop thinking about Diana. He had to admit that he still hadn't really come down from the sheer joy of making love to her – and twice in the space of a few hours too! But she had taken the time to listen to him, and her advice seemed so genuine and heartfelt that he warmed to her all the more. What's more, it was sound advice too – and he damn well knew it!

Once out of the shower he changed into t-shirt and shorts again, and then made out a list of the provisions he needed from the supermarket at Grimley. Painkillers were top of the list as he was desperately short of them and he still had a slight headache, but he had ensured that another bottle of Laphroaig wasn't too far behind.

It was almost noon, and in an effort to put the events of the last twelve hours or so behind him for the time being, he was determined to spend a few minutes putting his mind to the murder of Keith Jackson and what his further lines of enquiry would be.

Sitting on the open deck of his narrow boat sipping at a glass of fresh orange juice, he was again convinced that Jackson had been blackmailing someone, but whom? The two prime suspects had alibis – or did they? And what about the so-called witness? Call it a gut feeling, but something was not quite right there, he told himself again. There and then he decided to call on this witness himself. He would do this first thing in the morning – and before going into work too!

Happy with his decision, he went back inside the narrow boat to rinse out his glass before locking up and heading for the supermarket at Grimley. As he sped off in the silver Ford Focus, he felt happier than he had done in a long time.

At 12.30 p.m. Simon Collins sat alone at the bar in *The Wheatsheaf* and he was not at all happy. It was as if he had been thrown out of his own home by an alcoholic wife, and one who had taken out shares in Gordon's gin; such was her addiction to the bloody stuff! Because of this he was now sleeping in the spare bedroom at *The Wheatsheaf* – compliments of Tony and Sally Dawkins. On top of that the Old Bill were snooping around and asking questions. He seemed to have spent his entire life trying to keep them bleeders out of his hair, but he'd done nothing wrong; well, nothing worth shouting about. If Arthur Daley was a little dodgy but alright underneath, then so was he! But this was a different kettle of fish though. There were other things that troubled him, but one thing was for sure – he simply couldn't carry on like this. As he was trying to think of ways to resolve his problems, Christopher Ibbotson entered the bar.

'Cheer up,' he said to Collins as he patted him on the back. 'It might never happen!'

'Don't even go there,' replied a very disgruntled looking Collins, who had barely touched his pint of Guinness.

'Still *persona non grata* back at the old Hacienda, I take it?'

'I don't know and I don't bleedin' care!'

This was certainly going to be a lively conversation, thought Ibbotson as he called Tony Dawkins over and ordered a glass of wine. As Dawkins returned with his drink, Ibbotson turned the conversation to the subject of the previous night's punch-up.

'I see you managed to clear the mess up after the little fracas last night?'

'It's always the bloody same when him up at the Hall comes in here,' replied Dawkins.

'Yes, he can't hold his drink, that's for sure.'

'A breed apart if you ask me.'

Suddenly Collins ears pricked up. 'What did you just say?'

The look on Dawkins face seemed to suggest that Collins had just threatened him. 'Nothing…just that Rupert and his like…well, they're a breed apart, aren't they? Sort of …different from us mere mortals. That's all I meant...I wasn't being personal.'

Collins reaction took everyone by surprise. He stepped off his stool, and leaning across the bar he took a terrified-looking Dawkins by his collar and kissed him on the forehead. 'Tony, you're a bleedin' genius!'

Understandably startled, Dawkins was at a loss to grasp what had brought about this sudden change in Collins mood. 'What have I done now?' he blubbered.

Taking a wad of notes out of his pocket, Collins threw them on the bar. 'There you go,' he shouted. 'Get everybody a drink on me – and that's *everybody*!'

To Clarke's disappointment there were quite a lot of people already at the supermarket at Grimley when he pulled up. He was never very comfortable with large crowds, but the one thing that he hated about going to the supermarket more than anything was the prospect of being surrounded by irresponsible parents and their screaming, out-of-control little brats. Fortunately for him he never spent too much time with his shopping; he knew what he wanted, he got it and then he was out pretty damn smartish. Simple! It was just the noise coming from the kids, who were either perched on top of their mother's trolleys or running loose up and down every bloody aisle! Today was no different.

He was heading towards the cereals when up ahead there was a young girl stamping her feet and screaming at her mother. 'I don't want Rice Krispies!'

'But I thought you liked Rice Krispies?' replied the mother patiently.

'I don't want Rice Krispies!' repeated the little girl hysterically.

'Well, what would you like, precious?'

'I don't want Rice Krispies!'

Jesus Christ, thought Clarke. If he had spoken to his elders like that or behaved in such a petulant manner, then he would have got a damn good hiding when he got home. He wanted to say something, but he merely shook his head and moved on. As he turned the corner to go down the next aisle, he almost bumped into a woman and her trolley.

'Ooops, I'm sorry luv,' he said apologetically and without looking up.

'That's alright, Allan,' replied the woman he had once known as Maria Bukowski.

He apologised again. 'Maria, I'm so sorry. Fancy bumping into you again.'

'I know, twice in one week.'

Again he felt slightly uncomfortable and unsure of what to say. 'I'm surprised I haven't seen you in here before?'

'I usually come here after work on a Friday, but I had to attend a meeting this week and it ran a little late.'

'I see,' he replied.

Their shopping trolleys suggested that they were both single, and it was Maria who picked up on that. 'You live alone I take it,' she said nodding towards his trolley.

'Is it that obvious?' he replied.

'Well you can tell that I live alone from the few items that I've purchased, so it's not too difficult to deduce that you do too.' It was then that she saw the bottle of Laphroaig partially hidden by a loaf of bread and a carton of orange juice. 'You like a drink?'

Now he was embarrassed. 'Occasionally,' he lied.

Maria guessed that he was being just a trifle economical with the truth, but she didn't press the matter. Instead she rather clumsily asked him for a date. 'Look, I was wondering if we could maybe get together sometime – maybe chat about old times?'

The question caught Clarke completely unawares and put him on the back foot. 'Well, I…erm…I…don't…'

She persisted. 'I know you're very busy right now, what with this murder, but I'm free on Thursday evening if you can find the time?'

Christ, he'd made love to Diana only a few hours previously, but what if that was just a one-off? What if Diana only wanted him just

157

that one time? Before he could even think about it he found himself reluctantly accepting Maria's request.

'Okay, that's fine by me', he replied with a shrug of his shoulders.

Maria was delighted. 'That's great,' she said with some relief. 'Do you know *The Horse and Jockey* over at Manningley?'

'Yes, although it's some time since I've been there.'

'Their food is wonderful. Shall we say 7.00 p.m. Thursday?'

'I think I can manage that, yes.'

'Good, I'll see you Thursday then. Bye for now.'

'Okay, bye.'

So they parted company, but almost immediately Clarke regretted his decision. He felt an enormous sense of guilt; as if he was betraying Diana's trust. But then he'd initially felt guilty about having it off with another man's partner. Besides, it wasn't as if he was going to do to Maria what he'd done to Diana! 'Bloody hell,' he heard himself say.

'Sorry, Sir, what was that?' said the girl at the checkout.

'Oh…erm…just talking to myself,' he replied with a look of embarrassment.

Given half the chance he would have opened the bottle of Laphroaig there and then, but that would have to wait until he got home. And so it was with a little more urgency that he sped away from the supermarket. As he did so he was completely unaware that his conversation with Maria *and* his purchase of the bottle of whisky was witnessed by a fellow shopper. At the end of the day, Clarke was not the only member of Leverton CID out shopping at Grimley on that Sunday afternoon.

Chapter 26

Monday, 10 July, 2017 (a.m.)

It has to be said that Clarke was as good as his word and he pulled up outside Ken Watson's bungalow on Gold Crescent at 8.00 a.m. Monday morning. It was going to be another scorcher, and he decided to leave the bomber jacket in the car.

Strangely enough, although he had regrets about accepting Maria Bukowski's invitation to join her on the forthcoming Thursday, he never touched a drop of whisky the previous afternoon or evening. Perhaps it was Diana Marshall's words of wisdom that came to mind, but the Laphroaig remained untouched. Consequently he had a good night's sleep, and when the alarm went off at 7.00 a.m. he woke with a very clear head. Furthermore, he put the events of the past two days behind him – albeit temporarily – and concentrated his efforts on finding out who killed Keith Jackson. Convinced that this witness was lying, he had set off for Brockley determined to get to the truth.

The old man was eating some toast and marmalade when the knock came at the door. With a puzzled look on his face he turned to his beloved "Wilf". 'Who could that be at this time of the day?'

Rising from his chair, he made his way out into the hallway and on opening the door he was confronted by what he considered to be a rather scruffy-looking middle-aged man in a shirt and tie, who was clearly in need of a shave.

'Mr. Watson?' asked Clarke politely. 'I'm Detective Chief Inspector Clarke of Leverton CID and I'm the Senior Investigating Officer looking into the murder of Keith Jackson.' He proffered his identity card. 'May I come in?'

The old man admitted the detective readily, but he was clearly anxious to make it known that he had fully co-operated with the police.

'I've already made a statement, Inspector.'

'So I understand,' replied Clarke. 'It's just that there are one or two questions that I'd like to ask pertaining to that statement, Mr. Watson.'

'Okay. Please take a seat, Inspector.'

'I'd prefer to stand if I may.'

The old man shrugged and then returned to his chair. 'Fire away, Inspector.'

So Clarke began with the vehicle that almost forced the old man off the road whilst he was walking down Blackthorn Lane.

'I think we can agree that it was a large black vehicle, Mr. Watson, but are you sure that the registration number of that vehicle began with an "M"?'

Sensing that he had been rumbled, the old man attempted to feign ignorance. 'Well it all happened so fast, Inspector.'

Clarke picked up on the old man's discomfort. 'You know what, Mr. Watson? I don't think that you caught the registration number of that vehicle at all, did you?'

The old man jumped up from his seat. 'Are you suggesting…'

'Yes, Mr. Watson. I'm suggesting that you were lying when you said that the registration number began with an "M". And I'm suggesting that you did so in order to frame someone.'

'Preposterous!' spluttered the old man.

'No, not preposterous at all, Mr. Watson!' Clarke now had the bit between his teeth and leaning forward he went on. 'Tell me, Sir. What is it that you've got against Mr. Christopher Brian Ibbotson of Thraplow Lane, Brockley?'

The question clearly caught the old man on the wrong foot, and he sat back down again looking utterly deflated. 'I can't stand the man, Inspector.'

'And yet you were prepared to see an innocent man taken into custody for something he didn't do?'

The old man nodded. 'I'm sorry. I'm so sorry.'

Clarke was clearly in no mood to take any prisoners. 'I have to warn you that under Section 5, Paragraph 2, of the Criminal Law Act 1967, it is an offence to waste police time, and you could face up to six months in prison and/or a fine.'

The old man buried his face in his hands. 'Oh God, what have I done?'

'Make no mistake, Mr. Watson. We *will* be in touch again!' With that Clarke turned to go, but as he did so the old man called him back.

'Inspector?' he sighed. 'The registration number of the vehicle almost certainly began with an "S", and it had what appeared to be animal stickers on the bumper.'

'And this is the truth?' said Clarke brusquely.

'Yes, Inspector. I can't be sure, but they looked like hedgehogs.'

Detective Sergeant Fletcher arrived at the Incident Room that morning just before 8.30 a.m. and she was in a buoyant mood. That was hardly surprising following the revelations that were made by her friend on Saturday evening. She had even persuaded Izzy to accompany her around Wollaton Park on the outskirts of Nottingham on Sunday morning, when it was obvious that the latter would have much rather spent several hours gliding around John Lewis or the House of Fraser! Now Izzy had returned to London and Fletcher was itching to impart her secret to the Chief Inspector.

Webster had preceded her by about five minutes. Attired in a light blue shirt and dark blue tie, he was making a cuppa in the kitchen when Fletcher walked in wearing a dark brown trouser suit.

'The boss not here yet?' she asked the young detective.

'Not yet, Sergeant,' he replied. As he watched her make her way to her desk, he couldn't help but notice that she seemed more upbeat than usual. 'Have a good weekend, Sergeant?'

'Yes, and I've discovered something that I think will be of great interest to Inspector Clarke.'

Webster turned away and muttered under his breath. 'Don't bank on it!'

Fifteen minutes later and the man himself strode into the room with something of a swagger following his meeting with Ken Watson, and having greeted everyone with a casual 'Good morning' he entered his office and closed the door behind him.

That was the key for Sergeant Fletcher to make her move, and she promptly rose from her seat and confidently headed for Clarke's office. Hoping that he would at last start to take her seriously, she knocked lightly on his door.

Seated at his desk, Clarke was clearly making notes at the time. 'Come in,' he said without looking up.

Fletcher entered and in a state of some excitement attempted to impress Clarke with news of her discovery.

'Sir, I think that I've made a breakthrough in the case.'

Clarke continued to scribble away. 'Good, get it typed out and have it on my desk by ten o'clock.'

'But Sir, I think that you should hear this.'

Clarke now looked up and in a calm and assured voice began to rebuke her. 'And I think that you should do what I told you to do, and that was to co-ordinate the efforts of the whole team from here.'

Pausing for a few seconds, he then resumed his put-down of Fletcher. 'Or is that beneath you, Sergeant?'

Fletcher leaned forward and placing her hands on Clarke's desk she finally snapped. 'What is it with you? What have you got against me,' she shouted. 'Not content with giving me menial tasks, you never even speak to me, for crying out loud!'

Clarke was clearly taken aback, but he had been expecting just such an outburst. 'Who the hell do you think you're speaking to, Sergeant?'

By now everyone outside Clarke's office could hear the row and Webster buried his head behind his PC as Fletcher continued.

'I'm not responsible for the breakdown of your marriage, so don't take it out on me because your personal life is a mess!'

At that Clarke stood up and exploded with rage. 'I won't take any bloody crap from a jumped-up, middle-class, university-educated wannabe, who thinks that she can run before she can bloody well walk!'

Unbeknown to everyone at the Incident Room, it transpired that Superintendent Annable had chosen to pay an unexpected visit, and upon hearing the unholy row coming from Clarke's office he burst in.

'What in God's name is going on here,' he bellowed.

Clarke suddenly realised that he was facing a dilemma. He didn't want to work with Fletcher and he wanted her off the case, but if he said as much and issued an ultimatum then his worst fears could materialise, and Annable would force him into early retirement. What's more, it also dawned on him that he had forgotten his promise to Diana and allowed his personal feelings to come to the fore. He was just about to open his mouth when Fletcher beat him to it.

'Sir, I tried to tell Inspector Clarke that…'

Annable wasn't having any of it. 'I will *not* have my officers at each others throats! Is that understood?'

To Clarke's surprise – *and* it has to be said grudging admiration – Fletcher bravely continued.

'If you'll both bloody well listen!' If Clarke was surprised by her outburst, then Annable's jaw appeared to drop below his waistline, but still Fletcher ploughed on. 'I have some information – *about the badge*!'

Annable was about to reprimand Fletcher, but Clarke's antennae were well and truly alert at the mention of the badge and he caught the Superintendent's arm.

'You have our attention, Sergeant,' he said with some conviction.

And so Fletcher went on to reveal what her friend had told her about the *Tom and Jerry Club* at Cambridge, and it was as if Clarke was a different man. Annable, on the other hand, was still as impatient as ever.

'This is all very well,' he said a trifle condescendingly, 'but do we have any suspects in this case?'

Clarke mentioned his interview with Tony Dawkins, and then he also appeared to rule out Christopher Ibbotson for the time being. 'But we do need to talk to Simon Collins,' he suggested, 'although I don't think he went...'

Annable cut him short. 'Right! Bring the man in for questioning,' he barked.

Clarke attempted to continue. 'But Sir, I am fairly sure...'

Annable clearly had no intention of discussing the matter further. 'At the end of the day, the sooner we get our man the better.'

Clarke's head was bowed as Annable made this final statement, but when the Superintendent strode imperiously out of the office he cast a sideways glance at Fletcher, who turned to look at him, frowned and then shook her head.

'But it's not him,' she muttered.

Saying nothing, a wry grin then appeared on Clarke's face.

Shortly after the departure of Superintendent Annable, Fletcher and Clarke remained seated in the latter's office. The silence was broken by Fletcher.

'What do we do now?' she said staring into space.

'You heard the man,' replied Clarke rising from his chair. 'Get off to chez Collins and bring him in!' As Fletcher made her way out of his office and down the corridor, Clarke shouted after her. 'And you can do the questioning, Detective Sergeant.'

A rather self-satisfied grin appeared on Fletcher's face on hearing this, but Clarke wasn't sure that he'd made the right decision. Of course there was an outside chance that she would make a balls of it. That brought a smile to *his* face! He poked his head out of the office door.

'Webster,' he bawled. 'Get your arse in here – now!'

Webster had a good idea what was coming, but he foolishly tried to make light of it with one of his flippant remarks. 'Do you require my services, Sir?'

'Shut the door behind you and sit down, Webster,' said Clarke calmly. Webster duly did as instructed, but almost as soon as he had parked his backside on the chair, Clarke leaned forward and with his face barely inches away from the young detective he snarled at him. 'If I discover that you've been telling others about my private life again, Detective Constable, I'll make you wish that you'd never been born!'

About the same time as Clarke was giving Webster a bollocking, Simon Collins set off from *The Wheatsheaf* in his Nissan sports car and headed for his home at Armisfield. He was in a buoyant mood too, although everything depended on how his wife would greet him and what her reaction was going to be to his latest whim.

An innate optimist, relying on hunches and his intuition, this wasn't the first time that he'd decided to throw caution to the wind, but on this occasion he owed it all to that one conversation with Tony Dawson the day before. His mind was made up. Once everyone had put this bleedin' saga regarding Keith Jackson behind them, he was going to risk everything in pursuit of a *new* vision!

This was on his mind as he pulled off Church Lane, Armisfield, and turned into the driveway of the *Hacienda Jalisco*. To his astonishment, however, there were two police cars parked outside the main entrance to his home. Furthermore, it appeared that both uniformed and plain-clothes police officers were just about to leave, having been making enquiries as to his whereabouts from his wife.

'This is 'im now,' screamed a clearly intoxicated Dawn Collins as her husband climbed out of his car and headed towards everyone. 'What do you want 'im for – 'e ain't done nuffin wrong?'

Collins himself was not too pleased to find the Old Bill on his property for the second time in a matter of days. 'What's all this about then,' he growled.

Trying to make herself heard above the screeching Dawn Collins, Sergeant Fletcher introduced herself before telling Collins that he was being arrested and taken in for questioning regarding the murder of Keith Jackson. 'You do not have to say anything,' she began. 'But, it may harm your defence if you do not mention when questioned something which you later rely on in court. Anything you do say may be given in evidence.'

Collins made no attempt to protest or struggle, but as the police bundled him into one of the cars he merely shook his head. 'You've got the wrong geezer!'

'Leave 'im alone you barstards,' screamed his wife as the cars sped away.

Within fifteen minutes the convoy had arrived at Leverton Police Station. Whilst there, Collins was read his rights, searched and his possessions kept. Things just hadn't quite turned out as he had hoped – or expected. Told he was entitled to legal representation, he put a call through to a number in Grimley.

'Rupert?' he asked with some frustration. 'It's Simon Collins 'ere. I 'ope you've sobered up since the weekend. Looks like I'm gonna need your 'elp!'

Chapter 27

Monday, 10 July, 2017 (p.m.)

Clarke had made the journey to Leverton in time for the questioning of Simon Collins, and although he had delegated this to his subordinate, Sergeant Fletcher, he had made the decision on the proviso that he should be present. It might not have been one of his better decisions, but with any luck the woman would come unstuck and it would be left to him to rectify the situation. At least that was the general idea.

The task of conducting the interview had clearly given Fletcher renewed confidence; or should that be over-confidence, for she left Clarke in no doubt that *she* believed Collins was totally innocent of the crime of killing Keith Jackson. These were sentiments that Clarke undoubtedly shared, but they had to follow proper procedure and eliminate the man from their enquiries. Annable had given his orders, and like it or not Fletcher was going to have to follow them. All that remained now was the arrival of Collins legal representative.

For the most part Clarke had always had a deep antipathy towards the legal profession, but especially defence lawyers. And as he looked through the canteen window and watched as Rupert Frankland-Moore climbed out of his black open-top LaFerrari Aperta, he knew instinctively that he wasn't going to like the man. The fact that he had what appeared to be a plaster over his nose did nothing to dissuade Clarke that he could be wrong in his estimation.

Frankland-Moore strode into the building as if he were God Almighty and duly announced himself to the custody officer. He was then taken to see his client in the interview room and the pair were left alone to confer. Voices were raised during their time together, but whilst Collins sat at the desk shaking his head, Frankland-Moore paced up and down the room impatiently. Eventually the door opened and in walked Fletcher followed by Clarke. The reaction of Frankland-Moore was immediate.

'Here they come at last,' he said with a large degree of sarcasm, 'and led by a lady detective too. What's more, quite an attractive one if I may say so?'

Fletcher ignored the ingratiating smile that came with the last remark and proceeded to make the introductions. 'I am Detective Sergeant

Fletcher of Leverton CID,' she announced, 'and I will be conducting the interview. This is Detective Chief Inspector Clarke, who is here as an observer.'

Frankland-Moore barely offered a glance at Clarke, but instead kept his eyes firmly fixed on Fletcher. 'You must forgive my appearance – fell off the ladder whilst cutting the hedge, don't you know.'

Clarke couldn't resist a little aside to Fletcher as she took her seat at the desk and he made to stand by the door. 'Pompous prick,' he muttered under his breath.

With everyone ready to commence the interview, Fletcher switched on the tape recorder, gave the time and date, and then requested that all those present make themselves known for the benefit of the tape. As she did so, she was acutely conscious of the fact that Frankland-Moore seemed to be more interested in her than he was his client. This had not escaped Clarke's attention either.

And then there was the lawyer's aftershave. From the outset she found it almost unbearably overpowering, but there was something else about it too; something that reminded her of her childhood and filled her with nausea. Nevertheless, in spite of the fact that the man opposite made her feel distinctly uncomfortable she persevered, and went on to inform both Frankland-Moore and Collins why the latter had been brought in for questioning.

'Mr. Collins,' she began. 'You have been brought here on suspicion of the murder of Keith Jackson, at around 4.00 p.m. on the afternoon of Monday, 3 July. Would you care to comment on that?'

Collins was indeed prepared to comment. 'Load o' rubbish!' he replied.

Fletcher continued. 'Well can you provide us with your whereabouts around this time?'

'I was at my office in Grimley, and before that I was at my other office in Derby,' he said confidently.

'Can anyone corroborate this?'

'Yeah, ask any of my staff.' For some reason Collins then looked up at Clarke.

Fletcher persisted. 'What if we were to tell you that you were seen driving away from the scene of the crime at around 4.15 p.m. on the day of the murder?'

Collins leaned back in his chair and folded his arms. 'Bag o' bollocks,' he replied with a sneer.

'Well we have a witness who is prepared to come forward and testify that you almost forced them off the road on Blackthorn Lane at that precise time.'

Collins shook his head. 'Nah, it wasn't me.'

Fletcher looked at her notes. 'You do own a black 2016 Range Rover Autobiography SDV8, registration number SC13 TTT?'

Collins shrugged his shoulders. 'What if I do?'

'And that this vehicle has stickers on the bumper in the form of hedgehogs?' Nice one, thought Clarke as he leaned against the door.

At this point Frankland-Moore leaned across and whispered something to Collins, who then frowned and looked somewhat aggrieved. Turning back to Fletcher he conceded that he was at the scene at the said time.

'Okay, so I did go to visit Jackson. But there was no reply when I knocked on 'is door and so I left.'

'Do you expect us to believe that?' scoffed Fletcher.

Collins was clearly beginning to feel uncomfortable. 'Believe what you like – it's the truth.'

Fletcher pressed him further. 'But you've already been a trifle economical with the truth by denying that you were even there. So, what was your reason for going to see Jackson?'

Collins briefly looked at Frankland-Moore before answering. 'It was cricket club stuff. I went to make sure Jackson was gonna be sober enough to get the pitch ready, but like I said, 'e didn't answer when I knocked on the door and so I left.'

Clarke was watching Frankland-Moore at this moment and attempting to gauge his reactions.

Fletcher continued. 'So you knew he liked a drink then?'

This prompted Frankland-Moore to step in. 'Do you have any evidence whatsoever that my client committed the offence?' he snapped.

Fletcher brushed him aside and changed tack – much to Clarke's delight. 'Where you at any time at Cambridge University, Mr. Collins?'

Frankland-Moore began to show his frustration. 'Oh, this is getting ridiculous!'

But Collins had an answer for that one. 'No, darlin' – I went to the University of Life,' he replied defiantly.

It was at this point that Clarke decided to intercede. 'Tell me, Mr. Collins,' he said in a calm and composed manner. 'How long have you been having an affair with Patricia Jackson?'

The question took everyone by surprise, not least Fletcher, who had been kept very much in the dark on this matter by her superior. As they all looked up at Clarke, it was Frankland-Moore who broke the ice.

'I think now would be a good time for a break,' he said with some relief.

Fletcher switched off the recorder and followed Clarke out of the room. She wasn't happy with her boss.

'Why didn't you tell me about this?' she grimaced.

Clarke remained composed. 'In what I hope will be a long and illustrious career, Detective Sergeant, you'll find that there are times when it is necessary to keep *some* things up one's sleeve.'

He then went on to tell her about his meeting with Patricia Jackson and how he was sure that he had seen her before. And of course he had; when he left the *Railway Tavern* at Clavermill he had seen the pair together. Only he had no idea who they were at the time, or that they would both play a significant part in the case. Then Sally Dawkins had dropped a subtle hint when he called at *The Wheatsheaf* to interview her. And although her parents may have given her the money to buy the run-down buildings at Sapworth, how on earth could she afford to turn the riding school into even a 'moderately successful' (he chose Patricia Jackson's words) enterprise without further financial aid? No, Collins must have provided her with funding.

Fletcher was still slightly aggrieved at being kept in the dark, but for Clarke it was like scoring a try under the posts at Twickenham and knowing that it would be converted. As they both re-entered the interview room, Clarke could barely suppress yet another wry grin!

And so the interview with Simon Collins resumed. He admitted to the affair with Patricia Jackson, insisting that the couple first met when he, her husband and others were involved in a late night card game at the *Royal Standard* at Armisfield. The affair began some time later, and having encouraged her to go for the riding school, he then provided her with extra funding to expand and modernise the premises. Then one day in 2016 he was leaving the stables when Jackson drove by – he obviously saw the couple together. Shortly afterwards the blackmail began.

'If I didn't pay up, then Jackson threatened to tell my wife about the affair,' said Collins as he fiddled with his fingers and thumbs.

'And why would he want to do that,' asked Fletcher.

Collins sighed heavily. 'I told Patricia that if my wife found out about the two of us then she would take me to the cleaners. Jackson must 'ave overheard me tellin' 'er about this – could have been at the pub or at the cricket club for all I know.'

'How long had the blackmail been going on for?'

'Almost a year.'

'And how much did you pay him?'

'Enough to keep the geezer in booze – and able to 'ave a flutter every bleedin' week,' he grumbled. 'It was always cash in 'and. I'd go to 'is 'ouse on the same day every month. Only this time there was no van and no answer, so I pushed the envelope containing the money through the letterbox and left.'

Clarke interceded again. 'We never found any such envelope containing money.'

'Then whoever killed 'im must 'ave taken it,' replied Collins with a shrug.

'Or there never was any envelope containing money in the first place?' said Clarke leaning forward. 'Which means you could have killed Jackson?'

'Do me a bleedin' favour,' protested Collins. 'I shoved that envelope through the letterbox and pissed off smartish. End of story!'

Before anyone could continue Clarke suddenly concluded the interview. 'Okay, that will be all. Thank you, Mr. Collins.'

Collins looked at Clarke in stunned amazement. 'You mean I can go?'

'Yes, we shan't be holding you any longer.'

'Bleedin' waste of time,' said Collins as he attempted to brush past the detectives followed by Frankland-Moore.

'I shouldn't be too smug, Mr. Collins,' said Clarke somewhat laconically. 'We may need to speak to you again – and Mrs. Jackson.'

Both Clarke and Fletcher went over to one of the windows, where they watched as Collins and Frankland-Moore seemed to be engaged in a heated argument in the car park.

'I thought that you handled that reasonably well, Sergeant,' said Clarke still staring out of the window.

You wouldn't like to know what I think, thought his deputy as she too continued to watch the bickering couple in the car park.

Chapter 28

Monday, 10 July, 2017 (p.m.)

Dawn Collins was flat out on the sofa in the living room and dead to the world after yet another 'session' on the booze. She was genuinely upset that the police had taken her husband in for questioning and she had literally cried herself to sleep, but needless to say, two or three gin and tonics had contributed to her present comatose state.

However, shortly before five o'clock that afternoon she woke from her deep slumber with a start – and a splitting headache. Was that the front door? Rising gingerly from the sofa, she put her hand to her head and staggered over to the window, just in time to see a taxi disappearing down the drive. She then turned sharply on her heels and reeled to and fro as she saw her husband standing in the doorway to the living room.

'That you, babe?' she said with squinting eyes.

Simon Collins face showed no emotions as he made his reply. 'Yeah, it's me.'

'They let you go?'

'For the time being, but they may want to speak to me again.'

She then attempted to run over to him, but in doing so she knocked the coffee table over, sending her glass and other sundry items flying. Ignoring this minor mishap, she made her way over to him and flung her arms around him, pressing her head close to his chest. Unfortunately for her, he did not reciprocate in any way, but merely kept his arms dangling by his sides. Sensing that something was wrong, she slowly pulled away and backed off.

'Don't you love me no more, babe?' she slurred.

His reply was cold and to the point. 'It's over, Dawn. It was over the minute you started 'ittin' that bleedin stuff!' he said pointing to the empty bottle of gin beside the sofa.

'Please don't say that, babe,' she whimpered.

He was in no mood for arguing – or for reconciliation. 'I'm sellin' the business and movin' out,' he said emphatically. 'Don't worry, I'll see you right. Then you can do what you bloody like; sell the 'ouse, move back to London – whatever. But as of this moment we are finished. You got that?'

He then turned on his heels and headed up the stairs, ignoring the fact that his wife had sunk to her knees and was now breaking down uncontrollably.

In spite of his peccadilloes, she had remained loyal to him over the years and now it all counted for nothing. Perhaps she should have seen it coming, but for now she couldn't bring herself to launch into a fully-fledged attack on the woman who she believed was responsible for her pitiful situation. She was still on her knees when her husband came back down the stairs, dragging behind him a large suitcase crammed full of clothes. He also had a holdall, into which he now placed a laptop. He then made for a little side room off the living room where there was a safe. Removing all the documents from within, he rammed these into the holdall along with the laptop; he would sort them out later. And that was it – time to go!

He said nothing as he headed past his grief-stricken wife, but she found the strength to suddenly lunge at him in a fruitless attempt to grab at his legs and prevent him from leaving.

'Don't leave me now,' she screamed as her tears and what was left of her make-up combined to leave her face a discoloured mass! 'Please don't go – I love you, I love you, I love you.'

He merely brushed her aside and left her to slump once again onto the floor. He could be a hard bastard when he had to be. Slamming the door behind him, he ignored the sports car – he could always get another one. Instead he headed for the Range Rover. As he opened the garage doors, he glanced down at the bumper and the hedgehog stickers. He could have removed them there and then, but he decided against it. So he climbed into the vehicle, turned on the ignition and sped off down the drive to a new life. Anyone who had witnessed this spectacle would have sworn that they had seen the hedgehogs smiling away to their hearts content!

'Where are you?' asked the man with an uncharacteristically serious tone.

'I'm just doing a bit of shopping before going home and putting my feet up,' replied the woman curiously. 'Why do you ask?'

'You've finished work for the day and locked up then?' he continued.

'Yes, I have,' she confirmed. 'Is there a problem?'

'Look, can we meet up for a drink after you've done your shopping? Let's say the *Barley Mow* at Nedderton in thirty or forty minutes?

This did sound serious. 'Ye-es, I should be able to manage that,' she replied rather cagily. 'What's this all about?'

'We need to talk,' said the man. 'Just be there, okay?'

That was more of a demand, she thought to herself, but before she could reply the phone went dead. She was used to his somewhat capricious nature at the best of times, but this was obviously serious and when he was in that mood it was best to go along with him. She decided there and then to cut short her shopping expedition and meet him as arranged – albeit a trifle hurriedly. There was just one thing that she had to do before setting off to the *Barley Mow*.

About thirty minutes after this telephone conversation, Anna Frankland-Moore was completing her shopping at the Tesco supermarket at Grimley. She preferred to do the weekly shopping on a Monday afternoon as there weren't so many people about; not that she would have had much to say to anyone. She would have much rather been immersed in her books back at the Hall, but someone had to do the shopping and such a thing would have been beneath her mother-in-law. So she emerged through the automatic doors of the supermarket with a slightly morose demeanour and with her trolley barely laden with goods, and made for her white Ford Fiesta.

She approached the vehicle on the passenger side, unlocked it and opened the boot to place her bags carefully inside. Closing the boot and returning the empty trolley to the trolley bay, a look of horror appeared on her face as she came around to the driver's side of her car, for there was a horizontal scratch mark running along the length of the vehicle, including both doors. She closed her eyes and gritted her teeth with indignation. That mark *must* have been made within the last hour and whilst she was inside the supermarket! What's more, she had a pretty damn good idea who the villain was too!

Overcome with jealousy and rage, she contemplated reporting the incident to the manager of the supermarket, in the hope that the CCTV camera's would confirm the identity of the culprit, but just as she was about to head back into the building she stopped. No, she thought to herself. She would get her revenge when the time was right. After all, everything comes to she who waits!

Chapter 29

Monday, 10 July, 2017 (p.m.)

It was good to get back to the narrow boat, thought Clarke as he stepped wearily into the cabin before entering the galley and the saloon. He would have a good shower and then wind down with a glass of Laphroaig (maybe make that two glasses). Besides, the whisky helped him to concentrate, effectively clearing his mind of unnecessary and unwanted material (or so he always told himself); just as long as he didn't overdo it. However, there was little chance of that happening whilst he was on a case as important as this one. He wasn't feeling particularly hungry, which was unusual for him at this time of the day, so he made his way into the bathroom area where he gladly stripped off and stepped into the shower. What unparalleled bliss! Others may prefer a soak in the bath, but for Clarke this was a daily ritual that he welcomed wholeheartedly.

The day's events were trying to perforate his thoughts as he washed and then rinsed himself with the hot water, but he successfully dispelled them for the time being, and promised to give them his full attention once he was seated outside and armed with a glass of whisky. Neither Diana nor the forthcoming date with Maria came to mind either, but reluctantly stepping out of the shower he dried himself with a towel, and then changed into a white t-shirt and khaki-coloured shorts.

It was still a balmy summer's evening as he stepped out onto the deck. For a while he stood watching as a coot dived underwater to feed on weeds and algae, whilst a moorhen kept its distance and contented itself on the abundance of insects on the canal. How he loved the natural world. But he had a case to solve and someone had to be brought to justice, so he sat down at the table beside him, took a sip of his Laphroaig and began to focus his mind on what had passed earlier in the day.

He was becoming more and more certain that the badge was the key to solving the case, and he grudgingly admitted that Fletcher had made something of a breakthrough with her 'discovery' as to its probable significance. The owner of that badge had at one time attended Cambridge University and whilst there had become a member of this so-called *Tom and Jerry Club*. That ruled out Simon Collins; no question about that. But the interview with him *had* revealed that Jackson had been blackmailing him. What's more, he was at the scene of the crime at or around the time Jackson was murdered; not only did he admit it, but the witness eventually confirmed it.

'So what does that tell us?' Clarke said out loud before taking another sip from his glass of whisky. *There had to have been someone else already at the scene when Collins called and someone who remained unseen by the witness or others!* Therefore, was Jackson blackmailing others too? Furthermore, whoever killed Jackson *must* have been to the house before at some time, but for what reason?

He knocked back the last dregs of his glass of Laphroaig and went back inside the narrow boat to pour himself another one. Returning to his table on the deck a couple of minutes later, he suddenly hit upon an idea. Jackson had done gardening work for some of the locals and others; if it could be established who his clients were *and* if anyone of them had been to Cambridge University, then maybe they were onto something. It wouldn't be easy as Jackson was presumably paid cash in hand, but what if he kept a book with a list of his clients? Better still, what if this book *also* provided details of those he was blackmailing? Scenes of Crime Officers had failed to find any such book when searching through the house on Blackthorn Lane – *but that didn't mean that there wasn't such a book!*

Yes, he thought to himself, what's the betting that there *was* such a book and that Jackson kept the bugger hidden somewhere? It would be Fletcher's task to conduct a search of Jackson's house in the morning, he decided.

And what of Fletcher? Okay, he was willing to concede that there was very little evidence that the woman was a plant, as he'd originally surmised; and her questioning of Simon Collins was actually quite impressive. Furthermore, she was clearly unruffled by the unnecessary and unwanted attentions of his lawyer too. Nevertheless, he was still of the mind that she had ideas above her station – and especially above Leverton police station!

He felt that he'd played his cards right by keeping her in the dark about Collins affair with Patricia Jackson, especially after her revelations about the badge. So, there's the answer, he told himself; just keep one step ahead of her from now on. Another glass of whisky? 'Don't mind if I do,' he said to himself.

Oh, how wonderful, thought Jacqui Fletcher as she eased herself into the steaming hot bath and luxuriated beneath the water and the foam. If there was one thing that she looked forward to after a hard day's work then it was relaxing in her steamy tub. Not only was she able to burn off a few calories, but it gave her an indisputable feeling of inner peace. And after the kind of day that she had just had, peace would have been very welcome indeed. She wanted to think about the weekend and her friend Izzy, but that got her thinking about the badge and that in turn brought her mind back to the events of the day. So there was to be no peace for her, no matter how hard she tried.

And it was all because of that bloody infuriating man, Detective Chief Inspector Allan Clarke; "Mr. Misogynist", she'd started to call him. She'd gone into work so upbeat too; she should have known better. For crying out loud, he'd sidelined her for the past week, so he was almost sure to continue in the same vein. His outburst was not only proof of his loathing of the opposite sex, but it showed just what a pig-headed, cantankerous bugger he really was!

She was getting worked up and that was completely out of character. Bloody man – bloody men! They're all the same! She then stopped to contemplate this moment of misandry. Don't let him get to you, she told herself – but that was easier said than done.

And then at the mention of the badge he seemed to change; almost as if he was a different person. Is that why he decided to involve her in the investigation? Or was there a method in his madness? At least they were thinking along the same lines, in that they both held the view that Simon Collins was entirely innocent of the charge of killing Keith Jackson. But then he reverted to type and deliberately kept Collins affair with Patricia Jackson from her.

'Well, two can play at that game, Detective Chief Inspector!' she said to herself as she climbed out of the bath.

Having dried herself she wrapped the bath robe around her and then headed for the kitchen. Opening the fridge, she literally snatched at the bottle of Malbec and poured herself a large glass of wine. It was just what she needed after a long soak. Taking both the glass of wine *and* the bottle with her to the living room, she slumped onto the sofa and switched on the TV. She wasn't really watching what was on the screen; her thoughts were still on the days events. Another glass of wine? Why not!

'Bloody man,' she snarled. 'Bloody men!'

Chapter 30

Tuesday, 11 July, 2017 (a.m.)

Unlike the previous few days, Tuesday morning dawned rather cloudy as Detective Sergeant Fletcher set off for work. It was generally much easier getting out of Nottingham in the morning compared to getting back in again during the evening rush hour, but there were major roadworks on the Alfreton Road for the next two or three weeks, and this caused her to set off a little earlier than was usual. This gave her ample time to contemplate the day ahead and the possibility of a further clash with Inspector Clarke.

Nevertheless, she made it to the main incident room at Brockley without getting wound up about her boss shortly before nine o'clock, and said her good mornings to her colleagues. To her surprise there was no sign of Clarke, so she stepped into the kitchen and made herself a coffee before heading for her desk.

However, she was about to sit down when she noticed a yellow Post-it note attached to the keyboard of her laptop. It was from Clarke – and the coffee would have to wait. She was to go immediately to the scene of the crime and conduct a thorough search of the building, in the hope that Jackson had hidden evidence about his clients and probably more. Clarke himself had gone to see Superintendent Annable.

At first a frown appeared on her face. She understood that Jackson was likely to have a number of clients, but what could Clarke mean by 'probably more?' And surely Scenes of Crime Officers had gone through the building with a fine tooth comb? The frown turned to a look of suspicion as she began to suspect that she was being set up again, and she sighed heavily. At that moment Constable Webster appeared alongside her.

'Looks like you've been given an onerous task, Sergeant?' he said before taking a sip of his tea.

'Do you know anything about this, Webster?' she asked rather sternly as she passed him the note.

Webster cast his eyes over the note. 'No, can't say I do.' She looked at him sharply before he continued. 'Well let's put it this way, he certainly hasn't said anything to me about it.'

Snatching the note back, she glared at Webster and added a last request before setting off for Brockley. 'Make sure you don't let my coffee go cold, there's a good man.'

Webster watched her head for the door. 'What did your last bloody servant die of – ma'am.' he muttered under his breath!

By the time Fletcher had pulled up outside The Old Turnpike House there was a little light rain, and it had definitely turned cooler than of late. The building was still sealed off and a uniformed policeman stood guard outside. Her first impressions were not at all positive. It wasn't that the building was stuck in the middle of nowhere at the end of a narrow country lane; she had adventures in the Canadian wilderness, so this presented no problems. No, it was the building itself that she found so dispiriting. To her mind it was old and decrepit, and therefore in dire need of renovation – or pulling down altogether and starting again with a newer model! Climbing out of her car, she buttoned up her jacket, pulled her collar up and scuttled across to the policeman, proffering her identity.

Her spirits were not raised any having gained access to the building, for she felt an overwhelming desire to get out quick. Had *he* been there no doubt the Chief Inspector would have accused her of looking down her nose at the décor (or what remained of it), as it was most definitely not to her taste, but she was here for a purpose (or so she had been told), and that was to find evidence that might nail the killer of the guy who lived in this hovel.

Pulling on a pair of protective gloves, she began by looking inside the cabinet that lay at the foot of the stairs near the inside door. They had found the badge lying underneath, but she couldn't find anything of importance within. She then reluctantly began climbing the stairs and on reaching the top she gazed out of the window. The light showers had not abated and the town of Grimley loomed darkly in the distance. It looked *grim* alright; but then so too did what appeared to be the spare bedroom, which was literally crammed to the ceiling with paraphernalia.

'I sincerely hope he doesn't expect me to search through that bloody lot,' she muttered to herself!

She closed the door behind her and stepped into the main bedroom, which did little to raise her enthusiasm, especially when she saw the buff-coloured patterned wallpaper which was hanging off all over the place. There was a double bed and it was facing the window; it hadn't been slept in for a while, she guessed. The duvet cover and pillow slips were dirty, but she was able to make out that the design appeared to show a polar bear with young. At the foot of the bed and to the left of the window stood an oak veneer wardrobe that had clearly seen better days, and it had a drawer at the bottom. Opening the drawer first, she was surprised to find it empty and so she then tried the doors. It was sparse inside, with very few items of clothing. Several ties hung from a rack on the inside of one door, some of which were emblazoned with the regimental badge of the Worcestershire and Sherwood Foresters. Judging the wardrobe to be of no particular interest, she noticed that the bed base had room for storage, but when she opened this it came as no surprise to find that this too was empty.

In the right-hand corner of the room was a dressing table with mirror, and it had the same oak veneer as the wardrobe. There were three drawers down the middle and small doors either side, but again there was very little to speak of within other than bed linen and clothing. To the right of the bed and up against the wall were a cheap set of drawers, upon which lay a pair of jeans. Inside the drawers there was nothing other than underwear, socks and shirts. There was a small bedside cabinet between the bed and the wall, with a lamp on top and a pile of books within.

She then ventured into the other bedroom, which was slightly smaller but seemed to mirror the other one in that it had peeling buff-coloured wallpaper, a double bed, wardrobe and set of drawers. There was no dressing table, but there was a mirror on the right-hand wall. She checked behind that first, but found nothing. Jackson had no friends to speak of, but he did have children and she wondered if they might stay over from time to time. However, the drawers were empty and the wardrobe contained more books and magazines, mostly of the adult kind.

Leaving the small bedroom, she entered the bathroom which was filthy, especially the shower curtain, which had once been of a light-blue colouring to match the walls. There was a mirror above the sink and shaving equipment on the nearby window sill. At one corner of the bath there was a yellow sponge, upon which lay what was left of a bar of soap. A large, damp towel draped the bath itself, and a small one was hanging from the back of the door. Just below the sink was a basket, but on opening this she found nothing other than more damp clothing. It was time to head back downstairs, but she doubted that her search there would be bear any fruit either.

The first room that she came to on reaching the foot of the stairs was the living room, with more peeling wallpaper. More importantly, she was repulsed by the lack of cleanliness. Was this why Clarke had sent her in the first place, to turn her stomach? Wouldn't put it past him, she thought. Almost immediately her eyes caught the pornographic DVD's on the small table beside the easy chair, and a look of disgust appeared on her face. Her opinion of the late Keith Jackson was deteriorating rapidly. She quickly turned her attention to the easy chair, running her gloved hands over the cushion as if she was feeling for something, and then looking under the chair itself. Unsuccessful, she then did the same with the sofa, but met with the same result. The cabinet over towards the door was next, but surely this had been given a thorough search? Then again, we are talking about men, she pondered. However, here too her search was in vain.

Moving along the hallway to the back of the building she came to the kitchen. As with Clarke the previous week she was struck by the bare walls and a total lack of hygiene. The sink was still full of pots and pans, but at least she wasn't granted the luxury of witnessing the half-eaten plate of fish and chips, for someone had taken upon themselves the none-too-arduous task of disposing of them. The two empty bottles of vodka were still on the table – no doubt dusted for fingerprints. From what she had gleaned from the reports this was the victim's favourite tipple. Avoiding the damp patch on what remained of the cushion flooring, she searched through all the cupboards and drawers without success, but with every minute the utter pointlessness of her search was growing.

The only item of furniture in the kitchen which caught her eye (but didn't quite appeal to her tastes) was the old oak Welsh Dresser over to the left of the room, between the table and the wall. Adorned by an array of plates, most of these were in need of a damn good clean too from what she could make out. Curious as to the patterns on some of the plates, she made her way over to the dresser, but as she leaned upon the left hand side it wobbled forward and one of the plates came crashing down, smashing to smithereens on the floor.

'Bloody hell,' she swore to herself!

It was probably one of a collection and she looked up to determine if that might have been the case. As she did so, she noticed that where the plate had once stood the back panel of the dresser seemed to take on the appearance of a sliding door, for there was a slight gap on one side, as if this 'door' hadn't been closed properly. Could this be a secret compartment, she asked herself, and one that may have been missed or overlooked by the forensic team? There was only one way to find out, and so with one hand she held on to the dresser to prevent it from wobbling, and with the other she attempted to open this sliding door. Initially it seemed to stick, but after a few seconds it gave way and slid along to reveal what was indeed a secret compartment. What's more, within this secret compartment was what at first looked like an ordinary exercise book, but in fact turned out to be a diary for the year 2017.

Removing the diary from the compartment, she proceeded to take it to the nearby table to look through it. As she did so a flurry of ten pound notes fell to the floor from within. Bending down to retrieve them, she counted them twice and reached a figure of three hundred pounds. So much for being in debt, she said to herself. Could this be some of the blackmail money from Simon Collins?

She returned to the diary, and Clarke had been right. Jackson had written down the names of his clients and the dates he was due to carry out work for them. Needless to say, the spring and summer months were his busiest – or would have been of course; not that any of the names meant anything to her.

But wait a minute – what's this? Flicking through the pages as if to check and double-check her findings, she established that on the 3rd of every month Jackson had written the initials "SC". That had to be Simon Collins, she thought. She continued with her search and then stopped again.

'Hang on,' she said to herself. 'There's another one here.' Sure enough, on the 28th of every month were the initials "CBI". 'Was the bugger blackmailing somebody else?' At that moment a frown came upon her face. 'What does "CBI" stand for, I wonder?' She could only think of Confederation of British Industry, but whatever it stood for it was bound to be of some importance.

She carefully placed the diary into an evidence bag, sealed it and decided it was time to return to the incident room. Bidding farewell to the uniformed policeman standing guard outside, she jumped into her car, but before setting off back up Blackthorn Lane she slumped back in her seat. This wasn't a set-up by Clarke after all, she thought. Could it be that the old bugger is mellowing? No, he's up to something if truth were known. Turning on the ignition at last, her immediate concern was whether or not Webster had kept her coffee warm!

Reporting to Superintendent Annable on the progress of *any* case was not one of Clarke's favourite tasks, and this morning was no exception. It wasn't that he was petrified of the man, unlike some of his fellow officers who had bestowed upon him the sobriquet "Annable the Cannibal"; he could handle the more belligerent side of his character. No, it was his refusal to listen to reason and his demands for a quick result. Not forgetting his habit of inserting 'At the end of the day' into every bloody sentence! And of course now he had to tell him that he'd released one of the main suspects.

'But I thought that you'd got your man?' squealed Annable. 'What was his name?'

'Collins, Sir. Simon Collins,' replied a bored-looking Clarke. 'No-o, we merely brought him in for questioning. And when it was discovered that he hadn't attended Cambridge University…'

'Cambridge University!' bellowed Annable. 'What the bloody hell has that got to do with it?'

'I told you, Sir. The badge is the key…'

'Badge?' interrupted Annable once more. 'What bloody badge?'

Clarke felt like holding his head in his hands in despair. 'The *Tom and Jerry* badge found at the scene. As I was trying to say, it is the key to solving this case, and the owner of that badge went to Cambridge University.'

'Well, it sounds rather tenuous to me.'

Clarke decided to change tack. 'You'll be pleased to know that I've sent Sergeant Fletcher to the victim's house in the hope of finding more evidence that will lead us to catch the killer.'

Annable was indeed pleased. 'Well, I'm glad that you appear to be getting along together at long last.' But he still wanted results. 'Nevertheless, it's time that this case was solved, Clarke.'

Clarke rose from his chair. 'If that's all, Sir?'

Annable hadn't quite finished. 'By the way, Clarke. Who was that woman I saw you talking to at the supermarket yesterday?'

Clarke was clearly unaware that there had been a witness to his conversation with Maria. 'Erm…she's just an old school friend from many years ago, Sir,' he said somewhat sheepishly. 'We've arranged to meet up later this week, but…'

Annable interrupted again. 'Good! It's about time that you settled down.'

'We'll just be chatting about old times I suppose,' replied Clarke. 'I do value my independence, as you know, Sir.'

Clarke wasn't expecting Annable's response. 'You never had kids, did you, Clarke?'

Clarke began to feel his hackles rising. 'My then wife was against the idea and I went along with it – Sir!'

'You don't know what you're missing, Clarke.' And then it came. 'At the end of the day, every man should settle down and have kids.'

'Yes, Sir,' said Clarke with gritted teeth as he left the room. Annable was not accustomed to having his senior officers slam the door behind them – and he jumped a mile in the air as Clarke did just that!

Chapter 31

Tuesday, 11 July, 2017 (p.m.)

Tuesday morning had turned into Tuesday afternoon by the time Clarke left Leverton and his meeting with Superintendent Annable; the fact that it was still raining did little to assuage his feelings of anger towards his boss.

'Who the hell does he think he is?' said Clarke out loud as he pulled away from the station. 'Bloody arrogant...' He suddenly stopped short of adding to any further expletives and decided not to let his anger get the better of him. Indeed, by the time he reached Brockley his mind was back on the case, but instead of heading directly for the incident room he pulled into the car park of *The Wheatsheaf*; he could do with a swift half, he told himself.

There were very few people in the pub when Clarke entered, and Tony Dawkins was alone behind the bar; his wife Sally was nowhere to be seen.

'You're becoming a regular, Inspector,' shouted Dawkins in his usual light-hearted manner. He clearly wasn't expecting Clarke's response.

'I wouldn't bank on that, Mr. Dawkins,' replied Clarke with a dismissive smile. 'However, I would like to have a word with you about *your* regulars if I may? And whilst I'm here I'll have a half of Peculiar, please.'

The smile was indeed knocked off Dawkins face and he grudgingly poured Clarke his drink. Money was exchanged and after taking his first sip of the ale Clarke launched into the first of his questions.

'As far as you know, Mr. Dawkins, did the late Mr. Jackson do any gardening work for any of the regulars?'

Dawkins sighed and thought hard. 'Some of the cricket team are regulars, but most of them live outside the village, and yet he did do work for one or two of them.' He then seemed to warm to the situation. 'I do know that he did some work for Mr. Ibbotson now and again.'

'That would be Mr. Ibbotson, antiques dealer and head of the parish council?'

'Yeah, that's him,' replied Dawkins with a sneer. 'Lives in the big house just along Thraplow Lane, standing back from the road – the one with all the big trees either side the driveway.' Rubbing his chin, Dawkins continued. 'Funny, but he doesn't get many visitors. Keeps himself to himself, and yet he don't half think a lot of himself.'

Clarke listened intently and took a large gulp of his beer before continuing. 'Do you know if Mr. Ibbotson went to university by any chance?'

'Do me a favour; the guy is always going on about his time at university,' replied Dawkins with a hint of sarcasm.

'Have you any idea which one?'

Dawkins pondered for a few seconds. 'Cambridge I think,' he said rubbing his chin again. 'Yes, that's it, because he boasted about opening the bat for the Cambridge eleven against a Somerset team containing Botham, Richards and Garner!'

Clarke finished his beer. 'Thank you, Mr. Dawkins. You've been very helpful.'

As Clarke headed for the door, he literally winced as he heard the raised voice of Sally Dawkins, evidently berating her husband again. She must have been listening, thought Clarke, and he was mightily glad to close the door of the pub behind him!

The rain had practically stopped by the time that Clarke pulled up at the car park outside the incident room, and yet he had to step over one or two large puddles as he got out of his car. There was no sign of Fletcher's car, so he assumed that she was still at the scene of the crime as directed. However, Webster's car was there, and so he must have finished questioning Patricia Jackson about her affair with Simon Collins. Indeed, Clarke had just entered his office when Webster came over to inform him that she had corroborated Collins story.

'She made no attempt to deny the affair, Sir,' began Webster. 'She and Collins have been at it for some time.'

'I get the picture, Webster,' replied Clarke somewhat irritably as he draped his jacket around the back of the swivel chair. 'No need to be so sordid – and close the door behind you.'

Webster did as requested. 'Sorry, Sir,' he grinned awkwardly and took out his notebook. 'Yes, Collins did pay towards the riding school and the blackmail started after Jackson spotted the two of them together. It's been going on for about a year.'

Clarke sat back in his chair and placed his hands behind his head. 'I think we can definitely rule out Collins then.'

'How did the meeting with Superintendent Annable go, Sir?' enquired Webster with an element of trepidation.

Clarke looked up at him sharply as if he had touched a nerve. 'My meeting with Superintendent Annable is of no significance.' He then seemed to relax once more and stared ahead. 'It's what I've just learnt from the landlord of *The Wheatsheaf* that has put a whole new perspective on the case.'

Before he could expand further on his meeting with Tony Dawkins there was a knock on the door and in stepped Fletcher.

'Oh, I didn't realise you had company, Sir,' she said awkwardly.

'That's alright, Fletcher,' replied Clarke. 'Do come in.' He couldn't help but notice that she seemed rather pleased with herself, and assumed that she had found something important during her search of The Old Turnpike House. 'Your search yield anything by any chance?' he asked a trifle knowingly.

'Oh yes,' she replied in an upbeat manner, before proceeding to give an account of her visit to the victim's house. Clarke listened with a growing sense of tedium before she finally produced the diary and placed it on his desk before him. 'Take a look at that,' she boasted proudly.

Clarke began to flick through the pages of the diary. 'Where did you find this then?' he asked without looking up.

'Hidden in a secret compartment on the Welsh Dresser,' said Fletcher excitedly.

Clarke was impressed by her determination and diligence, but he wasn't going to show it. 'Clever bugger our Mr. Jackson,' he said somewhat indifferently.

'What? Oh, yes,' replied a puzzled looking Fletcher before continuing. 'As you can see, not only did he provide details of his clients and when he was due to carry out work for them, but look at the 3rd and the 28th of each month, Sir.'

As Webster peered at the diary over his shoulder, Clarke did as Fletcher requested. 'I see what you mean,'

'The SC must stand for Simon Collins, but for the life of me I have no idea what the CBI means,' she said with a degree of irritation.

Clarke decided to bring an end to the suspense. 'Christopher Brian Ibbotson,' he said calmly and somewhat smugly. 'Antiques shop owner *and* he went to Cambridge!'

Fletcher was again taken aback. 'How the hell did you discover that, Sir?' she said with a look of stunned surprise on her face.

If Clarke was honest he wouldn't have cared two hoots if Fletcher had come back empty-handed; he had trumped her once again and kept one step ahead of her, just as he'd intended. 'The landlord of *The Wheatsheaf* can be very helpful at times,' he replied with that smug grin still on his face.

Frustrated and irritated by Clarke's manner, Fletcher rose from her seat and made to leave. Just as she reached the door she turned to face the Inspector once more. 'Are you suggesting that Ibbotson *might* be the killer, Sir?'

'Well, we know that Collins was being blackmailed and why,' replied Clarke pensively. 'It now looks like Jackson was blackmailing Ibbotson too. Aren't you curious as to why that might be, Sergeant?'

'But I thought he had an alibi for the time of Jackson's death?'

'Then it's our job to find out if he was telling the truth, isn't it?' Fletcher nodded her head and turned to go, but Clarke hadn't finished. 'Well done, Sergeant – finding the diary.'

As she closed the door behind her, a huge smile came to Fletcher's face. Maybe the Inspector wasn't such a misogynist after all, she thought to herself.

Chapter 32

Wednesday, 12 July, 2017 (a.m.)

Wednesday morning loomed overcast and blustery, with the likelihood of more rain later in the day; a bit like Clarke's mood as he drove to Derby shortly after 9.30 a.m.

He had never liked Derby even though he had been born there. Someone had once suggested to him that he must have been proud of where he was born, but he replied in the negative. 'I might have spent the first three or four days of my life there,' he had said with undisguised contempt, 'but other than that I have no connection with the place whatsoever.'

This was before 1994, when he was posted to the Drugs Squad in Derby, but that did nothing to alter his perception of the place. He and his family were Leverton through and through and from coal mining stock, and he was convinced that this was why he was never made to feel welcome by his colleagues in Derby. 'I wasn't one of *them*,' he had lamented one day to his former sidekick, Detective Sergeant Coates. 'From the outset I was made to feel very much an outsider.' Even his dialect and accent were 'frowned upon' to put it mildly, and that continued long after he was promoted to Detective Sergeant in 2002 and transferred to the Derby CID. Then came his suspension in 2009; his being from Leverton didn't help his case, he had said to Coates. And so it was a huge relief when he finally 'came home' to Leverton in 2011, after being away for almost seventeen years. Now he was returning to the place that had brought him so much unhappiness and misery.

He had placed a call to Ibbotson's antique's shop shortly after 9.00 a.m. The female voice on the other end of the phone was undeniably polite but succinct.

'You will find Mr. Ibbotson at the Auction House this morning,' she had said.

And so that's where Clarke was heading as the wind whistled through the open window of his Ford Focus, and the sky above seemed to grow more melancholy.

Situated on Chequers Road, alongside the A52 – or Brian Clough Way – as one heads out of Derby, the Auction House contained three salesrooms, nine departments and a coffee shop. The latter was unlikely to appeal to Clarke as he never drank the stuff, so as he entered the building shortly after 9.45 a.m. he collared the first member of staff who crossed his path and enquired as to the possible whereabouts of Mr. Ibbotson. Glad to oblige, the staff worker duly pointed out the unmistakeable figure of Ibbotson standing on the right-hand side of the room, engaged in conversation with one of the auctioneers.

At six feet and two inches in height, Ibbotson towered over the other man, and he looked every inch the antiques dealer in his tweed jacket and bow tie. What's more, he seemed to be constantly brushing his wispy grey hair from his forehead with his left hand as Clarke approached.

'I do hope that you will excuse me for interrupting your conversation,' said Clarke politely and apologetically. 'But would you be Mr. Christopher Brian Ibbotson by any chance?'

A few words were exchanged between the two men before the auctioneer walked away, and then Ibbotson turned to face Clarke. 'Yes, I am he,' he replied with what Clarke put down as a rather false smile. 'How can I be of assistance?'

Clarke produced his identity card and introduced himself. 'Detective Chief Inspector Clarke, Leverton CID. I was told you'd be here,' he said calmly and with a false smile of his own. 'I just wonder if you could help with our enquiries into the death of Mr. Keith Jackson.'

Ibbotson suddenly seemed uncomfortable. 'Well, as you can see I am about to take part in an auction.'

'Just a few questions, Sir – won't keep you long.' Ibbotson sighed and grudgingly nodded his head before Clarke continued. 'How well did you know Mr. Jackson, Sir?'

'Other than his duties as groundsman at the cricket club, there was very little contact between the two of us,' he sneered. 'I suppose we bumped into each other at the pub now and again.'

'Would that be *The Wheatsheaf* at Brockley, Sir?'

'It would.'

'And yet I am reliably informed that Mr. Jackson undertook gardening work for you personally. Is that right, Sir?'

'Who told you that?'

'Just answer the question please, Sir.'

Ibbotson sighed heavily again. 'Yes, now and again. I'd let him get on with it and then pay him on match day or when he came in the pub.'

Clarke then stared directly into Ibbotson's eyes as he asked his next question. 'Have you ever been to Mr. Jackson's house by any chance?'

'Once or twice maybe... but only to discuss the maintenance of the cricket pitch with him.' Now we *are* telling porkies, thought Clarke. But Ibbotson was clearly becoming more and more irritated by the questioning. 'Look, where is this leading, Inspector?'

'Just routine enquiries, Sir.' Clarke continued in spite of Ibbotson's discomfort. 'Can you tell me the make of your vehicle, Sir?'

'Oh, for God's sake!' Ibbotson was now becoming exasperated. 'A black Range Rover Sport!'

Clarke suddenly changed tack. 'I understand that you went to Cambridge University, Sir?'

'What if I did?'

The next question caught Ibbotson completely by surprise. 'Where you at any time a member of the *Tom and Jerry Club* by any chance?'

'Good God no,' spluttered Ibbotson. 'What do you take me for?'

'So you do know what I'm referring to?'

'Yes, of course, but I had nothing to do with those reprobates. Cricket and a love of the Impressionists was all I cared about.' By now Ibbotson had clearly had enough. 'Look, if you want to ask me any more questions then it will have to be in the presence of my solicitor!'

As Ibbotson made to move to his seat, Clarke thanked him for his time, but he did have one last question. 'Are you buying or selling, Sir?'

'Selling, Inspector,' replied Ibbotson barely able to contain his anger. 'Today we are selling – and *this* is one of ours. Now if you don't mind?'

Clarke put his hands up as if to concede the argument, but just before leaving he looked across at the item up for sale. It was a painting of a woman holding a fan by Charles Willmott, entitled *E=mc2*. It was valued at between £2,500 and £3,000, although it was likely to fetch more. He turned to go, and as he walked through the door and back to his car his face lit up. He could hide the smile no longer.

By the time he pulled up back at the incident room the heavens had opened, and as he bolted for the door the rain lashed across the car park. Relieved to be under cover once more, he first entered the kitchen and retrieved a small bottle of sparkling Buxton Water. Making his way into the main office, he spotted Webster dozing at his desk.

'All getting too much for you, Detective Constable,' he bellowed!

Webster jumped a mile. 'What the…' he shouted. 'Oh, very sorry, Sir. Didn't realise you were back.'

'If I catch you sleeping on the job again, Webster, I'll have you doing traffic duty or some other menial task.'

Webster apologised again. 'It won't happen again, Sir. You have my word.'

'Too bloody right it won't happen again.' Clarke then appeared to calm down. 'Now that you're back in the land of the living, Webster, you can do something for me.'

'What would that be, Sir?'

'I want you to do a PNC check for me – the National Mobile Property Register to be precise.'

'Right you are, Sir.' Webster complied. 'What are we looking for, Sir?'

'Scroll down under the heading "Report My Loss" and then I'll let you know you when to stop.' Webster duly obliged, until after two or three pages Clarke suddenly barked out the order. 'Stop!' Leaning forward, he read the description before him and another smile came to his face.

Webster pointed to the screen. 'Is this what you were looking for, Sir?'

'Indeed it is, Webster. Read it out for me, please?'

'Stolen from a property in the Peak District three months ago, painting by Charles Willmott entitled $E=mc2$. That it, Sir?'

'That's it, Webster,' replied a jubilant-looking Clarke. 'Looks like we'll be applying for a search warrant!'

Chapter 33

Wednesday, 12 July, 2017 (p.m.)

Whilst Clarke and Webster were conducting their PNC check and the wheels had been set in motion for an application for a search warrant from the magistrate's court, Fletcher in the meantime had broken off from typing up her reports and popped out for some sandwiches, amongst other things.

Despite the encouraging words from Clarke as she left his office the day before, he had now trumped her twice on this case, and she was still feeling a trifle peeved. She was determined to prove her worth, not only to him and to her superiors, but especially to herself. After all, it was still a bloody man's world – or so she was always telling herself! Nevertheless, perhaps Clarke did have a point though; perhaps she did have a tendency to be overly-ambitious – sometimes.

These were her thoughts as she returned to the incident room and contemplated continuing the tedious task of typing up her reports. So she was somewhat surprised to find Clarke sitting in his office with his feet on the table when she returned. What was even more remarkable was the fact that he called her into his office, not only to fill her in on his meeting with Ibbotson earlier, but also to provide an insight into the likelihood of a possible scam involving the head of Brockley Parish Council. Before he could finish, however, she still couldn't resist the temptation to cut him off in mid-flow.

'Do you think we've got our man then, Sir?' she asked rather tentatively.

Clarke glanced at her and he seemed rather annoyed at first, but then he removed his feet from the table, rose from his chair and stood staring out of the window, almost as if he was thinking out loud.

'Mmmm…Ibbotson knew the victim and had visited his home on more than one occasion.' He then turned to face her once more and continued. 'He had even employed him on his garden, for crying out loud!' Then he turned to look out of the window again. 'And yet he *was* educated at Cambridge *and* he knew of the *Tom and Jerry Club*…although he denied ever being a member.'

Fletcher was incredulous. 'And you believed him,' she shouted!

Clarke still appeared to be in a world of his own. 'Too tall and wiry for my liking,' he said barely audibly. 'And yet Jackson was drunk, so it's possible I suppose. He turned to face Fletcher yet again. 'We should be able to arrest the bugger for being an inveterate, jumped-up snob!'

Fletcher had got the bit between her teeth. 'It's my belief that he employed someone else to do his dirty work,' she argued vigorously. 'After all, if as you believe we are going to find more stuff at his home, then there is every likelihood that he had an accomplice to do the stealing, and he could have paid *him* to do the killing.'

Clarke appeared to grudgingly bite his lip before proceeding. 'Good point, Sergeant,' he grimaced, but then reverted to type. 'However, when conducting *any* investigation I make it a policy of pursuing every line of enquiry, and I suggest that you do likewise before jumping to any conclusions. Ambition is a fine thing, but as I have seen all too often it can lead to burnout, pig-headedness *and* a shorter life!'

Fletcher leaned forward and placed her hands on his desk. 'But intelligence without ambition is like a bird without wings – Sir,' she said calmly.

Checkmate!

There was silence for a few seconds, and then Clarke told her to close the door before appearing to offer her an olive branch. Could it be that Diana Marshall's words were at long last sinking in?

'Look, I know you think I'm a misogynist,' he muttered whilst fiddling with his pen.

'Perish the thought,' muttered Fletcher under her breath.

'The fact is I'm really just a sad, bitter old bugger!'

Not one to admit her own flaws and weaknesses, it was at this stage that Fletcher chose to reveal that she was aware that his marriage had failed. 'I did hear that you and your wife had parted company some years ago, Sir,' she said looking at the floor almost apologetically.

'So I understand,' replied Clarke without referring to his reprimand of Constable Webster.

Fletcher then proceeded to enquire as to why he was suspended from duties back in 2009. Realising that Webster was almost certainly the source of this unfortunate incident in his career, Clarke went through every detail from start to finish, ending with the imprisonment of his old boss, DCI Maxine Greenhough.

'Must have been a very worrying time for you, Sir,' she said with sincerity.

'It was indeed,' he admitted, almost as if he was in a trance.

Ever inquisitive, she then asked why everyone referred to him as "Sniffer". 'Is it because you're good at sniffing out the criminal?'

Before he could reply, Webster suddenly burst into the room looking as white as a ghost.

'Haven't I told you to knock before entering, Webster?' grumbled Clarke.

'Yes…I mean no, Sir…I mean…' Webster was clearly lost for words.

'Well, what is it man?'

'You'd better get down to Leverton, Sir!'

'What on earth for?'

'There's been an incident at *The Wheatsheaf*, Sir!'

'What do you mean "incident"?'

'It's Mr. Dawkins, Sir. He's tried to strangle his wife!'

Chapter 34

Wednesday, 12 July, 2017 (p.m.)

The Duty Sergeant at Leverton police station, Bob Scattergood, decided to have a quick fag outside while he awaited the arrival of Inspector Clarke. He'd barely had time for a smoke all day and it wouldn't take the man long to get there, so now was as good a time as any.

He was looking forward to the weekend, when his daughter and grandkids were coming over for Sunday lunch. Actually his daughter would be doing the cooking – roast beef with Yorkshire pudding, new potatoes and greens, she had promised; he would have his hands full playing with the grandkids. She had been a Godsend since the death of his beloved wife, and he was just contemplating the delights of her culinary expertise when he saw the familiar outline of the silver Ford Focus come through the gates over to his left. Stubbing out his cigarette, he vainly attempted to brush the ash from his uniform before scuttling back inside.

Clarke had recognised the ginger-haired, rather portly figure of Sergeant Scattergood the moment he arrived at the station, but he wasn't going to begrudge him a crafty fag even at a moment like this. Nevertheless, he burst through the doors of the station like a hound straining at the leash.

'Where is he?' he barked without seeming to look at Scattergood.

'He's in Interview Room 1, Sir,' replied a nervous-looking Duty Sergeant.

Clarke suddenly stopped and turned to face him. 'Tut, tut, tut, Scattergood,' he said shaking his head. 'Don't let Superintendent Annable see your uniform in such a state!' Realising that he had put the wind up the uniformed Sergeant, Clarke continued on to the interview room with a mischievous grin upon his face.

The smile had gone from his face by the time he opened the door to the interview room and saw before him the miserable figure of Tony Dawkins twiddling his fingers nervously. He wasn't wearing a tie either; that had been used in the attempt to kill his wife.

Dawkins looked up at Clarke. 'It's a fair cop,' he said flippantly with a stupid-looking grin on his face.

'You won't be laughing much after today,' replied Clarke as he took his seat opposite the erstwhile landlord of *The Wheatsheaf*.

'Dare say I won't.'

Clarke rested his forearms on the table and leaning forward he brought his hands together. 'I don't suppose it takes a genius to work out what prompted you to strangle your wife, but I'm obliged to ask the question regardless?'

'Have you ever been married?' asked Dawkins through gritted teeth.

'Actually I'm…'

Dawkins cut him short. 'Must have,' he said almost dismissively. 'Bet *she* never wore the trousers though?'

'We had our up's and down's,' replied Clarke somewhat sheepishly. 'But no – she didn't wear the trousers.'

'Then you don't know what it's like,' he snapped. 'I'll tell you what it's like. It's like being a bloody captive twenty-four hours a day, seven days a week. That's what it's like!'

Clarke regretted his response almost immediately. 'Yes, I can imagine it is.'

Dawkins glared at Clarke with eyes blazing, and yet he waited several seconds before he continued. 'My sex life has been non-existent for as long as I can remember, and all because of a cruel, heartless woman – a woman I have come to loathe and despise with a passion!'

Clarke was forced to acknowledge to himself that sex had come to a shuddering halt during his marriage, but he wouldn't have called Lesley cruel and heartless, in spite of the self-inflicted bitterness that he underwent in the years after the marriage ended.

'I left my wife,' he said quietly, looking down at the table. 'Why didn't you leave yours?' he asked looking up at Dawkins again.

Dawkins didn't answer, but he asked another question of his own. 'Do you appreciate beauty, Inspector?'

'But of course,' replied Clarke.

Again, Dawkins hesitated awhile before continuing. 'There was a woman at the pub – one of the regulars. Her name's Angela.'

'What about her?'

Dawkins appeared to salivate as he replied. 'Well, she's fit – a right little goer,' he said apparently warming to the theme. 'You'd know what I mean if you saw her yourself, Inspector.'

What that had to do with "beauty" was anyone's guess, thought Clarke. 'Go on, Mr. Dawkins,' he said with a modicum of exasperation.

'Well, she came in the pub a bit earlier than usual today – her partner was there as always though.'

'Her partner was there, you say?'

'Yeah, that's right. His name's John Sheldon.'

Clarke's ears pricked up immediately at the mention of the name. 'Do go on, Mr. Dawkins.'

'Well, I'd been chatting her up a bit – she always seems to like my attention,' he said (and rather arrogantly in Clarke's opinion). 'All of a sudden she goes to the loo, like. And, well, I thought I'd follow her.'

'In other words, you fancied your chances, Mr. Dawkins?'

'Well, yeah. Suppose I did.'

Clarke knew what was coming, but he was obliged to ask the question. 'What happened next?'

'Well, as she came out of the loo I tried to kiss her, didn't I?'

'And she was having none of it. Am I right?'

'She pushed me away and called me a dirty old man,' snarled Dawkins.

'She rejected you?'

Clarke's words seemed to touch a nerve. 'The bitch had been stringing me along all the time, hadn't she?'

'And you found that hard to take?' Dawkins merely shrugged. 'So where does your wife come into all of this, Mr. Dawkins?'

The reply was barely audible. 'She'd been watching us all the time.'

'I'm sorry, but I didn't quite catch that?'

'I said she'd been watching us all the bloody time,' shouted Dawkins!

'She'd witnessed everything?'

'She'd been standing on the bloody staircase all the time,' sighed Dawkins. 'I tried to pull myself together – recover my composure – when she suddenly charged down the stairs and started mouthing me!'

'And that's when you snapped?'

'I just saw red and lost it, Inspector,' he admitted as he picked up the pencil before him. 'All those years of being nagged at, belittled and starved of affection. All that pent up frustration…' Such was his rage that he snapped the pencil in half.

A few seconds elapsed before Clarke continued with the questioning. 'What happened *exactly*, Mr. Dawkins?'

'It was when my wife started to climb back up the stairs,' he said as his eyes began to moisten with tears.

'What did you do?'

'I removed my tie and went after her.'

'You tried to strangle her?'

'Yeah, I tried to strangle her,' he repeated.

'What made you stop?'

Dawkins went on to describe how one of the girls behind the bar appeared on the scene having heard the commotion.

'Well, she started screaming and before I knew it several of the customers arrived and pulled me off – including Sheldon. Someone called the police and an ambulance, and the next thing I knew I was being cuffed and bundled into a car.'

Clarke looked at him shrewdly and then suddenly changed tack. 'Have you ever tried to strangle anyone before?'

The question puzzled Dawkins. 'No – never,' he replied with a deep frown.

'So you didn't kill Keith Jackson?'

'Of course I bloody didn't,' protested Dawkins loudly! 'I told you – I never left my car. I dropped him off and then drove away. Why would I want to kill Jackson? It was my wife that I wanted to kill!'

'And you very nearly did,' muttered Clarke, who then rose from his chair. 'Tony Dawkins, I'm charging you with an offence under section 1 (1) of the Criminal Attempts Act 1981, namely the attempted murder of your wife, Sally Dawkins, for which the maximum penalty is life imprisonment!'

'Anything is better than being with that cold-hearted bitch,' grumbled Dawkins as he was led away to his cell.

As Clarke emerged from the interview room he noticed Fletcher in conversation with Sergeant Scattergood; she had evidently made her way from Brockley to Leverton whilst he had been questioning Dawkins.

Fletcher broke away from her conversation. 'Presumably you've charged Dawkins with attempting to kill his wife, Sir?' she asked eagerly.

'Indeed I have,' replied an exhausted-looking Clarke.

'Did he admit to killing Jackson?'

'He's not our man either!'

At this point Scattergood intervened. 'Your search warrant has arrived from the magistrate's court, Sir,' he said holding the document up for all to see.

Thanking Scattergood, Clarke turned to Fletcher once more. 'I've got a little job for you tomorrow, Detective Sergeant,' he said with a satisfied grin on his face.

At first Fletcher had premonitions of being sent on a wild goose chase or that she might be sidelined again. 'What might that be, Sir?'

'Let's just say that it involves an arrest!'

Perhaps she had been wrong to think ill of him. Perhaps now might be the time to give him the benefit of the doubt!

Chapter 35

Thursday, 13 July, 2017 (a.m.)

Christopher Ibbotson was feeling reasonably pleased with himself as he took another bite out of his toast and marmalade. Even the fact that it was an overcast start to the day did little to diminish his sense of well-being and general contentment, although it has to be said that the wind had dropped considerably overnight.

Looking out of the kitchen window he couldn't help but smile to himself. It had been six years since he had left his London town house and bought the large period detached house worth £325,000 on Thraplow Lane, Brockley, and perhaps he could be forgiven for thinking that he was now master of all he surveyed.

It all seemed a far cry from the day in 1976 when he entered Cambridge University as an undergraduate in the History of Art. There followed a PhD in the same subject in 1982, and then four years as a Teaching Fellow at the University of Edinburgh. And then in 1986 he joined Sotheby's, firstly as a course leader, then as a programme co-ordinator and finally as the Director of Master of Art Programmes. He was with Sotheby's for eighteen years, and then in 2004 he set himself up as an art dealer and antiques expert in London. So it came as something of a surprise to his friends when in 2011 he inexplicably sold his business and moved to Derbyshire, buying the property at Brockley and opening an antique's shop in Derby. However, the move did come with its advantages.

Within the space of six years he had become head of the parish council *and* captain of the village cricket team; he wouldn't have been able to have achieved that back in the capital! He put it all down to his background and education, although competitiveness and a will to succeed undoubtedly played a part, enabling him to become emotionally detached when necessary. Furthermore, his experience in the world of antiques taught him to be decisive, cool and calm under pressure, not to mention mindful and alert. And yet all was not what it seemed.

The business wasn't going anywhere near as well as he would have liked for starters. He had been prepared to take calculated risks throughout his career, and this at times led him to misuse his power to further himself financially. In other words, he had allowed himself to be taken advantage of – for the right price. And yet throughout it all he had never allowed himself to be duped, which was the one thing that he feared above all else.

Having finished his toast and marmalade, he made his final preparations before proceeding to work. Teeth were cleaned, shoes were brushed and bow tie straightened before he donned his tweed jacket, picked up his briefcase and left the building. He had just locked the door behind him and was heading for his Range Rover when he looked up to see a procession of vehicles coming along the driveway towards him. As the lead car pulled up alongside, he was mortified to see Clarke step out from the passenger seat in his bomber jacket and tie, looking like the cat that got the cream.

'Christopher Brian Ibbotson,' said Clarke firmly. 'I have here a warrant to search your property, because I have reason to believe that you are guilty of handling stolen goods!'

'This is preposterous,' protested a stunned-looking Ibbotson, but having produced the warrant Clarke ignored him and ordered him to open up the house to his men. As he grudgingly complied with Clarke's order, uniformed officers poured into the house to conduct their search.

'In you go lads,' shouted Clarke.

Ibbotson followed the men inside at first, but then stepped back outside and tried to reason with Clarke. 'Look, surely there's been some mistake or misunderstanding?' he implored.

But Clarke ignored him again and then cast his eyes around the exterior of the building. On the far side of the house there appeared to be a large garage which was padlocked. 'What's in there?' he said nodding over towards it.

'It's…it's…my workshop,' said Ibbotson unconvincingly.

Doubt if you know the difference between a tenon saw and a handsaw, thought Clarke, as he strode purposefully towards the garage with a uniformed officer and Ibbotson following behind them, the gravel crunching beneath their feet.

'Key, please, Mr. Ibbotson,' he asked as they reached the garage door.

'But…'

'Key, please – now,' demanded Clarke with some vehemence!

Ibbotson sighed heavily before placing his hand inside his right-hand trouser pocket and dutifully producing a set of keys.

Clarke selected the smallest of the set and tried the padlock – it worked. He dragged the garage doors open, and as he stepped inside it soon became clear that it was no ordinary garage unit. It was a storage facility; and judging by the temperature a climate-controlled storage facility. Down the right-hand side and to the rear there were wooden storage units – some rectangular and some square-shaped. All were draped with blankets or covers of some kind. Whilst on the left-hand side of the garage there were pallets, on top of which appeared to be furniture; these too were draped with covers. Clarke went over to these first. Pulling back the covers he whistled softly to himself.

'What have we here then?' he said turning to Ibbotson and pointing to a beautifully manufactured velvet-covered set of chairs wrapped in plastic. 'Chippendale perhaps? Maybe Sheraton? Or Hepplewhite, by any chance?'

The latter shrugged. 'I'm an antiques dealer and I have a shop – there's not enough room to store everything there, so I keep the excess here.'

'I wonder,' replied Clarke dubiously. 'It may interest you to know that some of my officers are searching your shop as we speak and…'

'How dare you,' snapped Ibbotson!

'And *if* – as I strongly suspect – they find that your business is failing, then you've got some explaining to do,' continued Clarke with considerable authority.

Clarke continued along the left-hand side of the garage and pulled the covers back to reveal tables, cabinets and other valuable items of furniture. He then did the same along the rear of the garage and down the right-hand side, discovering a wooden box lined with cotton cloth and containing porcelain, and a watertight box containing rare first editions, such as *The Wind in the Willows* and *On the Origin of the Species*, amongst others. It was the last box that truly astonished Clarke, as it was full of valuable paintings, all of which had been carefully wrapped. The two policemen and Ibbotson eventually stepped outside of the garage, and Clarke turned to the latter.

'You know what I think, Mr. Ibbotson?' he said calmly but with a degree of perspicacity. 'I think that you were planning to sell all of these online. What's more, I shouldn't be surprised if you were planning to sell them to collectors – particularly those from the other side of the pond?'

Ibbotson finally seemed to realise that he'd been rumbled, but said nothing. As they headed back towards the house another police constable came striding towards them with what appeared to be a large painting.

'This was hanging above the mantelpiece, Sir,' said the constable, barely able to contain his excitement. 'Is this the kind of thing we're looking for?'

Ibbotson reacted as though he was about to go into an apoplectic seizure. 'Don't damage that, for Christ's sake,' he screamed.

'Why would that be, Mr. Ibbotson?' taunted Clarke.

Ibbotson was still frozen to the spot. 'It's a Sisley,' he said wide-eyed and with what he considered to be some authority.

Not especially *au fait* with the great Impressionists, Clarke continued to taunt Ibbotson. 'Worth a bit then, is it?' Before the latter could reply, Clarke turned once again to the police constable with the painting. 'Just make sure it gets back to the station in one piece lad. Oh and when you've done that, seize the gentleman's laptop – I think we'll find more incriminating evidence on there.'

'Yes, Sir,' said the constable with a smile from ear to ear.

Clarke turned once more to the by now crestfallen antique's dealer. 'Christopher Brian Ibbotson,' he began. 'I am arresting you on suspicion of handling stolen goods, in relation to Section 26 of the Theft Act of 1968.'

As Ibbotson was being led to a waiting police car, John Sheldon was preparing to set off for work from his semi-detached home just up the road, in the neighbouring village of Thraplow. He was due to conduct a preliminary inspection of a potential client's property up at Lamleydale, in the Peak District, ostensibly with a view to providing a quote for the installation of CCTV camera's and an alarm system. Just as he was about to climb into his van, two police cars arrived on the scene and prevented him from driving off. Two uniformed officers jumped out of the first vehicle and pinned him to the side of his van.

'What the fuck,' he growled menacingly.

Sergeant Fletcher then appeared. 'John Sheldon?' she shouted triumphantly. 'I'm arresting you on suspicion of burglary.'

As he was led away snarling and spitting into one of the waiting police vehicles, Angela Radford came storming out of the house. 'Where are you taking him,' she screamed. 'Leave him alone – he's done nothing wrong!'

'That will be for a court to decide, madam,' said Fletcher as she attempted to restrain the woman.

Clarke *would* be pleased with her now – wouldn't he?

Chapter 36

Thursday, 13 July, 2017 (a.m.)

As it approached noon on Thursday, 13 July, Leverton police station was a veritable hive of activity. By the time Clarke arrived, Interview Room 1 had already been taken up by Sergeant Fletcher, who was busy questioning John Sheldon in the presence of a duty solicitor. This was apparently a matter of some disappointment to Christopher Ibbotson's lawyer, Rupert Frankland-Moore, who swaggered into the station in the expectation of crossing swords with the attractive female officer once more, but whose demeanour suddenly became somewhat lugubrious when it transpired that his client was going to be questioned by Detective Chief Inspector Clarke.

Indeed, it was a rather subdued-looking Frankland-Moore who was directed into Interview Room 2, to be given some time with his client. Eventually, however, they were joined by a clearly more upbeat-looking Clarke, especially when he saw the smartly-dressed, ginger-haired solicitor sitting alongside the erstwhile antique dealer.

'What a surprise to see you here again, Mr. Frankland-Moore,' said Clarke cheerfully as he removed his jacket and hung it up behind the door. 'I can see by the look on your face that you were expecting my colleague, Sergeant Fletcher. I'm so sorry to disappoint you, but she is otherwise engaged – with your client's partner in crime!'

Frankland-Moore merely responded to Clarke's derisive joviality with a sneer, but as the latter glanced at the two men before him he would have been prepared to swear that they had been engaged in a vociferous argument beforehand. One thing was for sure – Ibbotson was not a happy chappie!

Having carried out the preliminary aspects of the interview, Clarke then proceeded with his questioning.

'You understand why you've been brought here today?' he began. Ibbotson shrugged and Clarke continued. 'You have been brought in for questioning on suspicion of handling stolen goods.'

Frankland-Moore butted in. 'My client wishes it to be known that he was only involved through the intimidation of a second party and that he was not motivated by personal gain. Furthermore…'

Clarke cut him off. 'That more than one individual was involved is beyond question,' he retorted sharply. 'It is for us to determine whether or not he was intimidated or coerced by others. And if he wasn't motivated by personal gain, then what was the painting by...' He turned to Ibbotson. 'What was his name?' he asked politely.

'Sisley,' replied Ibbotson imperiously. 'Alfred Sisley.'

'Thank you, Mr. Ibbotson,' said Clarke graciously. 'As I was saying, what was the painting by Alfred Sisley doing hanging above the mantelpiece in the living room?'

Frankland-Moore ignored that question and continued. 'Furthermore, my client wishes it to be known that he played only a peripheral role in this affair and that he had limited awareness of the extent of any fraudulent activity.'

Clarke wasn't impressed. 'Limited awareness my arse,' he scoffed! 'This "affair" clearly involved significant planning, and whoever played the leading role must have been well-educated and someone with a vast knowledge of antiques.'

Frankland-Moore attempted to go on. 'It was an opportunistic and...'

Clarke cut him off again. 'Mr. Frankland-Moore,' he bellowed! 'Would you *please* stop interrupting and allow me to question your client?'

The solicitor sank back into his chair and grudgingly acceded to Clarke's demand. The latter then shuffled through several papers and documents in front of him before proceeding with the interview.

'As I suggested earlier,' said Clarke shifting his gaze from Frankland-Moore to Ibbotson, 'we have reason to believe that your business had been going through some financial difficulties. Is that true?' Ibbotson seemed loathe to answer the question, so Clarke continued. 'Your bank will no doubt tell us all we need to know in that regard, Mr. Ibbotson, so you might as well tell us sooner rather than later.'

The ploy seemed to work. 'Yes, if you must know,' replied Ibbotson through gritted teeth. 'I was forced to take out a loan – the people of Derby don't appear to appreciate works of art or collect items of great antiquity,' he sneered.

'And you struggled to pay back the loan?' Ibbotson simply shrugged in response to the question. 'So when did you come up with the idea for your great scam?' continued Clarke.

Frankland-Moore stepped in again. 'This "scam" – as you call it – was the brainwave of John Sheldon, and *not* my client,' he said disdainfully.

'Oh, please don't insult *my* intelligence,' scoffed Clarke once more.

There was a few seconds of silence before Clarke went through his papers again and brought up the subject of Sheldon's criminal past.

'This man Sheldon has a record for petty burglary *and* actual bodily harm,' he said without looking up. He then raised his eyes and shot quick glances at the two men before him. 'He wouldn't know a Rembrandt from a Warhol, so he's hardly the kind of guy to formulate and instigate such an intricate enterprise as this, is he?' There was no reply from either Ibbotson or Frankland-Moore, so Clarke continued. 'And I still find it ironic that a man with *his* record was able to set himself up installing security and alarm systems – but that's what gave you your idea, wasn't it Mr. Ibbotson?'

Again there was no response from across the table, but Clarke was clearly gaining in confidence has the interview progressed.

'It was either at the cricket club or at the pub – probably the latter – when you first approached Sheldon,' he said as if in deep thought. 'And of course he went along with it, didn't he?'

Ibbotson turned to Frankland-Moore and whispered something in his ear. The latter shook his head, but then turned away in exasperation as it became clear to him that his client was going to open up.

'I persuaded Sheldon to target potential wealthy clients,' admitted Ibbotson frankly.

'This would be throughout the East Midlands region I take it?'

'And beyond,' replied Ibbotson. 'He would case the joint (Clarke cringed at the very mention of the phrase) on his first visit, take photographs of possible artefacts and send them to me for analysis. If I considered them to be valuable I would give him the go-ahead to install the security and alarm systems, and then he would carry out the burglary at a later date – having disabled the systems beforehand.'

'Very clever indeed,' confessed Clarke.

'The items would be stored in my garage, and of course Sheldon would get a cut of the proceeds if and when they were sold.'

'This must have been going on for some time judging by the number of items in your garage?' Ibbotson merely nodded and so Clarke continued. 'Did you ever sell any of the stolen items from the shop?'

'That would have been *too* risky!'

'And yet you were willing to put the buggers up for auction – as I saw for myself!' said Clarke with undisguised scorn. 'Surely that was downright bloody stupid!'

This time it was Ibbotson who cringed. 'That was Sheldon,' he replied uncomfortably. 'He was getting agitated because he hadn't had his share of the proceeds for some time. He actually threatened me if I didn't do something quick. And so I decided to gamble on putting the painting up for auction.'

Clarke shook his head, if only in bewilderment. 'But it was online that you conducted most of your business, wasn't it?'

'Our American friends are *always* willing to cough up copious amounts for items of quality and value; even if those items have been – shall we say – purloined.'

Clarke smiled ruefully. 'And yet it would appear that Sheldon was "purloining" the items faster than you could get rid of them!' Again, a shrug of the shoulders was all that Ibbotson could muster.

Clarke then decided to turn to the murder of Keith Jackson and was surprised that Frankland-Moore made no attempt to intercede on behalf of his client.

'Let's digress, shall we?' said Clarke deftly. 'Let's talk about Keith Jackson some more.' Ibbotson looked up to the ceiling and sighed heavily. 'You've already admitted that Jackson did some gardening work for you. That's right, isn't it?'

'What if he did?' replied Ibbotson with a degree of irritation.

'Did he find out about your scam?' Ibbotson now looked Clarke straight in the eyes, but he made no attempt to answer the question. 'Is that a yes or a no, Mr. Ibbotson?' demanded Clarke.

'No, he did not,' snapped Ibbotson!

As the pair continued to glare at each other, Clarke's eyes suddenly lit up and he leaned forward. 'No, he didn't, did he?' he said somewhat smugly. 'He wasn't blackmailing you about the scam; it was that bloody painting by Sibley!'

'How many times do I have to tell you?' bellowed Ibbotson. 'It's Sisley – Alfred bloody Sisley!'

'That was "purloined" too it would appear!'

'To have in my possession a painting by one of the foremost artists of the Impressionist movement was something that was beyond my wildest dreams,' admitted Ibbotson. 'I simply had to have it.'

'And it's been authenticated?' asked Clarke.

'*I* authenticated myself,' was Ibbotson's conceited reply!

'So tell me, Mr. Ibbotson. How *did* all this lead to blackmail?'

Ibbotson sighed heavily again and then proceeded to reveal all. 'It was back in March of this year,' he began.

'Go on, I'm all ears,' said Clarke attempting to hide his impatience.

'Jackson came to do some work for me. I was upstairs in my little office when I heard a noise, so I immediately went downstairs to investigate. When I entered the living room there was Jackson looking up at the painting. I'd made it abundantly clear that he wasn't to come inside the house under any circumstances.'

'I dare say he took no notice?' said Clarke.

Ibbotson nodded and continued. 'When I asked him what he was doing there he pointed to the painting and said that he'd seen it before. He then went on to say that he used to do some gardening for this wealthy chap at Grinsleydale Hall, up in the Peak District. Know where I mean, Inspector?'

'Yes, I know the place,' replied Clarke somewhat wearily.

'Apparently this chap was forever going on about how his father had been part of the occupying forces just after the end of the war, and that he and his mates had come across stolen Nazi loot.'

'And they decided to help themselves I suppose?'

'The chap's father managed to smuggle the painting back home to England without anyone knowing, and now it was pride of place in the living room. Would he – Jackson – care to see it? And so of course Jackson went along with him.'

'And how did you come by it exactly, Mr. Ibbotson?'

Clearly enjoying this part of the questioning, Ibbotson continued. 'Well, one day Sheldon showed me some photographs that he'd taken whilst visiting a potential client, and among them was a photograph of this painting. I recognised it as a Sisley immediately, so I gave Sheldon the go ahead to break into the property and steal the painting, which he duly did. Jackson evidently recognised it and knew where it had come from.'

'Did he ask you how you came about it?'

'No, but I think he had a good idea.'

'And you decided to keep this one for yourself and not flog it like the others?'

'As I told you before, Inspector, there are two loves in my life and one of them is the work of the Impressionists,' Ibbotson stressed in his pompous and pretentious manner. 'Numerous works by Sisley were known to have been seized by the Nazi's and have still not been found. This was one of them and it is absolutely priceless!'

'And you're certain it's genuine?'

'I haven't spent a lifetime studying the Impressionists and not knowing a Sisley when I see one!'

Clarke hadn't spent a lifetime studying human nature and not knowing a snob when he saw one, but Ibbotson surpassed himself in that regard! Nevertheless, the questioning continued.

'So, Jackson knew of your little secret and that's why he took to blackmailing you?'

'Yes, it was a trifling amount admittedly – and always on the same date every month. I had to put the money in an envelope, go around to his place and simply put it through his letterbox.'

'No doubt your little scam suffered as a result?'

'Let's just say I decided to put it on hold. Sheldon wasn't happy about that – we disagreed – but I was adamant.'

'So with Jackson out of the way, you would be able to resume the enterprise?' inferred Clarke. There was no response, merely the shrug of the shoulders once more. And then Clarke suddenly leaned forward again. 'Is that why you killed him, Mr. Ibbotson?'

Ibbotson was clearly taken aback. 'I didn't kill the man,' he spluttered.

'Or did you get John Sheldon to do the job for you?'

'What arrant nonsense,' scoffed Ibbotson!

Suddenly Frankland-Moore sprang to life. 'Where is your evidence for this, Inspector?' he snapped. 'I was led to believe that you were merely charging my client with handling stolen goods?'

'And so I am, Sir,' replied Clarke without looking at the solicitor. 'So I am!'

To the surprise of both Ibbotson and Frankland-Moore, Clarke then abruptly ended the questioning, and rising from his chair he duly charged Ibbotson with the handling of stolen goods – but nothing more. As Ibbotson was led out of the room, Frankland-Moore again pressed Clarke for evidence that his client had also committed murder.

'You haven't got a shred of evidence, have you?' gloated the solicitor.

'Let's just say I don't like playing cat and mouse games, Mr. Frankland-Moore!'

With that Clarke grabbed his coat and made his way out of the room, leaving the solicitor with a puzzled look on his face. Waiting for him at the reception desk was Fletcher, who had concluded her questioning of John Sheldon some twenty minutes previously. Webster was also there, having arrived at the station five minutes earlier. As he passed the group of detectives on his way out of the building, Frankland-Moore's swagger seemed to return on seeing Fletcher, but she blushed slightly before turning her head away. Clarke watched as the solicitor headed for his car, and then suddenly broke the silence.

'I've charged Ibbotson with handling stolen goods,' he said with his gaze still fixed on Frankland-Moore.

Fletcher attempted to butt in. 'But, Sir…'

Clarke turned to her and put his hand up as if to give her his assurance. 'He's denied killing Jackson, but now he's in custody we'll have more time to grill him on that score, Sergeant.'

There was silence for a few seconds as the three detectives seemed to be lost in thought. Again, it was Clarke who broke the silence.

'Webster?' he said without looking at the man. 'Find me the country's foremost authority on The Impressionists – with the exception of Christopher Brian Ibbotson!'

Chapter 37

Thursday, 13 July, 2017 (p.m.)

What a twenty-four hours! Three arrests – and yet the police *still* seemed no nearer to finding out who killed Keith Jackson!

The landlord of *The Wheatsheaf* had tried to top his wife; but Clarke had ruled him out of the murder of Jackson. He had charged Christopher Ibbotson with handling stolen goods, but although he had attempted to get the antiques dealer and soon-to-be erstwhile head of Brockley Parish Council to admit to having committed a graver crime, he hadn't got an ounce of evidence to prove it.

John Sheldon was evidently a tougher nut to crack, and yet although Fletcher *still* had him down as her prime suspect, Clarke couldn't be certain that he played a part in Jackson's murder either.

After she had finished questioning Sheldon, Fletcher had hung around the reception desk at Leverton Police Station waiting for Clarke to emerge from Interview Room 2. She had been joined by Constable Webster, but he had been sent on an errand shortly after Clarke had concluded his questioning of Christopher Ibbotson. To Fletcher's gratification and relief, it appeared that the truce between her and Clarke was holding, as he invited her into his office nearby and asked her to brief him on her questioning of Sheldon.

As she followed him into his office, she became aware of the series of posters adorning the wall to her left, all of which depicted well known figures and artists from the sixties and seventies music scene – Pink Floyd, Eric Clapton, The Who, The Eagles, Led Zeppelin, Santana, Yes, Free and others. Although music wasn't one of *her* great passions, it clearly played a major role in Clarke's life, and she scanned each of the posters with apparent interest.

'Quite a collection, Sir,' she said with her eyes fixed upon a poster of Led Zeppelin performing live at Earl's Court in May 1975.

Clarke's mind was elsewhere. 'What?' he said as if startled. 'Oh yes, my homage to what I call the Golden Age of music.'

'Have you actually seen any of them live?'

He threw his coat around his chair and then sat back with a look on his face that can only be described as pride. 'Some of them,' he gloated. 'Pink Floyd, Zep, Clapton, The Who, The Eagles.'

She turned to face him. 'And do you play any instruments yourself?'

'I have an acoustic guitar somewhere knocking about,' he said as Fletcher pulled up another chair and seated herself at the desk before him. 'But I don't play as often as I used to.' He then looked her in the eyes. 'Do you like music, Sergeant?'

Fletcher shrugged her shoulders. 'I can take it or leave it, Sir.'

'Music gives a soul to the universe, wings to the mind, flight to the imagination and life to everything.'

Fletcher's academic skills didn't stretch to the works of Plato, so for a few minutes it was as if the murder of Keith Jackson had been all but forgotten. But then she reminded Clarke why she was there.

'Erm, you wanted to know about my interview with John Sheldon, Sir?'

'Quite right, Sergeant,' he said as he crossed his legs and rested his left elbow on the arm of his chair. 'Quite right – please carry on.'

'To start with I reminded him of his previous convictions,' she began. 'As for his role in the affair with Christopher Ibbotson and the theft of valuable antiques, all he would say to every question was "No comment".'

'What a surprise,' said Clarke with a touch of sarcasm! 'Go on, Sergeant.'

'However, when I put it to him that he may have been involved in the murder of Keith Jackson, it was a different matter altogether.'

'Don't tell me,' interjected Clarke. 'He got a trifle agitated. Am I right?'

Fletcher nodded. 'To put it mildly he flipped and had to be restrained, Sir.'

Clarke leaned forward with an anxious look on his face. 'I do hope that you weren't hurt in any way?'

Fletcher was pleasantly surprised and mollified by Clarke's apparent concern for her well-being. 'Not at all, Sir. Besides, I can handle myself in such situations.'

Clarke sank back into his chair somewhat relieved by Fletcher's response. 'He denied killing Jackson of course?'

'He vociferously denied *any* involvement in the murder of Jackson, Sir; either for his own gratification or in conjunction with someone else.'

'Just as I expected.'

'He claims to have an alibi, Sir.'

'I dare say he does.'

'He claims to have been at a warehouse in Mansfield at the time, but we've checked and they say he left around 3.30 p.m. or thereabouts.'

'Could he have got to Brockley by 4.00 p.m. do you think?'

'*I* think so – if he put his foot down.'

Clarke shook his head. 'Nah, I just don't buy it!'

'But, Sir…'

'Where did he go after leaving Mansfield?'

'He went to visit a prospective client in Derby – he says.'

'No doubt with a view to "purloining" some of the contents of the house at a later date!'

'Pardon Sir?'

Clarke went on to provide Fletcher with a breakdown of his interview with Ibbotson, including details of how the scam was supposed to work and Sheldon's part in it.

'So you see the idea was Ibbotson's and so was the planning,' affirmed Clarke. 'But he didn't want to get his hands dirty – that's where Sheldon came in,'

'I suppose that Ibbotson's mistake was arranging for Jackson to do the gardening,' said Fletcher pensively.

'And yet he wasn't to know that Jackson would enter the house, recognise the painting by Sidley *and* where it came from.'

'It's Sisley, Sir.' Fletcher pointed out with some authority.

'What?'

'The painter – his name was Alfred Sisley,'

'Sisley or Sidley – does it matter?' Clarke was becoming irritated and so he turned his attention to Sheldon once more. 'What time did he arrive at the pub?'

'About 5.15 p.m.'

'You confiscated his mobile, I take it?'

'They're looking at it now…' Fletcher was determined to have her say. 'Look, Sir. Sheldon is capable of violence – we know that from his record and he would have attacked me earlier had he not been restrained. I still believe that he's our prime suspect for the murder of Keith Jackson.'

A week earlier Clarke would have jumped down her throat, but now he was prepared to hear her out; only he just couldn't agree with what she had to say.

'I understand where you're coming from, Fletcher,' he said somewhat benignly. 'But it just won't wash. We're looking for someone who went to Cambridge University…'

'*Ibbotson* went to Cambridge – we know that,' she stressed with some frustration. 'But I believe Sheldon carried out the killing on his behalf.'

'Then what about the badge, Sergeant?' Clarke reminded her. 'I hardly think that Sheldon was ever a member of the *Tom and Jerry Club*!'

Fletcher was getting exasperated. 'But what if Ibbotson planted the badge on Sheldon when he asked him to carry out the murder?' she implored.

Clarke was no longer listening. 'DNA results won't be available for at least forty-eight hours or so, but I think they'll prove conclusively that Sheldon wasn't at the scene of the crime on the day in question. As for Ibbotson...'

At that point Clarke's mobile phone sprang to life with the introduction of *Time* from Pink Floyd's *Dark Side of the Moon* album.

'Shit,' he muttered, before mouthing the word "Annable" to Fletcher, who looked up at the ceiling and yet remained seated! He then proceeded to answer the call with a cheerful 'Hello, Sir.'

Annable was evidently over at Division, where everyone had heard about the arrests and were absolutely delighted. Clarke clearly had difficulty getting a word in, but he tried.

'Yes, Sir. Thank you, Sir, but...' He tried again. 'That's very kind of you, Sir, but...'

It was Clarke's turn to look up at the ceiling as he waited until Annable had finished heaping praise upon him and his team.

Then he dropped his bombshell, as he was finally able to point out that none of those arrested had as yet been charged with the murder of Keith Jackson. He knew what was coming. He held the phone away from his ear at arms length as Annable blew a veritable fuse.

'Yes, Sir, I understand, but...' He had little option but to let Annable finish his tirade. 'Yes, Sir, at the end of the day we do indeed need results,' he intoned whilst looking up at Fletcher, who was struggling to suppress her mirth. 'Yes, Sir, I will indeed. Thank you, Sir,' he said with some relief as the conversation came to an end.

Fletcher was still barely able to conceal her laughter. 'I take it the Superintendent wasn't pleased, Sir?

'I don't know about you Sergeant, but I could do with a drink,' was Clarke's almost wistful reply. 'Care to join me?'

'Why not, Sir.'

As the pair rose from their seats, Clarke grabbed his jacket and made for the door, and then stood back courteously as if to allow Fletcher to exit the room before him. As he did so, he suddenly froze.

'Damn,' he said with gritted teeth!

'Anything wrong, Sir?' asked Fletcher anxiously.

'I forgot,' was his abrupt reply.

'Forgot what?'

Clarke realised he was in a tricky situation. 'Erm...I've got an appointment – later this evening.'

Fletcher seemed to sense some discomfort on the part of her boss. 'An appointment? What kind of appointment?'

Clarke realised it was better to come clean. 'If you must know, Sergeant, I've arranged to go on a date.'

And with that he parted company with Fletcher, who was left staring open-mouthed, and if truth were known somewhat incredulous that someone she had come to regard as a misogynist would find it in his heart to ask a woman out for a date!

On the second Thursday of every month, the Brockley Women's Institute held their monthly meeting at the local primary school, which lay between the Hall and Gold Crescent. Although membership had fallen in recent years, they were still able to boast a sizeable gathering and that certainly seemed to be the case as the women came together shortly before 7.00 p.m.

Needless to say, there was plenty to talk about – what with the events at *The Wheatsheaf* and those along Thraplow Lane – and predictably Vera Hartley was at the forefront of all the gossip.

Always among the first to arrive at the monthly meetings, she had scarcely removed her hat and coat before she was telling everyone how she had seen the police removing artefacts from Mr. Ibbotson's house.

'What she was doin' up there is anyone's guess,' whispered one of the women to another.

'Bugger's always shovin' her nose in where it's not wanted,' was the barely audible reply.

Someone then brought up the subject of Tony and Sally Dawkins, and Vera literally bristled with indignation.

'Well, I always said that there would be trouble with those two,' she scoffed. 'He didn't like work for one thing. And as for her...'

'What do you mean?' asked the vicar's wife, Rosalind Cox.

'Common as muck,' replied Vera with a sneer.

Unaccustomed to such derogatory put-downs, Mrs. Cox attempted to change the subject. 'I wonder who will replace Mr. Ibbotson now that he's – well – no longer head of the parish council.'

'More than likely him up at the Hall,' hinted another woman.

Vera saw an opportunity to voice her opinion once more. 'Well, like I said to Mrs. Briggs in the post office earlier, Mr. Frankland-Moore will no doubt have too much on his hands.'

'Yes, and if I know him it won't have anything to do with the law or cricket,' was the sarcastic reply of the woman who did the whispering earlier, reducing the other women into fits of giggles.

Not so Vera Hartley, whose face became as black as thunder as it dawned on her that the other women clearly knew something that she didn't!

Chapter 38

Thursday, 13 July, 2017 (p.m.)

There were still a few clouds about as Clarke pulled up outside the *Horse and Jockey* at Manningley, but at least it was a warm and dry evening. He hadn't been there for some years, and it was certainly long before the fire that destroyed the greater part of the pub. That was about five years ago, but it had since been refurbished and was now a very popular venue with those looking for a decent meal and a cracking pint of ale. Indeed, it was now recognised across the East Midlands as a popular gastro pub, and the beer was that good it had received the Cask Marque seal of approval.

The village of Manningley lay roughly five miles to the north of Grimley. Coal had been mined in the parish since the thirteenth century and granted, it wasn't one of the most picturesque of rural communities. Evidence of its past connection with the coal mining industry was still prevalent, particularly with regard to some of the housing, but the old terraced buildings were gradually being pulled down and replaced by more modern (and affordable, if the developers were to be believed) structures. Farming had always played an important role in the community too, and there were still three or four outlying farms in the area.

Apart from the *Horse and Jockey* there was one other pub in the village, namely the *Jolly Colliers*, which boasted live music at the weekends and Sky Sports almost every day. It was the more popular of the two pubs with the locals, but it was the *Horse and Jockey* that proved to be the greater attraction, particularly since its refurbishment, and it was here that Clarke had arrived shortly before 7.00 p.m. as arranged.

Punctuality was undeniably one of his stronger points, but he was still wondering whether or not he'd made the right decision to accept Maria's invitation when he saw the navy blue Fiat 600 turn into the car park and pull up forty or fifty yards away. Too late to back out now, he told himself. And so climbing out of the silver Ford Focus in his navy blue blazer, white granddad shirt and grey slacks, he locked the doors behind him and proceeded to make his way over to her. He'd selected a pair of black slip-on shoes at the last minute, but felt a trifle

218

embarrassed as he hadn't had the time to polish them. At least he'd trimmed his beard and had a shave – of sorts!

'Have you been waiting long?' she asked him as she stepped out of her car.

'I've just got here myself,' he replied somewhat nervously.

'You look very smart,' she said looking him up and down.

He still seemed uncomfortable and lacking in confidence. 'I wouldn't go that far,' he said with a brief smirk and hoping that she hadn't noticed his unpolished shoes.

'But you *do* look nice.'

It was a genuine compliment, and although she blushed slightly Maria recognised it as such. 'Thank you,' she said as the gentle breeze caught her neatly coiffed mousy-coloured hair and feathery fringe.

She had elected to wear a short-sleeved cerise jacket over a cream-coloured blouse, but she too turned up in grey slacks. She was never one to wear high heels as she found them utterly uncomfortable, so she opted for a pair of black low-heeled slip-on shoes, and they complimented the rest of her attire admirably.

'Shall we go inside?' asked Clarke tentatively. And with that they entered the pub and were shown to their table.

They were seated in a secluded alcove facing the bar, although Maria sat with her back to a small window that provided Clarke with excellent views across the fields outside and beyond. As they took their seats Clarke ordered a half of "Proper Job", which was a powerful pale ale at 4.5%, whereas Maria settled for a glass of red wine. Little was said whilst the menu was scanned, but Maria quickly plumped for the Super Green Salad with Char-grilled chicken. Clarke always had difficulty making his mind up at times like this, and it took him another three or four minutes before he finally settled for the Slow-cooked Beef & porcini Bourguignon.

'Could I have roast potatoes instead of the mash, please?' he pleaded with the waitress, who scribbled down his request before departing.

As they waited for their food to arrive, the couple seemed at a loss as to what to say. Clarke wasn't a "people-watcher", so he cast his eyes around and began to admire the décor. Maria seemed to notice this and suddenly broke the ice.

'They've done a good job, don't you think?' she asked.

'I'm sorry?' he replied as if he were coming out of a spell.

'The refurbishment – they've done a good job.'

'Oh yes, it's nothing like it used to be.' Several more seconds elapsed before Clarke spoke again. 'So, what did you do when you left school?'

At last we have lift off, she thought to herself. 'I trained to become a nurse,' she replied quite openly. 'But then I got married in 1987 and went to live in Derby.'

'But the marriage didn't work out I take it?'

'No, it didn't.'

'And there were two boys you said?'

'That's right – Stephen and Andrew.'

Clarke seemed to sense that she was holding something back. 'And they live with you?' he asked gingerly.

'No, they live with their father.'

'I see,' he replied unseeing. 'It's just that…'

She cut him short. 'Ours was not a conventional marriage,' she confessed with trembling lips. 'On the contrary, ours was…' She paused, coughed slightly and then continued. 'Start again. Colin was – and is – a very brutal man.'

Clarke listened intently as she went on to describe her former husband, Colin Nixon, as a violent, abusive control freak, who didn't want her to return to work after she'd had the children. The entire experience left her wounded and scarred – both mentally and physically. Indeed, she attempted suicide on one occasion. She eventually left her husband *and* children in 2008 and sought psychiatric help. Her divorce came through in 2011, so she reverted to her maiden name of Bukowski and moved to rented accommodation in Grimley. She found work at a care home in Nottingham a year or so later, and moved to the Little Orchard Care Home at Brockley in 2015.

Clarke was genuinely distressed by Maria's revelations. 'I'm so sorry to hear this. My heart goes out to you.'

'I haven't seen the boys for a number of years,' she said as if she hadn't heard his response. 'They take after their father.'

At that moment the waitress came over with their food, and although the couple continued to chat, nothing more was said about Maria's marriage.

It was still light by the time that Clarke and Maria finished their meal, and so having ordered another red wine for her and a Diet Coke for himself, the couple ventured out into the beer garden at the rear of the pub and seated themselves at one of the few empty tables remaining.

Others had followed their example and elected to sit outside too, but to Clarke's immense relief there were no screaming kids running around and creating havoc! However, childhood was very much on Maria's mind as she pressed him about his nickname at school.

'There's something I've always wanted to know,' she began. 'Why *did* the others always refer to you as "Sniffer"?'

Clarke had been expecting this all along, but he reluctantly obliged. 'There was this footballer by the name of Allan Clarke, who back then played for Leeds United and England,' he sighed. 'However, he had the nickname "Sniffer", apparently because of his predatory instincts in front of goal.'

Maria was puzzled. 'I don't follow you. What do you mean?'

'If there was even the remotest goal scoring opportunity, he – Clarke – would "sniff" it out.'

'Oh, I see,' said Maria unconvincingly. 'Did it bother you – the nickname?'

'Not really,' he replied honestly. 'But my mum wouldn't have liked it.'

'Why is that?'

'Because I was named "Allan" after Allan Clarke, the lead singer of The Hollies – my mum's favourite band!'

The comment caused momentary merriment, but Maria was determined to find out more about the man sitting beside her, so she broke off the laughter and came up with yet another question.

'What did you do after leaving junior school,' she asked abruptly.

To her surprise and curiosity he skipped his time at Grammar School. 'I joined the police straight after leaving school,' he revealed rather tentatively.

Not wishing to press him about his Grammar School days for the moment, she asked him why he joined the police. 'I had you down as a prospective teacher or author,' she suggested.

Clarke was flabbergasted. 'Me – a teacher?' he scoffed. 'No, I joined the police because... well... I had this thing about wanting to see justice done.'

Sensing that he had something of a chip on his shoulder, Maria returned to the subject of his time at Grammar School.

'Were you bullied at school?'

His head went down and he nodded. Without going into any detail his reply was short and to the point. 'I had three years of it – until I finally snapped.'

Maria deemed it appropriate to leave it at that and then went on to ask him about his marriage. Again, he was reluctant to talk about something that was clearly still a sore point, but he went on to describe how his wife let him down by having an affair, and that he had been the one to eventually walk out of the marriage.

'I left just about everything, but I made damn sure that I took my collection of Pink Floyd LP's and CD's,' he stressed vigorously and yet a trifle tongue in cheek.

Maria smiled. 'And there's been nobody else since?' she asked hesitantly.

To which Clarke shook his head. 'No,' he replied, conveniently neglecting the affair with Carol Vaughan in 2009!

Maria then turned to the subject of what was in his shopping trolley when they bumped into each other at the supermarket the previous Sunday, but all he could do was boast about his culinary capabilities.

'I meant the bottle of whisky, as you are well aware,' she said poking him in the arm with her finger.

He admitted that he did hit the bottle after his marriage broke up. 'It's been my closest friend, but I never let it affect my work.'

'Alcohol is never a friend,' she replied with some authority. 'I've been there.'

Clarke then tried to change the subject. 'And where is it that you live?'

'I told you,' she replied. 'I've been at Grimley for the last five or six years.

'So you did, so you did,' he repeated.

'What about you?' she asked. 'I can imagine you in a little cottage somewhere in the countryside.'

'Actually I live on a narrow boat on the outskirts of Leverton,' he boasted proudly.

Maria was genuinely surprised. 'Really?' she replied with a startled look on her face. 'I would never have thought that.'

'Yes, I like the peace and solitude of life on the canal,' he said in a somewhat trance-like state, but almost as soon as he'd said it he realised that he'd put his foot in it. Maria turned her head away for a few moments and Clarke winced – inwardly and outwardly!

She turned to face him once more. 'And how's the case going?' she asked with what Clarke thought was a slightly trembling voice.

'We have a number of suspects,' he replied with a sigh. 'But we still haven't caught the killer.'

'I see,' she replied nodding her head.

'How's your day been?' he asked after a few seconds.

Maria blew out her cheeks. 'Busy,' she replied earnestly, before going on to describe how one of the residents had claimed that some money and a diary had been stolen from her room, and that she and her colleagues had been turning the place upside down, but to no avail. 'The poor woman is suffering from dementia,' she said with a degree of sadness. 'She doesn't have a family – I believe her son committed suicide some years ago after being charged with murder.' She was about to point out that the woman was close to death when Clarke cut her short.

'I'm sorry,' he apologised. 'But this woman – this resident of yours. What's her name, if you don't mind me asking?'

'Fordham,' replied Maria. 'Mrs. Joan Fordham. Why do you ask?'

Chapter 39

Thursday, 13 July, 2017 (p.m.)

After their meal at the *Horse and Jockey*, Clarke and Maria parted company amicably before going their separate ways. However, although there was talk of the possibility of meeting up again some time, Clarke couldn't help feeling that he'd shot himself in the foot on that score, especially after his gaffe about liking the 'solitude' of life on the canal. 'Never was much good with women anyway,' he told himself as he drove away from the pub.

If truth were told he was relieved to get back to his narrow boat, where he immediately reached for the bottle of Laphroaig on top of the kitchen unit and poured himself a glassful. Actually Maria and the likelihood of another date with her were the last things on his mind as he drew the curtains and slumped into one of the armchairs in the saloon. It was what she had to say about one of the residents of her care home that preoccupied his thoughts right now, together with events of thirty years ago when he was still a uniformed police constable.

It was Monday, 5 January 1987 when the call came through that there was a missing schoolgirl out at Brockley. It was the last day of the Christmas break; the kids were due to return to school the following day to commence the Spring Term. The girls name was Emma Woodward; she was fifteen years of age and she lived with her mother and younger sister in one of the very few houses on Delves Lane, which was separated from Brockley by a public bridleway (a dirt track for the most part) leading from Gold Crescent. The girl's father had left a year or so before and now lived with his current partner in London.

Emma had left home just after lunch with the purpose of visiting her friend, Rebecca Tomlinson, who lived more or less opposite *The Wheatsheaf Inn*, on Main Road, Brockley. In order to get there she had decided to walk the half mile or so along the public bridleway from Delves Lane. This would lead her past Steadman's Wood and the pond or lake on her left, and the grounds of Brockley Hall off to her right, before emerging on Gold Crescent and then the Main Road. Her mother had told her to be back home by 4.00 p.m. as it would then be getting dark. When she had not returned by 5.00 p.m. her mother rang the Tomlinson's, who told her that her daughter had left their house shortly before 3.30 p.m.

Mrs. Woodward immediately rang the police and two uniformed officers were sent out to conduct a search of the area. However, as it was already dark by this time the search was called off, and it was decided to deploy more resources at first light the following morning. In the meantime, family liaison officers were to stay with Mrs. Woodward and her other daughter overnight, but naturally they feared the worst.

So it was that shortly before 8.00 a.m. the following morning the police began a thorough search of the area around Steadman's Woods and the pond. Forty minutes into the search, Clarke (then a young PC) had just descended the narrow valley within the woods known locally as "The Slope" when he thought he saw what looked like a human foot sticking out from the undergrowth. Upon closer inspection, Clarke was able to ascertain that it was the body of a young girl, just over five feet tall and aged about fifteen or sixteen with long brown hair. Her trousers and underpants were around her ankles, but it appeared that she had been asphyxiated and that her own scarf had been used as a ligature. It was fairly obvious to Clarke and to all those involved that the girl had undergone a sexual assault, and it was subsequently established that her body had been dragged to the site, where it was then covered with foliage.

A thorough search of the area had revealed very little and there was barely any forensic evidence (DNA was then in its infancy), leading the police to believe that the killer had covered his (or her) tracks well. One of the girl's items of footwear were initially shown to the mother and she was understandably distraught, but when called upon to identify the body of her daughter Clarke distinctly remembered her repeating the same words over and over again. 'Speak to me, my darling, speak to me.'

Door-to-door enquiries and witness reports led the team investigating the murder to believe that there was only one suspect, namely Peter Fordham, an autistic teenager who was known to the ignorant and less articulate as the 'village idiot'. He had been seen accompanying the girl to the home of the Tomlinson's on his bike, and then hanging around outside until she emerged later, when he accompanied her once more back to Gold Crescent and down the dirt track towards Steadman's Woods. He was duly charged with the girl's murder, in spite of the parents insisting upon his innocence.

Clarke recalled the celebrations when the young man was brought in, but he did not share the euphoria, believing that the team did not mount a thorough investigation. He didn't attend the trial either, but he remembered feeling that justice wasn't done. The youth had been unable to speak and his mother was inconsolable when the judge sentenced him to be detained at Her Majesty's Pleasure, and he was led away to begin his sentence at the Rampton Secure Hospital, in Nottinghamshire.

Within a year of the trial Fordham committed suicide (1988), by putting his obsession with Daedalus and Icarus to the test and jumping off the roof of one of the buildings at Rampton (believing he could fly). This literally broke the boy's father, Trevor Fordham, who took to the bottle in a big way and died just over ten years later (1998). Believing in her son's innocence, Mrs. Fordham presented what she believed to be evidence to the police that her son couldn't have been the killer on a number of occasions, but she was always turned away. Shunned by her neighbours, she eventually left the area to all intents and purposes, but evidently she came back a year or so ago and was one of the residents at the Little Orchard Care Home.

Yes, it all happened thirty years ago, but to Clarke it could have been yesterday. He turned to the pull-out table beside him, upon which lay the laptop, printer and lamp. There was a glass of whisky too, but he had barely touched it.

There was only one thing for it. Rising from his armchair he went over to the CD player and put on his copy of Pink Floyd's *Dark Side of the Moon*, beginning with the opening track, *Speak to Me*. As he sank back into his armchair the first words hit him immediately:

> *I've been mad for fucking years, absolutely years,*
> *Been over the edge for yonks,*
> *Been working me buns off for bands*
> *I've always been mad, I know I've been mad,...*

Shortly afterwards he fell into a deep sleep and dreamed of a woman with massive boobs – by the name of Maria!

PART 2

BREATHE

Chapter 40

Friday, 14 July, 2017 (a.m.)

It was 6.30 a.m. when Clarke woke the following morning in his armchair; and he was surprised to find that the whisky was still there beside him on the table – barely touched. What's more, he had a clear head and was able to recollect just about all the events of the night before – including his dream of the woman with the massive boobs. 'Aargh, let's not go there,' he told himself!

Leaving the glass of whisky where it was, he drew the curtains open before making his way up the steps and out onto the deck. There was hardly a cloud in the sky and a bright, sunny day beckoned. To his delight there was birdsong coming from every direction, and the canal seemed to be teeming with wildlife. It felt good to be alive on mornings like this; as if one was being reborn or taking one's first breaths – which in a way he was. He could have stayed on the boat all day long (strumming his guitar maybe?), but he needed to get out of the clothes that seemed to reek of slow-cooked Beef and porcini Bourguignon, and so he headed back inside for a shower.

He had only been under the water for several minutes when the words from *Speak to Me* perforated his thoughts, and something started to nag away at him. It was still nagging away at him as he dried himself off and then changed into his clothes for the day ahead. However, it finally came to him when he sat down outside for a bowl of cereal and a glass of fresh orange juice, and he knew what he had to do.

For a few minutes he marvelled at the sheer number of insects that seemed to make the canal their home, and was absolutely thrilled when a Red Admiral fluttered by and made its way downstream, especially as butterfly numbers were said to be on the decline. He reluctantly managed to tear himself away from this idyll and went back inside the boat, where he washed and dried the pots before locking up and making his way to the car.

Approaching the vehicle, he took out his mobile phone and rang the incident room to let them know that he wouldn't be coming in just yet. Sergeant Fletcher was to take over for the time being as he had an appointment elsewhere; he would be making an appearance later. It all seemed very clandestine, but no questions were asked, and he certainly had no intention of giving any answers – yet!

As manageress of the Little Orchard Care Home, Audrey Bostock always made a point of arriving for work at or around 8.00 a.m. every morning, and today was no different. By the time she entered her office, most of the residents had already been up and about for over an hour and enjoying breakfast; some in the comfort of their own rooms and others in the dining room area. Audrey operated flexible breakfast times, with rotating menu's, as it was not deemed acceptable to wait until all the residents were up.

Audrey's first task every morning was to undertake an inspection of every room, chiefly to make herself known to the residents, but also to see that everything was running smoothly. Needless to say, however, as staff scuttled around with the breakfast trolleys one or two incidents had occurred. Mrs. Birkin had spilt her porridge (again!), and Mr. Springthorpe was not at all happy with his kippers ('I've told you before not to put lemon juice on the buggers!').

Some residents preferred to go without a breakfast, in spite of Audrey's insistence that the 'nutritious and delicious choices' were good for their health and well-being. One or two were enjoying a crafty fag outside, but there were still others who were sound asleep. It had just turned 8.15 a.m. when a member of staff found Audrey in the dining room area chatting to some of the residents. Apparently there was a policeman in the reception area and he needed to speak to her urgently.

Slightly irritated, Audrey apologised to the residents and made her way briskly to reception, where she found Clarke admiring the tropical fish.

'Chief Inspector – how nice to see you again,' she said slightly out of breath and with a weak smile.

He turned to face her with a start and smiled apologetically. 'Ah, Mrs. Bostock, I'm so sorry to drag you away from your work once again.'

'That's okay,' she replied a little less breathlessly. 'And please, do call me Audrey.'

Clarke appeared somewhat bashful, but he acceded to her request. 'Very well, Audrey it is.'

'How may I help you Inspector?'

'Well…Audrey,' he began. 'I understand that you have a resident here by the name of Mrs. Fordham – a Mrs. Joan Fordham. Is that right?'

'Well…yes, as it happens.'

'I wonder if it would be possible to see her,' he said bluntly.

'It's very likely that she's still asleep,' replied Audrey somewhat taken aback. 'Besides, you really should have made an appointment…'

Clarke interrupted her. 'I really do need to see her, Audrey. It's a matter of great urgency.'

His persistence paid off as Audrey reluctantly led him to Joan Fordham's room. On arrival she tapped lightly on the door and entered, followed by Clarke.

'As I told you, Inspector, she's sound asleep.' She then stood to one side. 'See for yourself.'

Clarke took one look and recognised her instantly. It was only a brief glimpse, but everything came flooding back again – the tears, the grief and the sheer indomitability of the woman lying there before him as she set out to prove that her son was an innocent man. He turned to Audrey.

'Thank you, that was much appreciated,' he whispered.

'She is very ill, I'm afraid,' replied Audrey. 'And the chances of her surviving into next week are very slim.'

The pair took one last look before they tiptoed out of the room. Stepping out into the corridor, Audrey was just leaving the door slightly ajar when Clarke fired one more question at her.

'I also understand that Mrs. Fordham may have had some items stolen from her room – including a diary?'

The question took Audrey completely by surprise. 'How did you know that?'

Clarke sighed heavily. 'Please, Audrey, just answer the question.'

'Okay,' said Audrey grudgingly. 'She claims that a diary was taken from one of her drawer's and some money was stolen from her handbag. We spent all of yesterday…'

Clarke interrupted her. 'Never mind about the money,' he said shaking his head. 'I doubt if we'll see *that* again,' he said confidently. 'But I think I know where we'll find the diary!'

Moving across the corridor to the room opposite, he tapped lightly on the door and upon receiving no reply he entered.

Audrey followed him. 'Mrs. Jackson is in the dining room having breakfast,' she pointed out with a degree of impatience. 'I was talking to her when called away!'

Clarke was equally impatient. 'Get looking!' he said quietly but sharply.

'I beg your pardon?'

'Help me look for the diary – please!'

And so the pair began to scour the room for Mrs. Fordham's missing diary. Still shaking her head, Audrey started with the wardrobe, but seemed to be meeting with little success. Clarke began by looking under the bed and thereabouts, but he too found nothing of importance. He then moved over to the dressing table, and it was just as he was about to close the middle drawer that he suddenly uttered the word 'Bingo', and the search was over.

It was underneath some underwear that he'd come across the Tesco carrier bag containing the small, brown exercise book. Audrey came over as he briefly flipped through the pages.

'This is it,' he said triumphantly!

'Is this what you've been looking for all along?' asked Audrey, seemingly just as fascinated by the discovery.

'It is indeed,' replied Clarke. 'And I'm afraid that I must keep it as evidence for the time being.'

Audrey nodded, as if she understood the implications of what he had just said. The pair then left the room and headed down the corridor to the reception area.

Clarke thanked her profusely, offered her his appreciation and promised to return the book as soon as was conveniently possible. With that they parted company, and as she watched him leave Audrey could have sworn that he was actually skipping across the car park to his waiting Ford Focus!

There was somebody else watching his departure too. Through the window of one of the nearby rooms, Maria Bukowski had seen him leave and she came to a decision there and then. She was unable to act upon her decision immediately, but during her mid-morning break she sat down and wrote a letter. Fortunately she found several envelopes in her bag, and taking one of them she placed the letter inside, sealed it and before leaving work that day she placed it on Audrey Bostock's desk. She deemed it unnecessary to write any more letters on that day or thereafter. What was the point?

Chapter 41

Friday, 14 July, 2017 (a.m.)

'You have got to be kidding me, Sarge,' replied an inordinately astounded Constable Webster when informed by Fletcher that their boss had apparently been on a romantic assignation the previous evening.

The young detective's failed charm offensive the week previously had evidently been all but forgotten by his female counterpart for the time being, and she readily revealed to him what she knew of Clarke's tryst.

'He actually told me himself back at the station,' she said excitedly.

Webster was still coming to terms with the revelation. 'The crafty bugger...' he muttered to himself. 'Who'd have thought it?'

They were like a pair of excited schoolgirls sharing their secrets, and nobody else was to know. They were still chattering and giggling away at 10.00 a.m. when the outside door to the incident room suddenly slammed shut, and the footsteps down the corridor signalled Clarke's arrival.

'Don't say anything,' whispered Fletcher to Webster as the man himself entered the room.

'Good morning everybody,' was Clarke's uncharacteristically cheerful outburst, prompting Fletcher to cast a quick glance at Webster as if to say 'I told you so.'

Although Clarke had given the order that Fletcher was to take charge during his absence, it was Webster who came forward with some news for the boss.

'Sir, there's a guy from Christie's coming up to look at the Sisley painting,' he announced with a barely concealed smirk.

'From where?' shouted Clarke from his office as he hung up his bomber jacket.

'Christie's, Sir. You know – the auction people.'

Clarke seemed to be in a world of his own. 'Okay,' he mouthed, before promptly closing the door of his office behind him and placing a "Do Not Disturb" sign on it.

As he did so, Webster's smirk faded and he shot a puzzled look at Fletcher before returning to his desk. The two junior detectives then peered over their laptops and watched as Clarke produced what appeared to be an exercise book from his jacket. Glances were exchanged again and they continued to watch as he proceeded to read the book for the next half hour or so.

Now and again a smile lit up his face, and Fletcher would have been prepared to swear that she had seen him mutter the words 'Well, well' and 'Of course' to himself. Occasionally he was seen to nod his head too, and it was all very puzzling. What was he up to? Eventually he put the book down, and he was then observed making a couple of phone calls. As he rose from his desk and emerged from his office, Fletcher's head went down and Webster followed suit, as if neither of them had been taking any notice.

'Someone get me Parkside Police Station in Cambridge,' he barked out to no one in particular. He then turned to Webster. 'Did you or any of your colleagues call at Brockley Hall during your door-to-door enquiries?'

Webster popped his head up from his laptop. 'They were out at the time, Sir,' he replied somewhat nervously.

Clarke then returned to his office to consult the exercise book once more. Minutes later a member of the team came over to inform him that Cambridge were 'on the line', and he took the call immediately.

Fletcher and Webster were still perplexed as Clarke continued his telephone conversation. But he suddenly put the phone down, picked up the exercise book and grabbed his jacket before emerging from the office once more.

'I'm off to Brockley Hall,' he shouted to those present. 'Fletcher, you're in charge again for the time being.' He started to walk away but then turned back again. 'Oh, and I hope to have a job for you when I get back.'

As he strode purposefully out of the incident room, he was conscious of the fact that the atmosphere within had gone from mild mockery and amusement to complete and utter bewilderment, and a wry grin appeared on his face – he was determined that it should stay that way for the time being.

There was a cacophony of sound coming from the woods that surround Brockley Hall as Clarke passed through the gates. One or two grey squirrels scampered across the tarmac in front of him before ascending one of the magnificent lime trees that straddled the avenue leading to the Hall. This was the first time that he had actually been to the place;

he hadn't been tasked with calling there as part of the investigation into the death of Emma Woodward thirty years previously, in spite of its proximity to the scene of the crime. And yet it all seemed familiar to him.

Suddenly the woods just seemed to open up and there before him lay the 18th century Georgian mansion, complete with its large well-kept lawn at the front. It seemed ironic to Clarke that someone should be mowing the lawn just as he pulled up outside the building. Seated on a ride-on lawnmower was a man of some seventy-odd years, with receding grey hair and attired in navy blue overalls, and the moment he saw Clarke he stopped to dismount – albeit gingerly. Approaching the detective, he appeared to be limping slightly and carrying his left arm as if he had suffered an injury at some time.

'Can I help you, Sir,' he asked in what seemed to Clarke a rather condescending manner; almost as if he had no right to be there.

Clarke proffered his card and introduced himself. 'I'd like to speak to the owner of the house if I may,' he replied with some authority.

'Well, the master is at work in Grimley and Mrs. Frankland-Moore has gone to the library in Derby. There's only Mrs. Frankland-Moore senior here at the present.'

Clarke looked puzzled. 'Would that be the master's mother?'

'It would indeed,' was the rather curt reply.

'Then I'd like to speak to her if I may?'

'What would be the purpose of your visit, Sir?'

Clarke explained about the rather unsavoury incident on Blackthorn Lane the week previously, and added that his visit was merely part of routine enquiries. Following the man indoors, he was told to wait in the hallway whilst Mrs. Frankland-Moore was informed that a policeman wished to speak to her.

So he stood there with his hands behind his back and waited, but his eyes were almost immediately drawn to the large portrait paintings on either side of the hallway, depicting – he presumed – the forebears of the present occupant of the house, especially as they all appeared to be blessed with red hair!

As Clarke was dismissing the notion that any of the portraits were painted by a certain Alfred Sisley, the blue-overalled septuagenarian reappeared. 'Mrs. Frankland-Moore will see you now, Sir,' he said glumly as he ushered Clarke into the lounge, where he was confronted by an unsmiling elderly woman of some eighty years or so, with neatly coiffed collar length grey hair, heavily made up and wearing a black semi-fitted square neckline dress and pearl choker necklace.

'Good morning Chief Inspector,' sneered the woman seated before him in a very expensive-looking oak occasional armchair. 'I'm Monica Frankland-Moore.'

Clarke felt uncomfortable as she looked him up and down, as if he was being assessed as an applicant for a post at the Hall – and he wouldn't have been far from the truth. Very much the matriarch, Monica Frankland-Moore exuded authoritarianism, power and confidence, and it was as clear as daylight that she wanted it to be known that *she* was in complete control.

Born Monica Rawlinson to an affluent stockbroker in Kingston-upon-Thames, she met her future husband, Charles Frankland-Moore, whilst he was undertaking his National Service as a First Lieutenant in the 1st Battalion, The Sherwood Foresters. Soon afterwards he returned to the legal profession and his practice in Derbyshire, and following their marriage in 1960 she joined him at Brockley Hall. From the beginning, however, it was apparent that her husband couldn't keep his hands to himself, but she overlooked his transgressions for the sake of the marriage, which she always regarded as sacrosanct.

There was to be only one child from the marriage, namely Rupert, and she took to doting on him from the outset. When her husband eventually passed away in 2014, Rupert succeeded him as head of the family law firm and returned to Brockley Hall with his wife. The three of them live there together with a live-in housekeeper, Mrs. Dilks, and her husband, who now returned to his duties on the front lawn.

During her marriage and since her husband's death, Monica had always endeavoured to be the perfect host. Innately stylish, with a strong sense of occasion, every aspect of presentation had to be carefully considered, not just visually, but socially too. Needless to say, however, her obsession with appearances led her to become an inveterate snob. In her mind it was all about standards, but to others it was the rudest form of dismissiveness, as Clarke was about to find out.

'Oh do sit down,' she remonstrated sharply. 'I can't abide it when people loom over me.'

'Thank you,' grunted Clarke and he quickly seated himself.

'You don't look like a policeman,' she said with a deep frown.

Clarke ignored the comment and decided to press ahead. 'I'm here to talk about…'

She interrupted him. 'For goodness sake speak up – I can hardly hear you,' she said tersely.

He began again; only this time a little more forcefully. 'I'm here to talk about the unfortunate incident that occurred down Blackthorn Lane last week.'

'I take it that you're referring to that fellow Jackson?'

'Yes, that's right,' he shouted. 'I believe that some of my officers called here a few days later as part of our door-to-door enquiries, but unfortunately you were out.'

Not for the first time she looked down her nose at him. 'What makes you think that *I* can help?'

Clarke was beginning to get exasperated. 'Well, I'd be grateful for anything that you can think of that might lead us to catching his killer,'

'Such as?' was her brief but haughty response.

Enough was enough. 'The man outside – the one who introduced us.'

'You mean Dilks – what of him?'

'Does he do all the gardening work here at the Hall?'

'Of course he does…what kind of question is that?'

Clarke refused to let go. 'Has anyone else done the gardening at any time – Keith Jackson for instance?'

The question received a contemptuous response from Monica. 'I can assure you Inspector that we wouldn't require the likes of Jackson here!'

Her attitude irked him considerably, but his distaste for her overt snobbery was alleviated for the time being as his attention was drawn to what was obviously a wedding photograph over her shoulder on one of the cabinets. A look of puzzlement appeared on her face as he stood up and made his way over to it.

'Your son and his wife I take it?' he asked politely.

She eased herself around in her chair in order to see what had attracted Clarke's attention, and her attitude changed dramatically. 'Oh yes,' she replied proudly. 'That was taken shortly before he moved to Brussels.'

Curious as to why she neglected to mention her daughter-in-law, he nevertheless continued with the questions. 'Brussels, you say?'

'Yes, Rupert worked for the EU for a number of years.'

'And what of your daughter-in-law during this period – was she active in any way?'

'Oh yes, she did a little work for the EU from time to time,' she replied somewhat dismissively. 'You know, I'll never understand why they voted to leave.'

Clarke was among the 51.9% who fervently supported the Leave Campaign, but diplomacy and tact got the better of him, and so he bit his lip and persevered with the questions about her son's marriage.

'They were there a long time then – in Brussels?' he asked discreetly.

'Yes, they had a large house at Le Vivier d'Oie in Uccle – do you know it?' Clarke shook his head. 'It's an affluent suburb of Brussels,' she boasted. 'But they came back here following my husband's death in 2014, and Rupert took over the family business.'

'So he was a law student then – your son?'

'But of course.'

'Would that have been Oxford?'

'No, Rupert went to Cambridge,' she replied haughtily once more.

'When would that have been?'

Monica was getting slightly irritated by the questioning. 'Look, where is all of this leading, Inspector?'

'Just routine enquiries ma'am, as I said.' But he hadn't finished yet. 'When exactly was he at Cambridge?'

She sighed heavily. 'He went to Cambridge in 1984, but after two years there he took part in the Erasmus and Exchange Scheme from 1986 to 1987, attending the University of Regensburg in Germany.'

That was all he needed. 'I see,' he replied. 'Well, I think that I've taken up too much of your time.'

'Is that it?' she asked with some bewilderment.

'Yes, and thank you so much for your assistance. It's greatly appreciated.' She was about to call the housekeeper, but Clarke put his hand up. 'It's okay, I'll make my own way out.' He'd clearly had all he could take of Monica Frankland-Moore.

As the door closed behind Clarke, Monica rose steadily from her chair and made her way to the window in order to witness his departure. She watched him skip down the steps of the Hall just as another vehicle pulled up in front of the building – a white Ford Fiesta with what appeared to be a scratch mark along one side. Anna Frankland-Moore had returned from Derby and her assignment at the library.

As Anna emerged from her car, Clarke made his way over to her – and Monica continued to watch. The pair seemed to be engaged in conversation for quite some time before they shook hands, parted company and went their separate ways. It was as Anna entered the building and closed the door behind her that Monica appeared in the doorway to the lounge.

'Nice man,' said Anna sensing that Monica had been watching her conversation with Clarke.

'And what could he possibly want with you?' demanded Monica.

Anna remained relaxed in spite of Monica's apparent confrontational stance. 'He wanted to know how my car had come to have a scratch mark along one side,' she replied with a hint of sarcasm. 'When I told him he said that I should have reported the incident to the police.'

Monica had always reacted to any perceived threats to her authority with anger and spite, and as her eyes narrowed she launched into a tirade at her daughter-in-law.

'You're a liar,' she screamed! 'I don't believe a word you say!'

'So you *were* watching then?' replied Anna calmly. 'Believe what you like, Monica, but I'm past caring what you think.'

She then started to climb the broad staircase, but after a few steps she paused and turned to Monica once more.

'Oh, and he wanted to know if Dilks had had an accident recently, and so I told him that he'd fallen off the ladder whilst cutting the hedge a couple of months ago. Remember?' Monica's eyes narrowed all the more. 'Of course you remember,' Anna continued. 'Rupert had to go and grovel to Keith Jackson to finish the job and undertake any other gardening tasks until Dilks recovered!'

Monica mouthed the word 'bitch' at her, but Anna had made her point, and as she continued up the stairs to her little office a look of self-satisfaction appeared on her face. It had been a long time coming, but it was worth it.

Chapter 42

Friday, 14 July, 2017 (p.m.)

It was approaching noon when Clarke left Brockley Hall to drive the short distance to the incident room, but he was in a buoyant mood. His spirits were lifted all the more when he entered his office and discovered that the news he had been waiting for had arrived. He made a quick phone call and then burst into the main office.

'Where's Fletcher?' he shouted.

'Here Sir,' she called out from behind him. 'I just popped out to the shop down the road to get some sandwiches.'

Clarke spun around to face her. 'Bugger the sandwiches,' he snapped. 'That job I mentioned?'

'Yes, Sir?' she replied cautiously.

'I want you to shoot off to Cambridge – Parkside Police Station.'

Fletcher's jaw dropped and she let out a shriek that almost shook the foundations of the building. 'What!'

'You'll be meeting up with a Detective Chief Inspector Darren Green – he'll brief you.'

She followed him back into his office. 'Brief me on what?' she asked with a sense of increased exasperation. 'And what the hell does it have to do with the murder of Keith Jackson?'

Clarke glared at her. 'Just do it, Sergeant!' he bellowed. Barely pausing for breath he shouted again. 'Webster, get your arse here!'

Fletcher stormed out of Clarke's office with her tail very decidedly between her legs, and went to retrieve her handbag and car keys from her desk.

'His bark's worse than his bite,' whispered Webster as he passed her.

That certainly wasn't her impression of events, as it suddenly occurred to her that the temporary truce between the two of them had probably come to an end. Grabbing her bag, the door to Clarke's office was still open as she passed by and she heard him bark out yet another order to Webster.

'I want you to check out all unsolved rapes and murders in Nottingham between 1988 and 1990. Is that clear?'

Despite Webster's inference that the boss was a big softy at heart, his reaction to Clarke's order suggested that he probably wouldn't have been willing to have put his money where his mouth is on that score, and he emerged from his office like a scalded cat!

As he did so, Fletcher turned around and knocked lightly on Clarke's door.

'Sir, I'd like to undertake that task if I may?' she asked confidently.

'Any particular reason why?' grunted Clarke without looking up.

'No, not really – it's just that I know the Nottingham area very well and…'

'Well then, get yourself off to Cambridge like I said – and shut the door behind you.'

If she thought that Clarke would jump from his seat as she slammed the door behind her petulantly, then she was very much mistaken. On the contrary, he remained cool, calm and collected as he made the first of two overseas phone calls.

It took Fletcher just over two hours to get to Parkside Police Station at Cambridge in her cream-coloured Mini Cooper convertible with black roof. Coming off the M1 at junction 19, she then headed along the A14 until it merged into the M11, and exited at junction 12 near Grantchester to take the A603. Arriving at her destination just after 2.00 p.m., she was still in the dark as to why Clarke had sent her there.

Entering the four-storey building by the main door, she showed her identity card to the Desk Sergeant and then explained that she was there to see a Detective Chief Inspector Green. A call was put through to him, and a couple of minutes later he arrived and introduced himself.

He was pretty much as Fletcher had expected; just under six feet tall, with dark brown close-cropped hair and blue eyes. He was also very powerfully-built and thick set, but certainly not obese. He was smartly dressed too, with a two-piece brown suit and tie. It was a professional appearance – unlike that of Clarke – and it made a profound impression upon Fletcher.

As he led her through the building to his office, he joked with one or two of his colleagues along the way, and it was apparent to Fletcher that he was well-liked and well-received by everyone around him. Opening the door to his office, he asked her to pull up a chair before removing his jacket and seating himself behind his desk. There was what looked like a family photograph on one side of the desk, with Green, his wife and three children – all girls.

'Lovely picture, Sir.' said Fletcher nodding towards the photograph.

Green smiled. 'Yes, they all keep me on my toes,' he replied in a deep voice and with a slight Cambridgeshire accent.

Fletcher was keen to know why she was there. 'I haven't the foggiest reason what I'm doing here, Sir.'

He slowly took his eyes away from the photograph. 'Then I'd better fill you in then, Sergeant,' he said calmly but with authority. 'A young woman made an accusation of rape thirty years ago, back in 1986. However, to the surprise of everyone she subsequently retracted her statement.'

Still no wiser, Fletcher pressed ahead. 'Do we know why?' she asked.

'There was some suggestion that she had been got at, so to speak. She claimed that she had actually been drunk at the time, and couldn't remember much about the evening in general.'

'And what about the man who was supposed to have raped her – do we know anything about him?'

Green hesitated slightly before continuing. 'He was a student at the University, but he was also a member of this club.'

Fletcher's ears pricked up. 'That wouldn't be the *Tom and Jerry Club*, would it by any chance?'

'Something like that,' he replied with uncertainty.

Fletcher whistled before continuing. 'Do we know if she fell pregnant?'

Green seemed reflective, almost as if he were playing a game of chess. 'Can't be sure,' he said gazing out of the window. 'But we do know that she never married.'

'And what was the name of this woman?'

Green snapped out of his temporary trance-like state. 'Gemma Bateson – she lives in a flat on Fison Road, in the Abbey area of town.' He stood up to put on his jacket. 'It's one of the most deprived areas of the city. Oh, and she works at a pub – out at Fen Ditton. Shall we go and see her?'

The two detectives didn't have far to travel to the historic pub on the outskirts of Cambridge, although *The Ancient Shepherd's* (known locally as *The Shepherd's*) was actually more like a restaurant than a pub. Boasting a 'cosy and welcoming space, with various nooks and crannies,' lunch was coming to an end as the two detectives stepped inside, but there were still quite a few people still enjoying the last course of their meals. Introducing themselves to the manager, Green and Fletcher stated the reason for their visit and requested a few minutes to question a member of the staff, and pointing her out at the far end of the room the pair made their way over to the slim figure of Gemma Bateson.

At just under five feet and six inches tall, with blue eyes and her long fair hair in a pony-tail, Gemma was clearly showing the effects of drink and drug abuse, and looked much older than her forty-nine years. She wore little make-up to hide her wrinkles, only a light touch of lipstick. There was little evidence of eyebrows and she wore false teeth; but then she had been a heavy smoker since her early teens. Her nails were short due to constant biting, but at least she had made an effort to paint them. There was a stud in her right nostril and similar ones in both ears, and it was just possible to make out a tattoo of a seabird on the left-hand side of her neck. Other tattoos on her upper arms were hidden by the pub uniform, which consisted of a white, short-sleeved blouse with black neckerchief and black trousers. As already stated, Gemma was quite slim and relatively flat-chested. What's more, she wasn't pleased to see Green and Fletcher.

'What do you bastards want?' she asked in her local Cambridgeshire drawl. 'Can't you see I'm busy?'

Green was renowned for being something of a manipulator and he now turned on the charm. 'Let's just say that if you scratch my back, Gemma, then I might just scratch yours,' he replied with a winning smile. 'How about we go out to the garden at rear and have a chat.'

Gemma looked across at her boss who was nodding his head. 'Okay, I'll give you five minutes,' she said adamantly.

The trio went outside and although there were quite a few people sitting around and enjoying the sun, it didn't take them long to find a table. Almost as soon as they had sat themselves down, Green produced a packet of cigarettes from his inside pocket and offered one to Gemma. Accepting the offer, Gemma took one and inhaled deeply. Green returned the packet to his inside pocket ('I've never smoked myself,' he later explained to Fletcher, 'but I find they come in handy').

'Well, what is it that you want?' asked Gemma as she blew a mouthful of smoke just past Fletcher's right ear.

'We want you to cast your mind back to 1986,' said Green with a hint of gravity in his voice.

'Oh for God's sake,' she replied with some agitation. 'Not that again – it was thirty years ago! And like I told you buggers at the time, I was drunk, wasn't I?'

Green continued. 'Well, we have reason to believe that you were being economical with the truth, Gemma. Indeed, we have reason to believe that the man who raped you went on to rape again several more times and even commit murder.'

At that Fletcher turned to Green with a look of astonishment on her face, but he put his hand up as if to assuage her sudden feeling of shock and as a means of persuading her to bear with him for a while longer.

There was a look of shock on Gemma's face too. 'You mean the bastard did it again and got away with it?' she hissed.

Green nodded. 'It certainly looks that way, Gemma.' He was feeling much more confident now. 'So, tell us *exactly* what happened to you on the night in question – no holding back now.'

And so she came clean. She had been working behind the bar in *The Eagle* in Cambridge one night when a group of male students came in; they had apparently been thrown out of a restaurant earlier for rowdy behaviour. What marked them out was their blazer with a *Tom and Jerry* motif (Fletcher's eyes lit up at this). One of them kept trying to chat her up, but she wasn't interested. This group continued to be boisterous all night long, but at closing time she made her way home on foot.

However, she was conscious of the fact that someone was following her ('I could hear footsteps behind me'). She made her way down Trumpington Street onto Mill Lane and then onto the park at Laundress Green, which is where he struck. What's more, she recognised him as being the guy from the pub.

When it was all over he staggered away. She was eventually able to pull herself together and made for the nearest telephone box, from where she called the police. They were very good, and it wasn't long before the culprit was apprehended and placed in an identity parade, where she picked him out easily – his red hair. Needless to say, he was duly charged.

At this point Gemma asked Green for another cigarette, and then she continued with her story.

'A day or so later I had a visit from this woman. She said the man accused of raping me was her son and that what he did was right out of character – must have been the drink, she said. What's more, the accusation would ruin his prospective career and it would help everyone concerned if we forgot about everything. As a token of her esteem and best wishes she produced a package.'

'What was in the package, Gemma?' asked Green.

Gemma paused for a few seconds before replying. 'It was a thousand pounds,' she replied sheepishly.

'And what did you do with the money?'

'Well, I took it, didn't I?' she replied in a seemingly aggravated tone.

'And you subsequently told the police that you'd made the story up?

She nodded. 'Yeah, that's right. Got a warning for that, I did.'

She went on to tell the detectives that the money was going to be used to further her education, but she blew it all on drink and drugs. To their surprise she then revealed that the following year (1987) she gave birth to a son. That was when she turned to prostitution; to feed him and her habits. She eventually came off the drugs and quit prostitution.

Fletcher chimed in for the first time. 'And your son – what happened to him?' she asked politely.

For the first time a smile came to Gemma's face. 'He's in the Army now and doin' very well for himself,' she proudly boasted. Green leaned across and whispered something into Fletcher's ear. 'What are you two talkin' about?' asked Gemma anxiously.

Green turned to face her again. 'We were wondering if your son might be prepared to give us a sample of his DNA,' he said benignly. 'To prove who his father is.'

Gemma shook her head only for Fletcher to put something to her. 'And we also wondered if you might be prepared to be a witness at any future trial?'

Again Gemma shook her head and seemed close to tears. 'I just want to get away from here and put the past behind me!'

Green tried again. 'We realise that, but...'

Gemma stood up and interrupted him. 'You're telling me that the bastard is still free, aren't you?' she cried in an extremely agitated state. 'And you want me to face him again?'

'Well yes, but...'

She started to walk away. 'I'm not answering any more of your questions!'

Green thumped the table with frustration, but Fletcher put a hand on his shoulder and went after her.

'Gemma…Gemma please wait,' she shouted. Gemma stopped in her tracks as Fletcher caught up with her. 'Just one more thing – I promise. The man who attacked you? What was his name?'

Gemma sighed heavily. 'It was Robert – or something like that.'

'And the woman who gave you the money; what was her name?'

'I can't remember,' she shrugged. Fletcher thanked her, but just as she was turning to walk away Gemma shouted after her. 'But she was very "la-di-dah"; that I do know!'

Chapter 43

Friday, 14 July, 2017 (p.m.)

Fletcher and Green had spent much longer interviewing Gemma Bateson than the five minutes that she was going to give them, and it was almost 4.30 p.m. before the two detectives said their goodbyes and finally parted company. Realising that it would be close to 7.00 p.m. when she got back to Brockley, she decided to put a call through to the incident room before leaving Cambridge on the off chance that Clarke would still be there. It was Webster who answered the phone.

'Nah, he's gone home I'm afraid,' said the young Constable rather chirpily.

'Never mind,' replied a slightly disappointed Fletcher. 'You sound rather upbeat though. Have I missed something?'

'Guess what?'

Fletcher was tired and she wasn't in the mood for any of Webster's pranks. 'Well go on then – indulge me for crying out loud!'

'That painting by Sisley,' replied Webster.

'What about it?'

'It ain't – by Sisley I mean!'

'You mean it's a fake?'

'The guy from Christie's confirmed it!'

'So, the country's leading authority on the Impressionists isn't as bloody clever as he likes to think he is?'

It was a satisfying end to a conversation, and she climbed into her Mini Cooper convertible and set off back to Brockley a far wiser and happier detective than when she left!

Whilst Fletcher was making her way back from Cambridge, a rather tense-looking Rupert Frankland-Moore was climbing out of his black open-top LaFerrari Aperta at Brockley Hall. This was probably more to do with the fact that the cricket team were going to be without two of their star players the following day, one of whom was the Captain. It just so happened that he was also one of Rupert's clients and was now banged up in one of the cells at Leverton police station!

Nevertheless, his demeanour seemed to improve as he made his way up the steps of the Hall, for of course it was a foregone conclusion that he would be asked to lead the team by the others for the rest of the season at least; he was the obvious choice, *n'était-il pas*?

As the door closed behind him, he heard the distinctive voice of his mother calling from the living room.

'Is that you, darling?' she shouted expectantly.

Throwing his briefcase to the floor as he entered the room, he then approached her with arms open wide. 'Yes, I'm here, dear mama,' he said before bending down to kiss her gently on the right cheek.

It was always "mama" or "mummy" when he was in a good mood or when he wanted something, but "mother" when cross or irritated. However, he couldn't help noticing that she seemed to be troubled by something. Straightening up again, he made a beeline for the drinks cabinet with a puzzled look on his face.

'God, I could murder a Brandy,' he said with a deep sigh. 'Can I get you anything?'

'I'll have a G and T please, darling' she murmured. 'And don't forget the lime.'

He continued to look at her whilst pouring the drinks. There was only one way of finding out what was wrong with her. 'And how's your day been?' he asked with a degree of apprehension.

'Oh fine,' she replied nervously as she twiddled with her fingers. Pausing for a few seconds, she realised that she couldn't keep it from him any longer. 'Look darling, there was a policeman called here earlier.'

Cool, calm and collected under normal circumstances, his face betrayed the slightest hint of concern at the mention of the police. 'And what could he possibly want?' he sneered.

'He was asking about that *ghastly* man, Jackson.'

Rupert handed his mother her drink. 'What about him?' he asked before taking a sip of his brandy.

'He wanted to know if he'd done any gardening work here.'

'And what did you tell him?'

'I told him that Dilks did all the gardening work.'

Unbeknown to both mother and son, Anna had crept down the stairs and now stood in the doorway of the living room, listening to their conversation. They jumped with a start as she made her way towards the drinks cabinet and interrupted them.

'But if the pair of you remember, Dilks had a fall from the ladder,' she began. 'It was back in May and he was unable to carry out any duties for a few weeks, so Rupert paid a visit to Mr. Jackson.' Having poured herself a Scotch and Water, she turned to look Rupert straight in the eye. 'Didn't you, darling?'

Whilst Monica bristled with indignation, Rupert looked down at his drink and swirled what remained of his Brandy around inside the glass. 'Are you sure about that, dear?' he muttered.

She moved nearer to him. 'Yes, you were *so* put out because you had to shoot off to London on business later that day – or so you said.' They were now almost side by side. 'You even rang to say that you were going to be tied up over the weekend and wouldn't be back until the following Tuesday.'

With Anna's confidence growing, there were signs that Rupert was becoming more and more agitated, as his face began to flush. Gripping his glass tightly in his left hand he shrugged his shoulders. 'What if I did?'

That was all she needed. Throwing her drink into his face, she snapped at him. 'You weren't in London; you were at the Monaco Grand Prix with that slut of a secretary!' But she clearly hadn't finished. 'How do I know? Because I happened to come across your mobile phone a day or so before and saw the messages between the two of you! Slipped up there, didn't you?'

Not one to lose his composure in public, Rupert's face now became the embodiment of anger. His nostril's flared, his lips tightened and curled inwards, but it was his eyes that displayed the greatest rage as they practically bulged out of their sockets.

'You bitch,' he snarled!

As the back of his right hand came up as if to strike her, Anna screamed at him. 'Go on, hit me – that's your answer to everything!'

He had always felt the need to devour the woman he married and control every aspect of her life, but at long last Anna was coming out of her shell. Only just managing to control his temper, his hand came back down to his side. Returning the glass to the drinks cabinet, he ignored his wife and turned to his mother, who was standing beside her chair as if in a state of utter shock.

'I've just remembered,' he said between gritted teeth. 'I've left something important back at the office.'

As he stormed out of the building, Monica attempted to go after him. 'What time will you be back, darling?' she shouted.

But he ignored her and sped off in his LaFerrari Aperta down the driveway to the main road. Closing the outside door behind her, she returned to the living room just as Anna was pouring herself another

Scotch and Water. Monica stood in the doorway unable to look her daughter-in-law in the eye, but Anna wasn't in the least bit bothered. She took her drink with her and merely brushed past the woman who *she* had always regarded with unbridled contempt.

Chapter 44

Friday, 14 July, 2017 (p.m.)

The rush hour traffic in Cambridge was an encumbrance and patience was not exactly one of Fletcher's strong points. She had planned to head straight back to her home in Nottingham, but as she flew back up the M1 (outside lane all the way) she had a change of mind, and decided to call on Clarke at his "home" on the outskirts of Leverton.

It was shortly before 7.00 p.m. when she came off the motorway, and ten minutes later she was passing through Leverton on the way to Grimley when she saw the sign for Long Lane. There was still plenty of light, but she still chose to drive down the lane with a great deal more solicitude than when she did when on the motorway! Eventually she saw Clarke's Ford Focus up ahead and pulled over beside it.

Her first impressions of his "home" were not good. For one thing, she saw the name *Emily* on the side of the boat and under no circumstances whatsoever would she be using the word "she" to describe the damn thing! What's more, *she* decided that it was in dire need of a lick or two of paint, but *she* couldn't see the man ever getting around to completing the task. The windows to the boat were open and there was the distinctive smell of spices coming from within – no doubt a takeaway, she thought. Nevertheless, she climbed onto the boat and was surprised to see the pots of herbs on the open deck. It was with a hint of trepidation that she knocked lightly on the door to the cabin.

The response was almost immediate. 'Sergeant Fletcher,' said a clearly surprised-looking Clarke as he opened the door. 'I certainly didn't expect to see *you* here. 'Do come in and make yourself at home.'

Not expecting such a welcome, she seemed to frown momentarily and then gave a weak smile. 'Thank you, Sir,' she replied before climbing down the steps to the cabin.

On stepping inside, she was surprised how remarkably clean and tidy it was in contrast to the exterior of the boat. Clarke was busy hovering over the cooker and singing to himself, and it became apparent to her that the spicy aroma was the result of one of his own concoctions. Out of the corner of his eye he could see that she had taken an interest in his culinary prowess.

'Chicken Jalfrezi with spiced Masala rice, Sergeant,' he boasted. 'Care to try some?'

Somewhat pernickety with regard to her eating habits, Fletcher decided to decline the offer. 'Admittedly it does smell nice, Sir,' she replied truthfully. 'But perhaps I'd better not.'

Clarke was persistent. 'Oh, go on,' he insisted, and then promptly produced a piece of diced chicken coated in the fragrant sauce on the end of a fork. 'Here, try this.'

Unable to resist the temptation, Fletcher took the fork and bit into the tasty morsel. She was impressed. 'Actually, Sir, that's very good.'

'I tell you what,' replied Clarke excitedly. 'There's enough here for two – why don't you stay and have a bite to eat here, and we can discuss the events of the day over a damn fine curry?'

Fletcher couldn't be sure that this was the same man that had shown such hostility to her when she had first been posted to Leverton, but she found herself accepting his offer and his suggestion that she seat herself in one of the two armchairs whilst he finished cooking the evening meal.

He also continued with his rendition of *Peaceful Easy Feeling*, by The Eagles, but she shut her ears to it and began to cast her eyes around the cabin. The first thing that she noticed was the framed picture of Pink Floyd's *Wish You Were Here* album cover, but as with The Eagles she wasn't exactly *au fait* with the works of one of Britain's most successful rock groups of all time. Moving along, her gaze was caught by the pictures of wildlife and rural scenes, just as Clarke came over with the food.

'You like the pictures?' he asked tentatively as he placed the dishes of curry and rice before her.

'I love wildlife and nature,' she replied openly whilst still casting her eyes over the images. 'And I spend a lot of time outdoors – hiking and adventure holidays.'

Clarke was clearly impressed. 'Really? How wonderful! That must give you a lot of pleasure.' He paused to look at the pictures himself. 'I love all animals – they never let you down. Humans always do in my experience.'

She looked up at him as if to concur with his last statement, but he stood rooted to the spot for a few moments before he suddenly realised that there were no drinks. Apologising profusely, he seemed embarrassed by the fact that he had no wine.

'That's alright, Sir' she said calmly. 'A glass of diet coke will do if you have any?

'Yes, I've got plenty.' And with that he went over to the refrigerator.

This gave her the opportunity to ask the one question that had been at the forefront of her mind from the moment she came on board. 'So, why a narrow boat, Sir – I mean, as a place to live?'

Things were going so well that he was almost tempted to ask her to drop the word "Sir" from the conversation, but something told him that it wasn't right, so he paused briefly before answering her question.

'I've always preferred to take my holidays in the UK, Sergeant – the Lake District, Yorkshire Dales, Scotland, New Forest, Norfolk Broads. My wife always preferred the sun.' He hesitated and looked away for a few seconds, and then continued. 'I did persuade her to join me on a canal boating holiday once, but whereas I took to it, she hated it. Some time after moving back to Leverton, I got fed up with living in rented accommodation and decided to splash out on a run-down narrow boat. I renovated it to the best of my ability, and it's been my home ever since.'

Fletcher chose not to mention the fact that it was in need of renovation once more, but she did have one more question for him. 'Why the name *Emily*, Sir? Was that it's original name?'

'I can't remember the boat's original name,' he replied honestly. 'But the name *Emily* comes from a song – you probably wouldn't have heard of it.'

'Try me, Sir.'

'Okay, it comes from the song *See Emily Play*, which was released by the band Pink Floyd back in 1967. You heard of it?'

'Can't say that I have, Sir.'

It seemed like as good a time as any to begin tucking into their food, but it wasn't long before Clarke raised the subject of Fletcher's visit to Cambridge.

'How did things go,' he asked politely (if somewhat gingerly).

'You could have at least given me an insight into what I was to expect when I got there, Sir,' she replied tactfully.

Clarke swallowed another mouthful and shifted uneasily. 'Just tell me what you discovered, please, Sergeant.'

So Fletcher proceeded to tell Clarke about Gemma Bateson and the attack on her by a man calling himself 'Robert'. Fletcher went on to reveal that Gemma was paid off by the attacker's mother, in order to get her to retract her original statement.

'But I still don't know what all this has to do with the murder of Keith Jackson,' she said before scooping up another mouthful of curry and rice.

Clarke ignored her reference to Jackson. 'Is this "victim" prepared to come forward as a witness at any future trial?' he asked purposefully.

'I can't honestly say, Sir.'

'Damn,' snapped Clarke. He put down his meal, wiped his mouth and looked Fletcher straight in the eye. 'I think it's time that I put you in the picture.'

So he began to tell her about the original murder at Brockley thirty years previously, and how he always believed that the wrong man had been sent down.

'What was this man's name,' asked Fletcher inquisitively.

'Peter Fordham,' replied Clarke firmly. 'And he later committed suicide. His mother was convinced of his innocence, and she spent hours searching the woods in the hope of finding something that would incriminate the real killer. Unbeknown to us she also put together a diary,' he said waving the exercise book in front of Fletcher. 'In this diary she names the man who she believes committed the original crime – amongst other things.'

Fletcher's eyes widened. 'Wow!' she said excitedly. 'And who was that, if I may ask?'

'I'll come to that in a minute.'

'And what are these other things you mention?'

'Like I said, I'll come to them shortly.'

If Clarke was trying to stall her and frustrate her he was doing a damn good job, but she completed her meal nevertheless and thanked her host.

'That was delicious, Sir,' she said in all honesty. 'You should get that marketed.'

'You think so?' replied Clarke looking very flattered. He rose to get her another diet coke whilst he poured himself a liberal glass of whisky. 'I hope you don't mind?'

'Not at all, Sir,' she replied with a modicum of indifference. 'But I do wish that you'd go on with your story.'

Clarke took a sip of his whisky and obliged.

'Jackson is up to his eyeballs in debt, but he is constantly looking for ways to make money to feed his gambling and drinking habits. He has already taken to blackmailing Collins, having established that the man is having an affair with *his* wife. But he's also found out about Ibbotson's little sideline and taken to blackmailing him too. However, he considers these small fry. Ever the opportunist, he goes to visit his mother, but whilst there he broke into another room and stole some money.'

'And the diary?' interjected Fletcher.

'And the diary,' repeated Clarke.

'Go on, Sir – I'm all ears.'

'On reading the diary and seeing the name referred to therein, he realised that he was onto much bigger fish, and he saw a way of clearing his debts at a stroke if he played his cards right. Unfortunately he was dealing with a ruthless killer and he paid with his life.'

'But the killer didn't know about the diary?' said Fletcher with a deep frown.

'No, but he knew that Jackson must have found something that may have incriminated him,' replied Clarke confidently. 'That must have been what he was looking for when disturbed by the arrival of Collins. He obviously fled from the scene shortly afterwards *sans l'évidence*.'

'And how did he make his getaway?'

'Well he took a huge gamble, but I doubt if he used his own car.' Clarke sat rubbing his chin for a few seconds. 'He must have been parked up around the back of the building and out of sight – waiting for Jackson to arrive.'

Fletcher nodded her head as she weighed up everything that Clarke had just said, but then she suddenly sat bolt upright. 'Are you saying that the man who carried out the murder from 30 years ago and the man who killed Jackson are one and the same?'

'That's right, Sergeant.' said Clarke with a look of smugness on his face. 'The man we're looking for is Rupert Frankland-Moore!'

Chapter 45

Friday, 14 July, 2017 (p.m.)

Both Clarke and Fletcher had lost all track of time as they sat ruminating over what were up until now believed to be the two *known* crimes of Rupert Frankland-Moore. However, as dusk began to fall, Clarke continued to build on his case against the lawyer-cum-lord of the manor, and Fletcher was still all ears.

'Your visit to Cambridge has yielded several factors in this case,' stated Clarke firmly. 'For starters we know that a red-headed male student carried out an assault on a woman back in 1986.'

'It was rape, Sir,' insisted Fletcher.

'Rape or assault, this student wore a blazer with the *Tom and Jerry* motif. What's more, he *may* have been called "Robert", but I believe that this was Rupert Frankland-Moore.'

'I am in full agreement, Sir.'

Clarke nodded and continued. 'We know that the victim subsequently retracted her statement and that she was paid to do so by the young man's mother – a 'la-di-dah' woman. I believe that woman to have been Monica Frankland-Moore, and she confided in me earlier today that her son had studied law at Cambridge between 1984 and 1986.'

'What else did your visit to Brockley Hall reveal, Sir?'

Clarke knocked back the last dregs of his glass of whisky and poured himself another. 'That Rupert took part in an exchange programme between 1986 and 1987, and studied law for a further year at the University of Regensburg, in Germany.' Fletcher was about to say something, but Clarke had got the bit between his teeth now and he ploughed on. 'It was during the winter break that I believe he raped and strangled Emma Woodward at Brockley.'

'The bastard,' snarled Fletcher. 'So he'd got away with the attack on Gemma Bateson, and that gave him the impetus to go one step further and actually commit murder.'

'Precisely,' replied Clarke. 'And with him out of the way in Germany, my colleagues were free to reach the erroneous conclusion that Peter Fordham was the guilty party.'

'Poor lad.'

'Indeed, but the story doesn't end there.'

'You mean there's more?'

'I placed a call through to the Polizeipräsidium Regensburg in Germany earlier. They revealed an unsolved rape and murder in the Villapark area of the city – two months *after* the murder of Emma Woodward *and* during the time that Frankland-Moore was there!'

So that's what the phone calls were all about, thought Fletcher. And then the seriousness of Clarke's revelations suddenly dawned on her.

'Are we talking about a serial killer here?' asked Fletcher, almost as if she were talking to herself.

But Clarke still hadn't finished. 'We know that after he returned from Germany, Frankland-Moore was a trainee legal professional in Nottingham, and Webster has discovered that at Christmas 1988 there was an attack on a woman in the Wollaton Park area of the city...'

Fletcher cut him short. 'Yes, Sir. I...' She was about to say something, but she suddenly decided to bite her lip.

Seemingly irritated by her interruptions, Clarke repeated himself. 'There was an attack on a woman in the Wollaton Park area of the city, but the attacker was forced to flee when disturbed. This was shortly before Frankland-Moore met his future wife. They were married in 1990 and then they moved to Brussels.'

At this stage Clarke paused as if he was expecting Fletcher to intervene once more, but it was apparent that she had grasped the fact that one must not interrupt the Chief Inspector whilst he is taking the floor.

'Please go on,' she said somewhat timidly. 'I'm interested to hear what else you might have to say.'

Satisfied that there would be no further interruptions, Clarke continued. 'I also put a call through to the Police Station on the Rue du Marché in Brussels,' he boasted. 'They informed me that at Christmas 1992 the body of a young woman was found in the Espace Gaucheret park; she too had been raped and the case remains unsolved. Furthermore, at Easter 2010 the body of a woman was was found in the Parc de Laeken in Brussels; rape was again involved and as with other victims she had been strangled.'

Fletcher watched as he poured himself yet another stiff glass of Laphroaig, and by now she was expecting him to slur his words, but she was to be disappointed. Furthermore, he declined to offer her another diet coke. Having replenished his glass, he sat down once more and confidently resumed his dialogue.

'The Frankland-Moore's returned to England in 2014,' he said looking down at his glass. 'But during their time with the EU he travelled extensively to member states.' He now looked directly at Fletcher. 'You know something? I am certain that if we were to dig deeper then we'd discover other unsolved rapes and murders across the bloody Continent – from Paris to Madrid.'

Fletcher was in agreement once more. 'I'll bet you're right, Sir.'

'And I shouldn't be at all surprised if he's had numerous affairs since his marriage.'

'If that's the case, then why hasn't his wife left him?'

'Because the man is a control freak, and she has been scared shitless of him up until now – if you'll pardon my French,' he replied somewhat apologetically.

Fletcher shook her head. 'I still don't see how we can nail him for Jackson's murder.'

At this point Clarke reveals how contrary to what he had been told by Monica, Anna Frankland-Moore confirmed to him that due to an accident to their gardener, Rupert was forced to call at Jackson's house to plead with him to take the job on for two or three weeks.

'So you see, Rupert *had* been to the scene of the crime before. And I think that he returned there once more, only this time to commit murder.'

'And try to make it look like suicide?'

'Exactly!' exclaimed Clarke. 'And during the struggle one of them – I believe Jackson – dropped the *Tom and Jerry* badge on the floor.'

'Why do you say Jackson dropped it, Sir?'

Clarke sighed heavily. 'After Emma Woodward's murder, Mrs. Fordham spent days combing the woods and the scene of the crime, in the hope of finding *anything* that would exonerate her son. She found the badge, showed it to my then colleagues, but they didn't want to know. However, she kept it, along with her diary, and Jackson took them from her room. He hid the diary, but kept the badge on his person. As I said, it must have fallen out of his pocket during the struggle, and ended up underneath the cabinet at the foot of the stairs – all unseen by Frankland-Moore.'

Fletcher was impressed. 'When will you be arresting him, Sir?'

'Well, I want to get hold of the vehicle he used on the day of the murder, because I'm sure that we'll find both his *and* Jackson's DNA all over it.'

'How do you propose to do that?'

A wicked little grin appeared on Clarke's face. 'I have a cunning little plan, Sergeant,' he smirked. 'In the meantime I've already given orders that Frankland-Moore is to be watched 24/7 from now on.'

Fletcher saw her chance. 'And where do I fit into all of this?' she asked eagerly.

Clarke rose from his chair swiftly and ignored her last question. 'Bloody hell,' he swore. 'Is that the time? I really ought to be turning in – and you too, Sergeant.'

Fletcher shot a quick glance at her watch – it was approaching midnight. She rose too and made for the cabin door, but she hadn't received an answer to her last question. 'What part do you want me to play in the arrest of Frankland-Moore, Sir?' she asked rather impatiently.

Clarke was ready for just such a response. 'Well, I suggest that you get a good night's sleep to begin with, Sergeant,' he replied a trifle condescendingly. 'I want you to continue co-ordinating the case from the incident room.'

'But, Sir…'

He cut her short once more. 'Goodnight, Sergeant,' he smiled beatifically as he closed the door behind her.

It wasn't that difficult, was it? What's more, he'd still be keeping one step ahead of her – and that was the whole idea, wasn't it?

Chapter 46

Saturday, 15 July, 2017 (a.m.)

All was set for a glorious weekend in the town of Grimley, as Saturday morning broke with barely a cloud in the sky. By 9.00 a.m. the regular weekly market was already beginning to teem with people, and this in spite of the fact that it was nowhere near as big or as popular as in days gone by. It was the same with the shops and businesses around the market square and those along the main street that bisected the town – everyone had come out to shop!

Unusually for a Saturday, there was one business on the main street that was surprisingly open – or at least it seemed that way. If one peered through the large window of Frankland-Moore Solicitors, it was possible to make out the slim figure of a woman sitting behind a desk tapping away on her keyboard, answering the phone on her desk now and again or occasionally making her way over to a set of drawers on the other side of the room – amongst other things.

The woman in question was aged about thirty-eight, quite tall at five feet and nine inches in height, and her long, blonde wavy hair was piled up on top of her head. She wore a navy blue roll up sleeve blazer above a white blouse, together with jeans and high heels. Although casually attired, she *still* looked very secretarial and very attractive; what's more, she knew it!

Laura Brownlow was ostensibly putting in a few hours on a Saturday morning in the absence of the other staff and her boss, Rupert Frankland-Moore. It just so happened that he was also her lover and he had been very vague when they spoke over the phone the previous evening. She was to open up the business that morning, make a few phone calls and 'tie up a few loose ends' as it were, and then go home to pack her bags prior to meeting him at the East Midlands Airport around noon. There were one or two other minor details – so he said – but it all seemed very cloak and dagger to Laura.

She had been born in Derby, the daughter of a Rolls-Royce employee, but she was always deeply ambitious when it came to the pursuit of knowledge – and power. Having qualified as a legal secretary in her twenties, she worked for a number of law firms in the Derby area before landing the job with Frankland-Moore at Grimley in

2014. She has never married (her career has taken precedence), but there have been numerous boyfriends over the years. Attracted to powerful and assertive men, this was undoubtedly the reason why she unceremoniously dumped her previous boyfriend within weeks of becoming Frankland-Moore's secretary!

As much as she loves her work, she has quickly (and typically) developed a sense of loyalty to her boss, although others would say that this is because she is driven by the power it could bring. However, if dearest Rupert were to get into trouble in any way, then others would say that there is every likelihood that she would ditch him at the drop of a hat!

In many respects she epitomises the siren. She has developed her persona and charm on the premise that men are always looking for a variety of experiences, and she can present those experiences to Frankland-Moore. Her charm lies in an almost theatrical and sensually pleasing visual experience, which she creates through elaborate attire (although not today) and an air of seduction all around her. She is feminine, attractive and regal, but her strategy is to become even more physically attractive. It goes without saying that she had an instant effect on Frankland-Moore because of her sex appeal. There is an almost dangerous quality about her, and this has proved effective in making him pursue her.

There is a downside to all this of course. She greatly fears being rejected by him, and positively bristles with indignation that she might be considered inferior to his wife, who she sees as the enemy. Naturally jealous, malicious and vindictive; these characteristics have intensified since she began her affair.

For the time being, however, she is diligently performing the tasks that her boss and lover has given her, although it has to be said that she is still somewhat puzzled as to why he should want her to do them now and so suddenly. Still, it will be good to get away for a week or so and get him away from that bloody wife of his. And yet there was no mention of where they were going to; just that she had to pack her bags and meet him at the airport.

She was just extracting some documents from one of the cabinets when shortly before 10 a.m. a man wearing a short-sleeved shirt and tie entered the office. She turned to face him and noticed that he had a close-cropped beard.

'I'm sorry, but we're not officially open,' she said in a deep, sensual and well-spoken voice.

'That's a shame,' replied the man politely. 'My wife and I are getting divorced and I'm looking for an appropriate solicitor.'

'Well, Mr. Frankland-Moore is your man, but he won't be available for a week or so. It would be best if you made an appointment.'

The man was clearly disappointed. 'I see,' he said rubbing his chin. 'His he – Mr. Franklyn-Moore…'

'Frankland-Moore,' she corrected him.

'I'm sorry – Mr. Frankland-Moore. Is he okay to work for?'

A puzzled frown appeared on her face. 'Yes, of course,' she said suspiciously. 'He's a model professional.'

'A married man, I dare say?'

Now she was getting anxious. 'Yes…look…what's this all about?'

The man continued with his questions. 'Good looking, is he?'

'What are you trying to suggest?' she said bristling with indignation.

At that moment the man pulled out his identity card and introduced himself. 'Detective Chief Inspector Clarke of Derbyshire CID,' he said in a softly-spoken and yet authoritative voice.'I'm afraid I have some more questions to ask.'

Laura was clearly very put out. 'You could have said as much when you came in,' she snapped somewhat petulantly.

Clarke tried to suppress a wry grin. 'But that wouldn't have been half as much fun,' he said openly. His manner and his line of questioning then changed abruptly. 'Where was your boss on Monday, 3 July?'

She didn't even need to check the appointment books. 'Ah yes, that was when he was out for most of the day visiting a client,' she said confidently.

Clarke clearly sensed that she was lying. 'Well, perhaps you'd be so kind as to provide the name, address and telephone number of this client – if that's not too much trouble?'

Laura gave the impression that she was confused and befuddled. 'I'm afraid I can't do that,' she said nervously.

'And why not?'

'Because he didn't leave any details,' she snapped! 'He just said that he would be out for most of the day on business, and that if anyone called I was to tell them that he had gone to see a client.'

'There, that wasn't difficult, was it?' He paused briefly before continuing. 'Did he come into work in his own car?'

'Yes.'

'And so he used his car when he left the office that day on business?'

'No.'

'Well whose bloody car did he use?'

'He asked me if he could borrow my car for the time being as his was playing up.'

'Playing up?'

'That's what he said – playing up.'

Clarke shook his head in consternation. 'And your car – what make is it?

'It's a Renault Twingo.'

'Colour?'

'Silver.'

'Registration Number?'

Laura sighed deeply as if bored. 'HK15 TDG.'

'Thank you – you've been very helpful.'

'What on earth *is* this all about, Inspector?'

Clarke ignored the question. 'I'm afraid we're going to have to impound your vehicle, Miss Brownlow.'

Laura was now indignant. 'But you can't do that,' she snapped angrily.

'Oh but we can,' replied Clarke calmly.

'But why?'

'We believe that it was involved in a serious crime and so Scenes of Crime Officers will need to carry out a full forensic check of the vehicle.'

'Serious crime? What do you mean?'

'Your boyfriend has been a naughty boy,' he said mockingly. He then made for the door, but turned sharply on his heels and looked her straight in the eye. 'Oh, and you can forget about meeting up with him later!'

Laura protested vehemently. 'But *I've* done nothing wrong…'

Clarke opened the door and summoned a uniformed WPC from outside. 'You can come in now, Roper,' he shouted. As the policewoman stepped inside, Clarke continued. 'Caution her and then take her down to the station at Leverton.'

Laura was mortified. 'What am I being charged with?' she screamed.

'Didn't I say?' Clarke replied knowingly. 'You were caught on CCTV cameras at Tesco's causing wilful damage to another vehicle in the supermarket car park on Monday, 10 July!'

Chapter 47

Saturday, 15 July, 2017 (a.m.)

Clarke had been as good as his word and officers were mounting a twenty-four-hour watch on Rupert Frankland-Moore, and especially around Brockley Hall. One of those officers was a somewhat bored Detective Constable Webster, who had parked up at the village cricket club car park, and taken up position (with binoculars) on the lane between the Hall and Steadman's Woods.

He hated this sort of work, where one could spend hours attempting to watch the movements of an individual or individuals, and come away with bugger all. Okay, he had witnessed two vehicles departing from the rear of the Hall during his watch, about an hour or so earlier; one was a silver Range Rover driven by an old guy with a limp who had assisted a glamorous-looking elderly woman into the rear of the vehicle, and the other a white Ford Fiesta driven by a middle-aged woman with an older woman in the passenger seat beside her. And yet up until now there had been no sign whatsoever of the head of the family and the object of his assignment.

Unable to stifle yet another almighty yawn, he looked at his watch for the umpteenth time, and it was coming up to 11.00 a.m. Bloody hell – he had at least another three hours before his replacement took over! Reluctantly raising the binoculars to his eyes once more, he looked over the large garden to the rear of the Hall and at that moment the figure of a male appeared through the doors and came down the steps. At last, the man himself, thought Webster; and he was making his way towards one of the garages. Seconds later Frankland-Moore drove out of the garage in a black open-top LaFerrari Aperta and pulled up at the foot of the steps. Climbing out of the car, he opened the boot before returning to the house.

Suddenly Webster received an incoming message on his phone – it was from his colleague who was watching the gates to the Hall from the main road. Webster's eyes began to pop out of his head as he read the message with a sense of shock and horror:

A cream-coloured Mini Cooper convertible with a black roof was making its way down the driveway to the Hall!

'You gotta be kidding,' said Webster out loud. Snatching at the binoculars once more, he looked on in horror as the Mini Cooper emerged through the trees that lined the driveway and pulled up before the LaFerrari Aperta. 'What the fuck is *she* doing here,' he exclaimed. He wasted no time in calling Clarke and informing him that Detective Sergeant Fletcher had arrived on the scene.

Clarke exploded with rage. 'That bloody *stupid* woman,' he bellowed down the phone. 'I told her to stay away and not to get involved!'

'What are we gonna do, Sir?' shouted a clearly flustered Webster.

'I'm gonna see if I can get through to her – I'll call you back shortly.'

Webster didn't have to wait long. 'Did you get through to her, Sir?'

'Just as I expected,' replied Clarke. 'She's gone and turned her bloody phone off!'

'Oh my God,' replied an increasingly horrified Webster.

Clarke paused for a few seconds and then continued. 'I'll be on the scene as soon as I can, Webster – and with back-up!'

Unaware of the events now taking place around her – although conscious of the fact that her presence at Brockley Hall will have been noticed by now – Fletcher climbed out of the Mini Cooper just as Frankland-Moore came down the steps of the Hall with a couple of suitcases.

'Not playing cricket today?' she said standing beside her car with folded arms.

'Detective Sergeant Fletcher,' replied Frankland-Moore seemingly unperturbed by her arrival. 'What a *very* pleasant surprise – although you have caught me at an inopportune moment.'

'So I can see,' she said as she watched him put a couple of suitcases into the boot of the car.

'Cricket's off, I'm afraid,' he said raising his eyebrows. 'Well, with half the team missing – including the Captain... And of course the groundsman is sadly no longer with us.'

'Strangely enough, I was going to talk about the late Mr. Jackson, but actually I want to remind you of an event long before his demise.'

'You'll find my memory isn't as good as what it used to be, Sergeant – and I am in rather a hurry, as you can see.'

Fletcher unfolded her arms, stepped forward and positioned herself in front of the driver's door of his car. 'It will only take a few minutes of your time, Mr. Frankland-Moore.'

He looked at his watch. 'If you must,' he retorted somewhat impatiently.

'I'd like to take you back to the Christmas of 1988. You were then a trainee in Nottingham, were you not?'

His impatience was growing. 'What if I was?'

'There was a woman out jogging in Wollaton Park, when she was suddenly attacked and submitted to a violent sexual assault by a man wearing a balaclava. The attacker attempted to strangle the woman, but a man out walking his dog appeared from nowhere and the attacker fled from the scene. Oh, the woman survived the assault, but she was never the same again – as you can imagine.'

'Why are you telling me this?' he asked with increasing exasperation.

Fletcher dropped her bombshell. 'Because the woman who was assaulted was my mother, Mr. Frankland-Moore,' she replied as her eyes began to fill with tears. 'And you were her attacker!'

'What a preposterous suggestion,' snapped Frankland-Moore as he attempted to get into his car.

Fletcher refused to budge an inch and pressed on with her claim. 'It was the same time, the same place *and* the attacker was wearing *Joop* aftershave; the same aftershave that you were wearing when we questioned Simon Collins and the same aftershave that you are wearing now!'

'Utter rubbish,' he scoffed. 'Now will you let me pass!'

'My mother's attacker wore a balaclava, but the one thing that she always remembered was that bloody aftershave!'

As Fletcher tried to hold back the tears and Frankland-Moore glared at her with a look of sheer hatred in his eyes, a silver Range Rover came around the corner – followed thirty seconds or so later by a white Ford Fiesta. Monica Frankland-Moore had just returned from her weekly trip to the hairdresser, and the old man with the limp helped her out of the Range Rover. At the same time Anna Frankland-Moore had returned from a shopping expedition with the old man's wife, Mrs. Dilks. They climbed out of the Ford Fiesta, but it was Monica who spoke first.

265

'*Who* are you and *what* are you doing here?' she said in that haughty, condescending manner of hers.

Fletcher pulled out her identity card. 'I am Detective Sergeant Jacqui Fletcher,' she said continuing to look Frankland-Moore in the eye. 'And I am here to remind your son how he raped my mother and then tried to kill her!'

'What nonsense!' snapped Monica. 'My son would never do such a thing.'

Unseen by everyone present, Anna Frankland-Moore had stealthily stepped indoors, only to reappear several seconds later armed with a shotgun.

'I always knew,' she said calmly as she pointed the shotgun at her husband, who now turned to face her shaking with fear as he stood beside an equally stunned Sergeant Fletcher. 'Oh yes, I know how to use this,' she said confidently.

As she started to make her way slowly down the steps towards her husband, there came the distinct sound of police sirens in the distance, as a convoy of vehicles raced down the driveway to the rear of the Hall. Detective Chief Inspector Clarke had arrived on the scene at last – complete with back-up.

The first vehicle pulled up in a cloud of dust behind those already present, and Clarke stepped out of the passenger door with his hands raised.

'Please, don't do anything silly, Mrs. Frankland-Moore,' he said in a calm voice.

She was only several feet away from her husband now, but the barrel of the gun was still pointed directly at him. 'Tell them, Rupert,' she shouted. 'Tell them the truth, or I swear to God I'll pull the trigger.'

She had left him no option. 'Alright,' he bawled! 'It was me. I did all of them – Wollaton Park, Steadman's Woods and the others too!'

With those words Monica collapsed to the floor in a flood of tears. 'No, no, no,' she wailed. 'Not my beautiful boy!'

This was just what Rupert was waiting for. Sensing that this had caught everyone off their guard, he made to grab Fletcher by the neck from behind and use her as a shield against the gun. Dragging her towards the black Range Rover, he bellowed at Dilks. 'Give me the keys – now!' As Dilks fumbled around for the keys, Rupert held out his right hand to receive them.

It was a mistake.

Regaining her balance, Fletcher was able to grab Rupert's arm and spinning him around he was forced to release his hold on her neck. She then delivered a kick straight to his groin with her left foot, followed by another to his jaw with her right foot. All was done with lightning speed and in a manner that would have impressed the great Bruce Lee.

'Well don't just bloody stand there,' she screamed. 'Someone get the cuffs on him!'

Everybody had been watching spellbound by the proceedings and with mouths agape, but Fletcher's words had the desired effect upon one of her uniformed colleagues as he snapped out of his trance-like state to place the handcuffs upon a stunned Rupert Frankland-Moore, who was then bundled into a car and driven away.

However, a distraught Monica was being helped to her feet from the gravel by Mr. and Mrs. Dilks; her face unrecognisable due to the sheer volume of tears that had all but obliterated any signs of make-up.

Anna Frankland-Moore had willingly handed the shotgun over to another uniformed police officer, and she was now led away to another police car smiling from ear to ear.

At this point Clarke made his way nonchalantly over to Fletcher, whose eyes were still brimming with tears. 'I wouldn't recommend doing that sort of thing again without back-up, Sergeant,' he said softly but authoritatively.

She turned to face him with what could only be described as a look of guilt. 'I had to achieve justice for my mother,' she whimpered.

With those words, Clarke smiled at her and nodded his head as if to reassure her that all would be well and that he understood everything. 'I'll see you back at the station,' he said calmly.

She watched him walk back to the car to be driven away, and at that moment *she* fell to her knees, unable to stop the tears that now came flooding down her cheeks.

Chapter 48

Saturday, 15 July, 2017 (p.m.)

Having arrived back at Leverton Police Station, Clarke initially made for the canteen where he bought a small bottle of sparkling spring water. He could have murdered a glass or two of malt whisky (or even a small bottle), but that was going to have to wait. For now he made do with the water, and after exchanging pleasantries with Scattergood he made a beeline for his office. Shutting the door behind him quietly, he was still wearing his bomber jacket as he slumped into the chair behind his desk and closed his eyes. What a bloody fortnight, he thought to himself; and it still wasn't over!

The incident room up at Brockley would have to be wound up and closed down, and a search of the Hall conducted. He had delegated both tasks to Webster on his way back to Leverton. The next thing to do was inform Superintendent Annable of the events, and he sure as hell wasn't looking forward to that.

It transpired that Annable was playing a round of golf when the call from Clarke came through (who'd have thought it, thought Clarke), and he was not at all happy to have been interrupted. Indeed, he was already in a foul mood since he and his partner were four down after only five holes.

'This had better be good, Clarke,' he boomed in his deep, baritone voice. 'You know damn well that I don't like to be disturbed when on the golf course with friends!'

Another bunch of bloody Freemasons more like, was Clarke's immediate thought, and he was somewhat miffed that he couldn't very well reveal his innermost secrets to the Superintendent at this particular time.

'Actually it's good news, Sir,' he murmured through gritted teeth.

'Well, lets have it then!'

And so Clarke let him have it. 'We've got him, Sir.'

'Got who, for crying out loud?'

'We've got the man who killed Keith Jackson, Sir.'

The change in Annable's demeanour was instant. 'That's splendid news, Clarke – wait till I tell the Assistant Chief Constable!'

Irked that there was no word of congratulations for him and his team, Clarke dropped *his* first bombshell. 'It was the lawyer, Sir.'

'Lawyer?' boomed Annable in disbelief.

'Yes, Sir – Frankland-Moore from Brockley Hall.'

'You can't be serious?' he boomed again before pausing for a few seconds and lowering his voice substantially. 'Has he admitted it?'

Clarke was expecting just such a response. 'Well...not as yet, but...'

'Oh, for God's sake...!'

'As I was trying to say, Sir. We've got him in custody and we'll get the confession out of him, but DNA evidence will also back up our case against him.'

'You had better be right, Clarke!'

A rueful smile then came to Clarke's face as he dropped bombshell number two. 'There's something else, Sir,' he said knowing full well how Annable would react to the next set of revelations.

'What do you mean?'

'He's committed other serious crimes here and across the Continent, Sir,'

The response was deafening.

'*He's done what*!' bellowed an incredulous Annable.

Clarke held the phone away from his ear for a few seconds before replying. 'And I'm afraid one of those crimes involved a miscarriage of justice from thirty years ago.'

'Oh my God!'

It wasn't as if it had happened on Annable's watch, but one would have thought so judging by his reactions. But Clarke hadn't finished and he couldn't resist one last little dig at his superior.

'Well, Sir, I see it like this,' he began. 'At the end of the day, we must not be satisfied until justice rolls down like waters and righteousness like a mighty stream.'

Annable certainly didn't see the funny side of Clarke's comment. 'What the bloody hell *are* you on about man?'

'Martin Luther King, Sir – from his "I Have a Dream" speech in March 1963...'

There was a deathly silence at the other end before fully fledged atheist Clarke could add impressively that King's quote was taken from The Bible, Amos 5:24!

Clarke was glad to have got the call to Superintendent Annable off his chest, and for ten minutes or so afterwards he sat chortling to himself about his quote from Martin Luther King, amongst other things. His little reverie was brief, however, for there was suddenly a knock on his office door, and on his bidding in stepped Sergeant Fletcher. The tears had gone and since she wore little make-up it wasn't going to take her long to freshen up, but she still deemed it necessary to make an apology almost immediately.

'I'm sorry, Sir,' she began with a whisper. 'I let you down.'

Clarke looked her in the eye and gave his response after what to Fletcher seemed an eternity, but was actually only a few seconds.

'You have nothing to apologise for, Sergeant,' he replied with total sincerity. 'I would have probably done the same thing.'

She gave a weak smile. 'Thank you, Sir, but I can't imagine that you would.'

Clarke made no reply to her last comment, but he was naturally anxious to know why she had said nothing about her mother being a possible victim in the case. He took a swig of water from the bottle and proceeded to question her.

'Why didn't you tell me about your mother?' He asked in a softly spoken and placid voice.

Fletcher stared at him slightly stupefied. 'Because we were looking for the killer of Keith Jackson, Sir,' she replied with a frown and a shrug of the shoulders. 'And you *did* keep me and the others in the dark on this case, to put it mildly.'

Touché, thought Clarke. 'I rather asked for that, didn't I?' he said ruefully.

'Mmmm,' replied Fletcher nodding her head vigorously before a smile eventually lit up her face.

Clarke paused for a while before going on. 'Are you okay talking about your mother and what happened to her?'

Fletcher looked down at the floor. 'Like I said, she is still alive, but she has never gotten over what that bastard did to her.'

Clarke thought carefully about his response. 'That should come as no surprise to anyone under the circumstances.' He hoped that his comment was appropriate.

Fletcher then looked up and turned her eyes to the ceiling before going on to say that she was staying with her father at the time. Her parents had divorced when she was five, in 1986, and her mother had gone on to remarry soon after moving to Nottingham. She was out jogging in Wollaton Park when a man wearing a balaclava and gloves jumped out of the bushes and assaulted her. The man didn't say much, but her mother was able to recall that he had a 'la-di-dah' accent. More importantly, she recognised the man's aftershave – it was *Joop*. And the reason that she was able to recognise the aftershave was because her former husband (Fletcher's father) always wore it!

'It was when we were questioning Simon Collins that I first had my suspicions about Frankland-Moore,' she continued. 'I just didn't like the guy – the way he spoke to me and kept looking at me. And then there was his bloody aftershave – the same aftershave that my dad used to wear.'

'Go on,' said Clarke.

'And then of course my ears pricked up when you asked Webster to look into assaults in Nottingham between 1988 and 1990, and I knew he would come across the attack on my mother. When you confirmed it last night I almost revealed all there and then, but I held back because I just knew that you wouldn't let me get involved.'

Clarke nodded his head. 'Too right I wouldn't,' he admitted.

'So you see, I had to confront him myself.'

'Well, you certainly did that alright.' There was yet another pause, before Clarke asked her the inevitable question about the manner in which she disarmed Frankland-Moore. 'Where *did* you learn to do that sort of thing, Sergeant?'

'After the attack on my mother I started taking karate lessons,' replied Fletcher openly. 'I've been a black belt for several years now!'

Chapter 49

Saturday, 15 July, 2017 (p.m.)

Clarke's chat with Fletcher – albeit brief – had gone a long way to healing some of the divisions that clearly existed between the two of them; but then he had created most of those divisions himself. No doubt they still had their differences, but at long last Diana Marshall's advice seemed to be sinking in, and there was every reason to hope that it would serve him well in the future.

Strangely enough, he thought of Diana as he and Fletcher prepared themselves for the questioning of Rupert Frankland-Moore. It was a Saturday – what would she be doing? Indeed, what would she be wearing? No doubt very little on a baking hot day like today. His mind went back to the previous Saturday when they had made love, and he desperately wanted to do so again – and again.

He was shaken out of his brief little reverie by the knowledge that her partner would be back from his golfing weekend – and by another knock on his office door. It was Scattergood; Frankland-Moore and the duty solicitor were ready.

Duty solicitor! How ironic he thought, as he and Fletcher made their way down the corridor to the interview room. They said nothing to each other, but as he stepped aside to allow her to enter the room first he gave her a reassuring smile, and it was returned in kind. However, the smiles were gone seconds later as they came face to face with the man they had been after for the last two weeks; the man who now sat before them with folded arms and a look of pompous self-satisfaction from ear to ear.

Needless to say, most of his attention was reserved for Fletcher as she took her seat, and yet although she still found him utterly repellent, she no longer felt uncomfortable in his presence. Maybe it was the fact that she had immobilised him so decidedly. It was clearly still playing on *his* mind.

'You certainly know how to look after yourself, Sergeant,' he said to her out of earshot of Clarke – or so he thought.

'Well, she certainly knew how to look after you, didn't she?' interrupted Clarke as he removed his bomber jacket and hung it over the back of his chair before seating himself at the desk.

The comment produced a wry grin from Fletcher, but it also had the effect of wiping the one from Frankland-Moore's face, and he slowly turned his head and gave Clarke a look of undisguised malice. Completely disconcerted and unfazed, the latter switched on the tape and began by asking about him about his time at Cambridge.

'You were a member of the *Tom and Jerry Club*, were you not? He asked without looking up.

'Ah, great times we had back then,' replied Frankland-Moore nostalgically.

'You brought terror and mayhem to all the bars and bistro's of the bloody place, for Christ's sake.'

'It was all harmless fun.'

'I don't call assaulting and raping someone "harmless".'

'She was asking for it – all night long.'

Barely able to suppress his anger, Clarke pressed on. 'Is this when the attacks started – with Gemma Bateson?'

'Was that her name?' asked Frankland-Moore almost disinterestedly. 'Yes, I suppose she was the first – but then mummy came to my rescue,' he said nonchalantly as the smug grin returned to his face.

Clarke continued to make notes before moving onto the next question. 'But rape wasn't enough for you, was it? You had to take it one step further and resort to murder, didn't you?'

At this the duty solicitor stepped in. 'You don't have to answer anything…'

Frankland-Moore cut him short. 'I do know these things – I *am* a solicitor myself!' he snapped looking down his nose at the man who was representing him.

'Were,' said Clarke with unbridled sarcasm as he looked once more at his notes.

The comment caused Frankland-Moore to sneer at Clarke yet again, and he paused as if to compose himself before continuing.

'I suppose that I found the experience exhilarating, Inspector,' was his eventual reply to Clarke's previous question.

'Then tell me, Mr. Frankland-Moore,' said Clarke looking up and staring right into the offender's eyes. 'Tell me about the murder of Emma Woodward in Steadman's Woods all those years ago.'

Frankland-Moore sank back into his chair. 'It was the day before I was due to go back to Germany after the Christmas break.' he said with a sigh.

Fletcher looked at Clarke, and although nothing was said, the words 'Just like you said, Sir' were written all over her face. Frankland-Moore continued.

'I had been down to one of the bird hides in the woods, drinking and smoking a little Red Leb – I was high as a kite,' he boasted. 'As I emerged from the woods the girl in question approached – from there it was easy.'

'Would you care to elaborate – for the tape?'

Frankland-Moore sighed again, as if the proceedings were boring him. 'I dragged her into the woods, raped her and then strangled her with her own scarf – I have to say it gave me quite a buzz,' he grinned.

'I was the one who found the body,' replied Clarke after several seconds.

Frankland-Moore leaned forward. 'Were you really? he said as if fascinated by Clarke's comment.

'Oh yes, I got to see your handiwork at first hand.'

'Well there's a thing.'

At that moment Fletcher noticed that Clarke was visibly shaking and that his fist was clenched, so she leaned across and put her hand on his wrist as if to steady *his* nerves. It had the desired effect, although the incident clearly amused Frankland-Moore, who continued to grin like a Cheshire cat. Clarke composed himself and continued.

'What happened after you killed the girl?' he asked calmly.

'Luckily there seemed to be no one around, so I crossed the dirt track and entered the grounds of the Hall by climbing the wall.'

'You seem to have had quite a lot of luck with that case – the fact that your *Tom and Jerry* badge fell off in the attack and nobody found it during the ensuing search.'

'Frankland-Moore looked down his nose once more. 'Twas a trifle fortuitous, I must admit, but I didn't let it bother me.'

'And the fact that you were in Germany during the investigation – when we arrested the wrong man *and* so quickly?'

'Yes, that was a blessing too.'

There was a pause again before Frankland-Moore was asked about the murder in Regensburg, to which he confessed readily. Clarke then turned to the attack in Wollaton Park.

'What are your recollections of that day?' he asked glancing briefly at Fletcher.

'She could have passed for a much younger model,' replied Frankland-Moore with what appeared to be a degree of earnestness. 'But back then I wasn't choosy!'

'Stick to the point,' snapped a clearly irritated Clarke!

Frankland-Moore looked equally irritated that Clarke wanted him to talk about how he had been thwarted in his attempt to murder Fletcher's mother.

'Well, all was going to plan until that bloody man appeared with his dog.' He then leaned forward again and looked directly at Fletcher. 'How is your dear mother by the way?'

As Fletcher bristled with anger, Clarke decided that it was best to move onto the next set of questions. 'You met and married your wife, and then you both moved to Brussels...'

'We should never have voted to leave you know,' interrupted Frankland-Moore.

Under different circumstances, Clarke would have happily argued the merits of leaving the EU till the cows came home, but he had a job to do and so he pressed Frankland-Moore on his time in the EU.

'I take it that you were responsible for the murders in Brussels?' he asked confidently.

'*Mais oui*,' came the jaunty, cocky response from Frankland-Moore.

'And yet although you were based at the headquarters of that over-bureaucratised monstrosity for many years, you travelled extensively across the Continent during that time, so there must have been opportunities for further attacks and murders?'

Frankland-Moore clearly resented the attack on his former employer and was about to say as such when there was a knock on the door and in stepped Webster. As Fletcher announced his entrance for the benefit of the tape, he came forward and emptied a number of trinkets onto the desk in front of everyone – rings, earrings and necklaces, amongst other things.

'Found these up at the Hall, Sir,' said Webster in an uncharacteristically serious manner.

'Care to comment, Mr. Frankland-Moore?' said Clarke with just the merest suggestion of a smile on his face.

'Ah, you found them, I see. I thought you might.'

'Trophies by any chance?'

Frankland-Moore leaned forward and began pointing at each item of jewellery. 'That was Madrid,' he said pointing to an engagement ring.

'That one was in Rome – I can't remember where that one was from – but the earrings were a souvenir from Budapest.'

'So you do admit to further murders?'

'Working for the EU does have its advantages!' he said with yet another smirk.

Clarke scribbled a few notes on a piece of paper and then handed it to the uniformed policeman who had been standing beside the door. He left the room as Clarke stood up.

'I think it's time we had a break.' he said with a jaded, melancholic look on his face.

Chapter 50

Saturday, 15 July, 2017 (p.m.)

'You've got to hand it to him,' said Clarke as he slumped up against the wall outside the interview room. 'He *does* have a certain panache.'

Fletcher was more succinct. 'I just think he's a bloody arrogant narcissist, Sir!'

In spite of the seriousness of it all, her comment brought a smile to Clarke's face, and seconds later she followed suit before heading down the corridor to the canteen. She returned after a couple of minutes with a takeaway cup of coffee and a bottle of sparkling Buxton water for Clarke.

'I've been trying to think of that bloody case in Scotland many moons ago,' said Clarke as she handed him the bottle of water. 'They returned a verdict of Not Proven against the accused – you do know that they have such a verdict north of the border, Sergeant?'

Fletcher gave the impression that he had insulted her intelligence. 'Yes, Sir. I'm quite aware of that,' she replied.

He clicked his fingers. 'Got it,' he shouted triumphantly! 'The Ardlamont Mystery and the trial of Alfred John Monson. Do you know anything about it?'

'Before my time, Sir.'

He took the hint. 'Well, Monson was accused of murdering this guy, Hambrough, and he was represented in court by John Comrie Thomson. After the trial Thomson was alleged to have said "I don't know if he killed Hambrough, but he nearly killed me" – or words to that effect.'

'What's that got to do with *our* case, Sir?' she asked with a puzzled look on her face.

'Because that's how I felt when I walked out of the interview room just now.'

'Whatever you do, don't let him get to you, Sir.'

'I've confronted many a suspect over the years, Sergeant, but this bugger really is one of the most onerous adversaries I've ever...' He couldn't finish the sentence.

'But he's admitting to everything, Sir.'

'That's what's bothering me – and the manner in which he's going about it!'

'And we've still got to get him to admit to killing Jackson!'

He looked at her pensively for several seconds. 'Then I suggest we get back in there and finish what we started. You've got the diary and the badge?'

Frankland-Moore was in animated conversation with his lawyer as Clarke and Fletcher re-entered the room, but the smug grin returned to his face as he sat back in his seat with folded arms.

'Ah, once more unto the breach, dear friends, once more.' he said mockingly as the two police officers took their seats. 'Don't tell me – some more questions that you wish to fire at me?'

Clarke paid no heed to what he considered to be Shakespearean drivel and simply launched into the next line of questioning. 'Tell us about Keith Jackson,' he said unhurriedly.

Frankland-Moore's grin disappeared and he seemed to go into a sulk. 'What about him?' he sneered.

'Why did you kill him?'

'What makes you think *I* killed him?'

'The guy was trying to blackmail you, right?'

'No comment.'

'He'd already taken to blackmailing Collins and Ibbotson in a small way, but then he found something on you, didn't he?'

'No comment.'

'Yes, he found something that pointed the finger at you for the murder of Emma Woodward thirty years ago, didn't he?'

Frankland-Moore continued to sit back and listen intently to the accusations being made by Clarke. His legs were crossed and his hands were clasped before him, but he seemed to fiddle with his thumbs nervously as he paused briefly before replying to the last question.

'No comment,' he said once more.

Unabashed, Clarke continued.

'So when he contacted you on Monday the 3rd and demanded that you cough up or else, you decided it was best to go along with his little ploy for the time being, didn't you? But you made your mind up there and then that you weren't going to let this former Army veteran-turned-general handyman and degenerate alcoholic outsmart you. Am I right?'

Frankland-Moore appeared to shuffle uncomfortably in his chair, but his response was the same as before.

'No comment.'

'No, after you had deposited the amount that Jackson had demanded, you decided to lie in wait for him and parked up at the rear of The Old Turnpike House. After all, you *had* been there before – when you were forced to grovel to him and ask him to do some gardening work for you? But you couldn't use your Ferrari, could you? Which is when you came up with the idea of asking if you could borrow your girlfriend's car – the Renault Twingo?'

Frankland-Moore's eyes narrowed and a look of sheer spite and malice could just about be discerned on his face with these words, but once again Clarke had got the bit between his teeth.

'By the way,' he said leaning forward across the desk. 'Scenes of Crime Officer's are currently mounting a thorough search of the vehicle, and I am confident that they will find evidence of both your DNA and that of Jackson's.'

Frankland-Moore mouthed the word 'bastard' in response, but Clarke took no notice.

'Oh, and please don't insult my intelligence by insisting that you were out all day visiting a client. Your bit on the side is currently helping us with our enquiries on that and other matters, and she has already revealed that there was no client.'

'Women, eh?' replied Frankland-Moore as he cast a brief but furtive glance at Fletcher. 'Just can't trust them, can you?'

She looked down and ignored him as Clarke continued his line of questioning.

'So, you bided your time and waited – and then you heard a vehicle pulling up outside the house. To your initial surprise it was Tony Dawkins – and he'd come to drop Jackson off because he was absolutely rat-arsed. And then Dawkins drove off and you saw your chance. You waited until Jackson opened the door – and then using the washing line from behind the house you came up behind him and struck!'

Frankland-Moore *still* sat there with an odious smirk on his face and said absolutely nothing. It was as if the whole procedure was boring him and he couldn't wait for it to end. But Clarke was clearly in his element.

'It must have been over pretty quickly,' hinted Clarke. 'And especially so as Jackson was inebriate. But you weren't finished, were you? It was then that you came up with the idea of trying to make it look like suicide – and according to the pathologist a rather pathetic attempt for someone who considers himself to be smarter than the average bear!'

This reference to a cartoon comedy from the early sixties meant nothing to Frankland-Moore, but he got the gist of what Clarke was saying and the sneer returned to his face once more.

Clarke continued. 'And then you began to search in vain for the evidence – or whatever it was that Jackson had found that prompted him to blackmail you. But it was then that Collins arrived and knocked on the door. Mercifully for you he didn't hang around long, but he shoved his monthly quota through the door before departing. So you took that *and* the money that Jackson had extorted from you and scarpered from the scene.'

Frankland-Moore seemed to purse his lips, as if he was slightly aggrieved with one tiny aspect of Clarke's commentary and had made a mental note to correct him after the questioning was over.

But it wasn't over.

'However,' continued Clarke. 'During your struggle with Jackson – and your search for the incriminating evidence – you failed to notice this.' He turned to Fletcher. 'Could I have the badge, please, Sergeant.'

Frankland-Moore still showed little emotion as Fletcher produced the evidence bag, but when she tipped the contents out onto the desk and out fell the *Tom and Jerry* badge his whole demeanour changed at a stroke.

'Well, well,' he said as he leaned forward and tried to reach out for the badge.

Clarke put his hand out to stop him. 'Sorry, but that's evidence, as I'm sure you know.'

Frankland-Moore nodded. 'Where *did* you find that?' he asked.

'It was found under a cabinet near the door where you strangled Jackson. We believe it must have fell out of his pockets during the struggle.'

Frankland-Moore looked puzzled. 'But how on earth..?'

Clarke interrupted him. 'Ah, you're wondering how Jackson came by it in the first place? He found it amongst the possessions of a patient up at the nursing home, a Mrs. Fordham – a Mrs. Joan Fordham. That name mean anything to you?'

Frankland-Moore said nothing, but the look on his face suggested that the name was known to him – and Clarke sensed this too.

'Of course it does,' he growled. 'She is the mother of the lad who got sent down for the crime that *you* committed.' He paused briefly and then leaned forward to look Frankland-Moore in the eye once more. 'He later took his own life – did you know that?'

'What's that got to do with...'

Clarke interrupted him again and turned to Fletcher once more. 'Could I have the diary, please, Sergeant.'

'What have you got there?' asked Frankland-Moore anxiously.

'It's what you were looking for after you killed Jackson,' replied Clarke as he held the exercise book up before him. 'He found this amongst Mrs. Fordham's possessions too.'

'What is it?'

'It's a diary, Mr. Frankland-Moore. A diary put together by Mrs. Fordham.' He paused briefly and then continued. 'Did you know that she used to work at Brockley Hall?'

'What *is* all this about?'

Clarke ignored him. 'No, of course not – it was before you were born.' He then looked down at the diary and began to flick through the pages. Suddenly he stopped and looked up at Frankland-Moore again. 'Did you know that Mrs. Fordham was raped during her time at Brockley Hall – *by your father?*'

The look on Frankland-Moore's face was one of incredulity, but it was nothing compared to that which Fletcher gave her boss; not that he even offered to glance in her direction.

It was Frankland-Moore who spoke next.

'That's a bare-faced lie!' he snarled. 'How dare you...'

Clarke interrupted him again and pointed to the diary. 'It's all in here, Mr. Frankland-Moore. Mrs. Fordham fell pregnant and had no alternative but to leave Brockley Hall. Several months later she gave birth to a boy – *your father's son.*'

'Nonsense,' protested Frankland-Moore!

Clarke continued. 'But she was forced to put him up for adoption – and I think we'll find that the name of the family who adopted him was Jackson, and that they lived at Grimley.'

There was now a look of horror on Frankland-Moore's face as he attempted to take in what Clarke had just said, but he was quite literally speechless.

Clarke spoke for him.

'That's right, Mr. Frankland-Moore. *Keith Jackson was your half-brother!*'

Frankland-Moore was having none of it. 'Don't be ridiculous,' he snapped. 'You're talking absolute poppycock!'

Clarke placed the book in front of Frankland-Moore and pointed to the passage where Mrs. Fordham had revealed that she had been raped by his father, and had subsequently given birth to *his* son.

'Read that if you don't believe me,' he said forcefully. 'Go on, read it!' he bellowed.

Frankland-Moore looked down at the book and started to read. 'Oh my God,' were the only words that came out of his mouth.

'Needless to say, DNA from you and from Jackson will prove unequivocally that you were indeed brothers, Mr. Frankland-Moore.'

'I...I...just...can't...'

'What a strange quirk of fate that both Jackson's real mother and adoptive mother were residents of the same care home,' said Clarke as if he had taken the stand in court. 'Indeed, they still *are* residents. Both women were unaware of this, but then so was Jackson himself.'

Frankland-Moore continued to look down at the book, but it was clear to him that the game was up and he decided to come clean at last.

'I knew that it was Jackson on the phone that morning,' he said almost tearfully. 'I recognised his voice immediately. He said that he had evidence that I had killed the girl all those years ago. I didn't believe him at first, but when he started going on about the *Tom and Jerry Club* I realised that his intentions were serious.'

'How much did he demand?' asked Clarke.

'A small fortune,' replied Frankland-Moore as he sat twiddling his thumbs nervously again. 'Oh, I went along with his little ruse because he'd threatened to go to the police if I didn't, but I had no intention of letting him get away with it. A time and place were arranged for the drop and that's when I came up with the idea of asking Laura – my secretary – for the use of her car. I told her that something was wrong with mine and that it needed to go in for service. She was obliging of course, so I then withdrew the money and drove off to Brockley.'

'Where had you arranged to make the drop?'

'The toilets at the cricket club.'

'But you didn't park up there, did you?'

'No, I parked the car on Gold Crescent a good half hour or so before we had arranged, made my way on foot to the cricket club and deposited the money in one of the cisterns as instructed. I then returned to the car and waited until Jackson showed up.'

'Then when he reappeared you followed him?'

Frankland-Moore laughed mockingly. 'I still can't believe that he was so naive as to believe that I wouldn't follow him – and an ex-Army man too!'

'Then what happened?'

'I watched him go into the pub and then I drove down to his house and lay in wait. The rest is more or less as you implied.'

'You took an enormous gamble – what with it being a popular route for ramblers, cyclists and those out walking their dogs?'

'True – but I wanted my money back!'

Clarke sighed heavily. 'You should know that copies have been made of the diary, but we will be returning it to its original owner.'

As he rose from his chair and prepared to leave, Fletcher made her one and only contribution to the interview.

'Why did you do these things – the rapes and the murders?' she asked earnestly.

Frankland-Moore sat back and pondered her question for a few seconds before replying.

'When I was a child, I would watch my father assaulting members of staff at the Hall,' he said as if in a trance-like state. 'I would actually peek through the door of the bedroom, the kitchen or sometimes the living room and watch him doing it to them. I remember on one occasion mummy threw a sherry evening, and my father had one of the guests on the billiard table. It seemed such fun.'

The look on Fletcher's face was one of undisguised disgust. Clarke merely stood at the door, safe in the knowledge that justice had finally caught up with Frankland-Moore.

'Chip off the old block then, aren't you?' he muttered before turning to Fletcher. 'Charge him, Sergeant!'

Chapter 51

Saturday, 15 July, 2017 (p.m.)

The brewery had been very prompt in finding a temporary replacement for Tony and Sally Dawkins at *The Wheatsheaf*, and of course this was well received by the regulars. One would have thought that events up at the Hall would be the sole topic of discussion on this fine Saturday afternoon, but for some of those present there were far more important matters to discuss and debate.

Unable to field a full eleven for the game earlier, the village cricket team were declared to have breached the league rules (they were said to have been in 'non-attendance'), and twelve points had automatically been given to the opposition. Needless to say, having already lost their club Captain, star player *and* their fast bowler, this only added to the consternation of what was left of the side, most of whom had called into the pub for a 'swift half' earlier, alongside the most ardent of their supporters, and they were still there arguing over the future of the club a couple of hours later.

However, there was one member of the team who did not share in the concerns of the others or the looming crisis that now confronted the club. Indeed, he wasn't even sitting around the same table as them, for he was standing at the corner of the bar supping at his pint of Guinness and discussing *his* plans for the future with the woman seated at the stool beside him.

Attired in his claret and blue West Ham United shirt and white shorts, Simon Collins had entered the pub alongside Patricia Jackson, whose long, mousy-coloured hair was uncharacteristically loose and whose face and features no longer looked quite so weather-beaten. Wearing a short-sleeved cream-coloured blouse and jeans, she sat with her glass of diet coke listening intently, for Simon was now at his most animated.

'It's true, I tell yer,' he spluttered. 'I 'onestly thought that she would take every bleedin' penny, but she's goin' back to London. What's more, we reached a settlement yesterday and she's agreed to a divorce!'

284

Patricia had noticed the raised eyebrows from amongst some of those present the moment she entered the pub, but now she couldn't care less what anyone thought.

'That's fantastic!' she exclaimed.

'But that's not all, darlin',' he said excitedly. 'I've decide to sell up.'

'Sell up? What do you mean?'

'I'm sellin' the business – the whole bleedin' empire!'

'You must be mad!' she protested, albeit half-heartedly.

He ignored her and continued. 'I've been dreamin' about this for weeks and now I've decided to turn my dreams into reality. I'm gonna take a gamble with a new venture darlin'. I'm gonna go into 'orse breedin' – with you!'

Patricia almost choked on her diet coke. 'With me?' she shrieked. 'You're serious about this, aren't you?'

'Too bleedin' right I am!'

'But you need the qualifications?'

'Then I'll get 'em!'

'Then there's the land and…'

'Don't worry, I'll see to all that.' he said nonchalantly. 'You can still take care of the 'orse ridin' side of things, but I'll concentrate on the breedin'!'

'I have to admit, you've got some bottle – and confidence.'

'Well? What do you think?' he asked her persuasively.

She looked him in the eye for a couple of seconds and then a broad smile spread right across her face.

'How could I possibly say no?' she replied.

He punched the air, did a little jig on the spot and then bent down to give her a huge smacker full on the lips.

'Landlord!' he shouted after breaking apart. 'Bottle o' champagne over 'ere if you don't mind – we got somethin' to celebrate!'

At that point a rather sad looking figure approached the bar a trifle unsteadily to order another drink. Strangely enough, Ken Watson hadn't been sitting with the other members of the cricket team or the supporters either. Under normal circumstances he would have been sharing in their triumphs and tribulations, but he had been sitting at his usual table alone, without his beloved "Wilf" alongside him. What's more, he had said nothing all afternoon; he just sat there staring ahead and sinking pint after pint of John Smith's as if it was going out of fashion.

'You sure you can handle another one mate?' asked the temporary landlord as Ken ordered yet another pint. 'How many is that you've had now?'

'I'm alright,' snapped Ken as he stood there grimacing and swaying.

The temporary landlord shrugged and duly obliged by pouring Ken yet *another* pint of John Smith's, and then he watched as Ken counted out his loose change before offering the correct amount. As Ken snatched at his pint and staggered away from the bar, he attempted to make his way back to his seat, but in doing so he barged into the back of a member of the cricket team and caused him to spill his drink.

'Watch what you're bloody doing, you stupid old sod!' the man growled angrily.

What happened next stunned everyone present, for Ken did nothing more than place his drink on the nearest table and then unexpectedly swung for the man with his right fist. Unfortunately Ken missed the target completely, for the man had seen it coming and had backed off. Ken lost his balance and fell down onto the table before him, causing customers to jump out of their seats and sending glasses, beer and beer mats flying!

The temporary landlord rushed from behind the bar.

'Someone get him out of here,' he bellowed. 'He's had far too much to drink!'

Simon Collins came running over.

'It's alright, John,' he said grabbing hold of Ken, who was now mumbling incoherently. 'I know the geezer – we'll get 'im 'ome.'

With that Simon Collins helped Ken into his Range Rover, assisted by Patricia Jackson, who then drove the three of them around the corner to the bungalow on Gold Crescent.

Having found Ken's keys, Patricia opened the front door of the bungalow and let everyone in. The living room was off to the right and Collins took Ken inside and helped him into the easy chair. He was asleep within seconds.

'Fank God for that,' he said with some relief. 'Our Ken's a bleedin' dead weight.'

Patricia had followed them into the living room and she noticed some papers on the table beneath the window. Scanning them carefully she called out to Collins.

'Have you seen these, Simon?' she said with a sense of surprise.

Collins came over and looked over her shoulder. 'Bloody 'ell,' he exclaimed. 'No wonder 'e got pissed!'

It transpired that Ken had been issued with a fixed penalty notice under the Criminal Justice and Police Act 2001 *and* a ninety quid fine for wasting police time. There was no conviction, but his details would now be on the police computer, and for someone like Ken Watson that would be a disgrace and a stain on his character.

'Poor man,' muttered Patricia quietly, little realising that he would almost certainly be stripped from his post as head of the local Allotment Association. It also hadn't occurred to her that he would *never* be considered as head of the Parish Council too after this, and he must have felt as though the whole world had turned against him.

'Wait a minute,' whispered Collins. 'Where's the dog?'

In their rush to see that Ken was returned to his place of abode safely and without any complications, they had forgotten that Ken had gone to the pub alone and without his beloved "Wilf" for company.

'I'll go and have a look in the kitchen or see if he's been locked in the bedroom,' said Patricia anxiously.

'Good idea,' replied Collins. 'And make us a cuppa while you're out there,' he shouted after her.

Patricia headed for the bedroom first, but there was no sign of "Wilf" there, so she made her way into the kitchen and met with the same result. This was very strange; what could have happened to him? She checked to see if there was any food or water in his bowls, but they were both empty. There were one or two items on the kitchen unit that were obviously ready to be thrown out, but before she went outside with these she put the kettle on as Simon had suggested.

Opening the back door, she was just about to empty the rubbish into the blue bin when she thought she heard a noise. She stopped dead in her tracks and cocked her head to one side as if to listen for something.

There it was again – and it seemed to be coming from the nearby garden shed. As she approached the shed she heard the unmistakeable sound of a dog whimpering behind the door, which had been padlocked. She called out to Collins.

'Simon, come here quickly.' she shouted.

Collins came rushing out of the back door. 'What is it, darlin'?' he replied anxiously.

She began to sob. 'I think "Wilf" is in here.'

Collins put his ear to the door. 'You're right – the old bugger 'as locked 'im in 'ere!'

'What are we going to do?'

Just at that moment Collins spotted Ken's next door neighbour over the hedge, pottering around in his garden.

'ere mate,' he shouted.

The elderly neighbour turned slowly and seemed somewhat irked that someone had disturbed him. 'What is it?' he replied rather caustically.

'You got an 'ammer?'

'A what?'

'An 'ammer! You know, for knockin' nails in!'

'Reckon I've got one in me shed.'

'Well, could I borrow it – please?'

The man struggled to his feet and made his way gingerly over to his shed. He reappeared a couple of minutes later.

'This what you're looking for?' he said as he handed the implement over to Collins.

'Cheers mate,'

'What's the old bugger gone and done now?' asked the neighbour, almost as if he was used to Ken encountering some kind of mishap.

'Oh nuffin' much – only gone and locked 'is bleedin' dog in the shed!'

The neighbour shook his head and watched as Collins inserted two fingers into the padlock's shackle loop, before pulling up on the shackle to create tension. He then used the hammer and tapped the side of the lock with quick, short strikes. Seconds later he managed to 'bump' the lock open as the pins inside became disengaged. As he opened the door, out came a grateful "Wilf" wagging his tail and jumping up both Collins and Patricia.

'What possessed 'im to do such a thing?' said Collins angrily.

'The fixed penalty notice was probably the catalyst,' replied Patricia. 'Although it could have been a combination of events, I suppose. "Wilf" would have been in an excited state as he tried to tell his master that he was ready for his walk, and no doubt the constant yapping tipped Ken over the edge.'

'What are we gonna do with 'im?'

'Well he isn't staying here – not with Ken in that state.'

'You sayin' we should take 'im 'ome with us?'

'Yes, for the time being!' insisted Patricia.

As Collins handed the hammer back over the hedge, the elderly neighbour next door shook his head once more.

'Allus said that old bugger should be in a bloody 'ome by now!'

288

Chapter 52

Saturday, 15 July, 2017 (p.m.)

Unaware of the events at the pub and the tragedy on Gold Crescent, Clarke had returned to his office after the questioning of Frankland-Moore satisfied that he had now completed the case, and that his own questions had at last been answered. The where, when, what and how were known to him from the outset, but now they had discovered who had committed the crime and why.

He was mulling over these facts and other aspects of the case when there was a knock on his office door. He knew who it would be.

'Come in, Sergeant,' he said laconically. 'I've been expecting you.'

Fletcher entered and it was clear from her demeanour that not for the first time she was somewhat exasperated with her superior.

'Might I have a word with you, Sir?' she asked politely.

'By all means, Sergeant.'

'Why didn't you tell me that Frankland-Moore and Jackson were brothers?' she asked with a heavy sigh.

'What difference would it have made?'

'It would have been the courteous thing to do for starters.'

Clarke took the hint. 'Perhaps you have a point,' he conceded. 'But in my experience...'

She cut him off. 'Yes, I know – it sometimes pays to keep something back.'

'You catch on quickly, Sergeant – you'll go far.'

'I'll take your word for it, Sir,' she replied drily.

'Whilst he was always likely to boast about his sexual crimes and misdemeanours, I suspected that he would be much more reticent with regard to the murder of Jackson, and so it proved – he just wasn't going to play ball. That's why I felt it necessary to wait until the last minute to drop the bombshell on him that he and Jackson were brothers.'

Fletcher sighed again. 'Well your ploy worked, that's for sure.'

'And I believe that we now have a watertight case that we can present to the Crown Prosecution Service.'

'Well done, Sir.'

'Thank you, Fletcher. But it *was* a team effort.'

'Eventually!'

Clarke laughed. 'Yes, eventually.'

'What are you going to do now, Sir?

He held up the diary once more. 'I am going to return this to it's rightful owner.' He rose from his chair and donned his bomber jacket before opening the door for Fletcher. 'I suggest that you go home and have a few drinks – let your hair down.'

'You know something, Sir?' she said pensively before parting company. 'That doesn't sound like a bad idea.'

In the minutes after her husband's arrest, Anna Frankland-Moore had managed to find some time for self-reflection. For many years she had been unloved, duped and misled, but now that the truth had emerged the loyalty that she had previously shown him and his family were now gone. Perhaps she will find love and intimacy again with someone else? Perhaps not. One thing was for sure; she would be leaving Brockley Hall before the day was out.

She was busy packing her bags when she heard someone enter the room behind her. She knew who it was, but she continued to go about her business.

'So, you're leaving,' said a tearful Monica Frankland-Moore.

'That's right,' replied Anna as she glanced at her mother-in-law briefly before turning her attention to the wardrobe on her left.

'You blame me, don't you?'

'For turning your son into a monster?'

'Yes.'

'Of course I do.' replied Anna adamantly. 'You spoilt him and gave him everything he wanted – he could no wrong in your eyes.'

'Wouldn't you have done the same with *your* son?' said Monica almost apologetically.

Anna ignored the question – for now. 'You were married to a monster and you ended up creating one.'

Monica was struggling to fight back the tears. 'I know all about my husband,' she reluctantly admitted.

'No, I wasn't the only one to fall victim to your husband's lecherous debauchery, was I?'

'No, you weren't.'

As she finished packing her bags, Anna turned to Monica with a look of sheer disgust on her face.

'You may have come to my aid – on the day of my engagement. But what about the others? You admit to knowing about them and yet you did nothing?' she snarled.

'I am so very, very sorry.'

Anna ignored the apology. 'Well now the time has come for me to reveal my secret.'

'Secret? What do you mean?'

'Within a year of my miscarriage I decided to have an operation – for tubal ligation.'

The words cut through Monica like a chainsaw. 'You did *what*?' she cried with dismay.'

'That's female sterilisation to you,' replied Anna with what can only be described as a sense of schadenfreude.

'Oh my God, no!' screamed Monica.

'I'm afraid God had no part to play in *this* decision.' said Anna mockingly. 'I always wanted to have a baby, but it soon became apparent to me that your son wasn't fit to be a father. But that wasn't why I had the operation.'

'Then why?' whimpered a tearful Monica.

'I did it to spite you!'

'But *why*?'

'Because of your desire for an heir to this godforsaken place!' said Anna glancing around the room disdainfully. 'That was all that mattered to you. My welfare and well-being meant *nothing* to you, but if I had given birth then I knew only too well that you would do everything in your power to ensure that I had nothing to do with the child's upbringing. You would have created *another* monster – and I wasn't going to allow that!'

With those words Anna marched out of the room with her bags and left Monica to erupt into tears once more. Making her way down the stairs and out to her car, she threw the bags into the boot and set off down the driveway for a new life – destination unknown.

As Anna sped through the village in the direction of Grimley, she passed the Little Orchard Nursing Home just as Detective Chief Inspector Clarke was being admitted to the building.

Having announced the reason for his visit to the female member of staff who opened the door, he was reminded – rather too brusquely in his view – that he had to sign the visitor's book upon entering, which he duly did. She then directed him towards the manager's office, even though he tried to convince her – unsuccessfully – that he knew where it was from previous visits.

He knocked on the door, and upon entry found Audrey Bostock wearing a cream-coloured, short-sleeve blouse and busily tapping away on the keyboard of her laptop. It was clear that she was a trifle irritated to have been disturbed.

'What can I do for you now, Chief Inspector?' she sighed and stopped typing.

Clarke was slightly taken aback. 'Well, I...'

'I'm sorry, Inspector,' she replied apologetically. 'I shouldn't have reacted that way.

'You're obviously under a lot of stress at the moment.'

'Yes, as it happens, but I still shouldn't have reacted as I did and I apologise.'

'Think nothing of it.'

'So, what's the reason for your visit today?'

'I've come to return this to its owner,' he said holding up the diary.

'Oh dear,' she replied a little uneasily. 'You won't have heard.'

'Heard what, Mrs. Bostock?'

'Audrey, please,' she pleaded earnestly.

'I'm sorry – heard what, Audrey?'

'I'm afraid Mrs. Fordham passed away during the early hours of this morning.'

'Oh, I'm sorry to hear that.' He paused briefly and then continued. 'Does she have any family?'

Audrey explained that they had managed to contact a niece who still lived locally and that she had been in earlier to formally identify her aunt. The body of Mrs. Fordham had been taken away to Leverton hospital and laid out in the mortuary until the funeral directors came to collect it on the Monday morning. She would be registering the death herself on Monday, but at present she was sending an email to the local authorities, who had up to three days to stop paying the care home fees.

'I'll keep the diary in storage with the rest of her possessions. Was there anything else, Inspector?'

'Well, I wonder if I could just have a quick word with Mrs. Jackson, if I may?

'By all means – I believe that she's watching TV in her room.'

'Thanks, Audrey.'

'You know where it is,' she shouted after him as he made his way down the corridor.

He could hear the TV as he approached – the volume was obviously turned right up. He was going to have to knock loudly if she was going to hear him.

She did hear him eventually, and as she turned down the volume she invited him in.

'Chief Inspector,' she said with a surprised look on her face. 'How nice to see you again. Please, pull up a chair and I'll turn this off.'

Her words brought a smile to Clarke's face as he sat beside her bed and began to tell her about the events at Brockley Hall.

'I've come to tell you that we have arrested and charged the man responsible for the murder of Keith,' he said quietly and gravely.

She sat back and sighed. 'I'm so glad to hear that, Inspector.'

'It was Rupert Frankland-Moore.'

'Why am I not surprised to hear that?' she exclaimed bitterly.

'He is also responsible for a number of other crimes across the Continent and here too,' he said looking down at the floor. 'Including the rape and murder of Emma Woodward here at Brockley thirty years ago. Peter Fordham was innocent of the crime.'

A look of horror and anguish came to her face at the mention of Emma Woodward, and then she leaned across the bed as if she was about to reveal something very secretive.

'There is something I want to tell you, Inspector,' she said in a very low voice. 'When they arrested Peter Fordham all those years ago, my sister rang and told me what had happened, and I remember having this gut feeling that Peter's mother was also Keith's natural mother. I regretted doing it at the time, but I slammed the phone down on my sister.'

Clarke was clearly moved by her revelations. 'There's no need to feel any guilt, Mrs. Jackson, but what makes you think that Peter and Keith were brothers?'

'Well I grew up on the same street as the Chapman's – my best friend was Maureen Chapman, who was Joan's elder sister. I remember Joan becoming pregnant, and of course the fact that she later gave the baby up for adoption. I just...'

She was unable to finish her sentence, but Clarke seemed to gather his thoughts before continuing. 'We know from a diary that Mrs. Fordham left behind that she worked at Brockley Hall for a time, and that she had been raped by Charles Frankland-Moore, Rupert's father.'

Mrs. Jackson shook her head and sighed again. 'Would it surprise you to know that I too worked at Brockley Hall some years before and that he tried to assault me?'

'Charles Frankland-Moore tried to rape you?'

'Yes.'

'What exactly happened?'

'His mother came upon us before he could do anything,' she said as her eyes began to fill with tears. 'I had no alternative but to leave – although I did receive a sum of money as an inducement.'

It was Clarke's turn to shake his head. 'What a bunch of...' He couldn't finish *his* sentence.

'I was lucky, Inspector. The same can't be said for poor Joan Chapman.'

'No, you're right there.' He rose from his chair. 'Well thank you for your time, Mrs. Jackson. Please accept my condolences once more.'

'I'll be alright, Inspector.'

He placed his hand on her shoulder and then left the room feeling somewhat sombre. As he made his way down the corridor, Audrey Bostock emerged from her office.

'Ah, Inspector. I trust everything is okay?' she enquired cheerfully.

'Yes, thank you.' he replied none too convincingly.

'Will we be seeing you again?'

'I very much doubt it.'

'I see. Well, I hope that we have been able to assist you in your enquiries.'

'Yes, you have been very helpful,' he said appreciatively. 'Thank you once again and goodbye.'

'Goodbye to you too.'

With that he walked away briskly, but just as he reached the door he stopped and turned around.

'There was one thing, Mrs...,' He stopped and corrected himself. 'I mean Audrey,'

'What's that, Inspector?'

You have a member of staff – Maria Bukowski...or should I say Nixon? Is she here today by any chance?'

The look on Audrey's face said it all. 'I'm afraid she handed in her notice yesterday,' she said with a tinge of sadness. 'It appears that she's accepted a job with a care home at Hucknall.'

'I see,' he replied a trifle lost for words. He thanked her once again and then made his way out of the building.

Quelle surprise! He hadn't seen that one coming – and she had made no mention of it during their meal two nights beforehand. Perhaps it was for the best, he told himself. These things happen.

He climbed into his car and sat there for a few minutes contemplating what to do with himself that evening. He could have murdered a glass or three of Laphroaig; that was for sure. But then he remembered what Diana Marshall had said about his drinking; she did have a point, did she not?

His mind then went back to the previous Saturday when they had made love – oh to be smothered by her massive mammaries once more. But the knowledge that her partner was back from his golfing weekend brought him back down to earth.

At least if he went to the pub he'd get a chance to see Diana and perhaps have a chat with her; surely her partner wasn't to know what happened the previous weekend? It was a dilemma.

Or was it?

As he placed the key in the ignition and the engine fired up, a mischievous grin appeared on his face – Marilyn Monroe was winking at him again!

EPILOGUE

Thursday, 19 October, 2017

Having been charged with the murder of Keith Jackson, Rupert Frankland-Moore was also charged with the murder of Emma Woodward thirty years previously, the attempted murder and rape of Irene Cowlishaw (formerly Fletcher) in 1988, and the rape of Gemma Bateson in 1986. Brought before the magistrate's on Monday 17 July, it came as little surprise to anyone that he entered a plea of not guilty, thereby subjecting his victims and their families to the harrowing ordeal of having to listen to what happened to their loved ones in court. Of course that was his intent all along.

The trial opened at Nottingham Crown Court on Tuesday, 26 September, and from the outset Frankland-Moore showed no remorse for his nefarious activity whatsoever. He remained cool, calm and collected throughout, but then he'd always had a super-inflated ego, as many were willing to testify.

Among the witnesses was Gemma Bateson from Cambridge. It had been thought that she wouldn't attend, but she only agreed to do so at the last minute, thanks chiefly to the persuasive efforts of Detective Sergeant Fletcher. Mrs. Irene Cowlishaw – Fletcher's mother – also testified, although it has to be said that she did struggle to bring herself to look the defendant in the eye when she went into the witness box.

Perhaps the most moving aspect of the trial was the fact that some of the families of Frankland-Moore's victims from across Europe had come over to attend, including the family of the murdered girl from Regensburg, as well as those from Brussels, Madrid and Rome.

The police obtained from storage some of the clothing Emma Woodward wore on the day she was murdered, including her underwear; semen found using DNA was that of Rupert Frankland-Moore. Hairs and other evidence found on the clothing of Keith Jackson were found to belong to the defendant, and fibres found in Laura Brownlow's car also came from Keith Jackson's clothing.

On Thursday, 19 October, the jury retired to consider their verdict; it took them less than three hours. Frankland-Moore was found guilty on all four charges. The judge sentenced him to life imprisonment on all four counts, and there would be no possibility of parole. As he was led away, he turned to the gallery and gave one of his characteristically sickening smug grins, almost as if he was shoving two fingers up to those seated there and to the profession he had once represented.

He never even found the time to glance up at his mother, who sat alone shaking her head and dabbing her eyes. Someone had been heard to say afterwards that she should have saved her tears for the victims and their families, but it had been an ignominious fall for the Frankland-Moore's, and Monica was only too aware that no one would be shedding any tears for them.

There was a steady drizzle as Clarke left the building. He wasn't used to wearing a suit and tie, so it came as something of a relief when he quickly loosened the latter and undid the top button of his shirt. And yet he smartly fastened the buttons of his jacket as if to keep out the cold, damp air.

By the time that he'd undertaken these simple tasks, Fletcher had emerged arm-in-arm with her mother. Clarke turned and gave Mrs. Cowlishaw a chivalrous nod along with a sympathetic smile to accompany it, before asking if he could speak to her daughter alone for a few minutes.

'That can't have been a pleasant experience for your mum,' he said quietly as he nodded in the direction of Mrs. Cowlishaw once more.

'She's just glad it's all over,' replied Fletcher. 'Although the scars will always be there of course.'

'Of course. But justice as been done – of a kind.'

Fletcher chuckled to herself. 'Would I be correct in thinking that you would have preferred that he had been hung, drawn and quartered?'

'Wouldn't you?'

'I'm just happy that he'll be spending the rest of his life behind bars – that's where he belongs.

Clarke grunted. 'If you say so, Sergeant.'

'What I want to say…' she paused briefly. 'Christ, I'm hopeless at these things… I just want to say that it's been a pleasure working with you, Sir. We didn't get off to a good start I know, but...'

He interrupted her. 'I owe you an apology, Sergeant.' he said earnestly.

'You don't have to…;

He held his hand up again. 'My attitude towards you was out of order – at the beginning.'

'Well, perhaps I didn't help matters…'

'I know you think that I'm a misogynist, Sergeant…'

'Jacqui – my name is Jacqui,' she insisted.

Clarke paused briefly and she could have sworn that he looked at her in a manner that suggested that first name terms were not the done thing on his watch, so she was pleasantly surprised by his response.

'I know you think that I'm a misogynist, Jacqui, but I'm nothing of the kind. I just have a massive chip on my shoulder.'

'Webster said it was a sackful of King Edward's!'

That brought a rueful smile to Clarke's face. 'Did he now – I'll have his guts for garters on Monday morning!'

They both laughed heartily.

'I must be getting off, Sir,' she informed him cordially. 'Whilst you're berating Webster, I'll be back to my duties in Nottingham come Monday morning.'

'Well, that's not quite true actually,' he said with a slightly smug grin on his face.

'How do you mean?' she replied with a puzzled look on her face.

'I've spoken to Chief Superintendent Annable and insisted that your temporary post as Deputy Senior Investigating Officer with Leverton CID is made a permanent one.'

Fletcher was stupefied. 'You what!' she screeched. 'You're having me on?'

'I actually proposed the posting and Chief Superintendent Annable has sanctioned it.'

The look on Fletcher's face was one of sheer delight. 'Thank you, Sir,' she beamed. 'Thank you from the bottom of my heart.'

'So, I expect to see you *and* Detective Constable Webster in my office first thing Monday morning. Got that?'

'Yes, Sir!' she replied excitedly.

Clarke nodded and then turned away. As he started to make his way briskly up the street, Fletcher noticed a woman standing beside a car; a woman with wavy, shoulder-length auburn hair. And she appeared to be waiting for him.

'I didn't know you had a chauffeur, Sir?' Fletcher shouted after him.

Clarke continued walking, but shouted back over his shoulder. 'There's a lot about me you don't know – Detective Sergeant!'

Milton Keynes UK
Ingram Content Group UK Ltd.
UKHW040652140923
428670UK00001B/107